THE SAVING LIGHT

• Book III in The Endora Trilogy •

Thomas J. Prestopnik

9-25-07

To Uncle Walt & Aunt JoAnn,
Here's The Final Volume.
Best wishes and Enjoy!

With Love,
Tom

Copyright © 2007 by Thomas J. Prestopnik

ISBN 0-7414-4032-6

Cover design by Nathan Prestopnik.

Map by Thomas J. Prestopnik.

Published by:

INFIITY
PUBLISHING.COM

1094 New DeHaven Street, Suite 100
West Conshohocken, PA 19428-2713
Info@buybooksontheweb.com
www.buybooksontheweb.com
Toll-free (877) BUY BOOK
Local Phone (610) 941-9999
Fax (610) 941-9959

Printed in the United States of America

Printed on Recycled Paper

Published June 2007

CONTENTS

This book is affectionately dedicated
to my twenty-five nieces and nephews,

Matthew, Hayley, Abbie, Evan, Katey,
Kelly, Andy, Brenan, Alison, Ryan,
Meghan, Adam, Jenelle, Joe, Phillip,
Ben, Eddie, Stephen, Renée, Emily,
Andrea, Valerie, Nathan, Jason and Dan.

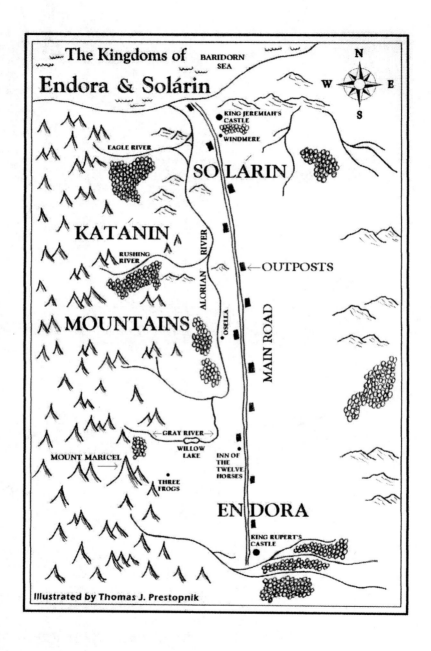

The Kingdoms of
Endora & Solárin

BARIDORN SEA

N
W   E
S

KING JEREMIAH'S CASTLE
WINDMERE

EAGLE RIVER

SOLARIN

KATANIN

RUSHING RIVER

OUTPOSTS

ALORIAN RIVER

MOUNTAINS

OSELLA

MAIN ROAD

GRAY RIVER
WILLOW LAKE

INN OF THE TWELVE HORSES

MOUNT MARICEL

THREE FROGS

ENDORA

KING RUPERT'S CASTLE

Illustrated by Thomas J. Prestopnik

CHAPTER ONE

Multiple Personalities

The wave lifted it higher and higher in a clumsy upward tumble. Like an out-of-control garden hose, it flipped and flopped and sputtered in a series of awkward somersaults–then suddenly stopped. For a split second it was poised high above the surface like a roller coaster balanced on top of a towering arc before a final plunge. Then it fell, plummeting like a dizzy brick in a wicked spiral toward the asphalt road. But a second wave of balmy air caught it like an invisible hand, hoisting it up above the street and treetops to again repeat the head-spinning process.

Belthasar wanted to scream, if only he could, caught like tumbleweed in a warm November breeze while trapped inside a mosquito's delicate body. He had managed to fly along the street at a good clip after escaping off that dog in a soapy stream of water. But a gust of wind severely tested him now and he wondered if he would survive his first flight.

As the breeze sent him plummeting toward the road one more time, its grip lessened slightly and Belthasar managed to sail straight ahead for a few yards, thinking he had regained control of the situation. Then when he saw a yellow delivery truck barreling directly toward him, he thought otherwise. A pair of unlit glass headlights looked like two huge deadened eyes, growing madly and eclipsing all else from view. Belthasar veered left at the last moment and flew between two trees along the sidewalk. The road below turned into a patch of green grass and Belthasar descended into the lush foliage for safety.

He alighted on a single blade to catch his breath, his tiny heart pounding and his ashen-gray eyes adjusting to this new perspective on life. He knew he had to get out of this bug's body soon so he could properly explore his new world. Though overwhelmed by the situation, Belthasar laughed to himself for outwitting his two greatest enemies–Christopher and Molly Jordan. He was in *their* world now, unbeknownst to them, and he could explore it at his leisure. What he would do here once he got his bearings, he still did not know. But Belthasar felt certain that his plans for domination and destruction would rival any he had made back in Endora and Solárin. He had gained much information from the thoughts of those individuals he had once inhabited who knew of this world's existence, so that was a big help for starters.

But now was the time for patience. Time to study the ways of this culture and determine exactly how one goes about becoming a giant among men in an exciting new world. Its citizens would never know what hit them. Belthasar savored the moment, brimming with vile and disdain, yet he knew there was much to learn if he wanted to do things right. He couldn't wait to begin.

Belthasar flew across the lawn of the nearest house to escape the hectic street, heading toward the backyard. The steady drone of car engines and the excited chatter of children getting out of school were soon replaced by the occasional caw of a distant crow or the sweep of a gentle breeze through a carpet of dried leaves. Belthasar sailed with ease from one yard to the next, darting over picket fences and hedgerows and sturdy walls built of colorful stones. He started to enjoy this new way of traveling and wondered if it might suit his purposes when he spotted a small pond in the next yard. Hovering above it in a mad dance were dozens of mosquitoes enjoying the warm autumn weather. Belthasar joined the frenzied mob, several times allowing his spirit to pass into the other insects.

"They're all the same!" he thought disgustedly. "They look alike. They *think* alike–not that there's much thinking going on here. Humph! Though their flying ability is superb, I need a grander host. I'm *better* than a bug!"

So Belthasar moved on, circling the crowd of mosquitoes one last time as they skated across the water. But he didn't get far. As he sped toward the grass on the opposite side, a dark wavy shape grew beneath him, growing larger and larger like a menacing shadow. Belthasar glanced into the water at the same moment that a large minnow jumped up, its eyes and mouth wide open as it swallowed the mosquito and splashed back underwater. Belthasar knew that he was doomed, and before the darkness completely engulfed him, his spirit passed into the minnow before it digested its mosquito snack.

"Disgusting!" he thought as he swam in the murky water. "Both the meal *and* this dreary place." A school of minnows zipped back and forth along the stony bottom of the pond, a few of them occasionally surfacing to feed on the buffet of flying bugs.

But Belthasar's disgust quickly turned into fear. He was trapped in this pond, only able to move from one minnow to another, doomed to swim in circles for the rest of his life. He wanted to scream or howl, but knew he couldn't do either. He sadly realized his dream of creating a kingdom in this world was about to burst like a soap bubble. Then all at once a dozen minnows brushed by, fleeing to one side of the pond. Belthasar wondered what had spooked them until he turned around and saw the disturbance.

Bubbles hissed and currents churned as something sinister roiled the water. A huge black shape was visible through the surface on the edge of the pond, its arm splashing through the water as if searching for something. Belthasar kept his distance but looked closer, not as intimidated as the other minnows. He was a tyrant after all, and had to keep up appearances, even if it was only among a frazzled school of slimy fish. Then Belthasar noticed the sharp claws and wet fur and knew what pursued them. He had seen this kind before–had *lived* in this kind before–and it brought back horrible memories of King Jeremiah's coronation platform. But now he saw the delightful irony of the situation and swam straight toward the creature to the perplexed horror of the other minnows.

"I hated you once, but you can save me now!" Belthasar thought with giddy excitement as he glided through the murky water directly toward the cat's paw that was causing such a commotion. "You may have me for lunch, furry beast, but I shall have *you* to do with as I will!"

Belthasar swam into the furious sea of bubbles as the cat's paw sliced through the water, but the sandy striped feline never got the chance to enjoy its tasty fish treat. For as soon as a few hairs on its paw had brushed against the minnow, the cat suddenly bounded away from the pond like a rifle shot, now possessed with the spirit of Belthasar. He ran through the grass from one yard to the next as the warm wind and sunshine swept across his whiskered face.

Then the backyards ran out.

The last yard lay adjacent to a narrow road with a small tract of woods just beyond. Belthasar sat in the grass, licking at his paws, wondering where he should go next. Into the woods? What danger or adventure might lurk there he couldn't begin to speculate. Perhaps he should travel the city streets again to await other opportunities. After all, he had his kingdom to think about again now that he wasn't reduced to a little fish in a big pond. Then Belthasar's ears pricked up and his spine tingled. He realized there was only one thing to do. Run!

Belthasar heard the growls and barks as clear as thunder as a large brown dog bolted from the woods after him. Belthasar spun around and ran back through the yards, searching for a place to hide or a tree to climb. He suddenly chided himself for thinking like a timid cat and not a ruthless despot. He needed no means of escape. Belthasar had exactly what he wanted, and all it would take was a split second. Belthasar stopped running and circled back in the grass and plopped down, waiting for the dog to come to him. It would never know what hit it.

As soon as the drooling, barking, tail-wagging dog charged at the cat like a furious bull, the cat sprang up and darted underneath the dog's legs. With the brush of fur upon fur, the dog's dark eyes instantly grayed as the cat's eyes filled with its previous yellow fire. Belthasar, now a canine, had no desire to chase a dizzy feline. He barked in victory and headed back to the woods.

Suddenly Belthasar felt tired to the core of his very bones. Passing from one animal to another so many times in a short span made him feel weak and disoriented. He needed rest, and the undergrowth among the trees provided the perfect spot. Belthasar crossed the road and traipsed through the cool, sweet-smelling leaves that littered the ground. He plopped down next to a tall elm tree, curled up and promptly fell asleep.

Dusky twilight had settled upon the city when Belthasar awoke. A bright swath of orange and purple clouds lay upon the horizon as the autumn air cooled. The dog stood and stretched his tired muscles. And though Belthasar felt steadier and more clearheaded, he was thoroughly famished. Dinner was in order.

Belthasar bounded out of the woods, crossed the road and wandered through the string of backyards once again. The houses and driveways were bathed in shadows and splashes of warm yellow light that flowed out of curtained windows. Belthasar sniffed the air and instinctively ran into the yard behind the next house and nosed about the back staircase. No one was in sight. All lay quiet except for the soft notes from a piano that drifted through an open window.

Then Belthasar discovered what had so delighted his senses. Three garbage bags were piled on a narrow cement sidewalk along the back porch steps. He buried his nose between the bags, pawing at the plastic with frenzied anticipation as a few flies buzzed about his twitching ears. When he ripped a hole in one of the bags, Belthasar's heart leapt with joy as the scents of crushed egg shells, decaying fruit rinds and rotting meat perfumed the nighttime air. His teeth locked onto a steak bone which he pulled out of the bag, only to drop it upon the sidewalk a moment later.

"What am I *doing*?" he thought in disgust. "I am not a dog!" he tried to convince himself, fighting off the urge to eat. "I can't behave this way as hungry as I am. I'll forget my true self if I don't get back into a real person soon." He walked backward a few steps, still drawn to the foul aroma but using every ounce of willpower to resist. Maybe just *one* bite? But any thought of an evening meal was driven from his mind when the back door swung open.

"Get out of there, Comet! I thought I heard you poking your wet nose through my garbage again!" A gray-haired woman in curlers and a bathrobe trudged down the stairs to shoo the dog away. "Take off before I swat you with a newspaper, you hear?"

As much as Belthasar yearned to exist in human form, he hadn't the slightest desire to use this woman as his host. Nor did he want to contend with her in any way as she darted toward him with a rolled-up newspaper, brandishing it like a sword. So in a desperate need for haste, Belthasar passed into a fly that had just landed on his nose and ascended into the night, leaving a confused and woozy Comet to fend for himself.

Soaring again. Belthasar cruised through the night shadows, more at ease this time with his flying skills. Since the afternoon breezes had disappeared, he was now able to fly high and low, blazing a trail of circles and loops through the darkness. But as no one could see him, Belthasar felt that his aerial skills were going to waste. He wanted an audience. He wanted to be noticed! That would come in time. When he was king, people would listen to his every word, and whether that was out of fear or loyalty, Belthasar didn't care. And best of all, people would obey him—or else! Oh yes, he *would* be noticed one day. Belthasar was determined to get his due.

But for now he was a fly and rose high into the air like a rocket, then plunged toward the earth in an exhilarating fall, feeling especially magnificent. He landed on a small rock near the edge of the pond where he had earlier swum with the minnows, feeling quite superior to his underwater friends. The cloud of mosquitoes had since disappeared and the air contained a crisp stillness punctuated by a few night noises. Somewhere a door slammed. Distant voices echoed in the gloomy darkness. A bulky shadow clumsily swished through the cool blades of grass.

Belthasar turned around, his multifaceted eyes scanning the low horizon, his senses attuned to every element of sound and scent swimming through the air. Something wasn't right and he prepared to take flight, but just a moment too late. Belthasar felt a wet slap across the side of his insect body and was pulled through the air toward a cavernous black opening. He screamed inside his mind as he appeared to sail in slow motion toward the frog's open mouth, stuck to its tongue like a ready-to-eat snack. Knowing that his flying time had abruptly ended, Belthasar's spirit passed into the frog an instant before it greedily consumed the fly, then it lazily hopped a few steps toward the pond.

"And I thought *mosquitoes* tasted revolting!" Belthasar mused, now trapped in the frog's bulging body.

But he had no intention of going back into the pond as his instinct seemed to direct him. So Belthasar turned around and jumped a few times through the grass toward the nearest house, pausing to catch his breath. The sudden shift from an acrobatic fly to a lumbering amphibian tired him out immensely, causing him to wonder how he was ever supposed to go anywhere in a hurry in *this* body.

"I'd rather be a minnow again," he sarcastically thought as he took another short hop through the grass. The house and driveway looked miles away as Belthasar peered over the grass tops through his bulbous frog eyes.

Then, just as he felt a cool touch upon his webbed foot, he saw a flash of light. Something approached. A beam of light swept across the lawn, bouncing this way and that, accompanied by chatter and laughter. Belthasar didn't know what to make of it and grew frightened, feeling trapped in a body that didn't want to move as fast as he'd prefer. But he found a chance to escape when he looked down and saw an earthworm gently glide through the grass and over his foot.

"He's much more mobile than *I'll* ever be," Belthasar concluded, and passed into the worm in the blink of an eye just as the light approached and landed on the frog's slightly stunned eyes. A young girl screamed and the frog jumped. Two other voices burst out laughing and the girl soon joined them. Belthasar weaved his long, sleek, wormy body through the thick grass to escape notice. But he didn't get far.

"Scared of an itty bitty frog?" her brother teased.

"Am not!" she shot back. "Dad, tell him not to pick on me. He's being—hey, look at this!"

The young girl aimed a flashlight into the grass, reached down and picked up one of the biggest earthworms she had ever seen, dangling it into the air like a prized trophy. She waved it in front of her brother's face, causing him to flinch.

"Ooooo! Scared of a wittle wittle wormy?" she teased.

"Just scared of *you*," her brother replied with a grunt.

"I'm just glad both of you aren't going to the lake fishing with me on Saturday," their father replied. "You'd frighten away all the fish!"

"Very funny!" his daughter replied, still holding up the worm. "Well, *this* one ought to catch you a whopper!"

Her brother removed the hole-poked cover off an old margarine tub and held out the container filled with a dozen worms and some soil. "Throw it in with the others."

As the girl extended her hand through the air to drop the worm into the bowl, Belthasar panicked, his body flailing like a streamer caught on a wire. *Fishing*! *Covered container*! What were they going to do with him? Belthasar knew he had to escape this undignified fate or else all would be lost—but something was wrong. His spirit was trapped, paralyzed inside this revolting worm. For some reason he couldn't pass into the girl as he helplessly dangled above the grass–and *now* above a container of worms slithering over and under each other like a brood of snakes. This couldn't be happening!

As the father aimed his flashlight higher up, Belthasar saw the reason for his predicament. The girl wore a pair of rubber gloves. Out of her fear of touching a night crawler, she had put on a pair of yellow dishwashing gloves to help in the search. Belthasar's spirit couldn't pass through the material. He needed to touch an actual living being in order to inhabit its body or he'd remain stuck in his current host. And a worm of all things!

"Now in you go with your little buddies, Mr. Worm!" the girl sweetly said, admiring her nighttime catch as she suspended it above the bowl. "Nighty night!"

She dropped the worm.

"Nooooooo!" Belthasar shrieked in his mind as he fell through the air and plopped on top of the slithering gray mass of worms and soil. "Get me out of here!" he tried to cry as he desperately crawled up the side of the margarine tub. But he couldn't get a grip on the plastic. All he could do was swim among the other worms, his spirit passing from one to the other in a last desperate attempt to control the situation. But his efforts proved fruitless. Then total darkness descended as the lid slowly covered the bowl and sealed it with the tiniest sound of deadly finality.

"Let me out at once!" Belthasar shouted at the top of his mind. "I demand it!"

But nobody paid attention. He felt his enclosed world rise gently up and down as the man holding his plastic prison walked across the lawn. Several minutes passed like hours, and since the cover had not been removed again, Belthasar assumed they had stopped searching for more worms. He listened for other noises as he jostled about among his slimy co-captives. Another door slammed shut. Voices faded.

"Go inside and wash your hands now. You both still have homework to do."

"All right..."

"I'll be inside in a minute," their father replied as he walked across the garage toward a small refrigerator beside a tool bench. He opened the door and adjusted the temperature control.

Belthasar felt his new prison drop with a thud, then all movement ceased. He wasn't swaying through the air in an ungainly manner anymore. Then the darkness, if it were possible, grew even deeper as he heard a door seal shut. He squirmed among the other worms, his mind still red-hot with fury, but after several minutes, he started to slow down. The others slowed down too. From exhaustion? From a sense of defeat? Belthasar felt a slight chill permeate the air. It gradually seeped into the soil and the other worms. And himself! An uneasy sleep gripped him as his body grew cooler, and there was nothing he could do to stop it. Belthasar tried to hold on to his dreams of conquest and domination to give him strength, but even those became a confused jumble as the seconds ticked away. His tragic end had arrived at last, he realized, and all his plans for glory were finished as he lay helplessly among a pile of worms. Even his thoughts felt frozen until he could barely think at all. Then his world went dark.

The following Saturday dawned like a warm sunny September. The city streets lay still as a car crept quietly out of the neighborhood, packed with a fishing pole, a tackle box and a small plastic cooler. Inside the red cooler was a bagged lunch consisting of a few ham and Swiss cheese sandwiches, some chocolate candy bars, a packet of sunflower seeds and a couple bottles of water. Next to the lunch bag was a plastic margarine tub with holes in its cover. The driver turned on the radio and smiled, delighted to get an unexpected day of fishing so late in the year at the small cabin in the woods. Life couldn't be better.

An hour later he stood on the shore of a tiny lake as the morning sunshine dappled a line of nearby white birch trees, their remaining yellow leaves as bright as sliced lemons. He set the cooler on the bottom of his rowboat tied to a post on the water's edge, then removed the bowl of worms, popped off the cover and set it on a wooden seat before returning to his car for the rest of his fishing gear.

The sun beat down like a gentle whisper, warmly touching the dark rich soil inside the bowl. Soon the last traces of imprisoning coolness evaporated and the spaghetti-like mass of worms started to move, jostling one another for space and heat and light. Moments later the man untied the rowboat, stepped inside and pushed off with an oar. He rowed out upon the gentle surface of the lake now splashed like an artist's palette with a reflection of autumn's vivid hues. He repeatedly dipped his oars into the water, moving closer to his favorite fishing spot, eager to cast his line. Minutes later he arrived and laid the oars inside the boat. Then, as if lifting a rare and priceless artifact for examination, he picked up his fishing pole and leaned it against his knee, fingering the hook between his thumb and forefinger.

"This beats a day at the office," he said to himself with a chuckle, extending the other hand toward the margarine tub now alive with earthworms.

The fisherman reached inside the slithering cluster, hooking a finger underneath a particularly long and wiggly worm. The others sensed the presence of the intruder as they fully awoke from their slumber, twisting and squirming to evade capture. Except for one worm. Belthasar, finding himself at the bottom of the pile, attempted to squeeze through the frenzied mob to reach the surface. As the fisherman slowly lifted the long worm out of the pile, it fought to stay with the others, curling one end of its body around the other worms so that the man had to tug at it a few times to try to free it. Belthasar struggled to reach that worm before it was pulled completely from the bowl, fearing he would be too late to make contact. As the end of the worm was slipping free from the others, losing its grip as it was being tugged, Belthasar regained his senses that had been dulled from the cold. He didn't have to find a path to that worm directly. He could go *through* the others! In a flash, his spirit repeatedly passed from one worm to another in a desperate search for freedom–back, forth, up, down and sideways–until finally Belthasar's spirit entered the very worm that was being pulled from the bowl at the instant it was yanked loose.

The man held up the worm to his large and amazed brown eyes, convinced it was the very last one that his daughter had caught a few nights ago. It wiggled wildly between his fingers like a live electric wire.

"You *are* a whopper of a worm! You're going to attract all kinds of attention down there," the man confidently said as he brought the hook closer to the bait. "Fish for dinner tonight!"

"Want to bet?" Belthasar thought with sneering contempt. A millisecond later, his spirit left the worm and passed into the fisherman's body.

The man sat up as straight as a soldier, his brown eyes clouding to gray. He dropped the worm and the fishing pole at the same time and slowly stood in the rowboat as it bobbed upon the lake.

"Ahhh... *That's* better," Belthasar said, stretching his arms and smiling with poisonous glee. "It's so good to have two legs again. And a *voice!*" he shouted with defiance across the water. He looked around the lake and studied his colorful woodland surroundings for a few moments, then sat back down and slowly rowed to shore.

"Now, where to from here?" he whispered.

CHAPTER TWO

Westward Bound

Belthasar pressed down on the accelerator, increasing his speed along the highway from a dizzying thirty-eight miles per hour to a staggering forty-five. And still other drivers passed him, honking their horns and throwing him dirty looks. He lowered the window and breathed in the fresh air, hoping to calm his jittery nerves. He had learned to drive only two hours ago.

"How can people move so fast?" he muttered, wishing he were riding a horse instead.

Though he possessed all the knowledge about driving an automobile from the fisherman whose body his spirit now inhabited, *knowing* and *doing* were two different things. Many cars sneaked up from behind, stalking him like wolves on a hunt. Fearing that a car might hit him, Belthasar bravely increased his speed, upping the digital readout to forty-nine, fifty-two and finally fifty-five. Noting that many of the highway signs indicated that exact number, Belthasar felt comfortable enough to stay at that speed. Though a few cars still passed now and then, nobody honked their horns anymore which made him feel better. Now he could enjoy the scenery on the way to his next destination. Belthasar knitted his brow. Exactly where *was* he going? He shrugged and kept driving, knowing he'd eventually stop somewhere to learn more about this weird and fascinating world.

Then something amazing caught his eye. Belthasar craned his head to the right like a cat spotting a mouse in the corner of the room. Belthasar's heart pounded. He slowed down and pulled off the highway. He stepped out of the vehicle and wandered over to a cyclone fence, his fingers grasping the metal rings as he gazed skyward. His jaw dropped as a mammoth white metallic flying machine landed in the distance on three sets of wheels, barreling down a runway like a gigantic eagle ripped out of a fantastic dream. About ten minutes later, another huge silver winged monstrosity roared into the air, the midmorning sun reflecting off a row of tiny windows along its side. Belthasar could discern the outline of human faces within the airplane. He shook his head in disbelief.

"These people can actually fly into the vast skies," he whispered. "How is that possible?"

Belthasar's thoughts swirled like a pile of leaves in October. Yet he realized that since the inhabitants of this world could travel over the ground at great speeds, it made sense that they would one day conquer the skies. A snake-like grin crept across his face. Only minutes ago he had ambitions to travel these lands to see where fate might take him. Belthasar imagined all of the additional places he could now go with those giant metal birds at his disposal. He wanted to get on board one as soon as possible.

Belthasar entered the airport terminal and sat down in the waiting area to observe the travelers and workers as they went about their business. As the sun shone warmly through a series of tall glass windows, several people milled about, some talking on cell phones or pay phones, others conversing with fellow travelers or flipping through magazines. Many people stood in long lines waiting to buy tickets while others prepared to board their flights. Belthasar soaked in the colorful blur of people as a faceless voice announced departure and arrival times over the loudspeaker.

An hour later he walked past a young businessman in a dark blue suit carrying a brown leather briefcase. By the look of his impeccably tailored clothes and serious demeanor, Belthasar concluded that this was a man of importance. At the moment, Belthasar inhabited a middle-aged man wearing a sweatshirt, blue jeans and sneakers, topped off with a red windbreaker. He definitely wanted to upgrade his appearance. So after the businessman slipped his plane ticket into his inside pocket and looked for a place to sit down, Belthasar casually turned around and followed. Moments later, Belthasar sat next to the man as he skimmed through the financial section of the day's newspaper.

"Excuse me, sir," Belthasar softly said, tapping the gentleman on the back of his hand. That was all that it took.

The man in the dark blue suit folded the newspaper and set it down on the empty seat next to him, his eyes now as dull and gray as winter clouds. He stood and walked away as the fisherman suddenly slumped down in the next chair, his world now a dizzying blur. He had such a headache as he looked about in utter confusion. Wasn't he supposed to be fishing? Was that a rack of suitcases that just rolled past? How on earth did he get *here*?

Belthasar settled back in his seat, having looked outside his window for the tenth time, still unable to believe he was actually this high in the air and heading for someplace called Los Angeles. He sipped his drink and watched the small television screen attached to the back of the seat in front of him. The fizzy beverage tasted sweet and energizing. The woman next to him had earlier asked for something called a diet cola from another lady who walked up and down the airplane aisle. When she returned with the drink, Belthasar asked for one too and enjoyed it as he watched the monitor while listening through a tiny set of headphones.

What *didn't* this world have, he wondered, as he absorbed a newscast and learned about the planet below, seeing events as they happened hundreds of miles away. What a day! What an education! Belthasar never wanted to leave.

This world offered everything he could want, and so many things he couldn't even begin to imagine. How could Endora and Solárin *ever* hope to lure him back through the timedoor?

Belthasar diligently studied life on the planet over the next several weeks through television, books, newspapers and radio. But what he enjoyed doing most was observing other humans in their daily activities. Belthasar would sit for hours in a coffee shop, pretending to read a book while drinking coffee, the whole time listening to three or four conversations bubbling around him. Other days he'd wander through a shopping mall or dine in a posh restaurant as he spied on the unsuspecting. On a few occasions he'd simply fly as a bird from tree to tree and watch and listen as life passed him by from below.

It proved to be an exciting learning process. But throughout the course of his studies, Belthasar came to one undeniable conclusion–not all power and influence in the world was wielded by politicians.

From businessmen to newscasters to entertainers–all held some sort of sway over segments of the population, for good or ill. Others, he noticed, who were swimming in riches and celebrity yet barely had a thought tucked between their ears, were nonetheless worshipped and adored. Somewhere in that mix, Belthasar thought he could find the right combination of wealth, power and leisure to enjoy life. He didn't necessarily have to run a country as long as he could be important and noticed and in control of others. After all, who would want to live life any other way?

Then he found his answer.

One day in early May while sitting on the sofa and aimlessly clicking the remote control of his wide screen television, Belthasar came across a tempting opportunity. His spirit had been inhabiting a real estate developer for the last week, enjoying life inside a spacious condominium. He had learned to drive with ease and tamed the highways of Los Angeles, savoring sun-drenched days along scenic ocean highways and balmy evenings of fine dining. But he still wasn't the center of attention. Nobody sought his opinion on issues of importance–or of *anything* for that matter. And he had nobody to tell what to do or when to do it. Above all else, Belthasar craved an audience.

He recalled how wonderful it had felt to stand on the platform outside the castle in Solárin, moments away from being crowned king, basking in the smiles of the adoring crowds and soaking in the pageantry of the ceremony. He so desired the power that had slipped through his fingers after he was foiled again by those pesky little children! Belthasar grabbed one of the sofa pillows and punched it repeatedly, snarling through his clenched teeth. Just the thought of Christopher and Molly Jordan and their alliance with King Rupert and that magician Artemas set his mind aflame. He vowed to repay them a hundredfold one day soon.

Belthasar sat back on the sofa and tossed the pillow aside. He had learned to control his emotions lately, at times even forgetting the wish to have his revenge upon the Jordan siblings. But thinking about his past life for a moment was sometimes enough to cause old wounds to surface. Belthasar knew that deep within his heart the desire for vengeance would always be there, waiting for the perfect time to strike. But the time had not yet arrived, nor was the plan in place.

Belthasar exhaled deeply, determined to get his new life in order first. So that meant not wasting time staring at the television like a wide-eyed owl. Belthasar grabbed the remote, preparing to click the OFF button when something caught his attention. He watched as a lady reporter chattered away, a smile steadily stretching across his face as he listened. The plan he was seeking had finally arrived. And this wonderful idea was compliments of actor Elvin L. Cooper. Belthasar turned up the volume.

...and movie critics and fans are sure to flock to the big screen when Elvin L. Cooper's first motion picture in two years is released in July. I'll have my interview with the movie's director Gordon Banks on next Friday's show, but as is typical with Elvin L. Cooper, the publicity-shy actor

will not make himself available for interviews. So we'll have to glean the latest nuggets of information about Mr. Cooper from his director and co-stars while he remains holed up in Clara Dú, his twenty million dollar oceanfront estate.

So there you have it, folks. The countdown has started to the July release of the action-adventure thriller TROUBLED WATER. And if the success of Elvin L. Cooper's two previous movies FOREIGN SOIL and HOT AIR is any indication, then TROUBLED WATER is sure to be a box office smash. This is yours truly, Eve Eloise, for this segment of BIG SCREEN BUZZ! I'll be back after these important messages.

Belthasar turned off the television, not eager to listen to any important message about headache tablets. He opened a sliding glass door and stepped out onto the fifteenth floor balcony as the late afternoon sun drifted westward. A warm breeze played through the leafy palm plants standing in the corners against the cast iron fencing. Belthasar walked over to the edge and gripped the top railing, staring aimlessly into the collage of buildings below as his mind calculated a dozen different human equations. One by one the pieces of his plan fell into place.

Belthasar smirked. Was there a better way to take center stage? So many people were fascinated with the lives of celebrities, he had observed. What if he inhabited an actor who the world loves to see yet continuously avoided the press? If he suddenly transformed into the most accessible actor in the business, then everyone would flock to him like seagulls along a littered shoreline. He'd instantly become the most sought after guest on television and the center of everyone's attention.

Belthasar liked what he was thinking, yet wasn't naïve enough to believe that public adulation could last forever. But a year or two would be fun. If he became the next Elvin L. Cooper, he could live a life of luxury and have thousands of people fawn over him, all craving to hear his latest opinion on just about anything. *That's* the life Belthasar desired, and it would be so easy to obtain. He stepped back inside and closed the sliding glass door. It was time to move on.

The hummingbird zipped from palm tree to palm tree planted in a gently curving line along the Olympic length swimming pool on the Clara Dú estate. The noon sun reflected off the crystal clear water like a burst of diamonds. Somewhere in the distance a cell phone rang and a glass pitcher of iced tea was being vigorously stirred. Elvin L. Cooper sat in the cool shade under the table umbrella, tapping at the keyboard on his laptop computer. Barefoot and dressed in khaki shorts and a black tee shirt, he looked closer to forty years old than the actual fifty he would be later that year. A pair of sunglasses covered his dark green eyes as they scanned the sentences he had just typed. He distractedly reached for an empty drinking glass when one of his housekeepers walked over and refilled the glass with iced tea and a fresh lemon slice.

"Thanks, Martha," he said, looking up. "You read my mind."

"That's my job, Mr. Cooper," she replied with a smile. "Anything else I can get you?"

The hummingbird landed on a wrought iron trellis wrapped in scarlet-red morning glories amid a sea of daisies and buttercups. A cloud of butterflies surrounded the fragrant blossoms. The hummingbird gently nudged one of the larger butterflies with its long curving beak and then wobbled precariously upon the trellis an instant later before flying off. That particular butterfly suddenly broke away from its companions and drifted toward the umbrella table.

As Martha walked away and Elvin L. Cooper returned to his laptop, one of his secretaries approached from the other direction, carrying a computer notebook and a cell phone. The rhythmic click of her high heels caused Elvin to turn his head. He removed his sunglasses as she spoke.

"Your wife called and wondered if it would be okay to change tonight's dinner reservations from six until eight. Her meeting at the art gallery was pushed back."

"That'll be fine, Linda. I'll have extra time to work."

"I'll inform her right away, Mr. Cooper," she said, flipping open the cell phone. "I thought I saw Gilbert heading this way," she added as she drifted away.

"Duly noted," Elvin remarked as he slipped his glasses back on and continued typing. The large butterfly, splashed with all the colors of an artist's palette, fluttered underneath the umbrella and landed on the rim of the tea glass. Elvin L. Cooper briefly observed it with an amused smile as another voice interrupted his quiet afternoon.

"I'm going back to my office, Elvin. Get a chance to sign those papers?"

Elvin reached over and grabbed a thin pile of letters and documents resting on the morning newspaper and handed them to his usually antsy and overly-caffeinated agent, Gilbert Staves. "As requested, Gil."

"Thanks." He noticed the butterfly balanced on the edge of the drinking glass and swished it away. "You've got butterflies in your tea, Elvin."

"Better than in my stomach," he joked, removing his glasses to speak as the butterfly returned and landed on the back of Elvin's hand.

"Looks like you made a new fan," Gilbert said flatly. "Well, I'll see you first thing in the morning, Elvin." He waved goodbye with the signed papers.

"All right, Gil," he said, eyeing the butterfly as he put on his sunglasses. Elvin sat up arrow straight in the next instant as the butterfly retreated in a graceless flight. Elvin called to his departing agent. "Wait a moment, Gil. I want to ask you something."

Gilbert Staves turned around and approached his boss, the shade from the table umbrella darkening his face. "What is it?"

"Why don't you arrange an interview with that enter-tainment reporter–Eve Eloise is her name, I believe."

Gilbert burst into a grin. "Good one, Elvin! I'll see you tomorrow," he said.

"I'm serious, Gil. I'd like to tape an interview for her

show to air when TROUBLED WATER is released."

Gilbert Staves looked as stunned as a student about to sit down for a calculus exam he had forgotten to study for. He stared at Elvin for several seconds, unable to speak. "You *are* serious," he finally uttered. "*Are you?*"

Elvin L. Cooper removed his sunglasses once again, his green eyes now slightly gray and lifeless. "*Deadly* serious. You arrange everything, okay?"

"Well... All right, Elvin. I– I can do that," he uttered, a puzzled look painted upon his face. "Sure... Sure..."

"You can fill me in on the details later, Gil."

"Sure... And then you can fill *me* in on why you suddenly want to speak with the press, Elvin."

"Just mellowing with age." Elvin L. Cooper waved him away with his sunglasses before returning them to his face. "See you in the morning."

Gilbert nodded and walked away in a daze, shaking his head all the way out the front door and continuing to do so as he drove his car down the long driveway and out the front security gate. He didn't know what to think.

Eve Eloise was sipping coffee at her desk and nibbling on a bagel when the telephone rang three days later. Her eyes popped open as large as clam shells and she nearly dropped her bagel when Gilbert Staves asked her if she wanted to interview actor Elvin L. Cooper. She said yes in a half dozen ways. Her heart pounded when Gilbert requested that the interview be taped in front of a live audience of five hundred lucky fans. Eve Eloise felt as if she had hit a Las Vegas jackpot.

Two months later, actor Elvin L. Cooper sat down in a makeup chair while people gawked at him as if he were a zoo exhibit. He smiled and joked and put them at ease. Twenty minutes later he sat on an easy chair opposite Eve Eloise, bathed in bright lights and the affectionate smiles of five hundred adoring fans who were chosen in a nationwide contest. Then the cameras rolled. The interview started. Eve Eloise took a deep breath, spoke for a few moments and then asked her first question.

"Why *now*?"

Elvin L. Cooper's movie opened in theaters two weeks later. On the week leading up to the premiere, Eve Eloise aired segments of her much envied interview every weekday on her live afternoon entertainment show BIG SCREEN BUZZ. She predicted that that week's show ratings would soar, even for the repeated airings at night. She couldn't wait to renegotiate her contract after scoring such a coveted interview. Even the commercials promoting the interview were a hit with the movie-going public.

"And is it true, Elvin, that you may show up at various theaters across the country unannounced to promote your new movie?"

"Anything is possible, Eve. I have a lot of years to make up for with my fans."

"I'll say. They'll congregate around you like moths circling a flame."

"It's the least I can do."

"And why this sudden change, Elvin? What has happened to that old quiet and shy personality of yours? Where did it go?"

"Oh, I still have it, Eve. But I have it folded away like an old shirt in the bottom dresser drawer. I have it stored behind glass like a dusty old trophy! I have it—"

ELVIN L. COOPER TALKS TO AMERICA! ALL THIS WEEK ON BIG SCREEN BUZZ WITH EVE ELOISE. AN EXCLUSIVE ONCE-IN-A-LIFETIME INTERVIEW YOU WON'T WANT TO MISS. SEE IT TONIGHT AND EVERY NIGHT AND FIND OUT WHAT THE BUZZ IS ALL ABOUT!

Elvin admired the tiny parakeet perched in the silver cage in the corner of his study as it preened its lemon-yellow and olive-green feathers. Elvin unlocked the latch, opened the tiny door and placed a hand inside, extending his index finger. The bird immediately hopped upon the actor's finger and Elvin slowly removed his hand from the cage and stared at his newest acquisition.

"I think buying this bird was a stroke of genius," he said to no one in the room. The spirit of Belthasar swam inside the heart and mind and soul of Elvin L. Cooper like a twisted choking vine. "*You* may not think so, Mr. Cooper," he added, still staring at the parakeet, "but *I* do. And that's all that really matters, isn't it?"

He walked over to a window, the morning sun gently washing inside. Elvin unlocked a latch and swung it wide open, inhaling a warm sweet breeze.

"Now things are going swimmingly here on the west coast, but I have another project back east that I need to check on. So I'll take my leave of you, Elvin, for a few days. You'll probably be a little confused, but that's all right. Just think of these last few months as a wild dream. But don't get used to your old ways again because I'll be back. You might try to loosen up on your own, Mr. Cooper. Everyone says you look much better for it."

Elvin stuck his arm outside the window, but the parakeet stood firmly upon his finger. Ocean waves swished hypnotically upon the shore in the background.

"Oh, and by the way–*don't* get rid of the birdcage."

In the next moment, the gray shading in Elvin L. Cooper's eyes dissolved and reappeared in the eyes of the parakeet which immediately flew off into the morning light. Elvin stumbled backward, caught himself on the edge of a bookshelf, and then plopped down in his desk chair. What had just happened? How'd he get in *here*? He slapped his hands to his face, a throbbing headache bubbling up at his temples, the likes of which he had never experienced before. He wanted some aspirin and a very long nap.

The hot dry breezes of July swept through the pine trees and willows planted around town. Orange and black tiger lilies basked under sapphire-blue skies. A week had passed since Independence Day and now everyone in the city eagerly awaited the upcoming weekend carnival–three days of games and music, food and rides, and plenty of good times. The Jordan family particularly looked forward to the annual summer celebration in the large field on the edge of town. It was always an event to remember.

But life went on as usual the day before the festivities. A white ice cream truck rambled slowly along a quiet road in one of the neighborhoods, its melodious chimes calling out to all who desired a frozen sweet confection on a sweltering afternoon. A young girl in a pink sundress waited near the edge of the sidewalk, money clenched in her hand as her mother watched from the front porch. She proudly made the purchase of a double scoop of strawberry ice cream after the white truck pulled up to the curb, then waved to the driver as he pulled away.

The girl beamed with joyous anticipation as she carefully walked back up the lawn toward the front porch, not wanting to taste the ice cream until she was comfortably seated in her favorite swinging chair with the print of singing frogs on the fabric. She smiled at her mother, quickly turning her head when a large black crow landed on a branch of a nearby sprawling oak. A sour grimace spread across the girl's face.

"Don't you even *think* about eating my ice cream cone, you old bird!" she sternly warned, pointing a finger at the crow before sprinting up the porch steps.

The crow cawed once and flapped its wings as it perched high above the silent street, its dull gray eyes reflecting the blazing summer sun.

"You're not the one I traveled across country to see, little girl," the crow thought, digging its claw into the oak branch. "I'm here to pay a visit to the Jordan family. Only question is—what shall I do when I *find* them?"

Suddenly the bird flew off above the rooftops in search of his prey.

CHAPTER THREE

An Unlucky Penny

The Ferris wheel turned slowly against the twilight sky, its metal spokes ablaze with alternating lines of icy blue and green lights. Stars peeked out in bunches over the field on the edge of town bustling with hundreds of carnival goers on a warm Friday evening in July. The aromas of sweet buttered popcorn and cotton candy drifted lazily through the air, competing with the calliope music from a twirling merry-go-round and the staccato pops of bursting balloons from the dart throw booth. The laughter of children and adults encompassed it all, rising from the festival grounds as lively as bubbles from a freshly poured glass of ginger ale. And as full darkness descended, the warm glow of the carnival lights increased as if keeping a silent and protective watch upon all who stepped within its radiant border.

Someone else kept watch from within the carnival grounds as well, observing the Jordan family stealthily and silently through ashen gray eyes.

Vergil dived into the sea of red, yellow, blue and green plastic balls, working his way to the bottom of the pile like a mouse digging a burrow into the soft earth. Sam and Sally Jordan kept an eye on their seven-year-old son from outside the lighted screen enclosure with some other parents, watching with amused grins as his dark brown head of hair popped up from under the colorful sea of spheres amid the other shouting and tumbling children. Vergil hooted and threw a fist in the air, then plopped backward and let himself sink underneath the plastic balls once again. He smiled and waved to his parents, beaming with pure joy as the last traces of his red, white and blue striped shirt disappeared beneath the surface. A woman in an orange blouse a few feet away also watched the activity through the screening, her gray eyes focused on Vergil.

"We should build one of these contraptions in the backyard," Mr. Jordan said to his wife as he adjusted the glasses on the bridge of his nose. "Think of the hours we'd save chasing after him!"

"But imagine how bored we'd be with all that extra free time," his wife joked, placing an arm around him.

"We could *use* some boredom," he replied, scanning the enclosure through the mesh screening. Suddenly he couldn't locate his son among the other children as they happily bounced about. "Hey, Vergil, where are you?"

Mrs. Jordan didn't spot him either and pressed her nose against the screen. "Vergil?" she uttered, a tinge of concern in her voice.

A few seconds passed and there was still no sign of his colorful shirt or the mop of hair usually in a wild tangle above his toothy smile. Mrs. Jordan pressed a hand against the tent. Her eyes darted back and forth in a maddening search. Mr. Jordan's stomach tightened. He was about to call Vergil's name again when a familiar voice shouted out.

"Here I am, everybody!" Vergil hollered as he burst like a rocket from underneath the pile of plastic balls. "I can hold my breath underneath all this stuff even longer than I can in the pool!"

"I guess you can!" his father said, flashing a thumbs up and exhaling.

"Warn us next time you're going to stay underneath for so long," Mrs. Jordan added, a slight quiver in her voice as her heart fluttered. She now followed the movements of her son with an eagle eye, amazed at his boundless energy.

"So maybe we *won't* build one in the backyard," Mr. Jordan commented to his wife as they watched Vergil dive again into the mound of plastic balls. "Besides, we probably wouldn't be able to keep Chris and Molly away from it despite their ages!"

"No doubt." She chuckled at the thought and looked at her watch. "It's almost nine-thirty. I wonder what mischief our other two handfuls are up to right now."

"You mean our two *teenage* handfuls," Mr. Jordan replied with a proud yet bemused smile. "Don't be concerned. Since there are no troll-infested castles nearby, I'm sure they're okay. Anyway, what kind of trouble can they find around *here*?"

"I just worry that trouble seems to find *them*," Mrs. Jordan said as she kept a close eye on Vergil, unaware that the lady in the orange shirt had quietly walked away.

Molly Jordan placed an index finger on either side of her face and pushed up, then sprouted a grin as wide as a pumpkin's.

"Look at this face, Betsy! What do you think?"

"I'll give it a B-plus," her friend replied as the pair continued to contort their faces in the distorted mirrors deep inside *Carnival Charlie's Amazing Funhouse of Monster Chills and Incredible Wonders*. Betsy folded her lips over her teeth to hide them, shut one eye and frowned. "What do you think of *this* one?" she mumbled.

Molly burst out laughing. "Excellent! Maybe you should go to clown school." She gathered up a handful of her shoulder-length blond hair and held it above her head while batting her eyelids. "I *love* this new look on me! Think it will impress Jake Towner?" she giggled, puffing up her cheeks.

"Only if he likes goofy looking space aliens!"

They broke out in laughter, making more ridiculous faces in the mirror until they heard the solitary footsteps in the distance. They went as quiet as church mice.

"Quick! To the next room," Betsy suggested with excited urgency.

They hurried along a brightly lit corridor awash in wild swirls of purple, silver and tangerine. The girls separated when the winding maze split into two passages. They promised to meet up in the next section.

Molly walked alone through one corridor, its walls aglow with a rich forest-green hue. The passage alternated between short sections that veered left, right or straight ahead. Molly had no choice but to walk along the crooked path as it switched its direction every few steps. She felt as if trapped deep within a cave. And there were those footsteps again. Was somebody following her? Then Molly screamed.

She quickly covered her mouth and laughed. The image of a giant fanged bat had suddenly appeared on the wall directly in front of her before instantly disappearing. Molly laughed again, thankful that her brother wasn't here. She knew Christopher would have teased her endlessly for being so scared. She moved anxiously through the remaining awkward bends in the corridor, eager to meet up with Betsy. Then she heard the deadly dull echo of footsteps once more, getting louder, getting closer.

Molly instinctively turned around. Perhaps an attendant was wandering through to make sure everyone was behaving. Or had Betsy backtracked to catch up with her? The footsteps ceased. Molly shifted her eyes left and right. All was still, almost *too* still, but she turned back around and plodded onward, wondering when this annoying corridor would end. Molly felt more frustrated than the time she had searched room to room on her first visit to King Rupert's castle. How tedious *that* little episode had been!

But before she could recall any more memories from her time spent in Endora, the monotonous thump of the footsteps returned. This time much louder. And now closer. Molly raced as best she could through the final turns in the crooked passageway. Left. Straight ahead. A quick right. Straight ahead again. And then–

Molly plunged into the gloom of the last chamber as

the footsteps boomed loudly in her head. Someone was closing in fast. She looked around wildly in the pale light. Suddenly a hand grasped her upon the shoulder. Molly shrieked and spun around. Another voice yelped liked a frightened pup. Then the lights turned up and a set of doors at the end of the room slid open. A draft of cooler evening air drifted inside.

"Betsy! You nearly scared me to death!" Molly said, half laughing to her friend.

"Sorry," Betsy replied with an apologetic shrug. "I thought you were part of the door frame. I heard someone following me and hurried to get to the end."

"Me too," Molly said, still aware of the steady beat of footsteps nearby.

She raised an eyebrow at the equally puzzled Betsy, then both girls turned around and spotted the answer. A pair of mechanically operated wooden shoes rose up and down upon a small square of oak wood in the corner of the room, stepping in place like a restless horse tethered to a post. Then the shoes stopped. For a few moments all was quiet except for the voices of other carnival goers drifting in from outdoors. Half a minute later the shoes moved again, though now not at all frightening in the glare of bright lights. Molly and Betsy giggled until a voice called to them from outside.

"Exit this way, ladies," a man said. "I have to close the door and dim the lights. Others will be through soon."

"Okay, mister," Molly said, signaling for Betsy to follow.

"You weren't scared, were you?" he asked while securing the doors.

"Hardly," Molly said with a roll of her eyes as she and Betsy scurried off toward the cotton candy booth.

The man observed them through a pair of ashen gray eyes as they disappeared into the crowd. "Perhaps *next* time," he whispered.

A single light bulb burned dimly above the desktop. The sheriff sat back in the squeaky chair, propped his feet up, then twirled one end of a long mustache around an index finger, grinning confidently. "Boys, expect some law and order from here on in," he muttered with an exaggerated southern drawl while polishing the star on his vest with the cuff of his sleeve. "I reckon that'd be the smart thing to do."

Christopher grunted, trying not to laugh at his friend. "I reckon that hat you're wearing is too tight, Robert," he said as he slipped on an oversized black and white striped convict's costume over his clothes. He adjusted the matching cap on his head of closely cropped light brown hair and grinned. "How do I look?"

"Like a weird zebra," his other friend Henry replied. He was similarly dressed as a convict in the mock sheriff's office on the carnival grounds as they waited to have their pictures taken in the jail cell.

"Why don't we stick *you* in the jail, Robert, and let me and Henry stand outside holding the key," Christopher suggested.

"No can do, you hooligan. I'm in charge in this town!" he said, hopping off the chair and clomping about in a pair of extra large boots. "Say, where'd that girl with the camera go?"

"She stepped out to answer her cell phone." Henry peeked through one of the windows but couldn't see her anywhere in the darkness. "Maybe she's on the side of the building. Probably gabbing with a boyfriend."

"Hope not," Robert said, adjusting his bolo tie and smoothing out his coffee-brown vest. "I was thinking of asking her out."

Christopher and Henry nearly choked with laughter.

"She's probably in college," Henry guessed. "Why would she want to go out with *you*? By the way, your mustache is crooked."

"I'm getting my driver's permit next month," Robert said in his defense while he properly reattached his mustache. "That'll impress *any* girl."

Christopher smirked. "Sure. *That'll* clinch it."

Henry sighed. "I'm going to see what's taking her so

long. This costume is starting to itch," he said, scratching behind his neck. He headed toward the door.

Robert followed him. "I'll go with you! We'll find her faster that way."

Henry turned to his friend, trying not to grin. "Robert, she'll go out with my sister's pet hamster before she'll even *consider* dating you."

Christopher waved them on. "I'll wait here," he said as they exited the tiny building. He removed his convict's cap, tossed it on the desk, then paced about the room. His watch read nine forty-five. Where *had* that girl gone?

He plopped down on the desk chair and leaned back with his hands behind his head, satisfied that he was one up on Robert in that he had already obtained his driver's permit last month. Christopher wondered if that *would* impress the camera girl. Yet for all the freedom that driving allowed him, it couldn't compare to traveling across the Endoran plains on horseback to rescue Princess Rosalind from captivity. But that trek had almost been for nothing after they were tossed into Malaban's vault far below the castle. Now *that* was a jail, Christopher concluded. Nothing like the tiny barred cell in this place. Luckily Mr. Smithers had tagged along and saved the day.

Christopher jumped up when he noticed a small window in the jail cell. He stepped inside and climbed on a wooden stool in one corner, peering out the dusty glass pane. The empty field behind the carnival grounds stretched on into the black of night underneath a canopy of bright white stars, another reminder of his time spent in Endora. Christopher's imagination swept him away to that faraway place as it had done on so many occasions. Suddenly a shadow moved just outside the window. Christopher flinched, thinking somebody was hiding behind the small building. Or was his imagination playing tricks on him? He wasn't sure as he looked again, unaware that the front door had opened behind him. Neither did he hear the footsteps that slowly approached nor see the hand that carried a large black iron key to the jail cell door.

Swiftly and silently the barred door was swung shut, the key inserted into the lock and turned, and then–CLICK!

"I finally have you," a voice whispered, startling Christopher from his daydream. "You're my prisoner and there's no escape!"

Christopher spun around and jumped off the stool. "Huh? What?" His thoughts were a thousand miles away.

"Earth to convict! You weren't napping in there while I stepped out, were you?"

Christopher shook his head and sheepishly smiled. "No, just thinking. My friends went looking for you." He grabbed hold of the jail cell bars.

"Don't worry. You're not trapped. I was just teasing you," the girl said, pulling the cell door open. "The lock doesn't even work. It's just for show."

"I could have busted out easily enough," Christopher said, pointing a thumb across his shoulder. "How many jails have an unbarred window in them?"

"Good point." The girl flashed a smile and set her cell phone and digital camera on the desk before adjusting a barrette in her stringy red hair. The words CARNIVAL STAFF were printed on the back of her shirt in bold black letters. "Sorry I took so long to get back. It was an important call. My grandfather's been in the hospital and my mother called to say he's doing much better. Probably going home next week."

"Great news," Christopher said.

"I feel better now after worrying for days that he might not make it." She blinked a few times. "Easy to take your family for granted until something like this happens."

"I know what you mean." Christopher grinned. "A family can seem off the wall at times, but it's nice to have them around."

She smiled. "Now where are your two friends? If you want three photos matted and framed, it'll be at least twenty minutes. We stop taking orders at ten-thirty."

"I'll round them up," Christopher said, heading toward the door. "Oh, so that means you *weren't* talking to your bo…"

"What?"

"Never mind," Christopher replied, opening the door and leaning on the knob. "By the way, I have my driver's permit," he casually added, making his voice sound deeper.

"Oh. Good. That's terrific," she said, concealing a grin as she checked the settings on her camera.

Christopher turned two shades of red. "Yeah, well… Back in a minute." He cleared his throat and scrambled out the door, shaking his head as he muttered, vowing to punch his friend Robert in the arm as soon as he laid his hands on him. As Christopher shot past, a figure emerged from the shadows on the side of the building, its ashen gray eyes following the boy as he drifted through the carnival crowd.

"Fifty doughnuts should be just about right," Vergil sleepily said as he leaned against his father while they stood outside the baked goods trailer.

"How about a half dozen of those huge chocolate covered butterscotch brownies," his mother suggested. "We can enjoy them on the back porch when we get home."

"I'm all for that!" Molly said, furiously clicking a penlight she had won earlier at one of the game booths. It flashed a bright ice-blue color. Her friend Betsy had left a while ago with her own parents. "Where's Chris?"

"He's going to walk home with Henry and Robert," her father said, sitting down on a nearby bench and plopping his son on his lap. "Vergil, I don't think you'll even stay *awake* for brownies."

"Bet I *will*…" he mumbled, unable to suppress a yawn. Distant voices of carnival goers and the monotonous drone of the amusement rides nearly lulled him to sleep.

Molly scowled. "How come Chris gets to walk home with his friends but I have to get carted around by my parents?"

"Because your brother is older," Mrs. Jordan said, fishing for money in her purse.

"Whoop-de-do!" Molly softly muttered. "I can climb

down a castle wall hanging from a ratty old blanket, but I can't walk a mile home at night."

"One and a *half* miles. Oh, and no more climbing down castle walls either," her mother replied matter-of-factly, still searching through her purse.

Molly sighed. "Whatever..."

Molly and her mother moved up to the window just after the last of the butterscotch brownies had been purchased by the previous customer. Mr. Jordan remained seated with his son.

"Fresh batch coming up shortly," someone inside the trailer said after Mrs. Jordan placed her order.

One of the bakers brushed a thick layer of double chocolate icing over a warm batch of brownies on a back counter, apologizing for the delay. Molly assured the red-cheeked women wearing a white paper cap that she didn't mind. Molly giggled to herself, noting the resemblance the lady had to Mrs. Rudkin who worked in the main kitchen in King Jeremiah's castle.

Molly nudged closer to her mother and stood on her tiptoes hoping to get a better glimpse of the brownie-frosting process, but was disappointed to see only a counter crowded with pre-formed bakery boxes, piles of white napkins and a small television to keep the workers entertained when sales were slow. The glowing TV screen currently showed a repeat of that afternoon's edition of BIG SCREEN BUZZ with host Eve Eloise. The low volume competed with the busy kitchen voices.

"They can't move any faster, Molly, even with your nose pressed to the screen."

"I know, Mom, but I'm famished! At least for brownies anyway."

"Me too!" her mother whispered with a playful grin, placing a hand on Molly's shoulder. "You can watch the TV to keep yourself occupied."

"Bor–ing," Molly said, smelling the chocolate wafting through the sweet July air. But her eyes settled on the television anyway and she listened halfheartedly with her mother as Eve Eloise continued her weeklong interview with actor Elvin L. Cooper.

"And is it true, Elvin, that you may show up at various theaters across the country unannounced to promote your new movie?"

"Anything is possible, Eve. I have a lot of years to make up for with my fans."

"Another whoop-de-do," Molly said with a click of her tongue.

"I'll say. They'll congregate around you like moths circling a flame."

"It's the least I can do."

"Some people have way too much ego and not enough space to store it," Mrs. Jordan said dryly.

"And why this sudden change, Elvin? What has happened to that old quiet and shy personality of yours? Where did it go?"

"Oh, I still have it, Eve. But I have it folded away like an old shirt in the bottom dresser drawer."

Molly turned her head and eagerly watched as one of the other bakers took the frosted tray of brownies and deftly sliced the batch into large perfect squares.

"I have it stored behind glass like a dusty old trophy!"

Mrs. Jordan looked up as the tray was carefully slid into the display rack in front for everyone to see.

"I have it caught like a helpless mouse in a hawk's iron grip! And I won't–let–go!"

Molly and her mother turned their heads and locked gazes. A simultaneous chill ran up and down their spines. For an instant, the warmth of this young summer evening felt as bitter and dreary as a rainy autumn night.

"And I don't think this audience wants you to let it go, Elvin. They're going crazy for the new you! What a treat for us all!"

Molly's heart pounded when hearing those jaw-dropping words. "Did that man just say what I *think* he said, Mom?"

Mrs. Jordan nodded. "I was about to ask you the same thing." She glanced at the television, studied the smiling and animated Elvin L. Cooper, and then turned again to her daughter. "I heard those exact words once before."

"Me too," Molly softly said. "About eight months ago on the coronation platform outside of King Jeremiah's castle."

Molly and her mother both recalled those horribly intense moments they had witnessed when Belthasar had taken over the mind, body and soul of Prince Jeremiah. He had uttered those very words to Princess Rosalind, who at that moment was trying to prevent her fiancé from sacrificing his own life to save his future kingdom. Solárin and its people were finally rescued from the scourge of Belthasar, but his malicious spirit had mysteriously escaped in the end. But to where, no one could say. Until now.

"That *has* to be him, Molly. *Here*! In our world."

"But how could it be?"

At that moment a lady in the trailer handed Mrs. Jordan a box with a half dozen freshly baked frosted butterscotch brownies along with a few napkins tossed on top. Mrs. Jordan hastily paid for the items and then sat down next to her husband and Vergil. Molly squatted in front of them as they huddled together to explain the news.

"What's going on?" Mr. Jordan asked, stunned beyond belief after he heard the details. "Are you sure it was the exact sentence you heard at the coronation?"

"Word for word," Mrs. Jordan assured him. "*Caught like a helpless mouse in a hawk's iron grip! And I won't–let–go!*" She sighed in disbelief. "Molly and I were both there on the platform. Only at *that* time Belthasar was referring to Prince Jeremiah and not Cooper's shy personality. When he repeated the phrase on television a moment ago, we both knew in an instant that Elvin L. Cooper was Belthasar."

"But taking over an *actor*? Why would Belthasar do that? And how did he get into our world in the first place?"

All were questions everyone wanted immediate answers to, but knew that none would be forthcoming any time soon.

"Hey, what's up?" a voice in the darkness called out. Christopher, Henry and Robert emerged from the shadows, dressed once again in their street clothes and proudly showing off the framed photographs of themselves in the jail cell. "What'd you buy?"

"Butterscotch brownies," Mrs. Jordan replied. "And as long as you're here, Christopher, I think you should come home with us."

"Now? It's not even eleven o'clock. I was going to walk home with these guys," he said, indicating Henry and Robert.

"We'll give them a lift back," Mr. Jordan added as he stood up, Vergil still clinging tiredly to his side. "Something's come up and we need to go home."

Christopher frowned. "What are you talking about?"

"A family matter," his mother said, trying to put a cheerful spin on the matter. But deep inside, she dreaded what the days ahead might bring. Like an unlucky penny, Belthasar had turned up again and she hadn't the slightest idea what to do about it.

"Aw, don't make me leave yet!"

"Yeah, we've hardly finished stuffing our faces, Mrs. Jordan," Henry pleaded.

Molly grabbed a napkin from the bundle her mother held and scribbled a few words on it with her penlight as Christopher tried to persuade his parents to let him stay. She folded it once and handed it to Christopher, glaring at him with a pair of steely eyes.

"You'll have all day tomorrow to hang out with your friends, Christopher," his mother promised.

Christopher took the note from Molly and hurriedly glanced at what she had written. "But you said I could–"

He flinched slightly when the words on the napkin registered in his brain. He reread them several times. Those three tiny words–*Belthasar is here!*–nearly took his breath away. He crumpled up the napkin and shoved it in his pocket, staring at his parents with apprehension. He looked sideways at Molly, raising an eyebrow.

"Oh, *I* remember now!" Christopher awkwardly exclaimed, snapping his fingers and nodding apologetically to his friends. "That's right, guys. We're supposed to, um–visit my Uncle George early tomorrow morning. It's a long drive. And we promised. Honest."

Molly turned away and bit her tongue, noting what a terrible fibber her brother was. They *had* no Uncle George. She wondered if Christopher could even convince a thirsty man to drink a glass of water. Then again, he needed only to persuade Henry and Robert, so Molly thought that it wouldn't be such a hard sell after all.

Several minutes later, the seven of them wandered through the carnival grounds, making their way to the parking lot on the east side of the field. The lilting music from the carousel filled the evening air, harmonizing with the glorious scent of fried sausage, peppers and onions dancing in the breeze. Nearby, a clown-suited balloon seller with a mop of orange frizzy hair, a huge red nose and a pair of oversized sunglasses attached a blazing yellow balloon to a helium tank and filled it until nearly bursting. Behind the sunglasses, a pair of ashen gray eyes focused on the Jordan family as they silently passed by.

"Spying on them was *too* easy," Belthasar thought as he watched the Jordans depart, delighted he could slip into their territory without them having the slightest clue. Yet before he devised a plan for their ultimate ruin, he wanted to get closer to the family and gather more information about how best to exact his revenge. After all, the people who had vexed him for so many years should suffer a defeat as equally memorable for himself as it was miserable for them.

"I'll slip into somebody to keep an eye on the Jordans, waiting for the right moment to strike," Belthasar mused as he filled up a blood-red balloon, deciding to return to the Clara Dú estate first and flesh out his plan. When he *was* finally ready to attack, Belthasar felt confident that the perfect candidate to serve as his spy would turn up.

CHAPTER FOUR

A Second Santa

Belthasar's ability to freely roam the planet hung over the Jordan family like a rain cloud. Only this cloud was the dreariest shade of gray imaginable and stretched on for miles and miles. They informed Mr. Smithers and his wife Emma about what they had learned, stopping at their newly remodeled restaurant late Saturday morning the very next day before business hours. The couple recoiled at the news, recalling those chilling words that Belthasar had uttered on the coronation platform.

"Everyone had appeared quite normal when we crossed through the timedoor last year," Emma said as she served her guests hot coffee and pastries at one of the restaurant tables. Smoky tinted mirrors and large leafy plants scattered throughout the dining area gently reflected the glow of ceiling lights tucked among wooden rafters. "How could Belthasar have gotten through?"

"And how do we stop him?" Mr. Smithers added.

They discussed contacting the police, but that possibility seemed unrealistic. Such a fantastic story would get them laughed out of the station. And as for revealing the existence of the timedoor to back up their claim? They agreed that such an action was out of the question. The chaos that might ensue while Belthasar had access to either world was frighteningly apparent. But the pandemonium that would result if the *world* knew of the existence of the timedoor was unimaginable.

Tracking down Belthasar themselves seemed equally daunting since he was a well-protected celebrity. In an instant he could shift to another host if he got the slightest bit suspicious that someone was after him. Until they developed a sensible plan to trap him, Mr. Jordan and Mr. Smithers concluded that they might have to leave him alone. Christopher, Molly, Emma and Mrs. Jordan reluctantly agreed, though nobody was happy about it. They drank coffee and ate pastries in silence. But food, for the moment, was as tasteless as cardboard.

The remaining days of summer wandered aimlessly from one outdoor barbecue to the next and from pitcher after pitcher of chilled lemonade and raspberry iced tea. From numerous trips to the library where armloads of books were plucked from metal shelves to backyard hammocks where they were breathlessly absorbed page by precious page. And from thunderstorms and humid mornings to twilight gatherings on front porches where pyrotechnic displays of skittish lightning bugs were viewed under the shady boughs of maple and pine.

But in all that time, Belthasar never showed himself.

Soon yellow school buses took to the roads and trees burst into flaming shades of orange and purple and gold. Temperatures dipped as days darkened and footballs sailed in perfect spirals against slate-gray skies. Ghosts and goblins wandered through streets as jack-o-lanterns glowed on front porch steps. Veterans saluted in local parks as flags proudly snapped under a crisp autumn sky.

And still Belthasar remained hidden.

In time families gathered to say grace and swap memories around tables laden with roasted turkey, fresh cranberries and warm pumpkin pie. Pine trees glittered with tinsel and lights while Christmas carols resonated from churches and shops. And powdery bursts of snowflakes swirled through the air with icy delight.

Yet Belthasar was nowhere to be found. Still, his loathsome existence was felt by the Jordan family every minute of every day, sometimes like an irritating buzz of a pesky mosquito hovering near an ear, other times like the overwhelming presence of the proverbial elephant standing center stage in the tiniest of rooms. He was *always* there.

Mr. and Mrs. Jordan relaxed on the couch the day after Christmas, enjoying some hot peppermint tea in front of the fireplace. It was seven-thirty in the evening. Shouts of success periodically erupted from the adjacent dining room as Christopher and Molly combated each other in a game of Battleship. Vergil had positioned himself upside down on an overstuffed recliner next to the Christmas tree by the front picture window, his feet propped against the headrest as he glanced through a booklet that came with his package of modeling clay. A dozen possibilities for his first project swam in his head like a school of frenzied fish. Magic lay in the corner of the room, munching on a bone-shaped dog treat, wagging his tail with furious contentment, oblivious to all else.

"Hasn't the blood rushed to your head yet?" Mr. Jordan asked his son.

Vergil opened his upside down eyes extra wide to see his father better. "Not yet, Dad. I'm still deciding what to make with my clay."

"That's fine," his mother said, standing to refill their mugs with tea. "But when you get to the actual building phase, your operation gets transferred to the kitchen table."

"Okey-dokey," he mumbled, flipping a page.

Mrs. Jordan headed to the kitchen and then paused when her eye caught sight of the ceramic Nativity scene displayed on a small table near the Christmas tree. She glanced at her son with a suspicious eye.

"Vergil, why is your Extraterrestrial Amphibian Android between the Three Wisemen and the kneeling shepherd? I don't recall him being at the first Christmas."

"Mom, I need a place to keep him until Dad finishes building his secret hideout. It's spread all over the den floor in about a thousand pieces!" he replied with an exasperated sigh. "Frogatron has to have *somewhere* to hang out."

"I'll have your web-footed robot's hideout finished tomorrow," his father promised.

"In the meantime, could you find a more appropriate place for your action hero, sweetheart?" Mrs. Jordan kindly asked, staring directly into Vergil's eyes so that he knew she meant business. "Perhaps Froggy can keep Magic company."

"It's *Frogatron*, Mom!" he muttered, closing his eyes and shaking his head.

Vergil dropped the booklet, pulled himself onto the recliner and ended up kneeling on the cushion while facing the back of the chair. He glanced out the frosted picture window into the gentle darkness of December. The bare bony branches of two huge maple trees on the front lawn were dusted with snowflakes. Heavier clumps of snow still clung to the sagging pine boughs on the side of the lawn to his left. The curving stone walk leading to the front porch lay caked with snow, awash in the gentle glow of a lamppost planted among the glittering snow banks rolling across the front lawn.

Vergil prepared to hop off the chair when he quickly did a double take. He craned his head closer to the frosted pane, standing on his tiptoes as he gazed hypnotically into the wintry evening landscape. A sudden night breeze blew a confetti-like burst of snowflakes in front of his eyes. Vergil's jaw dropped as he turned to his father.

"Santa's only supposed to stop here once a year, right, Dad?"

"That's the rule, Verg, no matter *how* good you claimed to have been in your three-page letter to the North Pole."

"Why do you ask?" Mrs. Jordan inquired as she reentered the room with two mugs steaming with fresh peppermint tea.

Vergil placed his hands to his hips and scrunched his face. "Because Santa's walking right up to our house this very minute!"

Vergil stared out the window again, wondering if his eyes were playing tricks on him. But he couldn't deny what he saw. An older gentleman wrapped snuggly in the folds of a thick gray cloak with a beard trailing down to his waist, trudged slowly up the front walk toward the porch. Though he was bathed in the light of the lamppost, the hood of his garment was draped over his head and concealed most of his facial features. The snow squeaked under the heavy steps of his large black boots.

Mrs. Jordan set the mugs down and joined her son at the window. Mr. Jordan walked up behind them and together the trio gazed into the night. An instant later, Mr. and Mrs. Jordan looked at each other and smiled with a mix of joy and relief.

"That's not Santa Claus," Mr. Jordan assured his son as the echo of footsteps sounded on the front porch.

"Then who *is* it?" he curiously asked as the doorbell rang.

"I'll get it!" Molly shouted from the dining room. She raced for the hallway door.

"Not if I beat you to it!" Christopher challenged, chasing after her.

"I better put on some more tea!" Mrs. Jordan said.

"For *who*?" Vergil exclaimed, marching in place on the chair cushion.

Mr. Jordan picked up his son. "Haven't you already guessed? It's–"

"*Artemas*!" Christopher and Molly cried out in unison from the other room. "Are we glad to see you!" they added as they dragged him into the living room after he hurriedly removed his boots.

"Oh, *him*!" Vergil shouted with a grin. "Arty Mouse!"

"The one and only," Artemas replied, delighted to see his friends again. "I hope I haven't arrived at an inconvenient time." He glanced at the snowmen and angels and holly decorations strewn about the house, particularly pleased with the colorful glow and sparkle of the Christmas tree. Some of the miniature lights matched the ocean-blue color of his eyes. "Not interrupting anything, am I?"

"Not at all," Mrs. Jordan said, greeting the magician with a hug.

"And it is *quite* a convenient time," Mr. Jordan added with a firm handshake. "We were relaxing from our usual hectic Christmas yesterday. It wore us all out."

"I can imagine," the magician replied, eyeing with bewilderment the piles of opened presents under the tree and in various corners of the room. "First it was carved pumpkins with candles in them, and now a pine tree in the middle of your house adorned with lights. I noticed them all over town. Quite beautiful. But I'll definitely have to research your holidays while I'm here on vacation!"

They sat in front of the fireplace after Mrs. Jordan brought out a tray of sliced cranberry-walnut bread and spreads to have with their tea. The Jordans were thrilled that Artemas wanted to remain in their world until the timedoor reopened in approximately eight days. The third and final opening would occur just over a week after that. Mr. Jordan invited him to spend his vacation at the house. Artemas agreed, but insisted that before his vacation started, there was something he must do. From one of the deep pockets in his cloak, he pulled out a folded note sealed with candle drippings.

"This message is from Queen Eleanor who asked me to deliver it to her sister Emma as soon as I arrived here," Artemas explained. "Do you know where she is?"

"She and Mr. Smithers reopened the diner near the timedoor," Molly said. "It's a really nice restaurant now and they live in the apartment above it."

"I hadn't noticed any lights in the downstairs windows when I passed by a short while ago."

Christopher grabbed a slice of bread and slathered it

with cream cheese. "They closed the place for Christmas and New Years."

"But they should be home upstairs," Mrs. Jordan added. "I can give them a call. And, Christopher, don't get crumbs over the rug."

"That would be wonderful. I need to speak with Emma before the timedoor closes." He held up the note. "I believe Queen Eleanor wants her to stop by for a visit between openings. It's been nearly a year since the two sisters have spoken to each other."

Molly did some quick calculating in her head. "It's been *over* a year, Artemas. More than thirteen months, in fact."

Artemas took a sip of tea and smiled over his mug adorned with candy canes and wreaths. "I was referring to the Endoran calendar, Molly."

"Oh, I forgot. *Your* day and year are longer than ours."

"How's the weather in your neck of the woods?" Mr. Jordan asked.

"Quite lovely. We're approaching the end of winter and eagerly await the return of spring and the start of another year."

"Your year starts on the first day of spring?" Molly inquired. Artemas nodded. "Ours starts in less than a week, right in the middle of all this cold weather. Maybe we should trade, then staying up until midnight outside wouldn't be so bad."

Artemas shrugged. "Why would you want to stay up until midnight in the cold?"

"Long story," Mr. Jordan said. "We should get Queen Eleanor's note delivered before the timedoor closes."

"The timedoor opened at seven o'clock and will close at ten," Artemas said, glancing at a clock on the wall that read seven-thirty. "So that gives us two and a half hours to take Emma back. I'm sure she and Queen Eleanor have much to talk about since they last met."

"As do we," Mrs. Jordan said, her tone now somber

and edgy.

Artemas noted the sudden change of expression on all their faces and tugged at his beard. "What's going on? Is something the matter?"

"More like *someone* is the matter," Christopher muttered.

Artemas wrinkled his brow. "I don't quite understand. *Someone*?"

"We have disturbing news to reveal," Molly whispered. She was sitting on the floor leaning against Christopher's chair, her arms folded across her chest. "Some *deeply* disturbing news. Part of a great mystery has been solved."

"Oh, don't be so dramatic!" her brother grumbled. "Getting those Sherlock Holmes mystery stories for Christmas doesn't *make* you a great detective."

"I'll be as dramatic as I *want* to, Mr. Dry-as-three-day-old-toast. And that's with*out* butter, brother!"

Christopher playfully punched Molly in the arm. "*You're* deeply disturbed!"

"Ooowww!" she moaned in exaggerated pain, rolling onto the carpet. "Mother, please lock up your son in his cage for the night. I think it's past his bedtime."

"Would you two delinquents behave," Mr. Jordan said, apologizing to Artemas with a roll of his eyes. "We have some serious business to discuss."

"Your father is right," Mrs. Jordan said. "Belthasar is no joking matter."

Artemas snapped his head up, stone silent for a moment as he carefully set his tea mug down upon the coffee table. "You have news of *Belthasar*?"

Instantly the living room walls seemed to close in upon them when hearing the deadly concern in the magician's voice. The house was so silent that the gentle ticking of the wall clock echoed in their ears. Artemas leaned back on the couch and sighed.

"We believe we've located him," Mr. Jordan said.

Artemas was flabbergasted by the information. His

eyes bored invisible holes into the rug before he finally looked up moments later. "Tell me everything you know!"

Artemas' shoulders slumped and the color drained out of his face as he absorbed the details of Belthasar's current whereabouts. Though the mystery of his disappearance after he had escaped from the cat in Endora was never explained, Artemas had hoped that Belthasar had simply vanished for good. But the chill in the magician's heart convinced him otherwise. Belthasar's evil spirit had survived, and now it infected the world of his dear friends. Artemas knew he had no one to blame but himself. If he had never created the timedoor, none of this would be happening. But now wasn't the time to wallow in self-pity. Something had to be done—and soon.

"There's not a moment to waste!" Artemas said with a clap of his hands, rousing himself from his drifting thoughts. "I must deliver this note to Emma, escort her to Endora to visit the queen, and then return at once. Belthasar must be dealt with posthaste!"

Mr. Jordan offered to drive Artemas to the restaurant, with Christopher and Molly insisting on tagging along, both hoping for a brief visit to Endora. Their father decided to indulge them, wishing to have a second look at King Rupert's castle as well.

"Too bad we couldn't stay there until the second opening," Molly suggested. "It's Christmas break after all. We wouldn't have to worry about missing school this time."

"Unfortunately, no," Artemas said. "Belthasar is in *your* world, so this is where we must plan our next move—whatever *that* is." He scratched his head and sighed. "Oh well. It seems my vacation has suddenly turned into a *working* vacation. And I had so wanted to catch up on my sleep!"

CHAPTER FIVE

A Budding Romance

"I must pack at once!" Emma gushed with exuberance after reading the elegant handwritten note from her sister. "How is she, Artemas? I've missed her terribly."

"She and King Rupert are doing splendidly," he informed her. All were gathered in the Smithers' apartment living room above the restaurant. Christmas tree lights reflected off shelves of ceramic knickknacks that Emma had collected over the last year. A large aquarium against a side wall glowed a subtle emerald green as handfuls of goldfish maneuvered around miniature sunken treasure chests, plastic frogs and swaying fingers of dark seaweed. "Queen Eleanor can't wait to see you again."

"And I can't wait to see her!"

"Emma hoped you'd return, Artemas, as if she could sense your arrival," Mr. Smithers said. "She was convinced that the timedoor would open soon."

"Her being on this side helped me to create another one sooner than usual," Artemas admitted. "In addition, I learned a few more things about magic timedoors after King Rupert's sword and crown were stranded here."

"Oh?" Mr. Jordan asked. "What'd you discover?"

"My calculations aren't complete, but I think I'll be

able to create a timedoor to this world *without* an object from Endora remaining behind. Or a *person*," he said, glancing at Emma with a smile. "It's still a learning process."

"That's great!" Christopher said. "The easier it is for you to open a timedoor, the more often we can visit."

Emma nodded. "Great news indeed! I so miss Endora, most especially those early morning conversations with my sister over hot raspberry tea," she replied with a distant smile. "Eleanor will hardly recognize me in my new outfit!" She wore a pair of blue jeans and a pullover sweater patterned with pinecones and snowflakes over a pink blouse. A silk poinsettia blossom was affixed in her long auburn hair. "I'll pack some of my old clothes or people will stare."

"Christopher and I know *that* feeling," Molly said.

"Then you can help me pack, Molly. I brought a few outfits from home that haven't seen the light of day since I arrived here," she explained, gleefully waving Queen Eleanor's letter in the air while leading the way down a narrow hall to the back bedroom. "Stanley, my dear, we'll be ready in the blink of an eye!"

"A jackrabbit's eye and not a turtle's!" his voice echoed from the living room.

Molly giggled at Mr. Smithers' joke as they walked into the bedroom. Emma made a beeline for the closet, grabbed a suitcase from inside and set it on the bed. She scoured through several dresser drawers for items to pack as Molly plopped down on a chair near the corner window.

"Artemas says it's almost springtime in Endora, so pack appropriately," Molly suggested.

"Then I guess I won't need the heavy winter coat I received for Christmas," Emma said. "I'll certainly miss Stanley even though we'll only be separated for a few days."

"He's not going to stay in Endora with you?"

"No. There's too much work at the restaurant before we reopen for the new year. I feel guilty for leaving," Emma said. "But he mentioned that I'd spend so much time with my sister that I'd probably forget he was there anyway!" She stopped folding a sweater and glanced at Molly over the rim of her open suitcase. "He's wrong, of course. I'll miss him terribly. And he promised to count the minutes until I return." Emma smiled and placed the sweater inside the suitcase. "He's always saying sweet things like that to me."

Molly nodded. "Mr. Smithers seems much happier since he met you, Emma. So different from when I first saw him in the diner five years ago."

"Well he was quite despondent after his first wife died, and running that business alone was the last thing he wanted to do. His heart just wasn't in it anymore."

"He never told us about his first wife," Molly said, quite surprised. "What happened to her? When did she die?"

"About seven years ago. She had been very ill for a few months." Emma gathered more items of clothing from another drawer. "Going through life wasn't easy for him."

"It's no wonder why he wanted to stay in Endora," Molly concluded. "I guess the diner held too many sad memories for him."

Emma nodded as a handful of socks tumbled over her fingers and into the suitcase. "But then he met me and..." She teared up slightly as she blushed. "Stanley often tells me that I erased the gray out of his life."

"I guess you mean the world to him," Molly said with a grin. "*Two* in fact!"

"We're a two-world family," she said, closing the suitcase and snapping the locks. "And though I miss my relatives in Endora, I do treasure my life here with Stanley."

"Believe it or not," Molly admitted, "I appreciate my family a lot more after all that's happened since our first trip through the timedoor." She gazed out the frosted window into the chilly winter night. "They're always there for you, one way or another."

"Don't ever forget that, Molly."

"I won't–even *with* Christopher and Vergil as my brothers!" she said with a laugh.

Six shadowy figures scurried down the snowy embankment leading to the stone support underneath the bridge by the river. In the cold December darkness, they entered the timedoor as quietly as raindrops sliding down a window pane. Soon a swirling, starry darkness enveloped the travelers, greeting them like an old friend and a mysterious stranger at the same time. Step by step they moved forward as if wandering lost through a blackened desert under a multitude of stars. Slowly a dim white light appeared ahead as if dawn were about to break. When they passed through the wavy opening in the solid stone wall and stepped into Artemas' chamber, the most wonderfully sweet and intoxicating fragrance greeted their senses.

Molly closed her eyes and deeply inhaled, smiling as if experiencing the sense of smell for the very first time. "Roses!" she whispered, standing still for a few moments. Then she opened her eyes and was flabbergasted.

Scattered around the room were the reddest roses she had ever seen, some arranged in glass jars and clay vases, while others lay in bunches upon tables and shelves and the fireplace mantel, all tied with gold or silver cords. Still others had been placed in Artemas' spare boots near the coat tree as he had apparently run out of room to store the flowers. Dozens upon lovely dozens of roses decorated the room, so many that Molly couldn't even begin to count them. The others looked on, equally impressed.

"Artemas, you've created a greenhouse in your chamber," Mr. Jordan said, gazing in wonderment. "Giving up magic to go into the flower business?"

"Not exactly…"

"It's a red jungle in here!" Christopher remarked as he wandered about, noticing a few parchment scrolls sticking out through a bundle of thorny rose stems leaning against one wall. "Why did you bring all these roses up here?"

"And where did you get them?" Emma wondered, bringing her hands to her cheeks in amazement while inhaling the sweetened air. "It's still days away until spring. Who could even *grow* roses this time of year?"

"I didn't *grow* them," Artemas hastily explained, opening the door into the corridor. "Hurry now! We can talk about this later."

Molly rushed to the set of double doors leading out onto the balcony, preparing to swing one wide open. "We need more light. I want a better look!"

"No! Wait!" Artemas cried, spinning around and racing toward her.

He was too late. Molly opened one of the doors and a blinding wave of morning sunshine splashed into the chamber. They all instinctively shaded their eyes for a moment to get used to the bright light and then looked around in utter astonishment. A wide swath of the roses had vanished. Wherever sunlight washed over the flowers, they silently disappeared like a fading bubble of soap. Any rose lucky enough to avoid the direct light remained unscathed, appearing as a fresh newly cut blossom.

Molly turned around and froze, her eyes wide with horror. She reluctantly shifted her gaze to Artemas, struggling to form an uneasy smile. "Oops..."

"Perhaps *double* oops might be more appropriate," Mr. Smithers said.

Christopher gently slapped a hand to his forehead. "That should be a *quadruple* oops with a half twist! Way to go, Molly!"

"I'm sorry!" she said, on the verge of tears. "I didn't know they weren't real."

Artemas dismissed the incident with a wave of his hand. "No harm done. More than half of the roses are remaining, so I can still monitor the test results for my experiment," he said, hoping to ease her concern. "I might have gone overboard anyway. The room *was* getting a bit cluttered."

"Maybe *just* a bit." Christopher plucked one of the roses on the mantel and dipped the top portion into a stream of sunlight. It faded instantly to nothingness. All he held in his hand were the remains of a thorny stem. "Neat..." He then tossed the stem into the sunlight so that it disappeared in midair as well. "I want to do that again!"

"Christopher!" his father said with a sharp glance

before addressing Artemas. "What kind of experiment were you performing?"

"Apparently a fruitless one. I'm still attempting to create a living thing that can exist on its own in direct sunlight," Artemas said. "I thought I was close to a solution."

"And I've ruined it," muttered Molly, closing the balcony door. She recalled how Artemas had trapped the cat containing Belthasar's spirit in a wildly growing patch of weeds and grass near the coronation platform. But as soon as sunlight peeked through the clouds, Artemas' magical handiwork disappeared like morning mist.

Artemas patted Molly on the shoulder. "Don't worry about it, young miss. I still have a few more spells to test. I may find a solution yet!"

"Why'd you choose roses?" Christopher asked.

"Because they don't move around like grasshoppers and crickets," Artemas replied dryly, eager to change the subject.

"I think they're lovely," Emma said, smelling one of the blossoms. "Stanley bought some for me on our last anniversary. It's a wonderful tradition in his world."

"So I learned during one of my previous visits," Artemas replied. "But we don't have time to chat about roses and failed magic spells. King Rupert and Queen Eleanor expect us to stop by their chamber before we go back through the timedoor to search for Belthasar. I recommend visiting the local library first thing in the morning to utilize one of those computer contraptions to go, *on-line*, is it?"

"That's right, Artemas. But what for?" Molly asked.

"So we can research the latest information about that actor whom Belthasar has inhabited. Maybe we can discover a clue to his whereabouts."

"Good idea," Christopher said. "But we can do that on our home computer."

"I suppose," Artemas said with a slight sigh. "But if we go to the library, perhaps that helpful librarian Miss Mayfield could–*help* us! She assisted me admirably last year on Halloween night when I needed to locate your new home," he fondly recalled. "And she *was* quite taken with some of my magic. That gigantic caramel cube really impressed her! Well, except for the broken table and the bits of candy corn splattered everywhere."

"She's a very knowledgeable woman," Mr. Jordan said, noting Artemas' apparent affection for the lady. "Miss Mayfield has invited me and several of my museum co-workers to give talks at the library from time to time. Eager to see her again?"

Artemas smirked. "I merely suggested that Mina might be able to assist us in our search. She *is* very smart. Any help would be to our advantage."

"*Mina?*" Molly asked with a teasing smile. "So you're on a first-name basis with our librarian?"

Artemas hooked a finger around his collar, tugging uneasily at his cloak. "If you must know, I had hoped to visit Miss Mayfield on my vacation. And it was *she* who insisted that I call her Mina." Artemas cleared his throat. "I also decided it would be proper to offer her a gift, and well, I figured a bouquet of roses created especially for her by me would be a thoughtful *and* spectacular gesture. So I practiced making them."

"And *practiced*," Mr. Smithers said with a grin.

"And practiced some *more*," Christopher added.

"Don't listen to them!" Molly said. "Roses are a great idea."

"Just buy her some real ones," Mr. Jordan suggested. "It's a lot less work."

"But a lot less personal too. Why settle for store-bought when you can have all of *these*?" Artemas waved a hand at what was left of his floral creation.

"Why don't you talk to Miss Mayfield first?" Emma asked. "Get to know her better before plying her with gifts."

"Well there's that, too. But a magic show and a roomful of roses might win her over at once. I have a timedoor schedule to compete with," Artemas reminded them. "Besides, I'm a better magician than a conversational-ist. I'd rather play to my strengths."

"You can always practice speaking," Molly said matter-of-factly. "Talk to yourself in front of a mirror."

Christopher burst out laughing. "How lame is *that*?"

"Hmmm…" Artemas said. "What an intriguing idea."

"See?" Molly replied, sticking her tongue out at her brother. "Artemas thinks it's a great idea!"

"What do *you* know?" Christopher replied with a scowl before turning to Artemas. "Buy Miss Mayfield a dozen roses like my dad said and take her out to dinner. That should do the trick."

"Maybe Chris can recommend one of his *romantic* hangouts for greasy burgers and fries," Molly said with a snicker, holding her hands to her heart.

"Hey, Miss Drama, who's even *listening* to you?"

"All right. Enough out of both you characters," Mr. Jordan said with a snap of his fingers. "Artemas can handle his own life. He doesn't need advice from us."

"I appreciate your suggestions," Artemas said. "But I'll handle things with Miss Mayfield as I best see fit. In the meantime, the King and Queen are waiting, and the minutes until the timedoor closes are ticking away. So if you would all follow me."

Artemas held open the door leading to the corridor and waved his guests through, then marched past them to the front of the crowd. As much as he wanted to renew his relationship with Miss Mayfield, he knew more important matters faced him now that Belthasar had been located. Magic roses might have to be put on the back burner. Perhaps magic timedoors should be placed there as well, he wondered, all too aware of the trouble he had caused because of them. The magician shook his head and sighed, already tired from the mountain of work ahead of him.

CHAPTER SIX

To Catch a Thief

They wandered through castle corridors and down several staircases on their way to find King Rupert. Christopher and Molly felt at home among the maze of stone walls adorned with flaming torches, fragrant pine boughs and numerous tapestries bedecked with gold fringe. Their voices echoed cheerfully off graceful stone archways and intricately carved statues scattered throughout the chambers. Then they turned a corner.

As they neared a secondary kitchen, the torches along that corridor had been extinguished. Shadows and whispers drifted stealthily between the narrow walls. A tense and suffocating silence gripped this section of the castle. Artemas quickly raised a hand as he approached the last burning torch, signaling for everyone to halt. Christopher and Molly scurried up to him, both painfully aware that something wasn't right.

"What's going on?" Mr. Jordan whispered, gently grabbing Christopher and Molly by the shoulder before they could shoot past Artemas.

"I'm not sure," the magician replied, pointing down the corridor. "But I think we're about to find out."

Mr. Jordan pulled his children close to him as the

silhouette of a man hurried toward them up the darkened corridor. Mr. Smithers held Emma's trembling hand. Artemas stepped in front of the group, preparing for the worst as the light from the last torch reflected off the eyes of the stranger.

"Stay where you are!" he whispered.

Though the grave tone of the man's speech ratcheted up the tension, everyone breathed easier nonetheless when they recognized Ulric's commanding voice. They smiled as King Rupert's chief guard stepped into the light, greeted by the familiar tangle of light brown hair rolling down to his shoulders and a pair of blue eyes set into his careworn face. He held a finger to his lips as he directed them away from the entrance of the corridor and back around the corner.

"It's good to see all of you again," he said when it was safe to speak, "though I apologize for my uncordial greeting."

"What in the King's castle is going on?" Artemas inquired.

"We're conducting a small-scale operation," Ulric hastily explained. "Several of my men are in position down that darkened hallway, waiting to catch a thief in the act. Others are stationed near the main entrance in the corridor parallel to it, ready to strike."

"Who's been stealing, Ulric, and what's been stolen?" Mr. Smithers asked.

At once, Ulric was peppered with a dozen questions. He finally agreed to provide a quick version of events so he could rejoin the operation at this critical time.

"Someone has been taking food supplies from the old kitchen down that passage," he explained. "It's only used as a storage room now, but Mrs. Pech, one of the head cooks, insists that items are being pilfered from inside. So after several days of complaints from her, King Rupert has kindly insisted that I look into the matter and resolve it one way or another."

"It's not exactly clashing with a troll army," Christopher said with a smirk.

"We must accept our battles as they present themselves," Ulric replied with an unenthusiastic sigh, "even *if*
they are occasionally fought over a missing bit of dried beef
or a sack of apples and chestnuts."

"You'll do your usual great job regardless of the circumstances," Molly said in an effort to cheer him.

"Anything I can do to help?" Mr. Smithers offered,
noting that he was still a member of the King's guard.

"Thank you, but I don't think that will be necessary,"
Ulric said. "I anticipate we'll have this matter solved–"

"We've got him!" a muffled voice shouted from
down the darkened corridor.

Ulric grinned. "–momentarily."

He rounded the corner in a flash with the others in
tow, grabbed the lit torch and headed down the passageway
toward the kitchen, igniting each blackened torch along the
way. The corridor was soon ablaze with light and ten other
soldiers were now visible, eagerly gathered near the back
entrance to the kitchen. The door had been swung wide open
as the young men, armed with swords, bows and daggers,
waited for their two companions who had charged into the
kitchen after the intruder. Moments later they emerged,
carrying a small wooden barrel once stuffed to the brim with
salted pork, but now containing the very trespasser itself.

"What's in there?" Molly asked as the two men, each
only a few years older than Christopher, gently set the
covered barrel onto the stone floor.

"We caught him, sir!" one of them proudly said to
Ulric as the barrel slightly rocked back and forth.

"Exactly *who* did you catch?" he asked, scratching
his head.

"Not *who*, but *what*!" the other soldier replied, prying
off the wooden cover. "Take a look!"

Though not everyone had a perfect view, they nonetheless craned forward hoping for a glimpse of the culprit.
Spinning around at the bottom of the barrel and clawing at
the sides was a fully grown raccoon. The creature looked up,
the dark patches just below the eyes giving it a bandit-like

appearance suitable for the occasion. One of the soldiers raced into the kitchen and grabbed a small piece of salted meat and dropped it in for the raccoon to feast upon and calm its nerves. The animal took a few cautionary sniffs before greedily devouring the treat, momentarily forgetting its predicament.

"Not exactly the thief I had anticipated," Uric said. "But at least we won't have to lock up the critter in one of King Rupert's prison cells."

"What shall we do with it, sir?" a soldier asked while the others watched the raccoon with fascination.

"Take it outside and release it in the woods. No real harm done," Ulric said. "The rest of you may return to your posts."

The soldiers sped down the corridor like a gust of wind and all was soon quiet. Ulric entered the kitchen, inviting the others to follow. He lit another series of torches inside to provide more light. All were amazed at the amount of food stored within the tiny room. Besides a few barrels of dried meat and sacks of apples and chestnuts, the countertops were crowded with fresh loaves of bread, wedges of cheese and an assortment of fruit pies.

"Even though I ate dinner a couple hours ago, I think I just found room for dessert!" Christopher said, his mouth watering at the display.

Molly shrugged. "Ulric, why are so many freshly baked goods stored in here? Won't they spoil?" she asked as he searched around the room with the torch in hand.

Ulric knelt on one knee in front of an old stone oven that hadn't been used in several years and held the torch inside for a closer inspection. The flame flickered. He smiled with satisfaction at what he had discovered and jumped to his feet.

"Correct, Molly. We don't ever store such items here. Then again, we don't often have to track down a thief."

"I understand," Mr. Jordan said. "You were trying to lure him back—or in this case—lure *it* back."

"Precisely. I asked Mrs. Pech to leave extra food here

that she wouldn't normally store in this room to tempt the intruder more than usual. And I just discovered a hole in the bottom of this old oven where some of the stones had crumbled away. I felt a draft flowing in from the next room that's not often used. It leads into the cellars," Ulric said, displaying all the confidence of a detective solving his biggest case. "No doubt someone had left the stairway door in that room ajar, allowing the raccoon to find its way up from the cellars and into this room. I will search below to determine exactly where our hungry friend found its way into the castle."

"Though I don't know much about military tactics," Artemas admitted, "it is as plain as snow on the mountains to see that your plan worked flawlessly."

"Sometimes to defeat an enemy you must seemingly give it what it wants," Ulric said.

Artemas considered the statement for a moment. "Hmmm... *Give the enemy what it wants.* That doesn't sound logical. Yet you *did* capture the perpetrator, so who am I to question your methods."

"Thinking several steps ahead of your adversary often helps," Ulric explained.

Christopher agreed. "Like the Boy Scouts say–always be prepared!"

"Always have a spare suitcase packed!" Molly added.

Artemas raised a finger. "And always keep an extra jar of blood beetles on the shelf!" he shouted with enthusiasm. He noted the baffled expressions staring back. "Sorry, but it's the only saying I could invent on the spur of the moment."

Emma giggled. "However Ulric did it, it was a job well done!"

"All in a day's work," Ulric modestly replied.

"If only you could track down *another* individual for us with such ease," Mr. Smithers added with an ominous tone in his voice.

"What's wrong? Do you require my assistance in some other matter? I assumed you had just stopped by for a social visit."

"Emma plans to stay here for a few days and spend time with her sister," Artemas explained, gazing pensively into the torchlight. "The others have only stopped by for a brief hello. And to clarify Mr. Smithers' worrisome comment, well..." The magician slowly raised his eyes while the firelight cast a devilish glow upon his face. "Something foul and wicked is lurking just beyond the timedoor."

They brought Ulric up to date on the latest news about Belthasar. And though Artemas and the others felt certain that their adversary still inhabited the famous actor Elvin L. Cooper, they couldn't be one hundred percent sure that he would remain there. Belthasar had the world's population for the taking.

"How we'll ever get him out of our world is anybody's guess," Mr. Jordan said. "And if we succeed, what then?"

"If anyone can figure out a solution, Artemas can!" Molly chimed in confidently. "Right, Artemas?"

"Hmmm... What was that, Molly?" the magician replied distractedly, again staring broodingly into the firelight. The quandary that was Belthasar hung heavily upon him like a lead weight around his neck. "We'll find a way, I suppose."

"Not if we stand around in this kitchen all day," Mr. Smithers said. "We're on a strict timetable."

"Quite right." Artemas clapped his hands sharply. "We were on our way to see King Rupert and Queen Eleanor before we got sidetracked. Let's continue before time runs out. I have a few duties to attend to in the meantime."

They took their leave of Ulric and hurried to visit the royal couple, eventually greeting King Rupert and his wife in one of their private chambers. And though it had not quite been a full Endoran year since Emma and Queen Eleanor had last met, they hugged each other amid tears and laughter as if it had been half a lifetime. King Rupert welcomed everybody to his castle, beaming with pride as light from the snapping flames in the fireplace reflected off the delicate crown of gold poised on his head of silver hair.

"I would have prepared a feast, but I know you have only enough time to escort Emma back here for her visit before you must return with Artemas," King Rupert said.

"Perhaps when the timedoor reopens the second time, you might be able to stay longer," Queen Eleanor hoped, her long red hair gathered atop her head and tied with a wispy ribbon of gold.

"However, we can share a loaf of currant bread and some winter ale before you depart," King Rupert insisted. "Both go particularly well with conversation among old friends."

"We'll definitely take you up on the conversation portion of your offer," Mr. Jordan replied. "We have much to tell you."

"How about a tour of your castle while we talk?" Molly suggested. "While King Jeremiah's castle is practically a second home to my brother and me, we really haven't had the chance to explore much of this place."

"Great idea!" Christopher said, urging King Rupert to give them a condensed sightseeing tour in the short time they had left.

King Rupert readily agreed and escorted Christopher, Molly, Mr. Jordan and Mr. Smithers on a whirlwind tour. Along the way, they updated the king on the latest information regarding Belthasar. Emma and Queen Eleanor remained behind to chat in front of the fireplace, catching up on the last year over a kettle of hot raspberry tea and fresh biscuits. Artemas excused himself from both gatherings to attend to a few items that he claimed needed his immediate attention. He promised to catch up with the others in a short while to accompany them back through the timedoor before it closed in less than two hours. Then he sped off to his chamber.

Artemas paced across the stone floor of his chamber, hands clasped behind his back, eyes affixed to the ground like nails into wood. Dozens of ideas fluttered about in his mind–beginnings, middles and endings of various plans to once and for all rid the two worlds of Belthasar. Artemas blamed himself for causing the entire mess by inventing the timedoor in the first place, thus creating Belthasar's spirit and giving it the power to wage his wars. But what to do?

Artemas flung both doors to the balcony wide open, allowing additional sunlight to enter the chamber. Bunches of the remaining roses previously protected in shadow faded into nothingness. Artemas sighed with disgust, chiding himself for wasting time on another failed experiment. Though he had nearly created a living thing with magic, he had no time to fiddle around on such spells now that Belthasar was on the loose, and even less time to conjure up a bouquet of magical roses to impress Mina Mayfield.

Artemas needed some fresh air and stepped onto the balcony and gazed out into the plains stretching northward. Though the last gray days of winter were shriveling up and allowing the green of spring to gain a foothold, patches of snow still clung to the higher elevations of the mountains in the west. Artemas gripped the balcony railing as a cool breeze washed through his long gray hair, feeling as alone and isolated as Mount Maricel, the tallest peak in the western chain that loomed in the distance. Artemas closed his eyes, imagining himself on top of that mountain and looking at the landscape below, wondering if his current plight would appear any different to him from that perspective.

The wind continued to gust cool and sharp. A blue jay's cry echoed among pine trees far below. Suddenly Artemas snapped open his eyes as an icy shiver shot up his spine. He gazed wide-eyed into the vastness before him as his mind fitted rambling thoughts together like the pieces of a floating jigsaw puzzle. He had an idea!

He ran inside and scoured through a dozen long pieces of rolled parchment, each tied with a silk cord. He fumbled through the rolls until he found the one he needed, untied the cord and spread the parchment on a table once piled high with roses but now flooded with sunlight. Artemas grabbed four stone jars of potions and placed one on each corner of the parchment to hold it in place, then studied the brown, blue and black etchings imprinted on the map before him.

The magician mumbled to himself, his thoughts in a whirlwind as his eyes scanned over the rivers, mountains, trees and plains representing a small section of terrain within the kingdom of Endora. Then he found it, a tiny spot on the map that grabbed his attention and wouldn't let go. He tapped his finger upon it then traced a circle around the spot several times with his fingernail, hardly aware that he had scratched a series of ringed lines into the map. He remembered this place from his previous travels, though he hadn't passed through that area in years.

"Hey, how's it going in there?"

Artemas jumped in surprise and quickly pushed aside two of the stone jars so that the map rolled up by itself. He spun around and saw Molly poking her head through the doorway.

"Dear me, child, but next time be sure to knock!" Artemas pleaded, stepping away from the table. "Is King Rupert's tour finished already?"

"Not quite, Artemas. And sorry for scaring you like that," she replied. "We're just around the corner in the next corridor, so I thought I'd stop by to see how you're doing. Maybe you can join us soon when you're finished in here."

"Actually, I *have* completed my work in this chamber, Molly. But there still remains a bit of research I must attend to in the library at the end of the passageway. It shouldn't take long. I'll catch up with your tour before we return through the timedoor." Artemas tugged uneasily at his beard. "Is it a deal?"

"I guess it'll have to be," Molly said, crinkling her brow. "You work too hard, Artemas. You *do* need a vacation! Hurry if you can."

"I'll try," he promised as Molly scooted away and the door closed, leaving the room in near silence. The whistle of a cool breeze swirled across the balcony and in through the open doors, carrying a hint of springtime. "I'll most certainly try," he softly said, leaving the remaining roses and the rolled up map behind as he darted out the door.

Over an hour had passed when Molly returned to Artemas' chamber, this time accompanied by Christopher and her father, Mr. Smithers, Emma, King Rupert and Queen Eleanor. Since Artemas had never joined them on their castle tour, everyone expected him to be in his chamber as the moment drew near for the timedoor to close.

"Where could that magician be?" Mr. Smithers asked, peeking out on the balcony.

"Busy as usual!" Molly said with a smirk, noting that her brother sprouted a grin as well. "He told me earlier that he needed to stop in the library down the corridor to do a bit of research. No doubt he's still there."

"Then let's go and drag him back," Christopher said, signaling for Molly to follow him out the door. "We'll be back in a flash!"

"Don't take any wrong turns," their father jokingly warned. "We'll keep an eye on the timedoor."

Christopher and Molly slipped out of the chamber and sped down the corridor toward the room at the very end. They had never been inside the castle library and were anxious to compare it to the one back home. A large wooden door was slightly ajar when they approached. Molly was about to call out Artemas' name before they entered the room, but had second thoughts, not wanting to startle him again especially if he was in the middle of something important. She put a cautionary finger to her lips, though her brother merely sighed.

They stepped inside the room ablaze with sunshine streaming in through five large oval windows along one wall, each pane crisscrossed with metal lattice work. The ceiling gently sloped upward on each side and met at a single line running the length of the room. Glass enclosed cabinets against the walls contained hundreds of scrolls and loose pages of parchment. A dozen wooden chairs were scattered about, and several hand-woven rugs sported elaborate geometrical designs in shades of red, blue, gold and green. Large lush and leafy plants sprouted out of huge wooden containers, some showcasing intricate carvings of sprawling oak trees or leaping deer, while others depicted the sun and the stars or a bird in flight.

Molly instantly fell in love with the room, imagining herself hiding out in here for hours while lost in the pages of one of her detective novels. How exciting it would be to sift through the clues of a daunting mystery, attempting to put together the pieces of the puzzle side by side with the great Sherlock Holmes–and *without* her brother around to bother her. In her rush of enthusiasm, Molly was surprised that nobody else was using the library at the moment. It looked completely empty.

She wondered where Artemas was hiding, ready to complain to Christopher when he raised a hand, cautioning her to be silent. He pointed toward the far end of the room. Molly steered her gaze in that direction, suddenly noticing what she had earlier missed upon first glance. In the back corner of the library, partially concealed behind one of the enormous potted plants, stood Artemas, his back to them, apparently talking to someone. Christopher and Molly quietly inched their way toward him. One of the larger cabinets helped to block them from his view.

Artemas spoke in hushed tones. Most of his words they could neither hear nor understand. When Christopher and Molly tried to get a better glimpse through the branches of the plant, they stopped dead in their tracks. Artemas continued to speak, unaware that they stood nearby, his face stone frozen in the most serious feat of concentration they had ever witnessed. What surprised the Jordan siblings most was the fact that Artemas was talking to *himself.* Except for his moving lips and occasionally blinking eyes, he stood as still as a tree in front of an elongated oval mirror framed within an oak stand. Christopher and Molly watched in perplexed fascination as he whispered his mysterious monologue into the mirror. Christopher finally nudged his sister, not feeling comfortable spying on their friend. With a slight turn of his head, he indicated that they should leave at once. Molly nodded in agreement and they departed.

Christopher and Molly returned to the library a couple minutes later, this time making enough noise to grab Artemas' attention. He emerged from the library just as they neared the doorway, appearing tired and disoriented.

"It's almost time, Artemas," Christopher casually said.

"So it is," he replied, rubbing his forehead. "I seem to have lost track of time while I was doing—my research." He smiled at Molly. "Sorry I missed the tour."

"Next time," she said, leading him back to his chamber.

Shortly after, King Rupert thanked everyone for visiting his castle, then he, Queen Eleanor and Emma said goodbye to Artemas, Mr. Smithers and the Jordans, looking forward to seeing them in another week or so. Emma hugged her husband tightly, having second thoughts about leaving him for the first time since their marriage. Stanley Smithers assured his wife that he would be counting the minutes until they saw each other once again. Moments later, the five travelers stepped into the timedoor and through the starry darkness. Several minutes after that, the timedoor closed with its usual thunderous clap.

"Back to *real* winter," Mr. Jordan said as a cold December gust greeted them underneath the bridge.

Molly shivered as they climbed up the snowy embankment. "A part of me always feels sad when I leave Endora, even if I've been there for only a couple hours."

"Me too," Christopher said, glancing at Artemas. "How do you feel after you leave *our* world?"

"I must admit that I experience similar pangs of melancholy," Artemas replied, gently rubbing his temples. "However, *now* I simply have a throbbing headache."

"Like I said earlier, Artemas—you work too hard!" Molly quipped.

"Perhaps so."

When they returned to the parking lot, Mr. Jordan started the car, and then everyone waited inside the restaurant until it warmed up. This allowed Artemas a few moments to run upstairs to the apartment and get some aspirin from Mr. Smithers while Christopher and Molly enjoyed a soda with their father at the front bar. While Artemas was gone, Molly told her father how she and Christopher had found him talking to himself in the mirror in the castle library. She wondered if Artemas had taken her advice about practicing what he wanted to say to Miss Mayfield.

"What else *could* it be?" she asked.

"Whatever his reason for talking into a mirror, it's none of our business," Mr. Jordan said, ending the discussion once and for all just as Artemas and Mr. Smithers returned.

"Feeling better, Artemas?" Christopher asked.

"Not likely," Mr. Smithers said with an apologetic shrug. "Out of aspirin."

"Mom will have some at home," Molly said.

"I'd much appreciate it," Artemas replied with a discouraging sigh, rubbing the back of his neck. "What a dreadful way to start my vacation!"

CHAPTER SEVEN

Endless E-Mails

Christopher, Molly and Artemas marched through the wintry streets to the public library the following morning. Blazing sunshine reflected off waist-high snow banks along city sidewalks, and every breath of air tasted frosty and dry. Bony maple trees creaked and moaned when catching breezes in their web of branches, while a pair of blue jays darted among the slender pines in the city park, their bending boughs lightly dusted with snow. A scattering of button-eyed and carrot-nosed snowmen congregated on front lawns throughout the neighborhood.

"How's your headache, Artemas?" asked Molly, warmly bundled in a yellow ski jacket and wearing a sky-blue hat and a matching scarf. She adjusted the sunglasses on the bridge of her nose.

"Slightly better," he replied, his face partially concealed in the hood of his cloak. "The aspirin your mother gave me last night is starting to kick in with the two tablets I took this morning. The drum-like throbbing in my head has been replaced with a dull pang. I *guess* that's an improvement."

"Try slapping a handful of snow on your forehead," Christopher joked, hoping to make him feel better.

"I'll keep that trick in mind."

They crossed the road at the end of the block and turned a corner. "Almost there," Christopher said, pointing to the library down the street. "Getting out of this bright sunlight might lessen your headache." He removed a pair of sporty sunglasses and offered them to Artemas. "Want to borrow these?"

"Thank you, but I don't think they're quite my style," Artemas said with a chuckle. "My hood is shielding my eyes well enough."

"Bet you'd impress Mina Mayfield wearing them!" Christopher slipped the glasses back on and raised the collar on his red fleece vest to fend off a biting breeze.

"That may be, but we have important business to attend to first," Artemas replied. "Locating Belthasar is on the top of our list."

"I'm still not sure what good that's going to do," Molly said, her boots squeaking as they passed along the snow-caked walks. "*Then* what do we do? Go after him? Or make him come after us?"

"Very good questions indeed," Artemas said. "And when I think of an answer to either one, I'll let you know."

"Better start thinking!" Christopher said. "We're here."

They bounded up the library steps and entered the toasty warm building. Christopher and Molly shed their hats, gloves and sunglasses and looked for a computer on one of the tables against the far wall. Artemas removed his hood and scanned the area around the main desk, hoping for a glimpse of Miss Mayfield. He frowned when he saw an older girl with short black hair and tinted blue glasses checking out some picture books for a mother and her two young daughters.

"Plenty of free computers," Molly said, tugging on Artemas' sleeve.

Christopher noted the disappointment on the magician's face, realizing that Miss Mayfield wasn't around. He nudged his sister and Molly quickly suggested that they inquire at the front desk first before attending to their business about Belthasar.

"This way," Christopher said, walking up to the checkout desk just as the mother and her daughters departed with a handful of books. Artemas and Molly followed as the girl behind the desk greeted them.

"May I help you?" she asked, intrigued by Artemas' long beard and flowing gray cloak lightly embossed with intricate designs.

"We're looking for Miss Mayfield," Christopher replied. "Is she—"

"What an awesome pair of glasses!" Molly interrupted, admiring the blue-hued spectacles the lady was wearing. "They go great with that necklace."

"Thanks," she said, holding up the piece of jewelry so Molly could get a better look. "It's a string of strawberry-pink topaz I received for my twentieth birthday last month. Amazing shade of color, don't you think?"

"With*out* a *doubt*!" Molly whispered, closely examining the gemstones.

Christopher glanced at Artemas and shook his head. He cleared his throat to get both of the girls' attention. "Uh, any idea where Miss Mayfield is today?" he politely asked, trying not to appear too impatient.

"Mina has the day off, but she'll be back tomorrow," the checkout girl replied. "I'm helping out over the next few weeks between semesters in college."

"Perhaps I'll return tomorrow if it's not an inconvenience," Artemas suggested.

"Sure. Suit yourself," she said, touching the cuff of Artemas' sleeve. "Nice threads, by the way."

"Excuse me?"

"She likes your cloak," Christopher quietly said.

"Oh."

"You don't see a getup like that everyday, at least not around here."

"This is, um—our great uncle Artemas," Molly chimed in. "He's from—Finland."

"Nice to meet you," she said, offering her hand. "My name is Lucy Easton. I'm a history major, but I must confess that I know very little about Finland."

"Well I wouldn't dream of boring you with the details just now," Artemas said, looking askance at Molly.

"We're here to use the computer," Christopher said, "so we'll stop bothering you. I'm sure you have more important things to do."

"No bother," Lucy replied. "I enjoy talking to visitors. It beats putting all the returned books back where they belong. So many numbers and letters!"

Molly laughed. "In that case, do you mind if I try on your glasses for a second? They'd go great with my scarf!"

"Molly!"

"Sure." Lucy removed her reading glasses and handed them to Molly, revealing a pair of soft brown eyes. "Let's see how they look."

"Don't mind my brother," Molly said as she slipped on the glasses. "He gets that way sometimes. Oh, but I *do* look good in these!" she added, admiring herself in a small compact mirror that Lucy had fished out of her purse under the checkout desk.

"If we applaud lightly and you take a bow, can we go?" Christopher muttered.

Molly smirked. "Told you he's like that," she whispered to Lucy as she handed back the glasses.

"My brother, too," Lucy softly replied.

"Then you *know* what I mean." Molly sighed as she turned to her brother and Artemas. "I'm ready now, gentlemen, if you would care to lead the way."

"Gladly," Christopher said, shaking the scowl off his face as he made a beeline for the computer. Artemas smiled a goodbye to Lucy and followed Christopher.

"Thanks," Molly said with a wave as she departed. Then she spun about for a brief moment. "By the way, my dad is a curator at the local museum. Since you're a history major, maybe I could get him to give you a special tour. There are lots of items in the museum cellars that aren't on display to the public."

"That'd be great!" Lucy said. "I've visited before, but I'm sure there's lots I missed. I'm on vacation for a few weeks. Stop by here if you can arrange something."

"Will do!" Molly said as she hurried to catch up with Artemas and her brother.

Christopher sat in front of the computer, already on-line. Artemas pulled up a chair next to him. Molly popped up behind them and glanced over their shoulders.

"Anything yet?"

"I just typed Elvin L. Cooper's name in the search box," Christopher said as he scanned the information on the screen.

"Let me offer you my chair, Molly," Artemas insisted.

"I'm fine," Molly whispered, gazing at the data Christopher had retrieved.

Artemas tugged at his chin as he stared in amazement. "All that information from a few touches of the keyboard. Astounding! But what does it all mean?"

Christopher leaned back in the chair and folded his arms. "Well, mostly it's information about Cooper's movies–plot summaries, reviews from critics, et cetera–some biographical material, links to fan websites and his own official site, lists of articles written about him and his films, and well–just *tons* of stuff."

"Where do we start?" Molly wondered aloud.

"Good question," Christopher said, drumming his fingers on the table. "Maybe we can find out where he lives."

"And go after him?" Molly skeptically inquired. "If Belthasar still inhabits Cooper, then he's probably hanging out at his California estate. Meanwhile, *we're* stuck in the middle of New York State in case you haven't noticed."

"I've noticed," Christopher replied, staring at the screen. "So flying across country is apparently not a convenient *or* inexpensive option."

"So what do we do?" Molly said.

Artemas looked his two companions in the eye. "Going after him *is* out of the question. It wouldn't be feasible, especially given his ability to move around at will."

Christopher shrugged. "So what are our options?"

A shrewd smile spread across the magician's face. "We let *him* come after *us*!"

Molly's jaw dropped. "Excuse me? Isn't that what we're trying to avoid?"

"For the most part–yes. But if we don't force the issue soon, Belthasar could spend years in your world destroying lives and acquiring untold wealth right under our very noses. He may enjoy *that* more than getting his revenge upon you two."

"What are you suggesting?" Christopher asked.

Artemas lowered his voice, not wanting to attract the notice of the other library patrons. "We need to get his attention! Belthasar knows you're both here and he can bide his time enjoying whatever life he chooses. But Belthasar isn't aware that *we* know he is in this world. Once we inform him of that fact, then his current situation is compromised. He'll want to make a move against us as soon as possible."

"Oh, *great* plan," Molly said sarcastically. "Why don't we stir up a hornet's nest with a stick in our spare time as well?"

"Rest assured," Artemas said with a wink. "We'll be doing *exactly* that!"

Christopher thought for a moment and nodded. "You're right, Artemas. I don't see any other way to find him. We have to let him know we're wise to his game and then wait until he makes his move."

Molly sighed in resignation, knowing that Christopher was right but not enthusiastic about waiting for Belthasar to catch them by surprise. She grabbed the mouse and scrolled down the computer screen, finally double clicking on a link to Elvin L. Cooper's official website. Up popped the homepage displaying a photo of the actor flashing a huge welcoming smile to his worldwide fans.

"What are you doing, Molly?" Artemas asked.

"If we're going to inform Belthasar that we know he's here, the easiest way is to e-mail him–over and over and over!" Molly located an e-mail address made available to his movie fans, briefly explaining to Artemas how they would be able to send messages to Elvin L. Cooper with the click of a button.

"Not meaning to sound negative, Molly–"

"Then don't, Chris."

"–but Belthasar, I mean Cooper, must receive hundreds of e-mails a day. Maybe *thousands*! Most of them probably aren't even read by him or his staff."

"That's why we have some major work to do when we get home," she replied matter-of-factly. Molly removed the penlight she had won at the carnival last summer from her coat pocket and copied the e-mail address on a piece of scrap paper.

"Don't you ever go anywhere without that pen, Molly?"

"Never. I might get a brilliant idea for a poem that I'll have to jot down. Or maybe there'll be a blackout," she added, playfully clicking the light on and off.

"A blackout, maybe," Christopher said. "But a *brilliant* idea?"

"Oh, so clever a comment, big brother," Molly dryly replied as she folded the piece of paper and slipped it into her pocket with the pen. "And I'd offer you a single laugh, but that would be *way* overpaying for such a microscopic joke."

Artemas suppressed a laugh by clearing his throat, hoping to get the discussion back on track. "Molly, explain your e-mail plan in detail. What exactly are we to do?"

"It's simple. We send Belthasar dozens upon dozens of e-mails, even hundreds if necessary in order to get his attention. In fact, it can be the same two or three messages sent over and over," she said. "We just want to get noticed."

"What should we write?" Christopher asked as he deleted the information from the computer screen.

"We mention all three of our names somewhere in

the note as well as Belthasar's. We could put his name in the subject line. With luck, someone on his end is sure to notice and bring it to his attention."

"It's an excellent plan," Artemas said with an encouraging tone in his voice. "Good work, Molly."

"Yeah, not bad," Christopher agreed.

"Thanks," Molly said, slipping on her hat and scarf. "Now let's go home and get started. We have some writing to do!"

"What do you think of *this* one?" Christopher asked.

FROM: Christopher, Molly and Artemas—Your three favorite fans!
TO: Elvin L. Cooper
SUBJECT: Great Movie Idea—"Belthasar Versus the World"

Dear Mr. Cooper,

We certainly love all your movies and can't wait to see you in more! So we've come up with a great concept and title we'd like you to think about. Please feel free to use either. No charge!

Belthasar, the self-absorbed multi-trillionaire protagonist with a slight anger management problem, decides to buy up all the land in the world and move everyone else to the moon. (FYI: It's that big round thing in the sky that keeps changing shape, not the bright hot yellow one.)

Please let us know what you think. Good luck!

Sincerely,
Chris, Molly and Art

"I like it," Molly said. "You have better writing skills than I give you credit for, Chris. Who would have thought? Send it!"

Christopher clicked the SEND button. "Done."

"Now it's my turn," she said, staring at the keyboard. "What *should* I type?"

"You're very creative," Artemas said. "Astound us!"

Molly grinned. "I've *got* it!"

FROM: Christopher, Molly and Artemas–Your three favorite fans!
TO: Elvin L. Cooper
SUBJECT: Dog Sidekick Named Belthasar

Dear Mr. Cooper,

As three of your biggest fans (and dog lovers, too!) we think your next movie should feature a dog as your co-star. It'll make millions!

Far be it from us to suggest a canine breed to share top billing with you, but we certainly feel that we have come up with the perfect name for you to consider using for the mutt–Belthasar! We can almost hear it growling now! And if you really want to stretch as an actor, perhaps *you* could play that part. Think about it.

Looking forward to your next movie!

Sincerely,
Chris, Molly and Art

"That's even better than mine!" Christopher said as Molly repeatedly clicked the SEND icon. "How about it, Artemas? Want to send Belthasar an annoying note?"

Artemas sat in front of the computer set up in the spare side room of the Jordan household. He gently touched his fingers to the keyboard, carefully considering his words.

"I *could* devise an elaborate e-mail to taunt our miserable friend," Artemas said. "Then again, a succinct note might have the same effect."

FROM: Christopher, Molly and Artemas–Your three favorite fans!
TO: Elvin L. Cooper
SUBJECT: Belthasar

Dear Mr. Cooper,

Hope to meet you soon!

Sincerely,
Chris, Molly and Art

"Hmmm… *That* should get his attention," Artemas said with a satisfied grin as he sent his electronic message on its merry way. He glanced at his co-conspirators. "Not bad for an amateur, don't you think?"

"Right on the mark," Molly agreed. "But do you think Belthasar will reply?"

"Do you think he'll even *see* our e-mails?" Christopher asked.

"He will if we send him hundreds of copies!" Molly cheered. "Shall we get started?"

Christopher nodded. "I'm ready, Molly, but I'm wondering about Artemas' plan." He glanced at the magician with a mix of curiosity and anxiety. "What will we do once we *get* Belthasar's attention?"

"Let's hope we're so lucky," Artemas said. "And after that, well–I'm making this up as we go along."

Mrs. Jordan prepared a spaghetti dinner early that evening, looking forward to a pleasant get-together with Artemas on his first full day in their world. Christopher and Molly bubbled with excitement though, hardly touching their tossed salad and garlic bread as they explained their latest tactic in the battle with Belthasar. Artemas listened for the most part and ate little from his plate, still silently suffering from a throbbing headache. Mrs. Jordan took note of his unease and offered him more aspirin.

"Thank you, Sally, but no. Perhaps I'll take a short walk later tonight before retiring. That might ease the pain," Artemas said. "I'm sure it'll pass."

By meal's end, Artemas felt better and asked Mr. Jordan if he could utilize the basement to work on a few spells. Though his magical abilities didn't seem to fade as fast the more often he visited the Jordan's world, Artemas was still not immune to losing his powers completely if he stayed here beyond a single opening of the timedoor. He needed to return to Endora to recoup his full strength or risk enduring the same fate that Malaban had suffered. Artemas couldn't imagine losing his powers forever like the sorcerer, hoping to practice and perfect his craft for as long as he should live.

The sun lingered above the western horizon three time zones away. Elvin L. Cooper relaxed in his study, perusing some movie scripts while sipping red wine. He leaned back in a swivel chair, his feet propped up on the desk. Mrs. Cooper was enjoying the month-long vacation in Europe that he had encouraged her to take with some friends while he searched for his next staring role. A tiny parakeet sat quietly inside a silver cage in the corner of the room, curiously watching its owner.

"Garbage!" he said, tossing a script into a wastebasket to join three others. "Who writes this drivel? I bet *you* could produce something better by tapping at a keyboard," he said to the parakeet, grabbing the next screenplay from a pile on his desk. He sighed when he heard a knock at the door.

"Sorry to interrupt, Elvin, but I wanted to let you know I'll be leaving now," his secretary Linda said as she bustled into the room. "Here's your meeting schedule for tomorrow and a few papers for you to sign."

"Fine," he replied with little interest, signaling for Linda to place the items next to the scripts. "Have a nice evening."

"Oh, one other thing," she said, approaching the desk. "It's probably a prank, but someone on the staff was going through your fan e-mails and found something curious."

Elvin leaned around in his chair to face her. "You know I don't have time to read that gibberish, Linda. Remember our rule–delete, delete, delete!"

Linda nodded with an awkward smile. "I know, Elvin. But there were three messages I thought you should see."

Elvin set his wine glass down, removed his feet from the desk and sat up straight. Though such details annoyed him, he realized that he had to play along with his employees in order to keep up his deception. He couldn't send *everyone* away on a vacation. "All right, Linda. What's so special about the three e-mails?"

"Other than their curiously strange content, each one of them was sent over two hundred times." She handed the three copies to her boss. "What do you think?"

Elvin L. Cooper scanned the printed e-mails, his heart pounding madly as soon as his eyes saw those three dreadful names—Christopher, Molly and Artemas. And there was *his* name too—Belthasar—being used like a sharp stick to taunt him. His secret had been discovered. Bad enough they knew he was hiding out in their world, but Artemas and those two inquisitive children had discovered *who* he was inhabiting. But *how*, Belthasar wondered with each labored breath. Since Artemas' name also appeared on the e-mails, Belthasar realized that the timedoor must be open again. He could return to his own world now if he wanted. *If* he wanted.

Belthasar considered the possibility. Though distant memories tugged at his heart, he had grown to like this world. He prospered here much faster than he had ever done in Endora or Solárin, with an endless array of technology and diversions to keep him entertained for the rest of his life. But now everything was at risk because of a few mischievous e-mails. Belthasar had to stop his enemies once and for all before they wrecked his life for a third time. He refused to tolerate another defeat.

"Elvin?" Linda's voice seemed to call to him from miles away. "What shall I do about the e-mails?"

"What? Oh, uh…" Elvin L. Cooper glanced at his secretary, for a moment at a loss for words. Then he smiled, pretending that everything was all right. "I'll handle these," he replied, waving the papers in the air. "Don't worry about it. Probably a prank, just like you said."

"I could look into where they originated from. It'd be no trouble," Linda said. "And I'm curious—what's the deal with that *Belthasar* name they kept mentioning? What does it mean? Any ideas?"

Belthasar shrugged with a clueless grin pasted upon his face. "Probably some bored kids with nothing better to do. Don't think about it for another second. You've done enough today, Linda. Go home and have a nice dinner. I'll see you tomorrow."

Linda thanked him with a smile. "I don't need to be told twice, Elvin. See you in the morning at nine. Have a nice night."

"I'll try to find *something* to occupy my time," he softly said as she departed.

He glanced at his parakeet when the door closed. "Looks like we'll both be flying tonight." Belthasar stood and walked to the window near the birdcage. He opened it wide, letting a soft twilight breeze drift inside. "I must leave you again, Mr. Cooper. I must travel east to take care of a problem. But I'll be back." Belthasar gently lifted the latch on the cage and swung open the metal door. "Please do keep up appearances, Elvin, while I'm away. I've done so much for your career in this short time that it'd be a shame if you reverted back to your dull and dreary ways." He placed his hand inside the cage, allowing the bird to perch on a finger. "Trust me. It would be a *disastrous* career move."

Moments later, Elvin L. Cooper stood alone in his study, his countenance glazed with bewilderment as he gazed at an open window and an empty birdcage.

A few hours later, the Jordan household was as still and silent as a layer of freshly fallen snow. Mr. and Mrs. Jordan and their children were sound asleep upstairs while Magic lay curled upon his oval rug in the kitchen, dozing to the gentle hum of the refrigerator. Moments later, Artemas left the guest room, tiptoed down the stairs, put on his cloak and boots and slipped out the front door into the chilly December night. Inside one of his pockets was a letter he had secretly composed in his room after dinner.

Artemas quickly walked several blocks along the deserted streets. And though his headache still bothered him, the brisk night air upon his forehead helped to alleviate some of the pain.

A few minutes later, Artemas approached a trash receptacle next to a mailbox on a corner above the city park. Artemas cast a few furtive glances then bent down on one knee and pretended to tighten his boot laces. He quickly removed an envelope from his pocket containing the letter he had written and placed it under the trash receptacle, leaving a corner of the envelope sticking out. Artemas casually stood up and walked back to the Jordans' house, feeling more exhausted than he had in quite a long time.

Half an hour later, an individual approached the same street corner, bent down beside the trash receptacle and retrieved the letter Artemas had left. The figure hurried off down the next block, the squeak of packed snow underfoot fading in the bitter darkness.

CHAPTER EIGHT

Shadowing

At the breakfast table the following morning, Artemas carefully spread a layer of cream cheese on a toasted bagel, followed by a heaping spoonful of raspberry jam which he meticulously distributed around the edges. Molly watched the magician with quiet amusement as Mrs. Jordan poured him a mug of hot coffee.

"Careful so you don't get any jam on your beard," Molly said, tearing a buttered bagel in half and dipping one piece into her orange juice before devouring it.

"I'll be quite vigilant," Artemas promised, adding a splash of milk to his coffee. "Nor will I splatter any on this fancy shirt with buttons that your father lent me." He glanced at Mr. Jordan at the opposite end of the table. "You don't think I'm overdressed, do you? I'm so used to my own attire."

"You look fine, Artemas," Mr. Jordan assured him as he stirred his coffee. "Throw on your cloak and you'll feel right at home. Mina Mayfield will be impressed. Maybe you two should make plans for New Year's Eve."

"Assuming she *remembers* me," Artemas replied with a raised eyebrow.

Christopher smirked. "After that Halloween magic

show you told us about, how *could* she forget!"

Vergil giggled as he ate his cereal, a few drops of milk streaming down his chin. "Artemas, make my cereal bowl spin around and grow *this big*!" he said, spreading out his arms.

"No magic spells at the breakfast table," Artemas replied. "What a mess *that* would make."

"Can't be worse than the mess Vergil already made," Molly said. "By the way, Dad, there's this girl Lucy helping out at the library over college break. She's a history major. I mentioned you might be able to show her some items at the museum not on display before she goes back to school. Best of all, she has great fashion sense!"

"Well in *that* case..." Mr. Jordan replied with a wave of his fork. "Maybe I can arrange something after the New Year, Molly. You're still off for a few days then."

"Great! I'd love a tour."

"Me too!" Vergil mumbled, his mouth stuffed with cereal.

Molly eyed her little brother with amused disgust. "Maybe Artemas can cast a *how-to-eat-properly* magic spell upon you."

"Yeah, well I have a new Frogatron shirt and socks and you *don't*!" Vergil replied before slurping up a spoonful of milk. "And don't ask to borrow them either."

"Hope *I* can," Christopher whispered sarcastically.

"Just your typical breakfast at the Jordan household," Mrs. Jordan commented to Artemas as she joined everyone at the table with a fresh cup of coffee. "Need a refill?"

"Not yet, thank you. But speaking of magic, I *did* make some progress last night while working on a few spells in the basement. I think I'm on the verge of creating a living entity that can survive in the sunlight," Artemas proudly announced. "After Molly inadvertently disrupted that project in my chamber—"

"Don't you mean *destroyed*?" Christopher lightly asked. "Perhaps *obliterated*? *Decimated*? *Wiped out*? Those roses didn't have a chance!" Mr. Jordan silenced his son with a searing glare. "Sorry."

"Anyway," Artemas continued after a sip of coffee, "because of Molly's action, I took advantage of our brief time back in Endora to research the properties of light refraction and the theory of double incantations. Well, to make a long and technical story short, I stumbled upon a magical detour I had never considered before. The prospects for success look *very* promising!"

"Excellent!" Mrs. Jordan said, raising her coffee mug. "Too bad you hadn't discovered this years ago. It would have spared that jar of grape jam I had placed on the counter in the sunlight. But no use crying over spilled milk."

"Good thing," Molly quipped. "We'd be doing *lots* of crying thanks to Vergil and his cereal bowl! I think Magic has better table manners than you, Verg."

"I don't *think* so!" he crowed as Magic bounded over toward Molly from his resting spot in the kitchen corner, hoping for a morning treat. "But I'm sure I have much better *library* manners. Take me with you?"

"Not today, Vergil," Mr. Jordan said. "You have an appointment to clean your bedroom. It's a mess!"

"Besides, I'm accompanying Artemas to the library," Molly explained. "He doesn't need you around while he's trying to have a few words with Miss Mayfield."

"Which is exactly why *I'll* be tagging along too," Christopher said, eyeing Molly. "You'll be more of a distraction than Vergil."

"Will *not*!"

"Times *ten*!" Christopher replied, repeatedly opening and closing his thumb and fingers on one hand to imitate a jabbering mouth. "Yakkety, yak, yak, yak!"

"Oh yukkety, yuk, yuk, funny man! Hurry or you'll be late for your comic tour," Molly said, dunking the rest of the bagel into her juice. "Your audience of *one* is waiting."

"Yep, just your typical breakfast, Artemas," Mr. Jordan said, repeating his wife's earlier comment with a bemused grin. He removed his glasses and lightly rubbed his eyes. "So if you're ever wondering why we keep aspirin in the house…"

Mrs. Jordan smiled and rubbed her husband's shoulder before standing up to get him more coffee.

Vergil tackled the mess in his bedroom later that morning after his father left for work at the museum. Since Mrs. Jordan was busy cleaning out a closet while monitoring her son's progress at the same time, Christopher, Molly and Artemas simply hollered a quick goodbye up the staircase. They ambled to the library once again in the chilly December sunshine under a cloudless sapphire-blue sky.

"Most of the time we've been with you outdoors, Artemas, we were either traveling across the plains between Endora and Solárin or sneaking through the woods," Molly said. "This is a nice change of pace."

"Not a troll or goblin in sight," Christopher joked.

"A fine morning indeed!" Artemas replied with a smile as he walked briskly along, the hem of his heavy cloak brushing against the snowy sidewalks.

Though he still suffered from an annoying headache, Artemas didn't want to complain and ruin their carefree moment together and tried to enjoy the scenery. Curling streams of blue and gray chimney smoke drifted lazily into the air from dozens of snowcapped rooftops. A gaggle of vacationing school kids, concentrating more on laughing than building, constructed a lopsided snow castle in the nearby park. A flock of blackbirds perched in an empty oak tree patiently observed the skies before flying off in unison like a swiftly moving storm cloud.

Nobody noticed as a single blackbird broke away from the others and alighted on a nearby telephone wire just as Christopher, Molly and Artemas passed by. It observed the trio with its ash-gray eyes while they walked along the sidewalk below, flying away several moments later but keeping them well in sight from high above.

"I'm going to check out Elvin L. Cooper's website again, Artemas, while Molly looks for a book," Christopher said. "It's probably a long shot, but if our e-mails had any effect, maybe they temporarily removed his web address from the site."

"Even if he did receive them, it's possible he'll do nothing just to keep us in the dark," Molly reasoned. "Why show his hand?"

"Always the optimist," Christopher muttered as they approached the library steps.

"Belthasar will announce himself when he chooses," Artemas said. "We can antagonize him as much as we want, but he still has the advantage. Don't forget that."

"We won't," Molly glumly replied as she grabbed hold of the cast iron railing and trudged up the stairs, kicking her boots against the cement to loosen the packed snow stuck to the soles.

Christopher and Artemas followed Molly up the stairs just as an older woman carrying an armful of books approached them from behind. She was bundled in a maroon coat with a fur collar and wore a pair of light red earmuffs. Artemas took her arm and assisted her up the stairs as Christopher opened the glass door for all to enter.

"May I carry your books, madam?" Artemas politely asked.

"You've done more than enough already," the woman replied with a smile as she stepped inside. "Thanks so much for lending a hand."

Artemas watched her walk toward the main desk then suddenly noticed Miss Mina Mayfield standing there staring directly at him. She nervously patted her chestnut-brown hair and straightened the lavender sweater she wore before greeting the woman with the stack of returns. Mina glanced at Artemas once or twice more as she put on the pair of reading glasses dangling from her neck by a thin gold chain. Artemas offered a slight wave of his hand and waited until the woman in the maroon coat stepped away to search for more books before he approached the desk.

"Well *there's* a familiar face," Miss Mayfield said with a cheerful smile. "The last time I saw you, our library

Halloween party was thrown into utter chaos!"

Artemas chuckled. "I do apologize again, Miss Mayfield, as I had no intention to turn your celebration into a
confectionery disaster."

Mina Mayfield grimaced slightly as she placed the
returned books on a cart behind the desk. "Now remember
our deal, Artemas. First names only."

"Of course, Mina. How could I have forgotten?"

"That's better."

They stared at each other for a few awkward moments, searching for something more to say. Then Mina
casually pointed past Artemas.

"I see you found who you were looking for," she
said, noticing Christopher and Molly standing behind him.
Mina waved at the children. "I know Molly Jordan by name
now, though I don't recall seeing that young man in here too
often. I guess the map I drew for you worked out after all."

"It did," Artemas replied, nearly forgetting that the
children had accompanied him. "Christopher and Molly are
here to, uh–help me with some research."

"And we'll be waiting by the computers when you're
ready, Artemas," Christopher said, taking Molly by the arm
and hurrying off."

"But, Chris, I wanted to…"

"Nice kids," Artemas remarked to Mina as Molly's
voice trailed off.

"Lucy told me you might stop by today," Mina said,
nervously straightening some papers on her desk. "I was
delightfully surprised that you had returned to our city. I
thought it would be nice to sit and have a pleasant
conversation since we never really had the chance last time
you were here. Your previous visit *was* sort of a mystery. I
still don't know where you're from."

Artemas nodded. "I was thinking the very same
thing. That we should have a nice *conversation*, I mean! I
wasn't referring to my mysterious visit," he quickly added, a
hint of uneasiness in his voice. "Or what you *thought* was a
mysterious visit. Nothing mysterious about it at all! And as

to where I'm from, well–that's no secret either."

Mina smiled curiously. "Where *are* you from, Artemas?"

Artemas took a breath and pondered the question for half an instant. "Finland!"

"*Finland*? Why, I can't detect the slightest trace of an accent in your voice."

"It comes and goes!"

"Perhaps it faded after spending so much time here," she politely said, not entirely believing him yet intrigued by his presence. "How long will you be here, Artemas?"

"For about a week, Mina. And I was wondering if–" He fidgeted with the folds of his cloak. "Just wondering if you might like to meet somewhere for lunch and talk. How about on New Year's Eve?"

"What a wonderful idea," she replied as the telephone rang. "But perhaps in the evening would be better, Artemas. The library is hosting a storyteller in the park at seven-thirty as one of the activities. There'll be a bonfire and hot chocolate and all sorts of things to do," she said as she reached for the telephone. "Excuse me for a moment."

"Of course."

Artemas stepped back while Miss Mayfield talked on the telephone. Two young girls strolled up to the desk to check out some books. Lucy Easton, who had been reshelving items in the science fiction section, returned to the desk to help out. She smiled at Artemas as she scanned the books for the girls.

"Hi again," she said, briefly raising her blue tinted glasses to greet the magician. "Glad you could make it. Mina was glad to hear you were back in town."

"Thank you for relaying my message, Lucy," he said with a nod of appreciation, observing how quickly she checked out the half dozen books for the two girls. "I'm looking forward to visiting with Mina again, and–oh, hello, Molly."

"Sorry to interrupt, Artemas, but I saw Miss Mayfield on the phone and thought I'd catch a quick word with Lucy," she said, stepping up to the main desk. Molly quickly explained that her father had okayed a special tour of the museum after the first of January if Lucy was interested.

"That'd be great!" she replied. "And thanks for asking your dad, Molly."

"I'll let you know an exact day and time soon. Happy to help."

"Happy to be a *nuisance* is more like it," Christopher said as he walked up behind his sister. "Are you bothering Artemas?"

"No."

"I'm waiting for Mina while she's on the telephone," Artemas said. "Molly's no bother."

Molly smirked at her brother. "*See?*"

"Done!" Mina said, hanging up the receiver. "Now where were we?" she asked, hoping to return to their conversation. A middle-aged gentleman in a brown leather jacket and scarf walked up to check out some books. A moment later, the woman in the maroon coat with the fur collar also approached with an armful of mysteries to check out. Christopher, Molly and Artemas simultaneously stepped back to give them some room.

"We'll get out of your way," Artemas said. "It's starting to get congested."

"I'll be done before you can recite the alphabet," Mina replied with a smile. "And how are you today, Mr. Porter?" she said to the man at the desk.

"Fine, thanks."

Mina opened the back cover of each book Mr. Porter had brought to the desk and scanned them into the computer one by one as he slipped on a pair of driving gloves and adjusted the scarf around his neck. Lucy assisted Mina by stamping the return date in every book and stacking them in a small pile. While the woman in the maroon coat waited her turn, she searched through her purse and mumbled to herself.

"Seems I could use a few more bookmarkers," she said with a slight laugh. "Always losing them around the house. I'll grab some more if you don't mind."

"Please help yourself," Lucy said as she inked up the rubber stamper.

"Thanks," the woman said. She reached over and took several bookmarkers from a small display on the desk, placed them carefully in her purse and patted it. "Those should last me a month," she said, winking at Christopher and Molly. She noticed Mr. Porter gathering up his books and quickly grabbed a few more bookmarkers. "Perhaps you could use some too, young man," she kindly said, placing them into his hand.

Instantly the woman took a step backward, somewhat off balance, and held onto the edge of the front desk, appearing as if ready to pass out. Molly ran up to her to prevent her from falling just as Lucy grabbed the woman by the hand to help steady her.

"Are you all right, ma'am?" Mina excitedly asked, about to scan the last book.

"I– I suddenly feel very dizzy," the woman softly said, looking around at everyone as if waking up from a deep and troubling sleep. "I'm a bit disoriented." She stood up straight and took a deep breath.

"Do you feel sick?" Lucy asked. "Do you need a doctor?"

"No. I don't think so, miss. I just feel, well, out of place, if that makes sense." She smiled and tried to shake off the strange sensation that overwhelmed her. "Perhaps I should sit down while you ladies finish checking out my books."

"A good idea," Artemas said, brushing past Mr. Porter to assist the woman to a nearby chair. Several people in the library craned their heads to view the commotion.

Lucy also went over to the woman to make sure she was comfortable while Mina checked out Mr. Porter's last book. He placed the bookmarkers the woman had handed him into his coat pocket and quickly gathered up his selections.

"I hope she feels better," he said.

"I'm sure she'll be all right," Mina replied. "I'll keep

you posted next time you stop by."

"Thanks," Mr. Porter said before heading toward the front door.

Christopher and Molly watched as the gentleman departed, both feeling pangs of uneasiness and somewhat disoriented themselves.

"Something strikes me as odd about what just happened," Molly whispered to her brother.

"Same here," Christopher replied, scratching his head. "Are you thinking what I'm thinking?"

Molly looked at her brother and nodded. "I can't help but recall Prince Jeremiah losing his balance on the coronation platform just as Belthasar's spirit left his body and entered into the cat that had leaped into his arms."

"And remember how Morgus Vandar stumbled about after he placed his hand into that cloud of moths? That's the moment when Belthasar's spirit had left *his* body," Christopher said suspiciously. He suddenly bolted toward the door and stepped outside just as Artemas returned to Molly's side.

"What's going on? Where'd your brother go in such a hurry?"

"He had to check on something outdoors," Molly said, gently taking hold of the magician's cloak sleeve. "And I think we should join him," she softly added. "Let's go."

They met Christopher outside on top of the library steps keeping an eagle eye on Mr. Porter. The gentleman climbed into his car parked halfway down the block and drove away through the bright and snowy streets. Christopher glanced at Molly and Artemas with a pained expression.

"Maybe I should run and follow him."

Molly shrugged. "And *then* what?"

Christopher merely shook his head and looked at Artemas for an answer. "We think Belthasar's spirit was in that woman in the library."

"And she nearly fainted when he passed into Mr. Porter," Molly added. She felt cold and empty inside knowing that Belthasar was so close to them in their own world.

"I can't deny that that was my suspicion as well when the woman lost her balance," Artemas said. "Or perhaps the woman is simply ill and our imaginations are running wild. Maybe we shouldn't make such a big deal out of this incident."

Molly crinkled her face, looking askance at the magician. "I'm having a hard time making myself believe *that*."

Artemas shrugged. "Maybe you're right."

Christopher exhaled deeply, his breath rising into the air like a swiftly moving ghost. "So our enemy is back," he said, folding his arms to keep warm.

"And he just drove away under our very noses," Molly glumly added.

Artemas draped the hood of his cloak over his head to fight off the morning chill. "So it would *appear*," he whispered to himself with a raised eyebrow, glancing through the glass library door at the individuals gathered around the main desk. "So it would appear..."

"What'd you say?" Molly asked.

"Oh, nothing. Nothing." Artemas clapped his hands, jarring everyone back to reality. "Forget about rescuing princesses and foiling false coronations. Now our task *really* gets difficult. In the meantime," Artemas said with a grin, "let's go back inside before we all freeze into snowmen!"

"I can't make up my mind," Artemas said at the dining room table later that evening, "whether this pizza meal is even *more* delicious than the barbequed pepper burger I ate in your backyard last year." He mentally debated the issue until his eyes lit up with a solution. "I guess I'll have to declare a tie!"

"I vote for chocolate cake!" Vergil exclaimed as he wrapped a stringy length of mozzarella cheese around his finger.

"Not until *after* dinner," Mrs. Jordan said, wiping off a spot of tomato sauce on Vergil's nose. "We should have named you Pizza Face."

"Or maybe *cheese brain*?" Molly quipped.

"That was *your* backup name!" Christopher said between gulps of soda.

Molly lightly flicked a finger at her brother. "Don't bother me, little gnat."

"Well I'm glad we can still laugh after all that's happened today," Mr. Jordan said. "It's important to keep our sense of humor and hold this family together. With Belthasar on the prowl, well…"

"I knew he'd return here sooner or later," Artemas said, "especially after all those e-mails we'd sent him. He has responded to our challenge in his own devious way."

"I probably should have followed him," Christopher said with a tinge of regret. "Maybe we should stake *him* out."

"Chances are that Belthasar is not even in Mr. Porter anymore," Mr. Jordan said. "From how you described the events in the library, it seems like Belthasar *wanted* you to know he was here. It was all a show to taunt you, I think."

"I think so too," Artemas said. "If he ever plans to strike, it will be without warning. That's why we have to be extra vigilant."

"And that's why some of us won't be getting a full night's sleep," Mr. Jordan added. "If Chris, Artemas and I each stay up for a two or three hour shift during the night, I'll feel a lot better. Just as a precaution," he said with a reassuring glance at his wife.

"Then please allow me to take the middle shift," Artemas said, rubbing his brow. "I haven't been getting a full night's sleep because of my persistent headache, so I'll be the least inconvenienced if I set an alarm for say, two o'clock?"

"A deal," Mr. Jordan agreed. "You'll find me catching up on some reading in the living room until then. Chris, you can set your alarm for five."

"Will do."

So several hours later at the stroke of two, Artemas relieved Mr. Jordan so he could get some sleep and took over the watch in the living room. The house stood still and silent. Magic lay in the kitchen near the door, sound asleep. Artemas uneasily flipped through a magazine, continually glancing at a clock on the wall. He set the magazine down after a few moments, not in the mood to read. He sat back in an easy chair and watched the clock slowly tick off each minute.

When two-thirty arrived, Artemas stood and listened for any sign of movement in the house. Everything was as quiet as could be. Artemas took a deep breath, tiptoed to the hallway and grabbed his cloak hanging upon a coat tree in the corner. He slipped it on, carefully unlocked the front door and stepped out into the chilly darkness.

Five minutes later he stood near a snow-covered park bench cloaked in the shadow of a towering pine tree. Artemas bent down and saw that a small rock had been placed beneath the bench to hold down a plastic grocery bag and a tiny envelope. He opened the bag containing two small items and carefully removed one of them, a photograph, and stepped out of the shadows to examine it.

"Hmmm... *That* looks manageable," he said to himself. "Not too difficult."

He removed the second item which had been wrapped in waxed paper and secured with a piece of tape. Artemas sniffed it a few times and nodded. "Unfortunately, *I* can't have this for a midnight snack."

He hastily placed the two items back into the plastic bag and stuffed it in one of his cloak pockets. Artemas next opened the envelope and removed a folded note, reading the three words scrawled upon the paper in red ink.

Everything is set.

Artemas crumpled the note. His heart raced. He tossed the piece of paper and the envelope into a trash can in the corner of the park before hurrying home to finish his watch. When he finally plopped back down in the easy chair, Artemas knew he'd be awake until dawn since not a speck of sleep would find him tonight. Too many unsettling things were about to happen. He grabbed a magazine and hastily flipped through the pages, his ocean-blue eyes staring at groups of words but reading none of them as the minutes of the bitter winter night slowly ticked away.

CHAPTER NINE

The Final Test

"Marvelous moats!" a voice boomed from the basement the next morning, followed by a stampede of rumbling footfalls up the wooden staircase.

"What's wrong?" Molly cried. She darted out of the kitchen where she was fixing herself a mug of hot chocolate. Magic followed her, barking up a storm as his tail waved like a dancing garden hose.

Christopher flew down the stairs and nearly collided with Molly and Magic as they barreled into the hallway. He grabbed hold of the railing to stop himself just as Artemas burst out of the basement door on the side of the staircase. His eyes were as wild as a madman's, yet his face glowed with an obvious sense of satisfaction. He gazed at Christopher, Molly and Magic for several moments, too giddy to utter a single word.

"Are you all right, Artemas?" Molly said, her heart racing. "You scared us half to death!"

Christopher sat on a lower step and petted Magic to calm him. "Yeah, what's going on? I bet our neighbors down the block heard that!"

"I apologize for my outburst," Artemas said, slightly out of breath. "But the most amazing thing has happened."

He buried his face in his hands for a moment, unsure whether to laugh or cry. "I just couldn't contain my excitement. I feel as if I could fly!"

"What *are* you talking about?" Molly knelt down to take her turn petting Magic. The dog licked her face a few times which she didn't appreciate.

Artemas stepped closer and squatted down, glancing from side to side as if making sure nobody was spying on him. "I finally discovered it!" he whispered. "I've at last perfected my spell!"

Christopher's eyes widened. "Do you mean...?"

Artemas nodded gleefully. "Yes! Yes! That's the one!"

Molly gasped as she held Magic close to her, gazing proudly at the magician. "You finally created something living that can withstand the *sunlight*?"

"I'm about to," he said. "I've conducted preliminary tests in the basement with your father's permission. There's a stream of sunlight pouring in through one of the windows. But I'd like to perform the final test outdoors just to be certain, perhaps in the backyard where it's still shady."

"Can we help?" Christopher eagerly asked.

"You can be a witness," Artemas said. "You too, Molly."

"Great. We'll even bring Magic along for good luck!"

"I wouldn't have it any other way," he agreed, gently scratching the wheaten terrier behind its ears. "Your parents and Vergil are invited too. I think they should witness this historic moment."

"Mom and Vergil are grocery shopping and Dad walked down to the hardware store," Christopher said. "But you can show them later. Let's not wait."

"I don't want to wait either," Artemas replied, "but this may be a one-time show. My powers are fading each day I'm in your world. Once I perform the final test, they may be too weakened until I return through the timedoor to recharge them, so to speak."

"If they have to miss the big event, so be it," Molly said, not wanting to wait another moment. "Grab your cloak, Artemas, and let's head outdoors. It's show time!"

Christopher and Molly rushed out the back door with Magic in excited pursuit. The dog raced around the snowy backyard dappled with sun and shadow, occasionally flopping on his back and blissfully making a canine version of a snow angel. Whenever he passed through a splash of sunlight, his beige and gray coat shimmered with faint traces of gold.

Before joining them outside, Artemas observed the trio through the backdoor window, nervously tugging at his beard. He reached inside a cloak pocket and removed the photograph he had retrieved in the park last night, quickly studying it a final time before placing it back. He then slipped his thumb into a second pocket, pulled it open and looked down inside. Artemas inhaled deeply and nodded.

"That *would* have made an excellent midnight snack," he muttered, removing his thumb. He took one more glance outside the window and sighed. "Well, let's see how good of an actor I really am." The magician stepped through the back door a moment later, quietly apprehensive like a student entering a classroom on final exam day.

Two feet of snow blanketed the yard, and a towering bare maple tree stood guard in the far corner. A row of hedges and small trees separated the adjoining property along the left side of the yard near the upper driveway. A four foot high stone wall stretched along the back and right borders with a small cast iron gate built into the right side. Tall evergreens in the adjacent yards perfumed the air with sweet pine. A picnic table and barbeque near the house were covered with large gray stretch tarps to protect them. Piles of fluffy snow lay undisturbed on each, patiently awaiting the warmth of a distant spring.

"I think I'll conduct my experiment along the back wall," Artemas said, pointing to the shadiest section as he trudged through the snow.

"What are you going to create?" Christopher asked. The late morning air was quiet except for the chirping of birds hidden in the nearby pines. Magic offered an occasional bark to get their attention.

"I suppose it would be appropriate to recreate another rose," he replied with a playful wink at Molly.

"You're never going to let me forget about *that*, are you," she said with a grin. "I promise not to interfere this time, Artemas. And as there are no balcony doors to open around here, I don't see how I can."

"We'll make sure nothing gets in the way," Christopher promised.

"Nothing will," Artemas said, burying his hands in his cloak pockets to keep warm. He took a deep breath and shrugged. "Well then, I suppose I should begin."

He walked toward the back wall, passing beside Magic as Christopher and Molly followed in his footprints. Magic barked and made a chaotic path through the snow, following Artemas and nudging him with his nose. Artemas petted the dog on the head.

"No time to play now, Magic. There's work to be done."

Magic wagged his tail and bolted past Artemas, then quickly turned around and blocked his way, whimpering while pawing at the magician's cloak. Molly scowled.

"Behave, Magic!" She slapped her hands just above the knees, trying to get the dog to run to her. "Get over here and quit bothering Artemas."

"He *does* seem rather playful today," the magician said, pivoting on one foot and taking a few awkward steps backward to get away from the dog. "Down, Magic! Down!"

"Should have left you inside," Christopher muttered as he grabbed Magic by the collar to keep him from burying his nose in the folds of Artemas' cloak. He held Magic in place until Artemas reached a shady spot along the back wall.

"Ah, this will do nicely," he said, sweeping off a pile of snow into the yard. "Now I need something to start with."

"Plastic grapes perhaps?" Molly joked. She fondly recalled the night when Artemas had produced a sprawling grapevine in the living room of their old house.

"I've got it!" Christopher said, grabbing hold of the tip of a pine branch leaning over the wall. He released Magic and removed the glove from his free hand with his teeth, stripped off a few of the soft green needles and handed them to Artemas.

Artemas held them carefully in his palm and set them gently on top of the wall just as Magic jumped upon him. The dog stood on his hind legs and pawed at Artemas' cloak, pinning the magician against the wall.

"Magic! What *is* the matter with you?" Molly cried, pulling the dog away and holding him in place. "I'll send you inside if you do that one more time."

"No harm done," Artemas said. "I think he's as excited about this test as we are."

Christopher knelt beside Magic and stroked his fur several times, whispering into his ear. "Now behave, Magic, and maybe I'll give you a treat when we get inside. Deal?"

Magic looked at Christopher upon hearing the word *treat*, but that only grabbed his attention for a moment. The dog remained as antsy as ever while he sat in the snow, gazing at Artemas the entire time, panting heavily with his tongue hanging out.

"I don't know what's gotten into that mutt," Molly said with an apologetic shrug.

"No matter," Artemas replied. "Let's proceed. Hopefully the adjustments to my spell will work."

"So you tweaked it a bit, eh?" Christopher asked.

Artemas peered at him out of the corner of his eye. "*Tweaked*?"

"Fine tune," he explained.

"Yes. That's *exactly* what I did!" Artemas said with a nod. "*Tweaked*. What an interesting word. Now let's see if all that tweaking produces a positive result."

He carefully swept the pine needles into a pile with his index finger before leaning back to examine the formation like an artist gazing upon an unfinished canvas. Christopher and Molly watched in silence, wondering what would happen next. Magic stood restlessly for a moment before sitting down again and licking his nose. He would have lunged at Artemas had not Christopher kept an arm gently around him.

Artemas placed one hand above the pine needles and whispered a series of nearly inaudible words which Christopher and Molly couldn't understand. The strain on the magician's face was apparent as he closed his eyes. Artemas then placed both hands above the wall and continued to speak before going utterly quiet. The shadows deepened in the thickening silence as if darkness had fallen in the middle of the morning. Suddenly the magician's eyes snapped open and he raised his hands, clearly enunciating the final word of the spell.

"*Coréniförsegro!*"

Immediately the small pile of pine needles started to wiggle as if ready to scatter in a mini explosion. But an instant later the tiny green spikes melted into one another, forming a liquid droplet about the size of a quarter that reflected the tree branches like a darkened mirror. The green liquid slowly migrated along the stone wall in a narrow stream about the width of a pencil, eventually forming a circular tube a foot in length that solidified into the stem of a rose. Several sharp thorns developed up and down the sides, making the stem roll back and forth as the emerging points took turns pushing off the stone. As the last thorn pierced through the woody fibers of the stem, a scarlet bud emerged at the tip, growing to the size of a large grape before blossoming into a fully developed and sweet-smelling red rose. The fresh flower lay tenderly upon the cold stone wall, a hint of spring quietly defying the bitter chill of the winter landscape.

Artemas took a step back, staring at his magical handiwork with subdued enthusiasm. Christopher and Molly, however, looked on in jaw-dropping amazement, shifting their stunned gazes between the magician and the rose. This simple demonstration was more spectacular than the sprawling grapevine which had overrun their living room five years ago. Artemas carefully picked up the rose and examined it.

"So far, so good," he said, rubbing his forehead with his free hand. "Unfortunately the effort hasn't lessened my headache any. It feels like a team of horses galloping around up there."

"Maybe you should rest before we go on," Molly said.

"No, I'll be all right." Artemas held up the rose. "Care for a closer look?"

Christopher and Molly stepped up to inspect the red rose in all its stunning detail, for an instant ignoring Magic. With no one holding him by the collar, Magic scrambled to his feet and squeezed between Christopher and Molly, charging directly at Artemas. He jumped up on the magician, pinning him against the wall once again and whimpering.

"Magic!" Artemas cried as he was pushed uncomfortably backward.

"Magic!" Christopher echoed as he and Molly raced toward the dog.

While Magic pawed at Artemas' cloak, the magician flailed his arms in the air, trying to prevent himself from performing a back flip over the wall. But just as Christopher and Molly secured Magic by the collar, the rose slipped out of Artemas' hand and fell into the next yard on the opposite side of the wall. Christopher and Molly tumbled backward into the snow with Magic falling on top of them, freeing Artemas from his canine captor. He couldn't help but laugh as Christopher and Molly got to their knees, trying to restrain Magic who wiggled like a fish in shallow water.

"Dear me, but if he doesn't like my magic tricks he should just leave the audience. No need to cause a riot!" Artemas joked as he scurried to the cast iron gate on the right side. "I better retrieve that rose before my entire act is ruined." He pushed open the gate into the piled snow just far enough to squeeze through, then walked along on the other side of the wall to where he had dropped the flower.

Magic calmed down as Molly rubbed the dog behind his ears. Christopher held him gently by the chin and stared into his eyes.

"What's with you, wild one?" he playfully asked before turning to Artemas. "Sorry about Magic. I don't know why he's acting so weird."

"Just being himself," Artemas said with an unconcerned shrug. He bent down and disappeared behind the wall for a few moments before popping up again like a jack-in-the-box. "But no harm done! Look, my experiment is still safe and sound," he added, holding up the rose he retrieved from the other side. He held it out for Molly as he casually leaned against the wall.

Molly jumped up and took the rose from Artemas, then closed her eyes as she smelled the fragrant flower. "I feel like I'm walking through a garden in summertime!" she said, examining the rose cradled in her hands. "This smells as lovely as the ones you created in Endora."

"Until you destroyed them," Christopher replied with a snicker. Molly inhaled deeply again, ignoring her brother's comment.

Artemas reentered the yard and closed the gate, keeping a watchful eye on Magic. As he swept past, the dog sniffed at the magician's cloak one time before swiftly turning away. Magic was no longer in the mood to bother Artemas and contentedly chewed at the bits of snow lodged in his paws instead.

Molly handed the rose to her brother and leaned against the wall to address Artemas. "Ready for the *real* test now?"

"I suppose," he softly said, stroking his beard. Broad patches of sunlight flooded the front section of the yard, yet Artemas seemed reluctant to leave the shadows.

Christopher walked over to Artemas and handed him the rose. "It's up to you now. Time to see if all that tweaking of your magic spell pays off."

Artemas stared at the rose for a moment then slowly

looked up. "I'm almost afraid to go ahead with my test," he admitted. "If it's another failure, then..."

Molly noted the apprehension upon his face and grabbed the sleeve of his cloak. "Let's go to the front of the house," she suggested to buy a little time so Artemas could collect his thoughts. "It's much sunnier out there. We can stand under one of the pine trees until we're ready."

"Good idea," her brother agreed, calling to Magic.

Christopher trudged through the snow near the wall as Magic followed, then continued along the shady side of the house opposite the driveway. Artemas and Molly hurried to catch up. Soon the three stood underneath a canopy of pine branches on the side of the front lawn while Magic ran about in crazy circles in the snow. Artemas slowly twirled the rose stem in his fingers, contemplating his next move. Molly looked up and offered an encouraging smile.

"Ready?"

Artemas smelled the rose and gently touched the tip of his finger to one of the thorns. "I still haven't the courage," he said. He handed the rose to Molly. "You do it for me, if you please. It'll be less of a disappointment if it, well, you know."

"All right," Molly said, taking the flower and gently touching the petals. "I'll be happy to help, Artemas. Wish me luck."

"*Much* luck," he whispered.

"Times *ten*," Christopher added, smiling at his sister. He indicated with a slight turn of his head that she should proceed at once.

Molly took a breath and nodded. Then holding the rose close to her chest, she stepped out of the shadows of the fragrant pine tree and into the blinding sunshine. Molly closed her eyes when the blast of heat and light hit her face, but continued to walk toward the center of the lawn. A moment later she stopped. She slowly opened her eyes, blinking several times in the snowy brightness. Molly turned to face Christopher and Artemas, still sheltered in the shade, before looking down at her hands. Her heart leapt. The fragrant red rose stared back at her, its thorny stem secure in her grip. Molly looked up with a mile-wide grin. The test had succeeded.

"Look at that!" Christopher cried, running into the sunshine to join his sister. Magic ran over to them upon hearing the excitement in Christopher's voice. Artemas remained standing under the pine branches, watching in subdued silence.

"I guess this means I redeemed myself," Molly said, handing the rose to her brother. "Now not another joke about that incident in Endora!"

"A deal," Christopher promised, holding up the rose directly in front of the sun. The tips of its petals glowed ruby-red against a deep blue sky. "Besides, I still have a boatload of other jokes in reserve."

Molly walked over to Artemas, motioning for him to join them. "Time to enjoy your success, Artemas. If that rose hasn't disappeared by now, it's *never* going to."

"I suppose you're right," he said, stepping into the light for a closer look. He carefully took the rose from Christopher and held it up for scrutiny.

"Pretty amazing," Christopher said, patting him on the back.

"That's one way to look at it," Artemas softly replied, lines of exhaustion and disbelief etched upon his face. He tried to smile as a weary sigh escaped through his lips. "Well, that's that, I guess, for what it's worth. I still can't believe it though."

"A fine accomplishment," Molly insisted. "First the timedoor and now *this*. You're quite the inventor, Artemas. How *do* you do it?"

"You know better than to ask that," Artemas replied, bending down on one knee and petting Magic who sat contentedly in the snow wagging his tail. "A magician *never* reveals his secrets."

They basked in the joy of the moment and the warmth of the sun for several minutes, for a while forgetting their battle against Belthasar. Magic ran circles through the snow as Christopher, Molly and Artemas took turns holding the delicate red rose. In time they retreated indoors, eager to recount the details with their parents and Vergil as soon as they returned. In the meantime, Molly made hot chocolate for everyone to celebrate while Artemas placed the rose in a small vase on the kitchen table.

And as the late morning hours drifted into afternoon, the blazing sun arched slowly through the sky beyond the towering pines, eventually sinking in the southwest. Warm splashes of sunlight filtered through the evergreen branches and glistened upon fluffy piles of snow along the stone wall on the opposite side of the Jordans' backyard. The heat of the sun rays focused upon the white flakes and melted them down a bit.

Water droplets also drizzled down the side of the wall as the snow on top thawed. The constant dripping formed tiny pools of water which encouraged more melting along the base of the wall. Layer by thin layer of snow disappeared in the progressive melting, eventually revealing an unusual object–a small strip of grilled steak that Artemas had earlier concealed in his cloak pocket and then hastily buried while retrieving the rose.

CHAPTER TEN

Dinner At Rupert's Place

The New Year's Eve bonfire gushed with warmth and light during the final chilly hours of the year, casting a ruddy glow upon the swirl of faces gathered nearby in the city park. Children drank hot chocolate from foam cups as parents sipped steaming coffee and strolled about. Helium-filled balloons swayed in the brisk air and glass bead necklaces sparkled in anticipation of a brand new year. Food vendors sold grilled burgers and hotdogs as folksingers, acrobats and storytellers performed to applause. Light posts resembling nineteenth century gas lamps were scattered throughout the park, softly illuminating the gentle waves of snow along the walks.

Near one large pine tree still adorned with Christmas lights, a face painter catered to a line of eagerly waiting children. One child sat proudly on a bale of straw while having a butterfly applied to her left cheek and a frog to the right. Others gawked and chattered as they waited their turn, discussing what color paint went best with a particular shade of glitter.

"So how do we look?" Molly asked as she and Vergil marched past the popcorn seller's tent. Mr. and Mrs. Jordan were talking to Artemas nearby.

"One dinosaur *here* and another one *here*!" Vergil exclaimed as he turned his face from side to side to display the fresh face painting to Artemas and his parents. "And look at *this*!" he added, pulling off his hat and raising the hair over his forehead. "A third eye! How's it look?"

"I-mazing!" his father joked.

"Molly only has butterflies and bumble bees on her face," Vergil said with a smirk before pointing to the stegosaurus on his left cheek. "Too late now, but she could have had one of *these*!"

"I think you both look perfect," Mrs. Jordan said, placing the hat back upon Vergil's head. "Now how about a hot drink? It's freezing!"

"Perhaps we should get closer to the bonfire," Artemas suggested, pointing toward the dancing flames in the distance surrounded by a ring of large rocks. The bright light reflected off the crowd gathered near it who were listening to a woman spin a tale about a grand adventure in a hot air balloon floating through the stars.

"I see Lucy and Miss Mayfield over there," Molly said as she excitedly waved to the two women. "They arranged the event for the library."

"What time is it?" Artemas asked. "Mina said she would be finished with her duties around eight-thirty. We're to meet afterward for a stroll through the park."

Mr. Jordan glanced at his watch. "It's only a few minutes after eight."

"This will give me a chance to introduce you to Lucy," Molly said to her father. "Did you find a good time to arrange a tour at the museum?"

"Thursday would be perfect. Around three o'clock," he said. "I'll be cataloging items in the basement storage area that day. It should be quiet then."

"Terrific!" Molly said, waving her hand again in an effort to get Lucy's attention. She signaled for Lucy to walk over and join them.

"Thursday afternoon is when the timedoor reopens," Artemas said, glancing at the bonfire. Mina Mayfield remained near the story time activities as Lucy approached. "It opens precisely at five o'clock and closes at eight. So if you don't mind, I'll stop by the museum shortly before then to meet you. And I won't have trouble finding you either," he added with a chuckle, recalling how he and King Rupert had spent many hours hiding out in the museum basement on their first visit to this world.

"That would be wonderful if you could stop by," Mrs. Jordan said. "This way we can accompany you back for a brief visit. I'd love to see Endora again."

"And I would love to show you," Artemas replied, glancing again toward the bonfire. "Coincidentally, that very day in Endora is the last day of *our* year, and also the last day of winter. But we don't celebrate the new year the same way as you. None of the fireworks or raucous celebrating that Christopher told me about. We usually sit down to a lovely breakfast to greet the first spring sunrise of a brand new year."

"Christopher will stay up until midnight no matter how cold it gets," Molly said, again waving at Lucy who swiftly approached. "He's running around with Henry and Robert, no doubt stuffing his face."

"I'm staying up until midnight too!" Vergil demanded. "I *am* seven after all."

"If you can keep those eyelids open that long, young man, you've got a deal. That's a promise!" his father said, certain that his son would be asleep well before eleven.

"And *I* promise to give you all a brief yet thorough tour through parts of King Rupert's castle you haven't seen yet after we go through the timedoor," Artemas said, raising his cup of hot chocolate with a smile before taking a sip.

"And what exactly is a *timedoor*?" asked Lucy with a smile as she arrived at their small gathering, squeezing in between Mrs. Jordan and Molly. She wore a long brown leather coat and matching boots with a heavy beige knit scarf wrapped about her head and neck. The soft glow from a nearby lamppost reflected off the deep blue lenses of her eyeglasses. Everyone stared back at her, momentarily at a loss for words.

"This is Lucy, everyone," Molly jumped in. "She's the history major I told you about and she can't wait to get a special tour of the museum." Molly introduced her to Vergil and her parents. "And you remember my great uncle Artemas."

"Of course," Lucy said. "From Finland."

Artemas nodded. "Thereabouts."

"I can tell you *all* about the timedoor!" Vergil chimed in. But an instant later, Mrs. Jordan pulled her son to her side and pleasantly laughed.

"Now, sweetheart, no need to bother Molly's friend," she said, kneeling next to Vergil and wiping his mouth with a napkin she had gotten with her coffee. "There's some face paint near your lip. Let me clean it off."

"Mom, I'm fine! I just wanted to tell that girl about the–"

"–*timedoor*!" Mr. Jordan interrupted. "I can tell you all about that, Lucy."

"You can?" she said.

"You *can*?" Molly repeated with a mystified gaze.

"I had told everyone to keep it a secret, but Lucy *is* a history major after all," Mr. Jordan replied. "And as I'll be giving her a tour on Thursday–if you're free, that is–"

"I am," Lucy said.

"–then there's no reason why she *shouldn't* know about the timedoor."

Mrs. Jordan stared at her husband, slightly in shock. "There *isn't*?" she managed to utter before glancing at Artemas and shrugging her shoulders. Artemas remained silent, curiously anticipating what Mr. Jordan would tell Lucy.

"I've been working on plans for a new exhibit at the museum," he continued. "I can't give you all the details yet, but I'm thinking about calling it *A Timedoor Into the Past*. It's still a working title, so keep it under wraps."

"No problem," Lucy said. "Sounds interesting, Mr. Jordan. I think it's a *great* title for an exhibit."

"I do too," Artemas agreed. "I'm sure it will be an astounding display."

Mrs. Jordan quietly sighed with relief. Molly grinned and gave a thumbs up to her father when Lucy wasn't looking.

"Maybe I could get a preview of this timedoor exhibit," Lucy suggested. "I'd love to see the items you're going to include in it. Maybe bounce a few ideas off me."

"Perhaps I will. How's three o'clock sound, Lucy? Molly will be along for the ride."

"I'll be there!"

"Me too!" Vergil insisted. "Why should Molly have all the fun?"

"If you're good that day, I'll take you," Mrs. Jordan said. "Maybe Christopher will tag along too. We'll make it a family tour. Care to join us, Artemas?"

"I won't have time for the tour, but I'll stop by before five o'clock. I'd love to take you all–*out to dinner*!" Artemas said with a strained smile. "Before I return to–Finland. There's a tiny restaurant a few miles from here that I've heard good things about. It's called *Rupert's Place*. Pencil it in. Thursday. Five o'clock."

Molly pulled the penlight out of her coat pocket and pretended to write upon a piece of imaginary paper. "We'll be waiting, Artemas. And don't be late!"

"Where's everybody going?" a voice softly said from behind. Mina Mayfield joined the small gathering, smiling at Artemas all the while. A smattering of laughter and applause floated through the brittle air as the storyteller neared the end of her tale. "We're almost finished so I sneaked over to let you know I'm just about ready, Artemas."

"I look forward to our stroll through the park," he replied, quickly explaining about Mr. Jordan's Thursday museum tour.

"I'd love to tag along," she said after Mr. Jordan invited her. "However, I'll be working then, so I must decline. But it'll be quite an opportunity for Lucy, so be sure to take advantage of it, dear."

"Trust me, Miss Mayfield, I will," Lucy replied, raising her coat collar to ward off a strengthening breeze. "I definitely know an opportunity when I see one."

"That settles it then. I'll see you in three days," Mr. Jordan said as Lucy waved goodbye to everyone and hurried back for the conclusion of the storytelling event.

"And I'll see you *now*," Artemas added, politely extending a hand to Miss Mayfield while at the same time keeping an eye on Lucy as she slowly drifted away through the crowd. "I'll accompany you back until your story time event concludes, Mina, then we can grab a bite to eat from one of the park vendors."

"A deal," Miss Mayfield replied, taking his hand. "And while we're walking and dining, you must promise to tell *me* a story about your life in–*Finland*? I'm so looking forward to hearing about the mysterious and magical Artemas. I'm sure you could weave an interesting tale."

"Oh, I assure you there's nothing *that* fascinating to report, Mina. You make it sound as if I'm from another world!" Artemas said, tossing a wink at the Jordans as he and Mina passed by and disappeared into the bustling crowd and the frosty darkness.

CHAPTER ELEVEN

A Helping Hand

January arrived gray and bleak, as if winter had tightened its grasp with no plans of ever letting go. Though the temperature had warmed slightly, the clouds thickened and snow flurries peppered the air like mosquitoes at a picnic. It was a miserable day to play outdoors, but a perfect day for an extended tour of the museum. Mr. Jordan guided Lucy and his family through several hallways, many containing long narrow windows that stretched to the ceiling. The dreary daylight reflected off smooth glassy floor tiles decorated with patterns of rich dark marble.

They viewed some displays about prehistoric times and the sights and sounds of the Middle Ages. At Molly's insistence, Mr. Jordan presented a brief star show inside the planetarium. Everyone sat back in cushioned chairs in the darkness and watched the constellations swirl about on a domed ceiling. Christopher and Molly fondly recalled using the planetarium to help King Rupert and Artemas determine when the timedoor would reopen while they were trapped in this world on their first visit.

"And now for something *extra* special!" Mr. Jordan said a short while later as he escorted everyone down a restricted staircase into the basement, a sprawling web of rooms and corridors containing crates and boxes of uncatalogued items. "I saved the best for last!"

"Dad, some of the sections down here look like a tornado passed through," Christopher said as he glanced about. "You need to hire more help."

"Everything's not as organized as it should be, but we're overwhelmed with items and there are only so many hours in a day."

"Maybe I could get a job *here*," Lucy said. "I would love losing myself in all these artifacts. What a treasure trove!"

Vergil snickered as he tugged on his mother's shirt sleeve. "And you and Dad tell me to keep *my* room clean? This is a super mess!"

"I'm not sure which place is worse," Mrs. Jordan replied. "It may be a tie!"

"This section isn't typical of everything down here," Mr. Jordan said. "There are several storerooms that are organized and spotless. Some of the really valuable items are locked up, and once something is catalogued, it is cleaned and maintained with tender loving care."

"I think it's fabulous!" Lucy said as they strolled through a cluttered and dimly lit corridor. Unmarked cardboard boxes sat piled on a row of narrow tables lined against a whitewashed cement wall. "What are you currently working on, Mr. Jordan?"

"We have a collection of oriental pottery loaned to us from another museum for one of our spring exhibits. Beautiful hand painted vases, plates and the like from the eighteenth century Far East," he explained. "They're in one of the lockups just around the corner. I've been going through the items to see which ones we should display."

"I'd like to take a peek," Lucy said.

"Me too," Mrs. Jordan added. "Any chance to use those pieces on our dining room table?"

"I don't think so, honey. I couldn't afford the insurance premiums to enjoy *that* plate of spaghetti!"

"Don't you have anything more exciting?" Christopher asked. "I mean–*pottery*?" he said with an exaggerated yawn.

"Maybe you'll learn something," Molly said, lightly jabbing him with an elbow.

"Maybe *you'll* run away and disappear if a mouse crawls out from behind one of those crates," Christopher muttered.

"Maybe *Lucy* will run away if you two don't put a lid on it," their father quipped.

"Don't worry about me. I have a younger brother," Lucy replied with a chuckle. "I know how it is. Most of the time bickering between siblings is just a big act."

"Sure. Chris is a *class act*!" Molly said with a roll of her eyes.

"And you're a *clown* act," her brother replied.

"Are you sure about that?" Mrs. Jordan whispered to Lucy as they turned the corner.

"Positive," she replied, fingering her necklace. "I know an act when I see one."

Mr. Jordan took them into a large room with white plaster walls lit with rows of overhead lights. A huge metal desk along one side served as a working station, equipped with a computer and digital camera, reference books, and most importantly, a coffee pot and a sleeve of foam cups. Shelves on both sides of the room were crammed with cardboard boxes and plastic containers marked with identifying stickers printed with strings of numbers and letters. The last third of the room was sealed off with a screen of black wire latticework stretching from wall to wall and ceiling to floor. A door of similar construction was built into the center. Mr. Jordan grabbed a key lying near the computer, unlocked the cage door and tossed it back on the desk.

"Not much into security measures around here," Christopher said with a smirk.

"We hide the key after hours, wise guy," his father replied, opening the door.

Vergil bolted past his father into the cage and pressed his face against the front, grabbing the metalwork and shaking it. "Let me out of this jail! Let me out! Let me out!" he hollered between bouts of giggling, staring at his sister on the other side.

"That's the perfect place for you," Molly said dryly as she followed Lucy and her parents inside. "It can be your new playroom."

"How you doing in there, Verg?" Christopher said as he passed by, shaking his brother's hand through one of the large diamond-shaped openings. He sat down in the desk chair, checking out the computer. "Got any good games on this thing, Dad?"

"Don't even think about it, Chris," his father replied as he searched the boxes on the shelves inside the cage for a pottery sample. "Join us in here for the big show."

"I'll rush right in," he muttered, leaning back in the swivel chair and turning from side to side.

"Okay, Vergil, enough with the convict act," his mother said as she pried her son's fingers off the metal enclosure. "Let's see what Daddy has to show us."

"All right," he sighed, trudging over with his mother.

"Could one of you girls grab that blue textbook lying open on the desk?" Mr. Jordan asked as he carefully set a red plastic container on a small table inside the cage. The sample had been sealed with a series of computer-generated stickers. "There's a photograph in that book of this very item I'm about to show you along with a small write-up. You don't know how privileged you are to view these things up close."

"I'll get the book," Molly said, heading out of the cage.

"I'm getting hungry," Vergil added, staring up at the staggering assortment of items.

"Mind if I grab a cup of coffee?" Lucy asked.

"Help yourself," Mr. Jordan said, carefully removing the stickers as his wife watched him work. She was pleased that her husband still enjoyed his job so much.

"Anyone else want some?" Lucy offered as she followed Molly out of the cage.

"Maybe later," Mrs. Jordan replied, still watching her husband at work while keeping a spare eye on Vergil.

"Don't say I didn't offer," Lucy whispered to herself, quietly palming the key to the cage as she swept past the desk. Then she stopped and turned around. "Suddenly I don't feel like coffee," she announced as Molly reached for the blue textbook and Christopher spun around in lazy circles in the swivel chair. Lucy walked back to the metal enclosure, nonchalantly closed the door and locked it.

Christopher dropped his feet to the floor and stopped spinning in the chair. "Lucy, what are you *doing*?"

Molly looked up and saw Lucy with the key dangling from her hand, perplexed for an instant until she noticed the cage door had been closed. "If that's supposed to be a joke, Lucy, it's not very funny."

"I don't *make* jokes, Molly."

"What's going on?" Mrs. Jordan said, turning around to discover that she and her husband and youngest son were prisoners inside the cage. She clutched the door and shook it. "Unlock this door at once, Lucy! What are you trying to prove?"

Mr. Jordan dashed to his wife's side. "What do you think you're doing?"

Vergil walked to the front of the cage and pressed his nose to the metalwork. "We really *are* in jail," he softly said.

"Not for long!" Christopher jumped up and stormed over to Lucy. "You have a strange sense of humor, girl. Now give me the key!"

"Here," Lucy said, holding it out. But as soon as Christopher reached for it, she tossed the key into the air toward Molly who grabbed it before it hit the floor.

"I think this tour is over," Mr. Jordan snapped. "Unlock this door, Molly."

"Right away, Dad."

"*Right away, Dad*!" Lucy mimicked with a sneer before she bolted from Christopher's side and charged directly at Molly. "After all, Molly, *you* know how awful it is to be locked up!" she added, lightly touching one finger against the back of Molly's hand as she swept by.

An instant later, Lucy staggered about, caught half-way between a run and a walk. The room spun in a dizzying blur as a faceless voice floating among her bewildered thoughts slowly faded. Lucy tried to grab hold of something and get her bearings, believing she was in the public library. She searched desperately for the edge of the checkout desk before her legs gave out, wondering where Miss Mayfield and the woman in the maroon coat had gone. She stumbled over her own feet and tripped on the leg of a swivel chair before crashing to the floor, seeing a white flash in her mind–then feeling nothing more.

"Are you all right?" Christopher cried as he brushed past Molly and went to Lucy's aid as she lay sprawled out on the floor. She had hit her head on the edge of the desk.

"She looks fine," Molly flatly replied, standing as still as stone with the key to the metal cage locked in her grasp. "There's a lesson to be learned here–*don't run before you're about to faint*! Not good for the balance."

"Quit making stupid jokes and unlock the cage!" Christopher said as he examined Lucy.

"Let us out of here, Molly!" Vergil demanded.

"Hurry!" Mrs. Jordan said.

Though Lucy had passed out, she appeared to be breathing normally and there was no sign of blood or a cut. Christopher felt somewhat relieved and glanced up at his sister. During all the commotion, Molly had not moved an inch.

"Why are you standing there? Unlock the door."

Molly sighed. "Like I said before, I *don't* make jokes–stupid or otherwise."

"Would you just–"

Then it hit him like a punch to the stomach. Christopher stared at Molly for several moments, observing the same cool demeanor that Lucy had displayed only moments ago. An eerie calm possessed his sister. A dull gray lifelessness filled her eyes. Christopher softly mouthed a single word. "Belthasar."

"So you *finally* figured it out," Molly said, tossing the key into the air and catching it. "About time! I've been inside Lucy for six days, ever since you, your sister and the great and mighty Artemas traipsed over to the library that one morning." Molly turned around and walked toward the cage, offering a contemptuous smile to Mr. and Mrs. Jordan. "As you can see, my acting abilities have improved ever since I took up residence in Elvin L. Cooper. I learned a lot from him about playing a personality."

"Well you've still got a lot to learn from *us*!" Mr. Jordan said, reaching through the cage to grab Molly.

She stepped back an instant before his hand could grasp her arm. "Not fast enough!"

"Neither are *you*!" Christopher said, wrapping his arms around Molly as he dashed at her from behind. "Always watch your back!"

"As if it *matters*."

Molly casually slapped the back of Christopher's hand and the spirit of Belthasar passed into him. He grabbed the key from Molly and pushed the slightly dazed girl aside.

"What's going on?" hollered Molly, rubbing her brow. Then she noticed Lucy sprawled upon the floor. "What happened to *her*?"

"Belthasar is in Christopher!" her mother cried. "Keep away from him!"

"You'd think I had the plague," Christopher said with a smirk, his eyes tinged with the color of wet ash as he walked toward an air vent in the floor near the door. He dropped the key through the metal grille covering the top. "That takes care of *that*!"

"Leave my children alone!" Mr. Jordan said. "Fight me instead—*if* you have the guts."

Christopher tilted his head and shrugged. "A year ago such a taunt might have provoked me. But I've learned a lot since then. I can get more accomplished when I control my anger *and* my ego."

"You may put on a good act, Belthasar, but in the end

your anger and conceit will spill out," Molly scoffed. "It always does."

Christopher took a deep breath. "Oh, Molly, how I truly miss all the lovely conversations we used to share when you visited my world–not!"

"And what do you plan to do now that you're in *ours*?" Mrs. Jordan asked as she stared through the metal latticework, one arm wrapped around Vergil's shoulder.

"*Plan* to do? Why, I've already accomplished quite a bit over this past year. I decided that I *like* living in your world ever since I arrived here in a mosquito on the back of that mangy dog of yours."

"Magic isn't mangy!" Vergil shouted.

"So *that's* how you managed it," Mr. Jordan said with a nod. "I must admit it was a clever move. You had us all fooled."

"Save the false compliments. I won't let my guard down," Christopher said with a raised eyebrow. "I still have much to do, only now I must do it sooner than expected thanks to your insatiable need to meddle in my affairs. I was happy living on the other side of this vast country, some days not even *thinking* about my desire to destroy you. But this family couldn't leave well enough alone."

"Did we put a crimp in your plan to enjoy a life of leisure at someone else's expense?" Molly said, pressing her hands to her face in mock horror. "Oops! Didn't *mean* to!"

"That brazen attitude will get you in trouble one of these days," Christopher said as the spirit of Belthasar churned inside him. "Mark my words!"

"I think it's gotten me *out* of a lot of trouble," Molly replied with a satisfied grin. "Most of it caused by you, by the way. That brazen attitude keeps me sharp."

"Well obviously not *too* sharp since I passed into Lucy right under your very nose," he said, plopping down in the swivel chair and planting his feet on the desktop. "I followed the three of you as a bird that day you walked to the library. A short time later I found another unwitting accomplice to assist me. In fact, Artemas helped me up the stairs by the arm while your brother opened the door for me," he said with a laugh.

Molly recalled an elderly woman in a maroon coat with a fur collar they had met outside the library that morning. She wore a pair of light red earmuffs, carried an armful of books–and housed the spirit of Belthasar. Molly scratched her head.

"We suspected you were inside that lady after she nearly fainted by the front desk," Molly said. "She handed that man, Mr. Porter, some bookmarkers, then became dizzy. Christopher ran outside after him, but Mr. Porter took off in his car. Artemas and I also watched him leave."

Christopher glanced at Lucy, who continued to sleep soundly on the floor, before flashing a snakelike smile. "I only *pretended* to get dizzy when I handed Mr. Porter the bookmarkers, wanting to make you think I had passed into him. Then you and Lucy, being such kind souls, both reached out to help the old lady. I took refuge inside Lucy when she grabbed my hand, and that's when the lady nearly fainted again, only *this* time for real. And so I, as Lucy, went about my business, using my acting skills to play the part of the wildly and weirdly dressed twenty-year-old college student and library assistant." Christopher crossed his arms, leaned back in the chair and smiled. "Clever, don't you think? And since you had offered to arrange a tour of the museum for Lucy through your father, she was the perfect choice to recruit as a spy, enabling me to keep an eye on all of you while I made my plans."

"Deviously clever," Mr. Jordan said.

"I'll take that as a compliment."

"Take it however you want," Mrs. Jordan chimed in. "But I'll ask you again. What *are* your plans?"

"Not that it's any of your business, but I think I'll take a trip to Endora for starters," Christopher replied, jumping up from his seat. "Now that I know the timedoor is reopening soon, a brief visit back might be enjoyable, especially since nobody will know it's really me." He grunted, recalling Artemas' words in the park on New Year's

Eve. "The old magician planned to take you to a restaurant called *Rupert's Place* on *Thursday* at *five o'clock*? Doesn't take a genius to decipher *that* bit of code!"

"Don't take my brother away!" Vergil said. "You *can't* take him to Endora!"

"Can and *will*!" Suddenly Christopher spoke very softly and wiped away a pretend tear rolling down his cheek. "And wouldn't it be a shame if your brother somehow got lost on the other side of the timedoor and never returned? It's a distinct possibility if I should find a more worthy subject to inhabit."

"Take me instead!" Mr. Jordan offered, keeping his rage in check, though all he imagined doing was ripping through the metal enclosure to get at Belthasar.

"Or *me*!" Mrs. Jordan jumped in. "After all, I helped ruin your coronation. You might have been king of Solárin right now if I hadn't interfered."

"How noble that you'd both sacrifice yourselves to save your children," Christopher said, his eyes pale and lifeless. "But as much as you have done to destroy me, your children have done even *more*! Let *them* pay the price. This one first," he said, pointing to his chest. "I'll deal with *you* later!" Christopher added, glaring at Molly as he slammed the chair into the desk with his foot. "And now, I must be off. It was *such* a pleasure to see you all again," he said with a hollow laugh as he headed toward the door. "Until next time."

"That's what *you* think," Molly whispered to herself as she rushed at Christopher and leaped up on his back before he could leave. "If you deal with one of us, bug brain, you deal with *all* of us!" she cried, covering her brother's eyes with one hand and leaning backward until they both tumbled to the floor.

"Don't toy with me, urchin, or I'll take *you* instead!" screamed the voice of Belthasar as they both struggled to their feet.

"You couldn't catch me, slow poke, if I drew you a map!" Molly taunted, scrambling across the room toward the lockup. Vergil and her parents helplessly watched with a heart-pounding mix of terror and fascination. "You'll never get the best of me, Belthasar. You don't have it in you, loser!"

"I'll show you, Molly Jordan!" he said, sprinting down the room like an angry bull. "There's no escape," the spirit of Belthasar gleefully cried as Molly backed herself against the metal latticework, unable to avoid her enemy's swift approach. "You're trapped! Nobody's here to save you now!" he cried, grabbing Molly's wrist with both hands as his body slammed against the metal cage.

"*We're* here!" a trio of voices shouted. Several arms reached through the openings in the cage like a flurry of binding ropes and grabbed hold of Christopher and Molly, holding them as if they would never let go. Molly latched on to her brother's wrist with her free hand as her parents locked their arms around her and Christopher. Even Vergil knelt down and wrapped an arm around one leg of each of his siblings, closing his eyes and holding on for dear life.

The spirit of Belthasar seethed with rage and tried to free himself from the Jordan family, passing with a blinding fury between Christopher and Molly. But he couldn't break the human chains that bound the family together. He attempted to subdue Mr. and Mrs. Jordan, but whomever he inhabited and tried to control, the other members of the family held on tightly and wouldn't let go.

Belthasar grew angry and bitter and frustrated as his spirit shifted from one person to the next, unable to establish his dominance in any individual. He felt as if he were trapped in a minnow's body at the bottom of that pond again, swimming in blinding circles with no escape. And amid breathing and heartbeats and the rush of blood, Belthasar heard a voice of defiance growing louder and louder. *You will never destroy this family*! How it enraged him. *Together we're stronger than you'll ever be*! The voice seared his mind like a white-hot fire. He grew tired and weak and couldn't think. The words echoed in his mind as the life was drained out of him.

"We're a family and we'll stick together no matter what!" Mrs. Jordan cried as she tightened her grip around the only thing in this world that mattered to her. "Make no mistake, Belthasar—we will fight you to the end!"

They continued to hold on as the wild storm whirled in chaotic fits, fending off black shadows of despair and destruction that circled like a hungry pack of wolves. Time seemed to evaporate as the Jordan family huddled together in the midst of the squall, wondering if the turmoil would ever cease or if the light of day would ever shine upon them again. Then suddenly Mrs. Jordan felt the warmth of a tender touch wash over her like a spring breeze. The caring words of a familiar voice floated among the mayhem.

"Allow *me* to lend a helping hand," Artemas said, his palm gently resting upon Mrs. Jordan's arm still securely wrapped around her family. The magician's face tightened and he took a deep breath, his voice now brimming with strength and determination. "Pick on someone from your own world, Belthasar, if you dare!"

Artemas instantly stood as straight as an arrow and stepped backward, removing his hand from Mrs. Jordan's arm. A crash of color swirled in his eyes, a mix of gray and ocean-blue fighting one another for dominance. The Jordans slowly looked up, dazed and tired, yet filled with undying hope. The first storm had abated.

"Artemas, what happened?" Molly cried, about to rush over to him.

"Stay– back!" Artemas uttered, his words forced and flat and his face muscles taut with pain. "Don't get– near– me."

Christopher clenched his jaw, his mind on fire with disdain for Belthasar. "He's inside you, isn't he, Artemas."

"Clever boy!" Artemas replied, his words now laced with spite. "He's figured out the obvious. But what are you going to *do* about it?"

"Just you wait and see!" Molly cried. "You haven't won yet, Belthasar."

"Oh, but I think I *have*. I've just acquired the mighty

Artemas and–"

"He doesn't– have me totally– yet, Mol–"

Artemas struggled to speak through the smothering spirit of Belthasar. Flashes of blue danced about in his eyes amid a growing gray storm.

"This magician is a tougher challenge to conquer than most," Belthasar replied, quickly regaining the upper hand. "A worthy opponent. And though it would be easier to retake one of you annoying children, I think I found a better deal. I–" His eyes suddenly widened and a sly smile crept across the magician's face. "What's *this* I sense? Strange words floating all about this wonderfully creative mind. *Findelgundygro*? *Grape vines*? I see images of colorful potions and elegant handwriting on parchment scrolls." Belthasar feigned an expression of concern as he tried to tap further into Artemas' mind. "Oh, and I see you have quite a fondness for a certain Mina Mayfield. How touching!" He gleefully rubbed his hands. "This *is* a better choice than either of you children. I'm going to get quite an education in the magical arts. I'll learn all sorts of things, though I sense, Artemas, that you're struggling to keep me out of your innermost thoughts. No problem. I'll have plenty of time to study."

"Leave him alone!" Molly said.

"Yeah, Belthasar. Why don't you inhabit a swamp rat instead?" Christopher suggested. "That's more your style."

"How predictably unamusing," Belthasar replied with a yawn. "I think you two are jealous that Artemas' mind presents more of a challenge than either of yours ever could. I absorbed your scattered thoughts in mere moments, though I never had any interest to closely examine them." Belthasar grunted. "Artemas offers me magic spells and timedoors and consultations with a king. All I got in the time I inhabited you two was, let's see–visions of amusement parks–*how exciting*!–echoes of your endless sibling bickering, and–" Belthasar gasped as he gazed at Christopher and Molly, unable to speak for a moment as he processed the information he now realized he possessed.

"What's the matter, Belthasar? Cat got your tongue?" Mr. Jordan said to egg him on.

"Don't say *cat*," Mrs. Jordan replied as she stood next to her husband inside the lockup. "I don't think he likes that word."

"Perhaps our children have a few thoughts your tiny brain can't grasp, Belthasar."

Artemas took a step closer. "On the contrary. Christopher and Molly both have some interesting memories–quite *recent* ones–that intrigue me very much. Memories about a rose." A serpent's smile spread across his face. "So after much trial and error, Artemas has finally learned to create a living thing. How extraordinarily amazing! But for some reason, he is using every bit of his strength to keep me from seeing those thoughts in his mind. Luckily I had *you two* to fill me in on the details."

"Why do you care about his magic anyway?" Christopher said. "You'll never have the talent to use it."

"I have plenty of time to learn," Belthasar replied, raising an eyebrow. "And wouldn't it be wonderful if..."

"If what?" Molly said with a trace of exasperation.

"Well, since Artemas has finally discovered how to create another living thing, imagine how wonderful it would be to create another one of–*me*!"

As bad a situation as they were in right now, the Jordans had never thought it could get any worse. But the cold, clammy ache simultaneously forming in the pit of their stomachs told them otherwise. Mr. and Mrs. Jordan locked gazes, knowing each other's thoughts. The only horror worse than the spirit of Belthasar roaming freely among the people was another Belthasar *himself* wandering about, only this time equipped with Artemas' magical abilities but with none of the magician's decency and honor. Christopher and Molly glanced at their parents and brother trapped behind the metal caging, feeling like prisoners themselves.

"Cat got *your* tongue?" Belthasar taunted at their loss for words. "No matter. You can stay here with your chins to the floor while I'll return to Endora. I must regain my magical strength, after all, before I can implement my new and *improved* Great Plan! And won't *that* be a sight to see when it's finished!"

"You won't get away with this, Belthasar," Christopher said.

"Already have."

"And don't think we're not going to try and stop you," Molly added, though clueless as to how to begin.

"I'd be disappointed if you *didn't* try," Belthasar smugly replied as he opened the door to leave. He briefly glanced over his shoulder. "But I think we all know that this tedious game is finally over, and you're stuck on the losing side. So until next time!"

Then without another word, Artemas stepped out of the room and closed the door behind him, whisked away by the triumphant spirit of Belthasar.

"Where's the key?" Christopher cried a moment later. He scoured the top of the desk and rifled through the drawers searching for it.

Molly knelt beside Lucy to examine her. She still slept soundly and her breathing appeared normal. "You tossed it down a ventilation duct, Chris! Don't you remember?"

"There's got to be a spare! We have to free Mom, Dad and Vergil and then go after Belthasar."

"Christopher! Molly! Over here on the double!" their father ordered.

"Hurry!" Mrs. Jordan said as Vergil clutched her side.

"We'll have you free in no time," Christopher promised as he and Molly hurried to the metal enclosure.

"That's the point," Mr. Jordan calmly explained. "There *is* no time. You have to go after him *now*."

Mrs. Jordan nodded as her eyes teared up. "You must warn King Rupert, Ulric and the others. With Belthasar in their midst, well, you know what can happen. He has to be stopped."

"But what about *us*?" Vergil asked, tugging on his

mother's hand.

"Someone will stop down here eventually, so don't worry," Mr. Jordan assured them. "You have to go back through the timedoor *now*. No time to lose!" He smiled for an instant and laughed. "I can't believe I'm saying *that*!"

"We'll follow you as soon as we can," Mrs. Jordan said, taking them each by the hand. "And be extra careful this time!"

"We will, Mom," Molly said, kissing her on the cheek.

"I know you can handle whatever Belthasar throws your way," Mr. Jordan said, taking Christopher's hand in his.

"Been there, done that," he replied with a wink.

"Still, this is a whole new ballgame, so keep a sharp eye. Both of you!"

"We promise!" Molly said.

Then she and Christopher hugged their parents and Vergil through the metal barrier as best they could before scrambling out of the room, expecting to face their most perilous trip through the timedoor.

CHAPTER TWELVE

The First Note

Christopher and Molly ran through the snow-packed streets toward the edge of town as a burst of flurries descended from battleship-gray skies. But as fast as they moved, dodging traffic and pedestrians along the way, they still found no sign of Artemas in the wintry landscape.

"It's as if he disappeared," Molly said, slightly out of breath. "How can someone his age run so fast?"

"That beard may make him look older than he really is, but I don't think Artemas is ready for a retirement home yet!" Christopher said. "I believe it's more *Belthasar* than Artemas who's running so fast right now."

"You're probably right," she said as they reached the road leading out of town. It would eventually take them past Mr. Smithers' restaurant to the bridge stretching across the river. At that very moment underneath it, the timedoor stood open for the second time.

"We're almost there," Christopher said. "A few more minutes and we'll be in Endora."

"Good. Then we won't need these heavy jackets anymore. Artemas mentioned in the park that today is the last day of winter in Endora—*and* the last day of their year. So tomorrow will be spring. I can't wait!"

"That doesn't always mean warmth and sunshine. We still might face some rocky weather ahead," Christopher cautioned. "In more ways than one."

Molly sighed. "Sometimes you're such a wet blanket, Christopher Jordan." She and her brother walked along the edge of the road to catch their breath as a line of bare and bony trees kept watch.

"Look on the bright side, Molly. Just think how happy you'll be to prove me wrong!"

"Well, there is *that*," she said, flashing a brief smile.

In time, they hurried past Mr. Smithers' restaurant. The building stood lonely and grim, its dark windows reflecting the swirl of black and gray clouds that drifted by. Not a car was in sight.

"I wonder where Mr. Smithers is off to," Molly said, scanning the empty parking lot. "Maybe enjoying some free time while Emma is visiting Queen Eleanor."

"That's the least of our concerns," her brother said as they approached the bridge farther up the road. "Look!"

They were quickly thrust back into grim reality when spotting a fresh set of footprints trailing down the snowy embankment toward the stone support underneath the river bridge. Christopher and Molly glanced at one another, acknowledging the difficult task ahead before trudging through the snow in utter silence.

After passing through a kaleidoscope of twirling stars, Christopher and Molly stepped into Artemas' chamber for the second time in eight days. A few candles had been recently lit which cast a dull glow in parts of the room. The fireplace stood cold and barren. Molly opened one of the balcony doors, curious as to the time of day. A cold damp breeze and the sooty darkness greeted her, so she quickly retreated inside.

"Maybe we *will* need our jackets," she said glumly, not sure at how late an hour they had arrived.

"We need to find King Rupert right away," Christopher said, heading out to the corridor. "And if we have to wake him up, so be it. Let's go."

They scurried down the passageway illuminated with a gentle flicker of torchlight, prepared to make their way to the lower levels. But a stern voice in the distant shadows halted their progress.

"Go no farther," a man spoke as he approached, the torchlight revealing him to be one of King Rupert's castle guards. "You must come with me at once."

"We have important information about Artemas!" Molly said. "We need to see King Rupert right away."

"It's very urgent," Christopher added, looking the man directly in the eyes. "The king will *definitely* want to speak with us."

"You're *certain* of that?" The guard sighed as a half smile spread across his face. "You must come with me at once," he repeated, turning down a side corridor and signaling for Christopher and Molly to follow. They reluctantly did so.

"Are we in trouble?" Molly whispered to her brother. "I thought we had free run of this place after saving Endora *how many times*?"

"Shhh," Christopher replied. "Save that speech for later."

"Wise advice," the guard muttered as he walked briskly ahead.

Minutes later they stepped into a room near one of the armories. A man sat hunched over a small wooden table sipping a mug of hot tea while looking over some words that had been hastily scribbled on a piece of parchment. Several candles burned on the makeshift desk, the only light in the room. He glanced up at the new arrivals and offered a tired smile.

"Even *I* don't ordinarily awake at this early hour, but Emmett here, one of the guards on the night watch, brought this to my attention," he said, briefly holding up the piece of parchment. "I had anticipated a visit from you after reading this note."

"What's going on, Ulric?" Christopher asked as he and Molly crowded around King Rupert's chief guard.

"But first, what time is it?" Molly inquired.

"Still a couple hours before sunrise," Ulric said, inviting them to sit down on a few wooden chairs nearby. "May I offer you a hot drink on a chilly morning?"

"Yes, please," Molly said.

Moments later, the three drank from steaming mugs of ginger root tea and nibbled on cold buttered biscuits. Emmett stood at attention on the opposite side of the table. Christopher and Molly briefly explained how Belthasar's spirit had secretly entered their world inside a mosquito, and how a short time ago he had overtaken Artemas and returned through the timedoor. Both hoped that their parents and Vergil were now free.

"Does this meeting have anything to do with that note?" Molly asked, trying to sneak a glance at its contents. Christopher nudged his sister with an elbow.

"Don't worry. I was planning to read it aloud to both of you," Ulric said, glancing at Emmett. "Artemas gave it to my guard a short time ago."

"That is true," Emmett replied. "I saw him just as he was leaving his chamber. He hurriedly placed the note into my hands with instructions to deliver it to Ulric. Then he sped away. I didn't get a chance to question him."

Before Molly could inquire about the contents of the note, Ulric held it near the candlelight softly reflecting off his weary wind-burned face. He read the brief message.

Go to the Inn of the Twelve Horses. Keep an eye out for the Jordans.

Christopher tapped a finger against the side of his mug. "I can decipher the second part of that message easily enough. But where is the Inn of the Twelve Horses?"

"It opened along the main road near the third outpost last autumn," Ulric said. "With increased travel between here and Solárin, people want places to eat and sleep to make the long journey less of a burden. Apparently Artemas wants us to go there."

"Why?" Molly asked.

"Your guess is as good as mine. After Emmett handed me this note, I sent a messenger to the guards at the main gate. They reported that Artemas had left on horseback, but he didn't say where he was going."

"Can we be sure it was *Artemas* who wrote that note and left the castle?" Christopher asked. "Belthasar is still inside him. This has to be some sort of a trick."

"You may be right," Emmett agreed. "When Artemas handed me the note he appeared to be himself. But as he was leaving the corridor, I sensed, well... He just seemed to be– *different*. Something about the eyes."

"This is a curious situation," Ulric concluded, "so we must be on our guard."

Molly dunked half a biscuit into her tea and ate it. "What do you plan to do?" she asked as Ulric offered a slight grin upon viewing her snacking habits.

"First we will consult with King Rupert to get his opinion," Ulric said, folding the piece of parchment and placing it in a shirt pocket as he stood up. "Then we'll pay a visit to the Inn of the Twelve Horses where I can get you a proper breakfast!"

"Considering that we didn't get to have dinner back home, another breakfast will hit the spot," Christopher said as he and Molly followed Ulric out of the room.

"We'll need all the energy we can get to track down Belthasar," Molly said, ready to pursue him. "Let's end this nonsense once and for all!"

"I am certain that *Belthasar* is thinking the very same thing," King Rupert said a short while later after Molly repeated her comment in one of his private chambers. All were seated at a large table, enveloped in the glow of a crackling blaze in the fireplace. Ulric and some of his fellow soldiers were also present. "So do not embark on this mission too lightly. Much danger lies ahead."

"I understand," Molly said, gazing at the dancing flames. "It's just that I'm eager to get underway. And I'm so worried about Mom, Dad and Vergil. I feel I have to do *something*–and soon!"

"That's exactly how I felt after Malaban's troops had kidnapped Rosalind," King Rupert replied, recalling those dreadful days. "I was trapped in your world, unable to rescue my daughter, and I felt as anxious and miserable as you are right now."

"How well I remember *that*," Christopher said. "Plus you knew Malaban was hiding out in our world and you tried to keep it secret. You were a wreck!"

Molly laughed. "Until Mr. Smithers spilled the beans after we tackled him at our campsite! That's when we found out the *whole* story."

King Rupert blushed. "Not my finest moment, I'll admit. But the point is we were successful."

"And we will be this time as well," Ulric added.

Molly nodded, trying to appear confident. "Only we don't have Mr. Smithers *or* Artemas riding along with us."

"Or me either," King Rupert said. "This operation is to gather information, at least at the outset. Ulric and his men can certainly handle that without my interference."

"We were hoping you would ride along with us," Christopher said, a tinge of disappointment in his voice. "Can't you change his mind, Ulric?"

Ulric grinned. "Change *his* mind? I have as much chance of doing that as I do changing *your* mind about *not* riding along. After all, neither you nor your sister have been recruited for this mission."

"Ulric!" Molly spouted with a sigh. "As if we *needed* to be invited along."

"You're right," he replied as a few of the soldiers laughed among themselves. "You and your brother would have followed us anyway, invitation or not. So now that that is settled, we will depart in one hour. I have sent word to the stable hands to prepare five horses for a swift departure. You two will accompany me and two of my men to the Inn of the Twelve Horses. And whether we find Artemas, Belthasar or some other mischief there remains to be seen."

"Well, it *will* be interesting," Christopher commented to Molly when everyone stood to leave. Some of the soldiers talked among themselves as they drifted out. Emmett, who had also attended the meeting and was about to go off duty, stayed back when Ulric signaled him to approach.

"Just like old times," Molly replied as she and Christopher headed toward the door. She craned her neck sideways at the last moment and noticed Ulric speaking to Emmett in private. Emmett nodded sharply and quickly departed through another exit as Ulric followed everyone else out the main door. "You never know *what* to expect around the next corner."

CHAPTER THIRTEEN

The Inn of the Twelve Horses

The five travelers departed King Rupert's castle on horseback as the last remnants of darkness clung to the landscape like a loose fitting cloak. Christopher, Molly and Ulric rode alongside each other, their three horses gently galloping northward along the main road that stretched across the plains. The low eastern hills and the majestic mountains looming in the west were still obscured by the last shadows of the night. Garrin, one of the two accompanying soldiers, took the lead while Collus, the second, followed and kept watch at the end of the line. A damp breeze swept across the fields dotted with stubborn patches of snow that refused to bow to the inevitable warm breath of spring.

"This reminds me of our first journey to Malaban's fortress to rescue Princess Rosalind," Molly said. "Except we're five years older now. Can you believe it?"

"Luckily, Malaban's fortress is now King Jeremiah's castle," Christopher noted.

"And in spite of this chilly wind, the weather is more pleasant overall. I'm quite comfortable in these clothes Queen Eleanor gave us."

"She thought you'd appear less *noticeable*, Molly, if you didn't wear those bright colorful coats from back home,"

Ulric said with a smile.

Christopher and Molly were each outfitted with brown riding boots that slipped over their blue jeans, and a long heavy woolen pullover shirt secured with a braided leather cord belt. Molly chose a forest-green hooded cloak to wear as an outer garment. Christopher donned a long jacket of the same material secured with a column of brown buttons. He covered his head with a gray and black knit ski cap which he refused to leave back at the castle.

"We'll only have to travel a few miles to reach our destination," Ulric said. "And a warm meal awaits us instead of an angry mob of trolls and goblins."

"What awaits us *beyond* the inn is what I'm worried about," Christopher replied.

"Me too," Molly said, tightening her grip on the reins. "We always had Artemas and his magic to count on. Now he has to count on *us* to save him. I hope we don't let him down."

"He knows we'll come after him," Christopher assured her. "He'd do the same for us in a heartbeat."

"I know. He's gotten us out of countless jams. I just hope–" Molly choked up for a moment. "I just hope he knows that we'll try. With Belthasar in command, well, I'm not sure how much longer Artemas will be aware of *anything* anymore."

They remained silent for some time, each dealing with a troubling mix of thoughts and emotions. The horses trotted briskly along the road as the wind whistled mournfully across the darkened landscape.

A gray and misty dawn inched across the eastern hills like a suspicious cat as the travelers arrived at the Inn of the Twelve Horses. The two-story building of stone and wood had been constructed to withstand the strongest winds that swept across the plains from time to time. Thin curls of smoke rose from its three chimneys, drifting to the northeast. Less than a quarter mile up the road stood the third outpost built between Endora and Solárin. A handful of maple and pine trees grew in the vicinity, providing travelers some cool shade when they visited in the summer months.

Even in the pale first light, Christopher and Molly immediately noticed the intricate carvings of horses in the huge uppermost beam of oak just below the roof. The artwork depicted a dozen noble stallions spread across the front of the building, some running like the wind itself while a few others rose proudly on two legs. Most of the horses, however, simply stood with heads raised or bowed in regal silence. The siblings gazed in awe at the lifelike beauty of the artwork.

"Wait until you look upon them in the sunlight, then you'll *truly* be impressed," Ulric said as he dismounted. "There's a small stream on the side of the inn. We can water our steeds and tie them up there before we go inside. Someone will feed them shortly."

"And us too, I hope," Molly said as she walked her horse across the grass. "I have a monstrous appetite in search of a three-course breakfast!"

"You won't be disappointed," one of the soldiers said. "Henry Droon and his family run a fine establishment. He'll feed you properly."

"Garrin is right. I've known Henry and his wife for many years, and both are excellent cooks," Ulric said. After tending to their horses, he led the group along a stone path to the front door. Since many of the overnight lodgers were still sound asleep, most of the wooden shutters on the second floor were closed.

They left the chilly morning behind when they stepped inside the Twelve Horses, greeted by a roaring fire and the subdued voices of a few visitors enjoying an early breakfast. Three long wooden tables and benches stretched along the length of the room, with a few smaller tables tucked into an odd spot where space allowed. A short counter had been built against the wall near the kitchen door, behind which were shelves of dishes, extra candles and a couple of small casks of ale. Various dried herbs hung upside down from the ceiling beams above.

Molly took a seat at the end of one table nearest the fireplace and signaled for the others to join her. A couple and their two children were seated at the other end of that same table and a half dozen unshaven men sat at the one farthest away, engrossed in their meal. Two of the men glanced at Ulric and his companions as they joined Molly. Another individual with his back to the crowd sat hunched over a tiny table near the far window, sipping on a mug of hot tea and picking at the dried beef and potatoes on his plate, ignoring everyone. He chewed his food noisily, his whiskered chin moving up and down like a well-oiled piece of machinery. One of his bottom front teeth was missing. A few other guests were scattered about the room as three servers drifted from table to table.

"What's on the menu?" Christopher asked.

Ulric pointed to a girl a few years older than Molly who hurried over to greet them. She wore a long blue apron over her clothes and a kerchief of the same material covered her head.

"She'll let you know," he said, waving at Henry Droon's youngest daughter Ella as she approached.

"Hello, Ulric!" she said with a surprised smile. "My father mentioned only a short while ago that he had a feeling you'd show up one of these days soon. How could he have possibly known that?"

"He knows I like the food you serve here," Ulric replied, quickly introducing Ella to everyone. "What's good for breakfast on this fine day for five hungry travelers?"

"Only the best we have to offer!"

A short while later they filled their plates from a large wooden bowl of steaming scrambled eggs mixed with bits of fried beef, diced apples and fresh herbs, accompanied by a bowl of wild mushroom gravy. A plate of biscuits, honey and butter were also served with a kettle of hot tea and dried spiced pear rings. Christopher and Molly merely smiled at Ulric in approval as they were too busy eating to waste time with words.

Midway through breakfast, a tall man with a shock of

graying brown hair and a wild mustache lumbered over to Ulric's table. A ragged towel was tossed over his shoulder and his shirt cried out with splatterings of butter and egg yolk. He extended a hand as Ulric stood to greet him.

"I'm always delighted when an old friend visits," Henry Droon said, joining the others at the table as Ulric made another round of introductions.

"I'm glad your new place seems to be doing so well," Molly said.

"Business is quite good. *Too* good sometimes," Henry said with a sigh. "Another hour and this room will be overflowing with hungry guests. I had to hire more help."

"That's great," Christopher said.

"Great for the cashbox, but not so good for my sleep," Henry joked. "Sometimes I tell my wife that we should have stayed in the village where life was simpler."

"You're doing a good thing," Molly said, recalling how she pitched a tent upon the plains in the middle of winter when taking part in Princess Rosalind's rescue. "I could have used an inn like the Twelve Horses five years ago when I passed through this area."

Henry Droon curiously raised an eyebrow. "You were *here*?"

"It's a long story," Christopher said.

"I'm *sure*."

"I'll give you the details some day," Ulric promised. "But in the meantime, what brings you to our table? Your daughter Ella said you had been expecting me to show up."

Henry leaned closer and lowered his voice. "I don't like to discuss personal affairs in public, but I was given a note a few hours ago and was asked to deliver it to you, Ulric, the next time you showed up. Only I didn't expect it would be *this* soon."

"Who gave you the note?" Molly whispered, brimming with curiosity.

Henry scanned the faces of his attentive listeners. "There was a pounding on my door in the dead of night, so I rushed downstairs thinking a tired traveler needed a place to sleep. Being the kind host that I am, I ignored my need for some shuteye, grabbed a candle and answered the door." Henry leaned in even closer, a puzzled look upon his face. "An old man stood before me, wrapped in a hooded cloak with a beard trailing down to his waist. He said his name was Artemas. But before I could utter a word, he shoved a note in my hand and told me to deliver it to King Rupert's chief guard, Ulric, when he arrives." Henry shrugged. "I couldn't respond because the gentleman immediately climbed on his horse and rode off west toward the mountains."

"A second note! What did you do with it?" Christopher asked, pouring a ladleful of mushroom gravy over another helping of eggs.

"*Second* note?" Henry asked, folding his arms and stroking his chin. "That must mean there was a *first* note. What did it say?"

Ulric cleared his throat and took a sip of tea, uncomfortably noticing a few of the other guests throwing inquisitive glances their way. "Perhaps we can finish this conversation in a more private location," he suggested to Henry.

"Certainly," his friend replied, quickly standing. "Meet me in the common room after you finish your meal. Through that doorway at the far end of the room. People don't start congregating in there until later in the morning. I'll bring the note with me." Ulric nodded as Henry departed and disappeared behind the kitchen door.

"More notes," Molly said, biting into a dried pear ring while mulling over a handful of explanations in her mind. "What is Artemas up to?"

"Or *Belthasar*," Christopher reminded her.

"The sooner we finish our meal, the sooner we find out," Ulric said, scraping up the eggs on his plate. He glanced at Garrin and Collus, the concern evident on his weary face. "At this point, I don't know what to think, so keep an extra sharp eye out in the wild."

Henry Droon handed a small piece of parchment to

Ulric when they gathered in the common room. The note was folded in thirds and sealed with candle wax. Ulric stood next to a window, bathed in the dim gray dawn. Christopher and Molly sat on a wooden bench near a fireplace with Garrin. Collus stood guard near the doorway.

"I must admit that the contents of this letter have had me intrigued ever since I received it," Henry said as Ulric carefully ripped open the wax seal with his index finger. He quickly scanned the handwriting.

"What does it say?" Molly asked.

Ulric ambled over to the bench and handed her the note. "See for yourself."

Molly held the piece of parchment close to the red-orange glow of the crackling fire as Christopher and Garrin peered over her shoulder.

Travel west along the Gray River toward the mountains. Rest at Willow Lake.

"Doesn't answer many questions, does it," Christopher said with a sigh of disappointment after rereading the words aloud for all to hear.

"I'm afraid it only raises new ones," Garrin said.

"I think we're being sent on a wild goose chase," Molly added with an assertive nod to Ulric. "Now I'm beginning to feel that *Belthasar* is penning these notes instead of Artemas." She scratched the back of her neck. "Then again, I *could* be wrong."

"Gee, what *brilliant* analysis," Christopher muttered.

"*Belthasar!*" Henry plopped down on a wooden chair opposite the bench and combed a hand through his hair. "I thought that menace had been driven from these lands for good. Why do you bring up *his* name?"

"I don't have time to tell you the entire story, Henry, but Belthasar is still in our midst," Ulric said, leaning against the mantel. A chunk of burning pinewood exploded in a mini burst of sparks. "Rumors you may have heard of his demise after King Jeremiah's coronation are sadly false."

"So what does that Artemas fellow have to do with this?" Henry asked. "Bad enough waking me up in the dead of night, but now I learn that *Belthasar* is still on the loose." He looked up with sad and tired eyes. "What is this kingdom coming to?"

"Ulric, is the Gray River the same river where we stopped that horseman from sending the smoke signal?" Christopher asked.

"No. That is the Alorian, a much longer river that flows south to north and empties into the Baridorn Sea," he replied. "The Gray River originates in the western mountains and snakes along for a couple miles, empties into Willow Lake, then continues on again and feeds into the Alorian at a point several miles north of here. If we travel west across the plains, we will reach the banks of the Gray River. It will be a two-hour journey from there to Willow Lake."

"Piece of cake!" Christopher said, hoping to dispel the slight sense of discouragement he felt creeping into their mission. Chasing after Artemas and Belthasar while trying to make sense of the notes felt as frustrating as grasping at feathers whirling wildly in the wind. He could see the restlessness in his sister's eyes. "Don't worry, Molly. We'll reach Willow Lake and solve this puzzle in no time!"

"I only wish I knew *why* we're going there in the first place," Molly said to her brother a few minutes later. They sat on a bench off to the side of the fireplace in the main dining room, waiting for Ulric to return. He and Garrin remained in the common room with Henry to discuss obtaining supplies for their journey west while Collus went outdoors to check on the horses. Christopher decided to enjoy another biscuit and some tea near the fire in the remaining time. Molly was too keyed up to eat and merely sat beside her brother, nervously tapping her foot.

"Eat some more. That'll calm your nerves."

"I'm not nervous, Chris. Just a little edgy." Molly scanned the faces of the other diners. A pair of eyes in the crowd briefly returned her gaze. "See *that*?"

"See what?" Christopher asked, leaning against the wall.

"Those six scruffy-looking men at the far table. One just peeked over at us," Molly whispered. "I don't particularly like the looks of them."

"Maybe they don't like the looks of *you*," he replied, casually glancing at the men still eating their breakfast. He did admit that they weren't the friendliest looking bunch. "I wouldn't want to run into them in a dark alley, but I think we'll be safe here."

"I suppose," Molly said, tapping her foot more loudly.

"Stop that!" Christopher said in a low voice, nudging Molly with an elbow. "You'll annoy the other diners."

"Will not."

She stopped anyway when the lone man who had eaten breakfast near the far window sat in a wooden chair in front of the fireplace, his back to Christopher and Molly. He extended his legs to warm his feet near the flames. His brown boots were caked with dried mud and wearing out at the soles. The man removed a pipe and a pouch of tobacco from his shirt pocket and stuffed the pipe. Leaning forward, he ripped off a sliver of wood from a piece of kindling on the stone hearth, stuck it in the flames and then lit his pipe. Soon puffs of acrid smoke drifted above as he sat back and closed his eyes.

Molly scowled when a whiff of smoke drifted her way, preparing to offer a sarcastic comment just as Collus walked back inside. "The horses are set," he said on his way to the common room. "We'll depart shortly."

"Join you in a minute," Christopher said, gobbling up the last of his biscuit and gulping down his tea. "Ready, Molly?"

"I guess," she said, waving her hand disgustedly in front of her nose. "I'm sure the air is much *fresher* at Willow Lake," she added in a louder voice, hoping to get a rise out of the man sitting near the fire. He apparently hadn't heard and didn't turn around.

Christopher glared at Molly for trying to draw attention to herself. "The air may be cleaner there," he softly said, "but *Belthasar* could be there as well, ready to ambush us. Remember that."

Molly rolled her eyes as she followed her brother to the common room.

Moments later, the man at the fireplace glanced behind him, noting that Christopher, Molly and their three companions were nowhere in sight. He jumped out of his seat, slapped a few copper coins on the counter, grabbed a ragged cloak from one of the wooden wall pegs near the door and exited the building. He exhaled a puff of gray smoke that matched the clouds floating overhead as he leaned against the side of the building, lost in thought. The sleeve of his cloak had slipped down to his elbow, exposing a faded scar running around his right wrist. A similar scar also encircled his left wrist.

"If this isn't an opportunity falling square into my lap, then I don't know what is!" Fennic said to himself with a mix of nervous excitement.

Christopher Jordan was the last person he had ever expected to see again, recalling with contempt how the boy had escaped from him nearly a year ago, leaving Fennic flopping about in a mud puddle like a crazed fish. He rubbed his wrist, the searing pain of those rope burns fresh in his mind. The boy must have succeeded in stopping one of the dozen horsemen Morgus Vandar had hired because the planned smoke signals had never materialized. Fennic had also heard stories of a young girl present at the coronation last spring when it was thrown into chaos. He wondered if she was the same girl he just overheard talking to the boy in the inn.

"*Belthasar*? *Willow Lake*? What's going on?" Fennic mumbled, furiously contemplating how to take advantage of the situation.

Ever since Fennic learned of Morgus Vandar's arrest at King Jeremiah's coronation, he knew the riches he had envisioned would never come to pass. Belthasar had disappeared after his ingenious plan to take over the two kingdoms had been thwarted. Fennic once hoped to make a fortune under the false King Jeremiah's reign since Morgus Vandar would have given him a steady supply of work. But now, with no desire to earn an honest living, Fennic couldn't even afford a decent pair of boots. He survived by wandering between the two kingdoms, scraping up bits of cash however he could.

Fennic drew a last puff on his pipe. If he could find Belthasar and apologize for his failure, maybe he could get into his good graces again and assist him in his current endeavor. Fennic tapped his pipe against a stone to empty out the charred tobacco. He thought for a moment, glancing west toward the distant mountains, and then walked over to his horse tied up by the stream. Fennic was determined to arrive at Willow Lake before the others. He had no idea what he would find there, but convinced himself that the smell of good fortune was once again drifting through the damp morning air.

CHAPTER FOURTEEN

Three Frogs

They left the Inn of the Twelve Horses in daylight, though the sun could not be seen through the thick layer of gray clouds drifting overhead. The horses were laden with extra provisions since none had expected this journey to take them beyond the inn when they had left King Rupert's castle. They headed west across the grassy plains until they came upon the banks of the Gray River, now running high and fast with the recent melting snow. Ulric halted briefly to allow the horses to drink.

"We'll follow the river to Willow Lake," he said. "I suspect it will be an uneventful two-hour journey. I can't imagine what awaits us once we arrive."

"I hope not another note!" Molly said. "If Belthasar is setting a trap, let him spring it and be done with it. Enough of the mystery."

"Patience, Molly. Sometimes in life you have to let a situation play out to its conclusion, like it or not," Ulric replied while scanning the barren landscape.

Christopher cupped some cold water in his hands and took a drink alongside his horse. The surging river reflected the gloomy skies above. He stood and leaned against the horse, gazing at the mountains looming in the west.

"This is the first time we're heading *toward* the mountains, Ulric. Every journey Molly and I have taken here, we've only traveled alongside them. Do they have a name?"

"Those are the Katánin Mountains, stretching south to north and marking the western borders of Endora and Solárin. Much of the land is desolate near the mountains themselves," he said. "The mountain chain veers slightly westward as you approach Solárin. The highest peak, Mount Maricel, is southwest of here." Ulric pointed the mountain out to Christopher and Molly. "Though it would appear more majestic in full sunlight, it is nonetheless a grand sight."

"It *is* beautiful," Christopher agreed, staring at it fixedly moments later as the horses gently carried their riders along the rushing waters of the Gray River.

"Unfortunately, we deal with the occasional band of trolls or goblins that inhabit parts of those mountains," Collus reminded them. "We patrol the western borders from time to time, but for the most part they are not a bother. There isn't any village in Endora or Solárin close enough to the mountains for them to attack."

"Trolls only seem to be a pain in the neck when Belthasar recruits them for one of his grand schemes," Molly said. "Hope we don't run into them again any time soon."

"What a treat *that* would be," Christopher said, recalling several close encounters they had experienced with the mountain creatures during Princess Rosalind's rescue.

Then Molly piped up, remembering a very important item she needed to know more about. "With everything that's happened, I never got a chance to ask anybody about Rosalind and Jeremiah's wedding last summer. How good a time did I miss, Ulric?"

"It was a wonderful celebration," he replied. "Actually *two*."

"*Two*? What are you talking about?" Waves of disappointment registered on Molly's face for the festivities long since gone. "If only Artemas could get some better timing on that timedoor!"

Ulric laughed before plunging into the details of the wedding. "Since the princess of Endora was getting married, the wedding was held in King Rupert's castle as tradition dictates. It was a two-day celebration with many guests and much food, music and dancing that is still talked about to this day." While Ulric wasn't much help in giving Molly specific details about Princess Rosalind's wedding gown, hair style and flower choices, she did get enough information to recreate the amazing celebration in her mind as her horse contentedly trotted over the grassy landscape.

"And what about the *second* celebration?" she quickly added.

"Since many people from Solárin could not attend the wedding in the next kingdom, the royal couple thought it fitting that *another* lavish reception be held there a month later. King Jeremiah and Princess Rosalind—or rather I should say *Queen Rosalind*—were honored to recreate their vows for all to witness," Ulric said, glancing over to see Molly daydreaming upon her horse.

Christopher noticed as well. "Keep an eye on the terrain, Molly. I'm sure Rosalind will tell you all about the wedding next time you see her."

"*Queen* Rosalind," Molly whispered, a delighted smile spreading across her face. "Imagine that!"

Christopher looked at Ulric and smirked. "Imagine what my family will have to go through when *she* gets married," he whispered. "If you think she's got her head in the clouds *now*…!"

Just as Ulric had predicted, the journey to Willow Lake proved uneventful. A gentle wind had picked up and the snowcapped mountains crept closer like a slow lumbering giant. But the monotony of the endless mass of gray clouds and the stretch of plains ready to come alive with the fresh green of spring remained unchanged. It was a visual feast to finally see the gentle lapping of tiny waves upon the grassy shores of Willow Lake. A scattering of trees around the small body of water had produced buds, patiently waiting for an extended warm spell to bloom and flourish in the otherwise drab region. The horses happily took another drink while everyone else stretched their legs.

Molly extended her arms and leisurely spun around in a circle, soaking in the surroundings. "Well, we're here. So *now* what?"

"I guess we take a seat in the grass and wait for a squirrel or rabbit to come along and present us with another note," Christopher joked.

"I wouldn't be a bit surprised," Molly said with a shrug, gently petting her horse on the nose. "What do *you* think we should do?" she playfully asked the animal.

"We'll split up," Ulric responded, quickly filling the group in on his plan. "Christopher, Molly and I will scout along the lakeshore. Garrin, continue riding west along the lake and look for signs of recent visitors. Collus, head south and do the same. Make a quick survey and return. If we are meant to find something here, I assume we will not have to look far."

Moments later, Garrin and Collus departed in different directions. Christopher, Molly and Ulric hiked along the south side of the lake, leaving their three horses behind to graze. Willow Lake stretched nearly a mile long from each mouth of the Gray River and extended almost a half mile wide. Christopher gazed across the water, looking for any sign of activity on the opposite shore, but saw nothing. He had an urge to shout out Artemas' name over the glassy surface, but in the eerie stillness he thought it wise not to announce their presence. So for several minutes they walked in utter silence.

Molly noticed it first a short while later, tugging on Ulric's sleeve and pointing ahead. "Look. Is that a wisp of smoke farther up shore, or am I imagining things?"

"Wouldn't be the first time," Christopher said, placing a hand above his eyes to reduce the bit of glare from the hiding sun. "But you may be right. There *is* something drifting in the air."

The trio ran less than a hundred yards before stumbling upon the remains of a small campfire near the edge of the lake. Thin curls of blue and gray smoke rose from the charred remains of a handful of sticks. Ulric closely examined their find.

"Whoever was here–and I assume it was Artemas– didn't stay long. Only a few small sticks were gathered for the fire, and some of them aren't fully burned," he said. "The fire was lit and then left untended, only to burn out."

"Why would Artemas build a fire for so short a time?" Molly asked.

"If he was cold, logic says he would have used it awhile to keep warm," Ulric concluded. "Yet there is no supply of wood nearby to keep the fire going."

"Maybe it's a signal," Christopher suggested. "Or perhaps he simply needed light. It would have been pitch-black when he arrived here."

"Excellent guesses. Perhaps one of them is correct," Ulric said as he surveyed the area. "Let's keep looking to be sure."

"I see some impressions in the grass," Molly said. "I guess they're footprints–man *and* horse. Then again, we already *know* someone was here because a fire was built, so what good are footprints?"

Ulric examined the prints, walking about in a small circle as he did so, eventually moving in a southerly direction. He paused for a moment and nodded before heading back toward the campfire. Then something caught his eye to the left and he wandered a few yards to where the grass was particularly low and dry. Ulric raised a hand, signaling for Christopher and Molly to join him.

"Find something?" Christopher asked.

"Learned something *and* found something," he said, turning to his companions. "First the footprints. Even though we're assuming Artemas stopped here and built the fire, all the boot impressions in the grass look the same size."

"Only one man," Christopher reasoned. "So he didn't meet anyone here."

"Possibly correct. The horse tracks that intersect with

the footprints appear to move to the south, so our magician probably did so as well."

"What else did you find?" Molly asked.

"I noticed another set of fresh hoof tracks close to the edge of the lake continuing west. Someone else recently passed by, but whether there was a meeting of some sort, I cannot say. It may just be a coincidental passing. But something else caught my eye," he eagerly explained. "I believe I know where Artemas is heading. Look."

Ulric pointed to a dry patch of ground surrounded by taller grass. Christopher and Molly took a step closer and craned their necks to examine the find. In the center stood a pile of three small rocks, each of them somewhat flat. The bottom rock was the size of a grown man's hand, on top of which rested another slightly smaller rock. The third and tiniest of the trio was set on top of the stack, the entire mini monument rising not much higher than Molly's ankle.

Christopher felt warmer as the morning progressed and undid a few of his coat buttons as he examined the pile of stones. "Okay, Ulric. What exactly are we looking at?"

"Same question," Molly said, examining Ulric's expression for a hint of an answer. "What is it?"

"Three Frogs."

"Excuse me?"

"Well, not the *actual* Three Frogs," he replied, squatting down and tapping a finger on the top rock as he pondered the stony message. "This is our next note from Artemas, so to speak."

Molly squinted in confusion. "What *are* you talking about?"

Christopher walked around the tiny formation and gazed at it with bubbling curiosity. "You're saying Artemas built this as a message for us to find?"

"Precisely. Perhaps the nearby fire was left to smoke as a signal to draw us to this area, just as you had guessed, Christopher."

"So what are the Three Frogs you referred to?" Molly asked.

Ulric stood and pointed south. "Several miles in the direction that Collus just rode stands a huge rock formation called Three Frogs. It actually looks like this small model on the ground, more or less. And it is much closer to the mountains than we are now, directly under the watchful eye of Mount Maricel."

Christopher gazed south across the plains. "How big *is* Three Frogs?"

Ulric pondered a moment for an apt comparison. "I'd say it is slightly larger than the Inn of the Twelve Horses and nearly twice as high. It's an impressive sight."

"And our new destination, no doubt," Molly said with a hint of boredom in her voice. "What should we expect to find *there*? Another pile of stones to decipher? Or perhaps some stick figure drawings in the dirt with arrows showing us where to go next."

Though Ulric empathized with Molly's sense of frustration, he was unable to conceal a grin. "Do not fret. I guarantee we will not find *any* pictures drawn in the dirt, Molly. The area in the immediate vicinity of Three Frogs is a rocky wasteland where not even a blade of grass can find a home. It is both desolate and dreary, but we are summoned to it, for good *or* ill."

"Then what are we waiting for?" Christopher asked. "Let's get this party rolling!"

Garrin and Collus returned within the hour and made their reports. As expected, Collus spotted one sign of recent movement south of Willow Lake where a set of horse tracks gradually veered southwest in the direction of Three Frogs. Garrin reported that a solitary set of horse tracks made a line parallel to Willow Lake, continuing along the upper branch of the Gray River where it reformed at the lake's western tip. Neither he nor Ulric could speculate why someone would ride alone so close to the mountains.

"Other than the King's scouting parties or a band of trolls, the area beyond this tract of land is uninhabited," Ulric noted.

"Maybe the fishing is particularly good upstream," Molly suggested. "Or perhaps someone simply likes to hike and explore near the base of the mountains."

"Possibly. But that's one mystery we have no time to solve," he said as he placed a foot in one stirrup and climbed on his horse. "Now we head south to Three Frogs to see what awaits us. Our horses have drunk and our water skins are full, so let us proceed. We should arrive in an hour or so, well before the sun is in the noon position."

"If only we could *see* the sun," Molly whispered, staring glumly at the bank of clouds drifting above. She draped the hood of her cloak over her head as a slight breeze stirred across the plains. With a gentle snap of the reins, her horse obediently followed the others through the vast and monotonous stretch of grassland ahead.

Happily for Molly, the hour swiftly passed. A few brief sprinkles of rain coupled with several corny jokes from Christopher made the next leg of their journey fly by as swiftly as the occasional crow that zipped across the lonely horizon. It was when the grassy landscape suddenly thinned out and turned rocky that Molly first noticed the dark formation in the distance. Three Frogs loomed stark, solitary and silent like a miniature mountain that had been dropped unceremoniously on a lunar landscape.

The Katánin Mountains had also crept uncomfortably closer, one of its stony spurs curling out like a crooked finger less than a half mile behind Three Frogs. Slightly to the north, more than a mile away and directly at the foot of the mountains, was a swath of green pine, a burst of rich emerald color thriving on the border of the dreary landscape. And overshadowing everything like a sleeping giant was the towering hulk of Mount Maricel, its broad rocky shoulders cloaked with the last remnants of winter's bitter snow.

"It's so quiet," Molly whispered. "I can't even hear a bird." The mournful clip clop of the horses echoed thinly across the stony surface.

"I'm afraid we are the only living things on this desolate patch," Ulric said, eyeing the dull green plains in the near distance that almost completely surrounded them. "As soon as we find what we're looking for, we'll retreat to a more hospitable location."

"It's an interesting spot, but I think I'd rather be exploring the inside of a castle," Christopher decided as he watched the Three Frogs monument gradually increase in size as they neared. "By the way, why is it called Three Frogs, Ulric? Where'd *that* name come from? The three rocks don't exactly *look* like frogs."

"I've heard many versions of the tale," Ulric said. "After all, it is an ancient formation, so it's not surprising that many stories have been told. The most popular account tells of how a huge river once flowed through this land, a river many times larger than the Alorian. One day a terrible rain storm swept through, raising the water and destroying all in its path. In order to save her child from being carried away, a mother frog instructed the child to hop on her back. But the river was still too high and treacherous, and before the wild waves washed them away, the father frog swam underneath at the last moment and lifted his family to safety. They swam to shore and waited for the water to recede. By daybreak, the river returned to normal. The frog family, still on top of one another and facing east, dried off in the warmth of the rising sun which they still watch each morning to this very day."

"Good story," Molly said with a smile, her heart a bit less troubled for the moment. "Unfortunately, the frogs only got an eyeful of clouds today."

"Oh well, every day can't be perfect," Ulric replied.

"I can't imagine *any* perfect days here," Christopher chimed in. "Isn't there another inn nearby that Artemas *or* Belthasar could send us to next?" he said with a chuckle, glancing at Three Frogs which grew considerably larger with every step the horses took. For an instant, Christopher thought something moved on top of the rock monument, now less than two football fields away. "Why would anyone in his right mind want to hang around *this* place?"

"*Right mind*? If we're talking about Belthasar, throw *that* phrase out the window," Molly said. "However, loopy, half-baked and crackpot are definitely appropriate."

"You'll get no argument from me," Christopher replied as their horses sauntered the last few yards toward Three Frogs.

Moments later, they stopped in front of the hulking stone structure. Its three huge layers, each smaller in size as they ascended, cast a faint shadow in the dim light. A series of cracks had formed on either side of the formation, allowing climbers access to the highest level. Christopher, Molly and Ulric, in the center of the group, craned their heads back and gazed up at the top of Three Frogs. Garrin and Collus, stationed on either end, scanned the area for any sign of movement.

"Well I *am* impressed," Molly said, taking a deep breath.

"But I don't see any sign directing us where to go next," Christopher said, steadying his horse who seemed slightly on edge.

"Where to go *next*?" a sharp voice called out in the gray stillness. "Why would you *want* to go anywhere else?"

Everyone again glanced up as a lone figure strolled to the edge of Three Frogs. He looked down upon the five horsemen, a crazed smile bursting from his narrow whiskered face. The man had a bottom tooth missing, and a mop of tangled hair framed a pair of narrow ash-gray eyes.

Christopher clenched his teeth and glared at the individual wrapped in a tattered and grimy cloak. "*Fennic*!" he muttered.

Molly and Ulric looked at him simultaneously. "*That's* Fennic?" his sister asked. "The man you had escaped from before you stopped that horseman by the river?"

"The very same!" Fennic shouted. "And yet, not *quite* the same."

"What are you doing here?" Christopher said, a trace of scorn in his voice. "I guess being defeated once wasn't enough. Ready for some more?"

"I can pose that very same question," Fennic said, his voice flying down on a cold breeze. "Why are *you* here?" Fennic smiled like a fox. "After all, who could have imagined that Christopher and Molly Jordan would willingly venture into the heart of my new enterprise on the very day of its creation?" Fennic raised his arms triumphantly into the air and shouted for the world to hear. "Behold the birth of the greatest empire in all of history! Witness the kingdom of all kingdoms and the realm of all realms! Welcome, my dear friends, to BELTHASARIA!"

CHAPTER FIFTEEN

Belthasaria

"My dear friends, my *foot*!" Molly scoffed, scowling at Fennic who stood atop Three Frogs like a hideous statue that existed in one's deepest and darkest nightmare. "We know that's you, Belthasar. Come down and tell us what you've done to Artemas before I go up and get it out of you!"

Ulric gently extended a hand in front of Molly, the other holding onto the reins of his horse. "I appreciate your enthusiasm, Molly, but allow me to handle the negotiations," he whispered.

Christopher shook his head. "Yeah, Molly, don't fly into dramatics like usual, at least not until we get information about Artemas."

"Oh, and I suppose you have some nifty scientific plan up your sleeve to do just that, Chris. We don't have time for this!"

"No, we *don't*," Ulric firmly replied, eyeing Christopher and Molly like a stern parent. "I am well aware of your skillful handling of Belthasar in the past, but for the moment, *I* will manage things."

"Sorry, Ulric," Christopher muttered.

Molly nodded. "You're right. We'll put a sock in it

for now."

"Thank you."

Fennic gazed down upon the small gathering and laughed. "Dissension among the troops, Ulric? Perhaps King Rupert's finest are a bit ragged around the edges. It's no shame to admit defeat."

Ulric raised his hand again, noting that Molly's face had darkened two shades of crimson. "I have complete confidence in my fellow soldiers," Ulric stated in a proud voice. "It is *you*, Belthasar, who make questionable choices in your associates. The stories I've heard about Fennic only reinforce the low opinion I already have about your competence, your judgment and, well, about *you* in general." Out of the corner of his eye, Ulric saw a grin spread across Molly's face. "So if it's a one to one comparison you seek between your side and ours, let's just say that I would not pursue that path. You would surely lose."

Fennic snickered, appearing unfazed by Ulric's comment, though his heart pounded furiously as a bitter anger rose inside him. "You have no idea of the loyalty my followers bestow upon me or the strength it provides. Fennic returned to me to assist in my cause the moment he learned that I was roaming the countryside."

"Some people will do *anything* for money," Christopher said, "even if it means crawling to the likes of you."

"For which I must thank you and your sister," Fennic said, his mind and soul whirling with the spirit of Belthasar. "You two, after all, led Mr. Fennic back to me."

"Tell us *another* story!" Molly said with a grunt.

"I speak the truth. You two just couldn't keep your conversation to a whisper at the Inn of the Twelve Horses this morning," Fennic said, stroking his whiskers beneath a snakelike smile. "As I can see from Fennic's thoughts, he sat by himself at breakfast when the five of you entered the inn. He recognized your brother from their encounter last spring. Fennic is still upset from his humiliating defeat in a mud puddle and the resulting injuries." He briefly examined the rope scars on both his wrists. "Ouch! That *must* have hurt.

Later, Fennic eavesdropped on you two chatterboxes while he sat by the fire enjoying a pipe. When he overheard the names *Belthasar* and *Willow Lake* in your conversation, he took off like an eagle to find me."

"More like a *vulture*," remarked Ulric.

"Good one," Molly said.

"Make your little jokes," Fennic continued. "They don't impress me, though I *will* grudgingly admit that your network of spies was quite efficient, tracking me to the Inn of the Twelve Horses, Willow Lake and finally here, all the while keeping you informed of my progress so you could follow. Very impressive indeed."

"*Spies*? What spies are you talking about?" Molly asked. "You practically drew us a map when you sent–"

Ulric quickly interrupted her, now realizing that Belthasar was not aware of the two notes they had received or the pile of three rocks left as a message near Willow Lake. He concluded that Artemas must have left those clues. But as to *how* or *why*, Ulric found himself completely in the dark. He glanced Molly's way and she suddenly understood.

"Let's not interrupt Belthasar when he gives us a compliment," Ulric lightly said, changing the subject. "It's not often that he does so."

"Another joke," Fennic said. "You spend too much time with that girl. Her irritating sense of humor is rubbing off. But the last joke, my friends, will be on *you*."

Molly smirked. "Oh really?"

"I guarantee it. You see, my original intent was to return to Solárin and get my revenge on King Jeremiah, now sitting on the throne that should have been mine."

"Is there anybody in this world or ours that you *don't* want revenge on?" Christopher said with a raised eyebrow.

Fennic sneered, ignoring the comment. "But as I neared the Inn of the Twelve Horses in the darkness, I was struck by a grand idea and an extraordinary vision at the same time. Why bother with Solárin *or* Endora, I asked myself? Why not create a kingdom of my own? So *that's* the grand idea I decided to pursue! After all, there'll always be time to conquer my neighbors."

"Quite an imagination you have," Molly said. "But with the likes of Ulric and his soldiers, you don't stand a chance."

"I'm shuddering in my boots," Fennic replied, gazing out across the stony vista that surrounded Three Frogs. "As for my extraordinary vision, a searing image of Three Frogs suddenly appeared in my mind. The beauty, majesty and splendor of this area instantly made me realize that Three Frogs should be the center of Belthasaria. So I raced along the Gray River to Willow Lake, waiting for the first light of day."

Christopher glanced around at the utter loneliness oozing out of every rock and stone. "Beauty, majesty *and* splendor?" he whispered aside to Ulric. "Is he delirious?"

"Shortly after I headed south toward Three Frogs, I was spotted by a band of trolls who had followed the river down from the mountains," Fennic continued. "After convincing them that I was Belthasar inhabiting the body of the magician Artemas, I quickly recruited them to my side. Memories of past defeats and the possibility of new victories made them eager to follow me once again."

Molly yawned. "Some trolls never learn."

"Is my tale boring you, young lady?" Fennic asked. "To make a long story short, I and a few of the trolls hurried here to Three Frogs. The others I sent back to raise a small army in the nearby woods for an immediate assault on the castle prisons in Solárin. We must rescue Morgus Vandar and those others still loyal to our cause."

"How'd you meet up with Fennic?" Christopher asked. "And where's Artemas?"

"At least one of you is interested in my story," he said, glaring at Molly. "The trolls I had sent to the woods soon came upon Mr. Fennic wandering along the river. They told him I was on my way to Three Frogs. Fennic met me here a short while ago which was a stroke of luck for my part. I've had a horrible time prying into the magician's mind to learn his magical spells, particularly the one to recreate another living me. He resists too much and I needed a break." Fennic rubbed his forehead as if suffering from a headache. "So I now inhabit Mr. Fennic's body, though he had little choice in the matter. It is a way to repay me for bungling his last job."

"Fennic should have had help guarding me in the wilderness last spring," Christopher said. "Then you wouldn't be in this mess right now."

"I've learned my lesson," Fennic replied. "This time I have a troll company guarding Artemas in a nearby cave." He casually pointed a thumb over his shoulder, indicating a series of caves in one of the curving rocky spurs at the foot of Mount Maricel less than a half mile behind Three Frogs. "I don't think he'll be escaping any time soon!"

"Nor will *you*," Ulric said, dismounting his horse. He stepped back to get a better view of Fennic. Garrin and Collus did likewise, keeping on either side of the group.

"What are you going to do?" Fennic asked, daring Ulric to make a move. "Capture me? I don't think so, considering there are only *five* of you–" Suddenly two groups of six trolls emerged from around the corner on both ends of the stone formation, armed with wooden clubs and daggers. "–and *twelve* of them!"

The dozen trolls quickly spread out in a semicircle to prevent anyone from escaping. A couple of the horses grunted and staggered about as the trolls advanced a few steps, their sharp yellow teeth and blazing red eyes intimidating the animals. Some of the trolls were dressed in faded remnants of the old coarse uniforms worn during the time Malaban had established his rule in Solárin. The rest wore animal skins, bits of leather or whatever other material they could make or steal. A few had even fashioned crude caps out of small animal pelts or pieces or rawhide.

Ulric, Garrin and Collus drew their swords as Christopher hopped off his horse. He quickly grabbed the reins of Molly's steed and led it closer toward Three Frogs to keep her as far away from the trolls as possible. The other horses restlessly followed.

"What are you doing, Chris? I want to stand and fight, too!"

"Don't worry. You may get your chance," he softly said to his sister. "Just stay on your horse and wait here against the rock."

As Ulric and his team stood their ground against the trolls, Fennic released a blistering laugh into the thickening silence. "Oh, I apologize if you misunderstood my earlier comment, but I had only sent a troll company of *one* to guard Artemas in his cave. A dozen trolls stayed with me to greet all of you while some others are stationed at the base of the mountain to await my orders."

"You may outnumber us," Ulric calmly said, "but your trolls are still no match. For their sake, I hope we don't have to demonstrate."

"Hmmm, I would enjoy a bit of entertainment right now," Fennic replied. "But I'd forgo all of that if you'll simply surrender to my troops. It would make the situation less unpleasant for everyone."

"We don't give up that easily!" Christopher shouted as he raced to Ulric's side. "Haven't you figured that out by now, Belthasar?"

Fennic scowled. "Humph! Stubborn as usual. In that case, I have no alternative." He signaled the trolls with a nod of his head. "Escort our new prisoners to the caves. And if they resist, you know what to do."

Several of the trolls laughed heartily while others growled and bared their sharp teeth. Rogus, the tallest troll and apparent leader of the group, raised his club and howled.

"Let's deal with this nuisance, boys! Take them!"

"I hoped you were going to say that," Ulric replied, his steely gaze fixed on the troll as he tightened his grip on a raised sword. "Stay behind me, Christopher," he added, watching him out of the corner of his eye.

The trolls advanced one more step in unison, and then another as Ulric, Garrin and Collus cemented their stances. The gray late-morning light dully reflected off their swords. Christopher grabbed two baseball-size stones and shadowed Ulric's movements, refusing to leave him at such a critical moment. But before anyone on either side could take a first swing, Molly snapped the reins on her horse, kicked in her heels and shouted at the top of her lungs as she bolted toward the center of the troll line. The other four horses burst forth at the same time in different directions, brimming with energy and crying with disdain at the towering enemy.

Like a rising ocean wave, Molly led the mini stampede and crashed through the advancing trolls, busting up the line and creating turmoil among the shocked and angry faces. Christopher and Ulric squeezed between two of the sprinting steeds as the troll in front of them dived sideways and tumbled to the ground to avoid being plowed over. Garrin fled to one side and pursued a fleeing troll as Collus raised his weapon against the club of another troll on the opposite end of Three Frogs. Molly continued to ride about, charging after a troll here and there as the other four horses galloped north toward the grassy plains for safety. Several skirmishes erupted around the rocky terrain at the base of the stone structure. Fennic looked down with rage as the clashing of swords, daggers and clubs filled the air.

"Don't let them escape!" he cried, pointing a finger in an attempt to direct the trolls in the midst of their battle. "And stop that girl on the horse!"

At that same instant, Ulric spun around to avoid a charging troll, but Christopher saw the enemy advancing like an angry bull and hurled two rocks at his ankles and tripped him up. The troll grunted as he lost his balance and fell forward, crying out in pain as he sailed into the stony ground.

"Nice shot," Ulric said, pulling Christopher to the side. "But you've got to get out of here now!"

"I'm not leaving!" Christopher said, surprised that Ulric would even make such a suggestion. "I can take care of myself."

Before Ulric could respond, two more trolls barreled toward them. But as Ulric raised his sword and Christopher was about to launch another rock, Molly blasted by on her horse, turning the trolls aside for the moment.

"I'm not worried about your fighting skills," Ulric said as he and Christopher scrambled around the base of Three Frogs. "I need you to go to the third outpost by the inn. Word must be sent to Solárin at once. King Jeremiah needs to know of the gathering troll army in the woods before they launch their attack to free Morgus Vandar and the others. Send word to Endora as well."

"You need my help here! I can't run away!" Christopher shouted, his words filled with hurt and frustration.

"You must go now before it's too late."

"But you're outnumbered. You can't afford to lose *anybody*!"

Ulric placed his hands on Christopher's shoulders and looked him squarely in the eyes. "Not to worry. As Artemas might phrase it–*I brought along an extra jar of blood beetles*," he said with a wink. "We'll be fine." Ulric spun around in the next instant and plowed into a troll who tried to sneak around the rock, sending him to the ground in an unconscious heap. "I heard his heavy breathing," Ulric casually said as he wiped his brow. "Now are we clear?"

Christopher nodded, realizing that Ulric must have some plan up his sleeve and was merely following his own advice by thinking one step ahead of the enemy. He still wasn't happy about leaving his sister and friends when the situation looked bleakest, but more lives would be at risk if he didn't.

"I understand," he softly said.

"Good," Ulric replied with a sharp nod before running back to the battle. "I know you won't let me down!" he shouted, his voice trailing off in the distance.

Christopher took a deep breath and bolted northeast toward the plains, planning to find the Gray River and follow it back to the third outpost. He hoped he would be fortunate enough to catch up with one of the horses Molly had let loose. It was the only positive thought he could conjure up at the moment, but it didn't last long. Fennic's voice rang out like the discordant clang of a rusty bell.

"Don't let him get away, Rogus! Don't let him get away!" Fennic cried, jumping up and down and waving his arms. He pointed at Christopher as he fled from Three Frogs. "Stop him NOW!"

Christopher craned his head backward as he raced across the rocky terrain, his heart skipping a beat when he saw an enormous troll bolting after him. He was frighteningly amazed at the speed that the lumbering Rogus could move and wasn't sure he could outrun him over the short distance. He would never reach the outpost in time with that creature on his back targeting him like an arrow seeking a bull's-eye. Christopher gulped when he took a second glance, wondering if he'd ever reach the outpost at all as he saw Rogus pull a dagger from his side.

"There's no escaping!" Rogus cried, raising his arm as he held the dagger firmly in his grasp. "Stop running now–that's the smart thing to do. Otherwise I'll take you down like a rabbit. Your choice!"

Christopher breathed heavily, his mind racing faster than his feet trying to figure out how to survive the next few moments. His footfalls pounded the rocky ground like hammers, though he could hardly feel the pain. Then, like a punch to his stomach, Christopher heard Molly scream in the distance. He knew in an instant that it wasn't one of her dramatic acts. He wanted to turn around and go after her. Suddenly the terrain dipped slightly downhill and Christopher nearly lost his balance. He could see the plains getting closer but knew Rogus would reach him before he could feel the soft grass beneath his boots. Turn around or continue running? He felt doomed in the next few seconds no matter which choice he picked.

"Last chance!" Rogus shouted, his arm lifted high, ready to launch the dagger. His eyes burned red with a devilish fury. "Stop now or *I'll* stop you!"

Christopher slowed a bit to keep steady on the downhill, saw Rogus crank his raised arm backward, ready to hurl the dagger while charging full speed, then did the only thing he could do. Christopher skidded to a halt and plunged to the ground just as Rogus was upon him. The troll's eyes widened in surprise when he saw the boy drop, but as he was still running downhill at a full clip and slightly off balance with his arm raised, Rogus had no choice but to leap over him. Christopher anticipated this and twisted one of the troll's legs as he flew over, sending Rogus into a tumbling freefall across the rocks. Christopher chuckled when he heard the troll's enraged cry as he sailed through the air, followed by a string of painful grunts and curses when the troll landed. But what also caught his ear was the metallic clank of Rogus' dagger falling upon the stone.

Christopher jumped up and saw the dagger lying a few feet away and scooped it up as Rogus struggled on the ground in a twisted heap. But the troll saw Christopher swipe his most prized possession, sending him into a howling rage and giving him the strength to get on his feet in spite of the stinging injuries. Christopher ran as fast as he could in the opposite direction.

"Give it back!" Rogus hollered as he scrambled up the incline after Christopher.

"Try and get it!" Christopher shouted, not turning around as he ran as straight as an arrow toward the western mountains. Only after several minutes had passed did he dare glance back to see Rogus still in pursuit, but now much farther behind. The troll's injured limbs and wounded pride had slowed him down considerably.

"That'll teach you," Christopher muttered, nearly out of breath. But even though he was heading in the wrong direction, he still ran westward, knowing he couldn't turn around with Rogus lurking somewhere behind.

Soon the rocky ground transformed into the grassy plains once again as the mountains neared. Mount Maricel towered to his left like a watchful giant as a billowing mass of gray clouds drifted overhead. A small pine forest at the foot of the mountains stood less than a quarter mile away. The invigorating scent of fresh evergreen drifted on a soft breeze, renewing Christopher's strength and spirit. He decided to take cover in the woods until Rogus was no longer a threat. When all was clear, he would travel north along the edge of the trees until he found the Gray River, follow it east past Willow Lake and beyond until he returned to the Inn of the Twelve Horses and the nearby outpost.

"Easy enough plan," he muttered to himself as his run slowed to a sluggish walk. His legs felt as heavy as lead as he slipped off his coat to cool down. His breaths were labored and deep as the memory of Molly's cry echoed in his head. He gazed up at the sky with pleading eyes, hoping all his efforts wouldn't be in vain.

CHAPTER SIXTEEN

Dramatics

As Christopher approached the edge of the woods, his fear and anxiety eased as the cool sweet fragrance of pine washed over him. He turned around, heartened at seeing no sign of Rogus on the horizon. Christopher concluded that the bruised and angry troll had probably limped back to Three Frogs to face the ire of Belthasar. Whatever his fate, Christopher was delighted to be rid of him. Now he could hike north along the edge of the woods until he reached the Gray River, then follow the water all the way back toward the third outpost. Once he sent word to King Jeremiah and King Rupert about the impending troll raid, Christopher believed there'd be no problem stopping it in its tracks.

He wandered in the shadow of the tall pines. The chirping of sparrows and the lush green of the trees and grass under the majesty of the mountains made the landscape a pleasant place to explore. The perfect location for a daring settler to build a cabin, he decided, until recalling that the area could be crawling with trolls. Maybe the average person wasn't *that* daring, Christopher concluded as he hurried along the tree line.

Several minutes later he stopped to rest, sitting against one of the pines as a heavy weariness crept over him.

Christopher knew he had to get to the outpost soon, but if he didn't take a moment to regain his strength, he wouldn't get anywhere. Though it was almost noontime in Endora, Christopher roughly figured that it was near midnight back home. His body craved sleep even though the light of day tried to convince him otherwise. The urge to close his eyes for a few minutes tempted him, but Christopher knew he couldn't give in for fear of falling into a deep slumber. So he struggled to his feet and continued his lonely journey to the Gray River.

A cool breeze picked up moments later and revived him, forcing him to put his coat back on. Christopher casually grabbed at some of the pine needles as he brushed past the trees, recalling the living rose that Artemas had magically created in their backyard. Now he was on a mission to save Artemas, uncertain whether the magician could save himself from Belthasar even with all the magic in the world. To make matters worse, Christopher glumly contemplated that Molly, Ulric and the others could very well be prisoners in spite of any backup plan Ulric may have devised. So any notion of a meal or sleep had to be blocked out of his mind. More important things were at stake.

Christopher halted for a moment, wondering if he had heard a noise. A wild animal swishing through the grass? Voices in the breeze? He looked about and placed a hand to his ear but didn't hear another sound and continued walking, his mind occupied with distant memories to combat his loneliness.

Christopher recalled wandering through the wild early last spring when he had to stop the horseman by the river from signaling Belthasar's troll army. Back then he was trying to save Endora from an invasion. Now he had to help Solárin from suffering a similar fate. Both times, though, he was weary and alone and felt as if he were battling the world–only nobody knew of his effort or of the danger that encroached upon their lives. He visualized the soldiers and policemen and so many others back home who risked their lives every day. Most of the time he never gave them a thought as he enjoyed life because of the security they provided. As Christopher trudged through the grass, a new respect grew in his heart for all of their unsung effort and sacrifice.

A short while later he spotted a ribbon of water gently curving in the near distance as the Gray River came into view. He planned to follow it east back to civilization, hoping on the way to find one of the horses that might have come back to drink. Christopher wished he had a canoe or a small raft to carry him down the currents, anything to buy a bit of time. He was about to sprint toward the water when the voices returned. He *hadn't* imagined them earlier, and the now familiar sounds grew closer.

Christopher gulped. Trolls! Some shouting, some guffawing, but every voice cantankerous and miserable. They approached from the north, circling around the edge of the woods toward Christopher and less than a quarter mile away. He slipped into the woods like a rabbit, hoping he hadn't already been spotted. The undergrowth was minimal this time of year, so Christopher ran deeper into the trees where the shadows would keep him safe. He veered north again, wanting to pass by the trolls as soon as possible. Their voices grew nearer, still situated outside the tree line.

Christopher stood still and silent behind a large pine about thirty yards into the forest. He could see the band of trolls clearly now as they marched noisily along, two dozen total. Most likely joining up with the raiding party, he figured. He waited for them to pass by, breathing a mountainous sigh of relief when they were gone.

Then his heart pounded inside his chest.

The trolls suddenly turned *into* the woods twenty yards farther away. Christopher could hear them squabbling. He feared they had spotted him and prepared to bolt. But as the trolls' arguing grew more heated, he realized that they were lost.

"Are you sure this is the spot?" one of them growled.

"Ain't stupid, you know!" another shouted back among the general grumbling.

"Should have entered the woods once we came out of the mountains!" another troll gruffly suggested. "Whose brainless idea was it to walk *around* the trees?"

Happy that the trolls hadn't spotted him, but definitely too close for comfort, Christopher plowed deeper into the woods, taking each step quickly and quietly, keeping hidden behind a tree as often as possible. He could still see the gray light of day streaming in along the edge of the woods, though little light filtered down through the treetops. Christopher had secured Rogus' dagger inside his belt and now drew it out, clutching the handle as he held it to his side. He wasn't quite sure how to wield the weapon if it ever came to a fight and hoped he wouldn't have to find out.

Christopher was sorry he had never asked Ulric for a lesson in sword fighting. Escaping trolls in a castle was one thing, but facing them while vastly outnumbered in the wilderness was a whole other ballgame. He was slightly amused as he plunged deeper into the trees, imagining Molly lecturing him that no amount of technical reasoning or scientific theory would get him out of this mess. Perhaps she was right, he admitted, but he couldn't imagine her theatrical displays working any better either. Right now running *away* from danger seemed the best bet as he weaved among the trees and over a soft cushion of pine needles and dried twigs. But moments later he stopped dead in his tracks. His lungs froze. His stomach knotted up. More voices!

"Where were they coming from *now*?" he wondered. Voices whirled in the darkness, a mix of gruff whispers and guttural complaints, some in the distance, others from behind, until finally Christopher couldn't pinpoint their origin. He felt disoriented and in danger as he continued to run, unsure where he was going as the minutes ticked by. The light on the edge of the woods disappeared as he burrowed into the deepening gloom, wanting only space between himself and the hideous echo of voices.

Beads of sweat dripped down his forehead as he dodged the trees and groping branches. Christopher felt he was blindly running through chaos, nearly suffocating in the darkness. He wished only to be free in the open air and the light of day. Then the hint of a red glow caught his eye at the same instant he tripped over a sprawling tree root.

"*Aaahh*–!" Christopher shouted, his cry cut short as he stumbled headfirst between two hulking figures onto the cold damp dirt. The scent of pungent pine needles filled his nostrils. He skidded on his left side, bruising his arm and wrist while still clutching Rogus' dagger in his right hand. He scrambled to his feet, suddenly aware of the bright flicker of firelight that reflected off the eighty pairs of eyes staring back at him. Christopher stood slightly off balance next to a bonfire surrounded by a ring of mountain trolls, all gazing in stunned curiosity at the new arrival.

Christopher instinctively raised the dagger as he scanned the monstrous faces–a frightening display of sharp teeth, blood-red eyes and dark leathery skin. The trolls breathed heavily and raised their clubs and daggers. One of the mountain creatures grunted and started to laugh.

"You and that dagger aren't going to escape *us*!" the troll said, wickedly grinning at his companions.

Christopher knew that only too well as he gazed at the creatures, seemingly in a dream. He could hear his heart beating. He could see the faces of his family. He had no idea what to do except stand there and wait for the wave of trolls to overtake him. Christopher wondered how Molly might escape, though believing that no amount of dramatics could save him. He knew brawn was required now, but realized he hadn't the strength or skill to fight his way out.

He was on the verge of giving up, ready to hand over the dagger, when he noticed that one of the trolls in front looked vaguely familiar. The creature wore a ragged leather vest with several dried squirrel bones attached to it for ornamentation. Christopher wondered where he had seen him before as he gazed into the troll's eyes.

"What are *you* looking at, little mouse?" the troll bellowed, his face knotted in a deadly scowl.

Another troll grinned. "He *is* a mouse compared to us giants. And we eat mice for breakfast!"

The trolls burst out in riotous laughter as Christopher looked on, suddenly realizing where he had seen and heard that troll before. It was Bolo, one of the two guards who had nearly captured him, Artemas and Mr. Smithers as they hid in the curtained alcove in Malaban's chamber during Princess Rosalind's rescue. Artemas had later knocked out Bolo and the second guard with a sleeping potion at the bottom of a staircase where they had been trapped. He assumed Bolo fled back to the mountains after Malaban's defeat. Christopher continued to gaze at him, a flurry of thoughts dancing in his mind as a plan quickly took shape.

"Do I have to tell you one *more* time?" Bolo complained. "Stop *staring* at me! You're already as safe as a fly in a swamp full of hungry frogs. Don't make it worse for yourself by annoying me—*or* by pointing that dagger at us! You don't want to see us when we get *really* mad. It's not a pretty sight!"

"*That* attitude is more like it!" Christopher snapped. "I thought you trolls had gone soft on me." He narrowed his eyelids and grimly smiled. "And as for this dagger? I have no intention of *threatening* you with it." He casually tossed the knife a foot into the air so that it did a somersault and caught it by the handle. Then he held the blade between his fingers and extended his arm, offering the knife to Bolo. "I intend to *give* it to you, hoping you won't lose it like its previous fool of an owner!" Christopher boldly marched toward the troll, eyeing Bolo as he shoved the dagger handle at him. "If you ever run into Rogus, you tell that incompetent bungler of a troll that he'll be scraping the mud off my boots the next time he works for me because that's the *only* job he'll ever get! Can you *remember* that, Bolo, or must I print it on a piece of pine bark for you?"

Bolo growled as he grabbed the knife. He was ready to attack Christopher with a raised fist, but a hint of confusion registered in his and the other trolls' eyes. "How'd you know my name?" he demanded. "And where'd you get Rogus' knife?"

Christopher stomped around in the circle of trolls, his

voice mimicking the tone of a whining child. *"How'd you know my name? Where'd you get Rogus' knife?"* Christopher stopped and gently rapped his knuckles against the side of his head. *"Hello!* Anybody *in there?* Are you dunderheads even paying the *least* bit of attention? Do you even *know* who you're talking to? Or must I get a *second* piece of pine bark, sit you all down like school children and draw you a map? I thought I recruited the best trolls the mountains had to offer when I met you on my way to Three Frogs early this morning."

"We met with *Belthasar,* not *you!*" another troll shouted. "Belthasar was inside the body of that old bearded magician."

Christopher dropped his chin to his chest, slapped his hands over his head and sighed. "Must I *spell* it out for you?" he muttered, raising an eye at the perplexed troll. A few others scratched their heads while some in back of the crowd whispered among themselves. "Can you work with me just a *little bit,* people?"

Bolo stared unblinkingly at Christopher, tilting his head slightly. A hint of a crooked smile formed on his face. "Are you–*Belthasar?*"

Christopher dropped to his knees and raised his arms to the treetops. "Green grasshoppers and chicken feathers–he *finally* understands! There's some gray matter in that noggin of yours after all!" Christopher jumped to his feet and grinned triumphantly as several of the trolls continued to exchange mystified glances with each other.

"Our leader is back!" Bolo explained, nodding his head. "Only this time as a young boy." He eyed Christopher with a hint of uncertainty still in his voice. "But *why?*"

"Why? *Why?*" Christopher pointed to the dagger he had just given Bolo. "Because thanks to the reckless actions of our featherbrained friend, Rogus, our plan to rescue Morgus Vandar from King Jeremiah's prison has been skewered like a roasted squirrel on a stake!"

"I *like* roasted squirrel!" commented a troll as he noisily licked his lips.

"Quit talking food!" another troll shouted as he pointed an accusing finger at Christopher. "Just how do we know if Belthasar is really inside *this boy*?"

Christopher spun around and fearlessly barreled at the troll like a steaming bull, grabbed him by the wrist and held up the creature's leathery hand. The troll looked on wide-eyed and speechless as Christopher glared at him, his jaw clenched and his grip tight like a vice.

"*This boy* I'm inside was one of King Rupert's spies who tried to disrupt my plans at Three Frogs when his warriors attacked!" Christopher said, his voice forceful yet steady. "And when Rogus carelessly mentioned that a band of trolls was secretly gathering inside these woods, *this boy* tried to break away to get word to King Jeremiah. A few others in his party escaped too and are no doubt sending out warnings as we speak. So I pursued *this boy* as Fennic and captured him, deciding to use his swift feet to get here as fast as I could to warn all of *you*, thank you very much!" Christopher looked with contempt at the troll whose wrist he still clutched, a mounting disgust in his voice clearly audible. "I knew *this boy* would be a much faster runner than Fennic, and *certainly* much faster than any of the trolls." Christopher stood on his tiptoes in an attempt to stand face to face with the towering troll, intimidating him like a drill sergeant. "But since I have now warned everyone that we have to change our plans, I no longer need to remain inside *this boy*! Perhaps I could use *you* as my next host?" he asked, squeezing the troll's wrist even tighter. "It'll only take a second for my spirit to inhabit you, and the others certainly won't care. And it would be *such* a favor to me." Christopher slowly raised his eyebrows. "So tell me, swamp breath, how does *that* strike you as a plan? Are you now convinced that I'm really Belthasar–or should we put it to the test?"

The troll leaned back as far as he could and rapidly shook his head. "No! No! No need to go *that* far, Belthasar. Of *course* it's you! I– I didn't know what I was saying. Ignore the words of a simple-minded troll. I meant no disrespect."

"Perhaps coming down from the thin mountain air has clouded your critical thinking skills," Christopher calmly said, lessening his grip. "It must take time to get used to all the extra oxygen in the forest."

"I– I *guess*," the troll said with a shrug, offering an awkward and anxious smile.

"Well, then, no harm done. At least *this* time," he replied, releasing the troll and stepping back into the center of the circle as the flames of the bonfire crackled. The fiery red and orange glow reflected off Christopher's face as the trolls looked upon him with a newfound fear and respect.

"So what will we do *now*?" Bolo dared to ask after a few moments of tense silence. "Are you killing our plan to attack King Jeremiah's prisons?" Many of the trolls grumbled when Bolo suggested such an idea.

"On the *contrary*," Christopher serenely responded, stretching out his upturned palms as if the answer was obvious. "This is an *opportunity* for us if only we look at it from the proper angle. King Jeremiah will *expect* us to abandon our scheme once he gets word of it. But we're not going to do that."

"We're not?" someone asked.

"Oh no! We're going to modify the plan just a bit," Christopher replied, moving about the circle of trolls as if he were a basketball coach explaining the next play to his team. "A little switch *here*, a little change *there*–and *ta da*! We have a new scheme."

One troll leaned over and whispered into the ear of the one standing next to him. "Grut, what is *ta da*?" Grut glanced back, scratched his head and shrugged as Christopher explained the revised plan of attack.

"Now listen up!" Christopher said with a clap of his hands. "We're going to grab victory from the jaws of defeat! Make lemonade from a bushel of rotten lemons! Rip a silver lining out of every cloud that comes our way! You all understand?" The trolls nodded vigorously among a ripple of shrugs, head scratching and raised eyebrows. "Good! Now does everyone know where the Alorian River is located?"

"Of course!" Bolo said, looking as if Christopher had asked him to point out the sky.

"And you also know the location of a large outcrop of rocks along a bend in that river?" he said, visualizing the place where he had stopped the horseman from sending the smoke signal.

"I know that spot," Bolo quickly added. "I could find it in the dark if I had to."

"That's the attitude I like!" Christopher replied, pumping his fist. "But can you find it in *secret*, avoiding all villages and travelers on your way there?"

"We can do *anything*," another troll said. "But why would we want to do that?"

Christopher wearily sighed. "To–keep–our–mission– a–*secret*!" he said through clenched teeth.

"Yeah! Pay attention!" Bolo snapped at the troll before glancing at Christopher apologetically. "Go ahead, Belthasar. Didn't mean to interrupt."

"I'm glad you did, Bolo. That shows me you have the intelligence and cleverness to lead this new mission."

Bolo's eyes widened as he stood up straight with pride. "You want *me* to lead it?"

"You bet I do!" Christopher said. "I trust your judgment, Bolo. In fact, I want you to pick two other trolls before you leave to be your seconds-in-command. I need only the best trolls I can find to help me establish my new kingdom of Belthasaria. And after *that* is accomplished, I will take over Endora and Solárin as well, finally making it into one grand kingdom!"

The trolls cheered when they heard this, raising their daggers and clubs into the air and howling like wolves. After a long and arduous winter, they were ready for some adventure in their lives, and conquering the two kingdoms once and for all was what they wanted to do more than anything else.

Christopher described the details of his new plan, instructing Bolo to lead the trolls to the bend in the river and wait there for a special messenger who would provide him with the specifics about raiding King Jeremiah's prisons. Bolo nodded as he carefully listened, eager to please Belthasar with his loyalty and attention to detail. Christopher sensed that the troll was trying to curry favor with him, so he made one last pitch to secure his trust.

"And if all goes according to plan, I will need some other men–or even *trolls*–to help manage my kingdoms," Christopher said with a gleam in his eyes. "Bolo, how would you like to be the chief guard of Belthasaria? Or perhaps *Prince Bolo* of Endora? I do so like to reward those who are loyal to me."

"Bolo at your service!" was all he could say, stepping forward with a stony expression as visions of power and riches swirled in his head. At this moment he was prepared to lead his fellow trolls across the Katánin Mountains if Belthasar asked him.

"Excellent!" Christopher said. "And the same offer goes for all of you. Give me your best and you could *all* be princes of Endora or Solárin. The sky's the limit as to the rewards awaiting you!" he shouted, jumping up and down and raising both fists in the air like a champion prizefighter before waving them off. "Now fly to the Alorian River to await my messenger! Run as fast as the swiftest horse and be as invisible as the wind! Let's *goooooooooo!*"

"You heard him, troops!" Bolo cried as the other trolls bellowed and roared like a pack of wild animals. "Follow me!"

They marched behind Bolo through the shadowy pines. Christopher watched them depart like a herd of buffalo as he stood next to the bonfire, his heart beating like a drum. He took a few steps backward and leaned against a tree, eyeing the trolls as they exited the woods and flew east under the gray light of day. When they were at last out of his sight, Christopher exhaled like a deflating balloon, sliding down the tree until he sat on the ground. His mind burst with exhilaration, knowing that he had pulled off such an elaborate deception. If only Molly could see him now.

He started to laugh, gazing up at the treetops while on

the brink of exhaustion. But Christopher knew he couldn't savor his victory for too long since he had to send word to King Jeremiah about where to find and capture the deluded band of trolls. How he would love to stand there by the river to watch it all unfold.

"That was quite a performance," said a voice in the darkness. "The *real* Belthasar would be impressed had he seen it."

Christopher jumped to his feet. He reached for the dagger at his side when he realized that Bolo now had it. He grabbed a burning branch from the bonfire and held it in front of him.

"Who's there?"

Two figures slowly emerged from the shadows and walked toward the snapping flames. The firelight reflected off their gruff countenances. Christopher felt his heart grow cold when he recognized the faces. They were two of the six men he and Molly had spotted eating breakfast at the Inn of the Twelve Horses.

"I just can't catch a break," Christopher muttered.

CHAPTER SEVENTEEN

The Scientific Approach

"Quit dragging your feet, pesky one! I have better things to do than cart you around from cave to cave," the troll complained. He led Molly to one of the many entrances in the curving rocky spur at the base of Mount Maricel, a half mile west of the Three Frogs formation.

"If you want something better to do, try a long walk off a short pier," Molly said as she marched along the stony terrain.

"Huh?"

"Think about it, brainiac," she muttered under her breath.

A few minutes later they neared a cave opening. Another troll sat guard, relaxing on a flat boulder that served as a seat. A large wooden club leaned against the stone and a dagger was strapped to the troll's side. He grunted when seeing the pair approach.

"*Another* one!" he growled, standing up and throwing Molly a cursory glance. His sharp teeth and blood-red eyes intensified the scowl on his face. "I'm busy enough!"

"Yeah, you *look* like you're working hard, Zrugga!" the troll replied with a grunt, pushing Molly toward the cave entrance.

"Why do I have to guard *her*?"

"Because she won't shut up!" he said. "Belthasar can't stand listening to her while he's interrogating the other prisoners. Neither can I! He wants her here for safe keeping."

Zrugga exhaled disgustedly through his clenched teeth as he eyed Molly. "You get in there and keep quiet, little worm. I've had a good day so far and you're *not* going to ruin it! Understand?"

Molly smirked. "Such a charming demeanor. But don't worry. You won't hear a peep out of me," she promised, walking into the cool shadows of the cave. "Like *that'll* happen," she whispered to herself a moment later.

Darkness surrounded her as she took a few more steps inside. Five hours had passed since the ambush at Three Frogs. Ulric, Garrin and Collus valiantly fended off the trolls as Molly swept by on her horse. When she saw Christopher run to the north on Ulric's command, Molly was pulled off her steed by a troll who had sneaked up from behind. She screamed as she fell, slightly bruising her shoulder. Fennic cheered from his perch on top of Three Frogs when the troll captured Molly. At the same time, a small host of reinforcements stationed at the base of the mountain had arrived and the battle was quickly over. She along with Ulric, Garrin and Collus were rounded up and sent to the caves to be interrogated.

Molly sighed, wondering how Christopher and her friends were faring. She had opened her mouth and flung one too many wisecracks at Belthasar earlier, finally being banished to this cave to await her fate. Maybe Christopher was right, she thought. Maybe she *should* think before she spoke at times. Perhaps carefully reflecting on her options instead of bursting into dramatics at the drop of a hat might make it easier to get out of a tight spot. Molly wondered if this was one of those times. Suddenly, a cool draft of air brushed over the back of her neck.

She looked up. The current of air wasn't flowing in from the cave entrance several yards away but from the blackness above. When it stopped, Molly wondered if there might be an opening near the top. Slowly a plan of escape started to take shape in her mind. She unbuttoned her cloak and reached inside one of the pockets of her blue jeans, retrieving the penlight she had won at the carnival last summer. She clicked it on and a bright ice-blue beam of light shot up to the ceiling.

"Wow!" she whispered, examining a clump of mini stalactites directly above, thin and curled like a bunch of arthritic fingers.

As Molly aimed the beam of light across the stony roof, a second larger bunch of stalactites was visible deeper inside the cave, looking as if someone had fastened a bizarre piece of abstract art to the ceiling. The dirty milky-colored mineral strands twisted in several directions, some curved and others coiled, and most partially hollowed out along their sides. Another draft swept against Molly's eyelashes, though she couldn't see any holes in the rock above. She guessed there must be a series of small fissures extending throughout the roof to the outside, allowing the wind to find its way inside. Molly concluded that the constant and chaotic gusts had prevented the stalactites from properly forming straight up and down. She'd explain her theory to Christopher providing she could free herself from her current confinement.

Then Molly took a deep breath as her eyes widened in panic. A deep growling sound suddenly saturated the air, reverberating off the cave walls and reaching into the depths of Molly's heart and lungs like an icy hand. She lowered the penlight, wondering if she had disturbed a giant bear at the end of its winter slumber.

"*Hello?*" Molly whispered, taking a step backward.

She aimed the light in several places to pinpoint the origin of the noise. Then it gradually changed, no longer a growl but instead a series of deep sluggish breaths. Molly gathered her nerve and moved toward the center of the cave. She pointed the penlight in various spots until the light beam landed on a dark lump lying on the floor just ahead.

"Way too small for an adult bear. Though I wouldn't rule out a wolf or a tiger," Molly said to herself with a faint laugh, hoping to boost her courage. Her voice echoed loudly off the walls though she spoke in nearly a whisper.

A few more cautious steps forward brought her to within an arm's length of the object lying curled up and wrapped snuggly in a cloak. She examined her find more closely with the light.

"Definitely a person," she said with a sigh of relief, noticing a pair of boots sticking out at the bottom. Several fingers curled around a fold in the cloak near the top.

However, the unusually loud breathing that continued to overwhelm the cave caused Molly to think that some strange being with an enormous lung capacity lay before her. She aimed the light into the air and noticed that the second larger bunch of twisted stalactites hung directly above. She curiously massaged her chin, intrigued by the cave's odd acoustics. Molly took a step back, pointed the light at the breathing heap and gently prodded it with the toe of her boot.

"Wake up," she softly said, "whoever you are."

The cloaked pile stirred. The breathing stopped.

"Rise and shine," Molly added in a braver tone, her voice ricocheting off the walls. "It's the middle of the afternoon. You can't—" Molly yelped as a hand suddenly grabbed her by the ankle.

"*Who's there?*" a startled voice cried. The figure rose up and the cloak dropped off its shoulders. Molly pointed the light on the man's face as he sat on the cold ground. He released his grip on her ankle and shaded his eyes. "Too bright! Too bright! Now I'm seeing spots." Molly smiled apologetically and lowered the light.

"Well hello there, Artemas," she said, squatting next to him. She placed a hand on the magician's shoulder, happy to see him alive and well. "It seems like weeks have passed since I saw you." She recalled when Artemas departed the museum basement under the wicked influence of Belthasar, though it had been only a half day ago.

"Quit making all that racket!" Zrugga bellowed as he

marched into the cave, his club held high in one hand and the dagger in the other. Molly extinguished the penlight as she and Artemas jumped up and stepped farther back into the cave. "I don't want to hear any more screams or loud talk, you hear?"

"We were just having a private conversation. And I *didn't* scream," Molly said defiantly. "It was just a slight– outburst."

"Not from where *I* was sitting!" Zrugga replied with a scowl. "Now I like it nice and quiet when I'm on guard duty. I'm busy enough and don't need you two complicating my job. So silence it up or I'll silence it up *for* you! Understand?"

"Perfectly," Artemas said, stepping in front of Molly to shield her from the troll.

"That's the right answer," he muttered before trudging out of the cave.

"I *didn't* scream," Molly whispered a few moments later as she and Artemas sat on the cold ground.

"No you didn't," Artemas replied with a grin. "And I see you've brought some light along. A handy invention, that pen of yours."

"Yes," Molly said, somewhat distracted. She turned the penlight back on and aimed it at the ceiling directly above them.

"What are you looking for, Molly? A way out?"

"Perhaps." Molly noted that the portion of the ceiling above them was simply made of rock now that she and Artemas had stepped farther back into the cave. The mass of misshapen stalactites was hanging just a few yards ahead. "Notice something peculiar about our voices now, Artemas?"

The magician considered her question. "They sound perfectly normal."

"Exactly! But when you were sleeping under that twisted bunch of stalactites, your breathing sounded as loud as a race car."

"I *was* very tired."

"Maybe not *that* loud, but it was quite noticeable. Now that I think about it, my voice seemed to magnify when I spoke to you from over there, too. That must be why Zrugga heard us." Molly stood up. "Let me try something."

"What are you doing?" Artemas asked, wrapping his cloak tightly about him to ward off a chill.

Molly stood directly under the stalactites with her back to Artemas and whispered. "Coconut cream pie with a side of sardines."

Artemas crinkled his face. "Though I'm not familiar with all the cuisine from your world, I must say that that combination sounds absolutely disgusting."

Molly sat down next to the magician. "So you heard me clearly?"

"Pie and sardines–*quite* clearly."

"And I whispered that phase *extremely* softly. Zrugga definitely would have heard it if I had spoken normally."

"I suppose," Artemas replied, rubbing his forehead. "But what is the point of your experiment?"

Molly frowned. "Headache still bothering you?" Artemas nodded. "Unfortunately I don't have any aspirin with me. And sleeping on cold rock can't help much either."

"Not really. But it'll pass," Artemas said, waving a finger at the ceiling. "Tell me more about your idea and those twisty things."

"Not much more to say," Molly said, folding her arms. "The stalactites seem to magnify sound when you stand under them, turning this place into an echo chamber. Don't know what good it'll do us, but I'll mull it over for a bit." Molly giggled. "Almost sounding like Christopher. I'd better be careful."

"Where is he?" Artemas asked. "And by the way, how did *you* get here?"

"Christopher and I followed you and Belthasar through the timedoor after you fled the museum. We met up with Ulric shortly after and the search began. Garrin and Collus, two of his soldiers, went with us. Luckily you were clever enough to leave us those two notes and the rock clue.

How did you do that, Artemas?"

Artemas stretched his arms to loosen a knot in his back. "*Notes*? *Rock clues*? What are you talking about?"

"Forgotten already?" Molly joked. But when she noticed the blank expression on the magician's face, her amusement evaporated. "Don't you remember building the model of Three Frogs near Willow Lake? And Henry Droon said you gave him a note in the middle of the night at the Inn of the Twelve Horses. Also, the first note you sent to Ulric said that–" Molly twirled a finger around a lock of her hair as Artemas looked on with a vacant gaze. "You have *no* idea what I'm talking about, do you, Artemas."

"I'm afraid not, Molly," he said, his face tightening. "Oh, this blasted headache!"

"How can that be?" Molly asked, feeling as if he had denied that two plus two equals four. "When we confronted Belthasar at Three Frogs, he admitted he didn't know how we had tracked him down, believing there was a network of spies following his every move. That just leaves *you* as the only logical explanation."

Artemas shrugged. "Sometimes logic isn't very– *logical*."

Molly looked at him askance, wondering for an instant if the spirit of Belthasar was still inside him trying to pull off another deception. She shook her head, concluding that that was impossible.

"Maybe the headaches are affecting your memory, Artemas. But the point is that you're safe now." Molly glanced at the cave opening, a dot of cloudy gray light punctuating the surrounding blackness. "If only I could find a way out," she said, trying to suppress a yawn. She was unable to keep her eyes open as a long string of sleepless hours finally caught up with her. Molly leaned against the cave wall to take a brief rest, and as uncomfortable as it was, she promptly fell into a deep sleep.

She opened her eyes to total darkness and a sore back. Molly stood up and stretched, hearing a soft steady breathing nearby. She assumed that Artemas had fallen asleep again. Molly found her penlight lying on the cave floor and clicked it on. Artemas apparently turned it off when she had dozed off. Molly glanced at the cave entrance and saw a flicker of light in the deepening gloom outdoors.

"How long have I slept?" she said to herself.

"About four hours," Artemas softly replied. "Not long enough, but you needed the rest. I took another quick slumber myself."

"What time is it?"

"Just past nightfall. And *way* past dinnertime," he said with a chuckle.

"I'll see what I can do about *that*," she muttered, making her way to the entrance.

"Molly!"

"It'll be all right, Artemas."

Molly poked her head through the opening into the cool night air. Zrugga was sitting against a rock with his arms folded, muttering to himself. A single torch wedged between two large stones provided the only light. The shadows of murky night settled upon the landscape. Molly could barely discern the silhouette of Three Frogs a half mile away, cloaked in dusky twilight.

"How about some dinner!" Molly demanded.

Zrugga jumped up with his dagger in hand. "Get back in there and quit disturbing me, little rat! How many times do I have to tell you that?"

"You're quite the poet. And you'll probably need to tell me at *least* a half dozen times before it sinks in," Molly replied. "But enough chit chat. Are we going to get anything to eat in this lovely establishment?"

Zrugga grabbed the torch and marched directly at Molly, the firelight bouncing off his bloodshot eyes and sunken cheeks. "You *might* get something to eat after *I* get something to eat!" he snarled, placing the dagger close to Molly's face. "Since you don't see any food around here, chances aren't good that you'll be supping any time soon!"

Molly flinched as she stood face to face with such

hideous peril, knowing instantly that a sarcastic comment or some splashy dramatics would only land her in a heap of trouble. This troll dripped with a seething hatred that Molly felt in her very bones. To engineer a meal *or* an escape, she would have to cultivate another approach.

"I guess we can wait," Molly gently replied as she stepped backward into the cave. She spun around and ran to Artemas, sitting next to him. "That is one *miserable* troll. Way crabbier than most–and that takes some doing!"

"He's unhappy with his current situation, sitting on cold rock with little food and lots of boredom," Artemas guessed. "Belthasar's promises of riches and victory are looking doubtful to him right now."

"He plans to build a kingdom right here. *Belthasaria* he calls it," Molly said. "Could he be any *more* conceited?"

"Belthasar told me of his intentions after his spirit left me and overtook Fennic. Then he banished me to *this* place," Artemas said with a sigh.

"This land is part of Endora," Molly said. "I don't think King Rupert will allow Belthasar to establish any kind of foothold here."

"I assure you, my dear, that he won't."

"Belthasar in control of *any* kingdom is a scary thought. But what's even scarier is another *Belthasar.*" Molly glanced at the magician with heartfelt concern. "He wants to create another of himself using your magic spell. Maybe he would retain some of your magic abilities if he did so. Is that possible, Artemas?"

"Anything is possible, Molly. Belthasar tried to tap into my innermost thoughts and learn the secrets of the magic arts. And I resisted as best I could, but..." Artemas tugged uneasily at the folds of his cloak. "A few strands of my knowledge *may* have been revealed to him by his constant prying."

"*May have?*"

"Most likely. But none of it really concerns him yet since all he desires is that one spell to create another living thing–another of *him.*"

Molly took a deep breath, composing herself before she asked her next question. She stared at the ground as she spoke. "Artemas, did Belthasar get *any* part of that spell?"

Artemas looked up at the ceiling and sighed. "Well, I'll put it this way–he didn't get the most important *part* of the spell. He didn't get the last word."

"Oh dear," Molly said. Suddenly her body felt cold and clammy as she dug her nails into the ground. If Belthasar learned most of that magical spell from Artemas' thoughts, how much longer would it take him to obtain the last word if given another chance? Then Molly sat up straight and grabbed hold of Artemas' arm.

"What is it, Molly? You seem as frightened as a mouse."

"I just realized something! You may have had the strength to resist Belthasar prying into your thoughts, but he already had access to Christopher's and mine." Her haunted eyes gazed helplessly at the magician. "He already *knows* the last word to the spell because my brother and I both heard you say it. Once Belthasar realizes that–"

"–then he'll be able to create a lovely red rose!" Artemas said with a chuckle.

"Huh?"

"Put your mind at ease, Molly. The last word of the spell that you and Christopher heard only applies to *that* particular spell. *Corénifórsegro*. That was the crucial word I used to create the rose from the tiny pile of pine needles in your backyard," Artemas reminded her. "It will be of no use to Belthasar in recreating another of himself. An entirely *different* word is the key to that spell–and I will not reveal it to anyone."

"Well thank goodness for that!" Molly said. "Still, it *is* only one word he needs to complete the spell," she added, her mind not completely at ease.

Artemas flashed a reassuring smile. "Fear not, my friend. Belthasar has a long way to go before I come close to giving up *that* piece of information!"

Molly wanted to feel encouraged but realized that if

Belthasar's spirit inhabited the magician once again, he would stop at nothing to get the final piece of the magic puzzle. He would attack Artemas' mind as if chipping away at a stone wall until it eventually collapsed. Then all would be revealed–and all would be lost. She couldn't allow Belthasar to *get* another chance.

"We have to escape!" Molly said. "Belthasar will be back to try again. It's only a matter of time. We have to overpower that troll."

"But he's well armed and we're not."

"I'll admit that's a minor flaw in my plan," Molly said. Then she turned to Artemas as a wide grin crept across her face. "Wait a minute! We're overlooking the obvious. Why don't you use your magic?"

"I have no potions to create a sleeping tonic if that's what you mean, Molly."

"Who needs potions? Can't you cast a spell on that cantankerous troll? Turn him into a lawn chair or an ice cream sundae. Anything!"

Artemas shook his head, his shoulders slumped in defeat. "Perhaps I could under ordinary circumstances. But I'm very tired right now, and my head aches so that I can't even think straight. My struggle against Belthasar has left me weakened. I couldn't shrivel a blade of grass right now, assuming you could find one around here."

Molly folded her hands and rested them on her bent knees, sulking slightly. "Sounds like you don't even *want* to escape, Artemas."

"I really just want to sleep, Molly, and regain some of my strength. I've had a hectic day," he said, attempting to joke about the situation to put her at ease.

Molly nodded dejectedly as she clicked off the penlight. "Then get some sleep, Artemas, while I think. I'm feeling as cooped up as a chicken in here," she said, jumping to her feet and wandering about the cave, her voice echoing off the walls when she walked under the twisted stalactites.

"Think away," Artemas lazily uttered in the darkness, lying down on his side. "Wake me if you think of something

192

good–preferably in the morning."

"Fine," Molly sullenly replied, clasping her hands behind her back as she paced across the width of the cave. She occasionally shot a glance toward the entrance, noting the flashes of firelight and picturing the huge troll Zrugga on his vigilant watch. How could she *ever* defeat that hulking brute?

Molly sighed with mounting impatience, frustration, and worst of all, hunger. Breakfast at the Inn of the Twelve Horses had been hours ago. Except for a quick bite from their provisions on the way to Three Frogs, that meal had been her largest in over half a day. What she would give for a grilled cheeseburger or a slice of pepperoni pizza right now with a strawberry milkshake to wash it all down. Even the *scent* of a cheeseburger wafting through the cave would be a welcome treat. Molly shuffled her feet and grimaced. Her imagination was making her even hungrier, leading her no closer to an escape. She plopped down on the cave floor and closed her eyes, at a loss as to what to do while listening to the sputtering flames of the troll's torch outside the cave.

Then Molly slowly opened an eye and turned her head toward the entrance. As hungry as she was, she imagined that Zrugga would be more famished and miserable than she could ever be. She briefly clicked on the penlight to locate the spot with the largest set of stalactites and then stood directly underneath them. Molly knew she couldn't overpower the troll, but maybe she could get *rid* of him.

"Artemas!" she cried, her voice echoing throughout the cave. Molly was certain Zrugga would hear her side of the conversation.

"What's the matter? I haven't even had a chance to doze!"

"I'm *hungry!*" she said, her words reverberating in the darkness. "I need to get some food in my stomach or I'll faint!"

"Maybe our troll friend outside will find something for us in the morning," Artemas said. "In the meantime, go to sleep. And quiet down. You're awfully loud."

"But I need *food*! Don't you understand? I'm not a magician after all," Molly complained. "Maybe *you* can go without a slab of grilled beef or steaming baked potatoes for days at a time, but I *can't*!"

"Enough, Molly!"

"At least the trolls in that *other* cave had food and were nice enough to give me some scraps." Molly smacked her lips. "I don't know where they got it, but one of the guards roasted some game over a small fire and the scent filled up the whole cave. One of the trolls must have brought some provisions from the woods. Oh, it smelled *so* good!"

"Shhh! Keep quiet, Molly, before Zrugga barges in."

"I don't care!" Molly replied. "All I can think about is that roasting meat–wild squirrel, no doubt–skewered on a stick over a fire as the juices dripped and sputtered in the flames. Who would have thought freshly skinned game could taste so good? But one of the guards tore off a sizzling strip and gave it to me to try. *Delicious*! And they even had a few juicy apples, too! Don't know *where* they got those from, but I saw the trolls devouring those like they'd never eaten an apple in their lives. They didn't give me one, but they sure smelled good. So sweet and crisp as if you had just plucked them from an apple tree on a cool autumn afternoon. I could go on forever."

"Please *don't*!" Artemas insisted, fearing that Zrugga might show up any moment.

Molly had the same fear at first, so she plunged into her food story as fast as she could, hoping her words would make the troll stop and listen. And they did so perfectly. For at that very moment, Zrugga stood outside the entrance listening in, hearing every word of Molly's that echoed throughout the cave. He was about to barge in as soon as her words drifted outside and disturbed his rest, but Zrugga was instantly captivated by Molly's description of an apparent banquet only a few caves away. The troll listened to the mouthwatering details as his imagination carried him away to the most splendid feast ever. His legs and knees quivered from hunger. How dare his fellow trolls send him off alone to guard this cave while they gorged themselves on the best fare the wild had to offer! It wasn't fair. He had to find a way to join them before he starved to death.

"Maybe you're right, Artemas," Molly sadly replied. "I'm only making myself feel worse with each roasted squirrel leg I think about or every seedy apple core I imagine myself gnawing upon. I think I *will* go back to sleep."

"Those are the first sensible words you've spoken in quite some time," Artemas said. "Now good night to you!"

"Good night, Artemas," Molly said, lying on the floor and curling up in a bundle. "Wake me when life is worth living again!"

Then she went silent.

Zrugga stood outside the cave entrance for nearly twenty minutes, listening to the heavy breathing within. Apparently his prisoners were fast asleep, but he knew he still had a duty to guard them. Zrugga turned around and gazed into the darkness, facing south where the other caves were located. He sniffed the air, believing he could detect a hint of roasted squirrel in the air, picturing the other trolls indulging themselves in two or even *three* meals until they were beyond stuffed. It really *wasn't* fair!

He could tolerate it no longer. Zrugga tiptoed into the cave and listened carefully again. Though he could see nothing, he clearly heard the breathing of two individuals. The girl's breathing was particularly loud. They were surely in a deep sleep, he was convinced, not to awaken for hours. The troll stepped out of the cave and fidgeted about for another ten minutes, debating what to do. But his growling stomach could take it no longer. After one more quick listen inside the cave to make sure his prisoners were indeed asleep, Zrugga grabbed his torch and trudged along the rocky terrain. He followed the mountains south, determined to meet up with his fellow soldiers in their cave to enjoy a well deserved meal.

Molly lay inside the cave as still as stone, facing the cave entrance. One eyelid was raised slightly all the while so she could observe the flickering glow of the torch outdoors. When the light faded and turned to darkness, she opened both eyes and smiled, picturing Zrugga marching along the barren landscape in search of a meal that didn't exist. She wanted to laugh but didn't dare, knowing her voice would carry. Molly contented herself with a sweet and silent victory.

"*Gotcha*, troll!" she thought, beaming with quiet pride. Then her mind quickly shifted gears. It was time to escape.

CHAPTER EIGHTEEN

Voices in the Dark

Artemas opened his eyes to a blinding light.

"*It's time!*" he shouted, sitting up in a cold sweat.

"Calm down," Molly gently replied, lowering the penlight. "You must be dreaming. We're still inside the cave."

Artemas wiped his brow, exhaling deeply as he looked about in the gloom. "I guess so," he said. "What time is it?"

"Still early in the evening. And speaking of time, what were you dreaming about? It's time for *what*?"

Artemas shrugged. "Um, I'm not sure," he said. "I seem to have forgotten the dream already."

"If you say so," Molly said, offering him a hand up. "Zrugga is gone, by the way. We have to leave now before he discovers there's no squirrel buffet at the other cave."

"Hmmm? I must have missed something."

"You mean you fell asleep as I recited my imaginary menu?" Molly said with a laugh, quickly explaining how her deception had gone off without a hitch. "Now, not meaning to be pushy, but on your feet. We have to leave immediately!"

Artemas stood, slowly stretching as he rubbed his

lower back. The glow of Molly's penlight revealed the worry and anxiety etched upon his face. "Do you think it's wise to leave right this minute? There may be other trolls wandering about."

Molly grabbed the magician by the hand and led him to the front of the cave.

"What has gotten into you, Artemas? I'm getting the feeling you don't *want* to escape," she said, shaking her head in confusion. "You've got to get out of here before Belthasar returns. We're doomed if *that* happens."

"Very well," Artemas replied. "I suppose I've had one too many adventures up to this point. Maybe I'm losing my nerve. We can hide among the rocks until morning."

"We'll make a beeline for the Gray River is what we'll do," Molly said as they bounded through the cave opening into a blast of cool night air. "There's no way we're hanging around this place!"

Molly aimed the penlight at the ground, illuminating the rocky terrain. The bright blue light cast an eerie glow upon the harsh and sterile landscape, overwhelming Molly with pangs of emptiness and isolation. But she knew she had to keep a sharp lookout. Though they weren't very high in elevation, one wrong step could mean a twisted ankle or a bone-breaking tumble. Then they both saw a torchlight approaching in the distance. Molly quickly turned off the penlight as she imagined Zrugga storming furiously at them with his club swinging through the air. Suddenly a fall upon the rocks didn't seem so bad.

"*Now* what do we do?" Molly whispered, looking frantically about. There was no place to hide nearby. Only the darkness could conceal them, though Molly felt certain that the penlight had already given them away.

"We should go back to the cave," Artemas suggested.

"No way!" Molly said, grabbing his cloak sleeve and heading left. "This way!"

They had only taken a few steps in the murky shadows when Molly saw the torchlight swiftly drawing near. Zrugga was running, no doubt having spotted them. Her pounding heartbeat echoed in her ears. Molly bent down, feeling for a loose rock to use as a weapon, but found none.

"Stones everywhere *except* when I need one!" she muttered, glancing up at the torchlight. "No more time, Artemas. We have to run!"

"But it's too dark, Molly!"

"Either that or face a troll. Your choice!"

"Since you put it *that* way…"

Molly and Artemas scurried down a small incline as best they could, ready to bolt as soon as the ground grew level. A cool breeze brushed against their faces as small breaks in the clouds opened above, allowing a handful of stars to peek out. But the torchlight continued to advance from their right, gaining speed.

"Get ready to run, Artemas," Molly said. "I think the terrain gets flatter up ahead. Are you with me?"

Artemas was about to reply but grabbed Molly instead, pulling her to a stop as the flaming torch sailed through the air in a series of fiery somersaults, landing several yards in front of them. The torch burst into sparks when it hit the ground, yet still burned, casting a red and orange glow upon the land.

"Don't go any farther!" a voice commanded as a dark shape raced toward them, scrambling across the rocks as agile as a tiger. "It's not safe that way."

Molly breathed heavily as Artemas stood in front to protect her, though they both now knew that it wasn't a troll who pursued them. The stranger picked up his torch and signaled them to approach. Molly clicked on her penlight as she and Artemas walked over, aiming the light near the man's face. She recognized him instantly.

"What are *you* doing here?" she said with a mix of surprise and caution, facing one of the half dozen men she had spotted at the Inn of the Twelve Horses.

"Trying to save your life, Molly Jordan," he said, slightly out of breath. "Look!" He pointed to the area that she and Artemas had been running toward. Just beyond it was a long and narrow crevice gently curving like a sleeping snake. "It's not very wide, but running straight at it in the darkness would have proved disastrous!"

"Who *are* you?" Molly asked, no longer suspicious of the man as she had been at breakfast. Though unshaven and weather-beaten, he didn't appear so threatening under these new circumstances.

"My name is Ardon. But if you follow me, Ulric will explain everything," he promised. "It is not far."

"He and the others are safe then?" Molly asked.

"Quite safe," Ardon said, walking alongside the crevice and signaling them to follow.

"There may be a troll on the loose," Artemas warned as he and Molly trailed after him. "A very *large* troll."

"I don't think you'll have to worry about that one," Ardon replied. "But as I said, Ulric will explain everything. Hurry now."

Molly deeply inhaled the lively scent of fresh grass as if it were a gust of pure mountain air. She smiled when feeling the spongy cushion of green under her boots, though it was now shrouded in darkness. And her heart nearly burst in joy when she heard her brother's voice and saw his grinning face in the gentle torchlight.

"About time you showed up," Christopher said.

Molly wrapped her arms around him. Also greeting her, Artemas and Ardon were Ulric, Garrin and Collus, along with four more of the six men she had spotted at the inn. They were on the edge of the plains north of Three Frogs, resting as a cool breeze swept by, slowly breaking up the clouds above. One by one the stars popped out, appearing like hundreds of winking eyes as the gauzy cloud remnants drifted eastward.

"What's going on?" Molly asked. "I thought *I* was the escape artist. How'd you all get here?"

"A little planning ahead," Ulric casually said as he lounged on the ground. "And now that you and Artemas have joined us, we can go."

"Go where?" Artemas asked.

"To the encampment." Ulric stood and pointed to an area left of Three Frogs.

Molly and Artemas turned around and looked. The soft glow of dozens of campfires lit up the southeastern edge of the plains less than a mile away. There, King Rupert waited with three hundred of his finest soldiers. Round tents with wide vertical stripes of green, silver and yellow had been hastily pitched as horses grazed in the tall grass and small meals were heated over snapping flames.

"Where'd *they* come from?" Molly whispered in awe, wondering what had happened in the last nine or ten hours since she had been pulled off her horse by a troll. "I get stuck in a cave for a while and the whole world changes."

Ulric happily explained as they walked to the encampment, staying just on the edge of the plains as they made a large semicircle around the eastern side of Three Frogs.

"As I mentioned before, it's wise to think a few steps ahead of your adversary," Ulric said. "That's why I sent Ardon and the others to the Inn of the Twelve Horses ahead of us. After our meeting in King Rupert's chamber, I instructed Emmett to prepare a team and send them to the inn. As we didn't know what to expect while following Artemas, I thought it best to have another set of eyes keep their eyes on *us*."

"Clever move. But you could have let us in on your little secret," Molly said.

"Not that I wouldn't have trusted you," Ulric replied. "But since it would be utter foolishness to reveal our tactics to the enemy, the fewer people who knew of the plan, the better."

"A wise policy," Artemas agreed. "*Very* wise."

"By the way, I'm happy to see you in such good spirits, Artemas. Belthasar's influence upon you seems to have faded," Ulric remarked. "Your clever dispersal of clues to find you proved very effective. How did you manage *that*?"

"As I told Molly earlier, I really cannot say," Artemas said with a sigh. "It is all a big mystery to me. Perhaps

Belthasar was laying a trap that backfired. After all, I *did* escape, thanks to Molly."

"We can discuss it in more detail at the encampment," Ulric said, noting that Artemas appeared tired and not in the mood to talk.

"I want to know how *you* escaped, Ulric," Molly inquired. "And what happened to you, Chris? I saw you run north just before I got pulled off my horse. And how did King Rupert's army get here, too?"

"Anything *else* you wish to learn before I begin?" Ulric asked with a chuckle.

He quickly explained that he had sent Christopher to the nearest outpost to send warnings to King Jeremiah about the impending troll raid, and to King Rupert about the situation with Belthasar. Ulric hoped that Christopher would meet up with one of the six men from the inn since they had been secretly following on the plains.

"Only Ulric didn't plan on Rogus chasing me to the woods," Christopher said, describing his encounter with Bolo and the other trolls and how he pretended to be Belthasar in order to escape. Molly was impressed as he detailed his dramatic acting skills. Then after Christopher met the two men from the inn who had secretly followed him into the woods, one of them, Tandrak, returned to the outpost to send warnings to the two kings. Ardon, the second man, and Christopher left to meet up with the four other soldiers from the inn.

"And then they rescued you from the caves?" Molly asked.

"Just as Ulric had predicted," Garrin said. "After Belthasar finished questioning us while inhabiting that Fennic character, he left me, Ulric and Collus tied up in one of the caves. Only two trolls guarded us. The other trolls went with Fennic to plan their strategy elsewhere."

"Those two guards were less than enthusiastic about their duties," Ulric pointed out as he walked through the grass. Molly attempted to keep up with his long strides. "When darkness fell, the remaining five of my men from the inn along with Christopher easily defeated the two guards and freed us. We left the trolls tied up in their own cave."

"We added a third troll to the mix, Molly, when we apprehended the guard who had left his post in front of *your* cave," Ardon said. "That was just before I left to look for you and Artemas."

"Zrugga. What a pleasant fellow *he* was!" Molly said with a grimace.

"Why did he leave his post?" Christopher asked. "Where was he going?"

"Well, I cleverly *nudged* him away, Chris, since he was a couple hundred pounds more than I could handle," Molly admitted. She explained how she had tricked Zrugga into leaving the cave in search of a nonexistent meal of roasted squirrel and apples.

Christopher playfully exaggerated a gasp. "Deformed *stalactites*? Cave *acoustics*? Why, your plan sounds delightfully scientific! Are you sure you're the *real* Molly Jordan?"

"Put a sock in it," she muttered, trying not to giggle.

"Yep. It's you all right."

"I'm glad you two are no worse for the wear after all the trials you've been through," Ulric said.

"I could use a bit of food," Molly responded, rubbing her stomach. "I'm a few calories deficient."

"We'll be at the encampment shortly. You'll get plenty to eat when we arrive," Ulric said. "We have already run into one of the scouting parties King Rupert has scattered around the perimeter of Three Frogs. The King is worried about your safety and will be happy to see you again."

"And we'll be happy to see him. I–"

Suddenly a bloodcurdling scream echoed off the rock and mountains, ripping through the darkness like a sharp crack of thunder. The group of eleven stopped dead in their tracks and gazed west toward Mount Maricel. The Three Frogs rock formation loomed in the near distance.

"What was *that*?" Christopher said.

"I believe Belthasar has just discovered his prisoners

have escaped," Ulric replied with a smile of satisfaction. "Now he will be having second thoughts about his next step." Ulric continued on through the grass. "It's not much farther to the encampment. Then we can launch our attack and end this trouble that has been festering in the kingdom for far too long."

"*Attack*? At *this* time of night?" Artemas asked with a hint of skepticism. "Shouldn't we wait until morning so we can see what's going on?"

"We want to catch Belthasar unaware," Ulric replied. "What better time than now?"

Artemas shook his head as he trudged through the grass, suddenly lost in thought.

Molly casually pulled Christopher aside as they marched on. She whispered to him out of earshot of everyone else. "I can't explain it, Chris, but Artemas has been acting strangely ever since I found him sleeping in the cave. He didn't even want to escape. Kept making excuses that we should stay put."

"And now he doesn't seem eager to launch an attack on Belthasar," Christopher replied, wondering what it might indicate.

"For a brief moment I thought Belthasar's spirit might still be inside him," Molly said in an even lower voice. "Think it's possible?"

She and Christopher glanced up at the magician as he walked ahead of them, the torchlight casting a gentle glow upon his cloak as it swept through the grass. They tried to ignore the pangs of doubt that pestered them like the buzz of an annoying mosquito. Everyone remained silent on the final leg of the journey.

King Rupert bowed his head in relief when he saw Christopher, Molly and Artemas walking among the campfires with Ulric and his men. He marched up to them, clasping his hands in victory, though waves of concern continued to wash over him.

"I am so glad to see you safe and sound!" he exclaimed as the glow of the fires reflected off his smiling face. "Perhaps I *should* have accompanied you to the inn with fifty soldiers in tow, but your excursion has turned out well after all."

"Ulric had the situation under control," Christopher said. "It was only a matter of letting things play out."

"Of course. Of course. Now we need to discuss the *final* play of this maddening game," King Rupert replied. "Ulric, I must meet with you and your closest advisors in my tent momentarily to discuss strategy. We have Belthasar and his trolls trapped against the mountain range and I mean to capture him one way or another. The sooner, the better!"

"He's still as slippery as a fish," Artemas warned. "I recommend that you not rush into a battle in the dead of night for fear that he might escape in the darkness."

"Duly noted," King Rupert said, though he had no intention of postponing the attack. At that moment one of his scouts rushed up to the king's side, slightly out of breath. "What have you to report?" King Rupert anxiously asked. "Speak quickly!"

"They are *still* nowhere to be found, sir. We have scoured the campgrounds and beyond another two times. We'll look again if you so command."

"Do so. And report at once if you find them," he ordered. "At *once*!"

"Yes, sir," the scout replied before hurrying off.

"What was *that* all about?" Molly asked. "Who or what is missing?"

"Nothing to worry about! Nothing! Nothing!" King Rupert gazed uneasily at Christopher, Molly and Artemas, preparing to say something then suddenly changing his mind. "Now not meaning to be rude, but I must return to my quarters and prepare for the meeting. Christopher and Molly, a tent has been raised for you just over there, and Artemas, yours is next to it. I suggest that you all have something to eat and then get some richly deserved rest. You have done enough today. Ulric's soldiers can handle things from this point on. The attack should be swift, so when you wake up, our nightmare will finally be over. I *hope*."

The king bubbled with eager anticipation to defeat his enemy, yet a subdued anxiety gnawed at him. King Rupert instructed Ulric and his men to grab a brief meal and meet him in his tent within the half hour. Then he bounded off in the darkness through a maze of busy soldiers, grazing horses and crackling bonfires.

Christopher tilted his head slightly as he watched King Rupert depart, a queasy feeling forming in the pit of his stomach. "Suddenly he reminds me of the King Rupert we found in Mrs. Halloway's barn five years ago."

Molly agreed. "He's just a bundle of nerves."

Christopher glanced at his sister with a raised eyebrow. "He's *hiding* something."

"But *what*?"

Ulric cleared his throat to get their attention. "Enough idle speculation. King Rupert is merely under a lot of pressure. I respectfully suggest that you two retire to your tent for some soup and some sleep as the King instructed. You too, Artemas."

"But we're not tired," Molly complained.

"Then you can lie on your cot and think," Ulric said with a smile. "I, in the meantime, will grab a meal if I can find one and then meet with King Rupert to discuss our mission. We must strike fast before our best chance for success withers away." Ulric said goodnight to Christopher, Molly and Artemas, dismissed his soldiers and departed.

Christopher glumly exhaled as he scratched his neck. "So I guess we're not needed at this point."

"Apparently not," Artemas softly said, gazing into the darkness. He turned to his two companions. "I'm going to retire to my tent."

"Still sleepy?" Molly asked.

"No, but I need to–think. Goodnight now."

Christopher and Molly waved goodnight as Artemas trudged away, then decided to scrape up a meal before heading to their own tent. Many of the soldiers were boiling small kettles of soup over open fires or roasting strips of beef and venison on a skewer. The mouthwatering aromas wafted through the campsite.

"I *am* hungry," Molly said. "Maybe a meal will help us decide what to do next."

"If there is anything we *can* do," Christopher replied as they shuffled through the encampment, occasionally bumping into a soldier who was sharpening a sword or pounding a tent stake into the ground. Both felt of little use at the moment.

"I wish we could accompany Ulric to King Rupert's meeting. Maybe we should crash it," Molly suggested.

"I don't think that would be a good idea," Christopher warned, pointing to a campfire up ahead. "We're not inside King Rupert's castle where they might take that kind of stunt in good humor. We're on the edge of a battle. Let's do as Ulric said. Let's get some soup."

Ulric, in the meantime, met with a few of his advisors and informed them of the meeting. Then after rounding up a bite to eat, he sat in the shadows by himself to think, munching on a biscuit and sipping from a mug of hot tea. A gentle breeze swept across the plains as the clouds above drifted eastward. The stars bloomed in bunches.

"*Psst!*"

Ulric spun around when hearing the sound emanating from the darkness behind him. He jumped up and unsheathed his sword, staring into the murky shadows.

"Who approaches?" he asked.

"Someone who needs to speak to you at once," the voice whispered. "In *secret!*"

Ulric wrinkled his brow and then suddenly recognized the voice, his eyes widening in surprise. He lowered his sword and approached the lone figure in the deepening blackness.

Ulric raised the flap to King Rupert's tent and entered several minutes later before the others had arrived. A small fire burned in a triangular metal container in the center of the enclosure, the smoke drifting upward and escaping through an opening cut into the ceiling. Shadows danced upon the walls of the large circular tent. A few low wooden seats had been set off to one side for the upcoming meeting.

"Thank you for stopping by," King Rupert said, inviting Ulric to sit down.

"There is something I need to discuss with you in private."

"And I with you. But you speak first," the king replied.

Ulric sat down and stared at the ground for a moment, then glanced up at King Rupert, his face tight and careworn. "I think maybe we *should* hold off on the attack until morning. I can't go into details about why, but–"

King Rupert raised a hand and nodded. "I agree with you on that point now, however you arrived at your conclusion."

A flash of surprise swept over Ulric's face. "You *do? Why*?"

"Something has happened, Ulric, that forces me to postpone any immediate battle plans." King Rupert sighed and sat down in front of his chief guard, unable to speak for several moments. The firelight eerily reflected off the side of his crown. He looked up as if the weight of the world had settled upon his shoulders. "There is some deeply disturbing news I must tell you."

A hint of gray light slipped over the eastern hills. The first day of spring and the Endoran New Year dawned with a damp and chilly silence. The sky stretched dark and clear as the remaining stars began to fade one by one. The sun still lingered below the horizon, not yet ready to warm the brittle rock and the grassy plains. Except for the soldiers on guard duty and those scouts patrolling the perimeter around Three Frogs, everyone else still wrestled with bouts of uneasy sleep and fitful dreams. A cool breeze rustled the sea of tents that had sprouted upon the grasslands as if a gentle hand was attempting to rouse everybody from their long and restless slumber.

Then a sharp and stinging voice crashed through the silence. Someone shouted from the top of Three Frogs. People rushed out of their tents, shaken fully awake by the chilly air and the grating noise. Word quickly spread that Belthasar wanted an audience with the king.

"And I want a word with *him*!" King Rupert muttered as a group of twenty-five soldiers was quickly assembled to travel the quarter mile or so to Three Frogs. King Rupert led the contingent along with Artemas, Ulric and a few of his top advisors. Christopher and Molly insisted on going too, and each rode a horse alongside the king.

They slowly approached Three Frogs which appeared to grow larger in the graying light of dawn. A figure stood on top of the imposing cold rock awaiting the opposition. Most figured it was Fennic under the mesmerizing influence of Belthasar, though his face was still shrouded in the lingering shadows.

"Maybe he wants to surrender," Molly whispered to her brother when they stopped in front of the rock formation. The soldiers formed a semicircle in front of Three Frogs.

"That'll be the day," Christopher muttered, gripping the reins of his horse. "Belthasar isn't the surrendering type. However, if he wants to demonstrate a graceful swan dive off his perch, well then, I'd be happy to cheer him on."

"Hush!" King Rupert whispered. "Let's hear what he has to say."

"Yes, please *do* listen!" Fennic shouted from up above, stepping to the edge of the rock and looking down. "I'm so delighted to see that my former prisoners are in such good health. Especially *you* two," he added, dripping with sarcasm as he pointed to Christopher and Molly.

"You just can't build a cage strong enough to hold me or a guard smart enough to watch me," Molly said with a laugh. "When will you realize that, Belthasar?"

Christopher grinned. "She's right, you know. For someone with designs on a new kingdom, you really don't know how to pick the right people for the job, Belthasar.

Perhaps you should join *our* side?"

Fennic twitched his lips and clenched his fists, then stood up straight, forcing himself to remain calm. "You two still can't resist flinging the wisecracks my way."

"If they are well deserved, can you blame them?" Artemas asked.

"And *you* are just as annoying as they are, magician! Though all three of you sit there smugly on your horses, don't think you have gotten the best of me," he said as the landscape lightened a bit more so they could see the bitterness etched upon his face.

"So you don't plan to surrender?" Ulric asked.

"I would think long and hard about doing just that," King Rupert added. "What you see before you is only a small portion of the soldiers I have waiting back at the encampment. My scouts have surrounded the area so no more troll reinforcements will be available to you."

Fennic chuckled. "*Reinforcements*? Who needs reinforcements when I have something even better," he slyly replied. "I have a bargaining chip!"

He signaled to some troll guards who had been standing near the back edge of Three Frogs out of the line of sight to those on the ground below. They quickly stepped forward, surrounding three individuals who had been under their constant guard. Christopher, Molly and Artemas gasped when they saw the bewildered faces of Sam and Sally Jordan and Mina Mayfield looking down upon them.

Christopher gulped. "*Mom? Dad?*"

Artemas clutched at his heart. "Mina!"

Molly shook her head, her thoughts floundering in a sea of despair. "How did this *happen*?" she whispered.

CHAPTER NINETEEN

A Rescue Party

On the day before Christopher, Molly and Artemas gazed up at Three Frogs in stunned horror, a lone figure sat in the museum lobby near the reception desk, buried behind a newspaper dated the third of January. Gray light filtered in through a series of square windows built into the ceiling above the carpeted area, warmly bathing a half dozen towering potted palm trees, an oval glass coffee table and several empty cushioned chairs. An enormous wall clock near the front doors was inching its way past four-thirty. A few people wandered through the museum, their whisperings and gentle footsteps echoing off the glassy tiled floors.

A pair of curious eyes occasionally peered over the newspaper, stealthily observing the surroundings before pretending to read some more. Moments later the inquisitive figure looked up again and received a surprising eyeful. A bearded gentleman in a flowing gray cloak, his face hardened with an arrogant determination, hastily strode across the lobby floor to the front doors and bolted outside. The figure behind the newspaper sat up straight, somewhat taken aback, contemplating for a few minutes what to do.

A short time later the frantic voices of two teenagers echoed through the main lobby. The figure in the chair quickly raised the newspaper aloft, all the while carefully listening and peeking around to one side. The young boy and girl, like the older gentleman before them, made a beeline for the main doors.

"Hurry, Molly, before we lose him!" the boy said as he pushed one of the glass doors open and stormed out into the cold January afternoon.

"I'm on him, Chris, like scales on a fish!" the girl replied, her voice cut off the instant she stepped outside.

The figure in the waiting area lowered the paper, wondering what all the commotion could mean, debating whether to follow the trio to where they were going or from where they had just left. One, two and three more minutes passed by and the figure stood up, placing the newspaper on the glass coffee table. Then a woman entered the museum, smiling as she brushed a few snow flurries off her coat sleeves. She had chestnut-brown hair and wore a delicate pair of glasses. As she walked toward the reception desk, the figure in the waiting area recognized her and sat down again, quickly picking up the newspaper to hide behind while listening carefully.

"How nice to see you, Miss Mayfield. Happy New Year," said the young woman attendant behind the desk.

"Sam Jordan invited me for a private tour with some others, though I said I couldn't attend," Miss Mayfield explained. "But I managed to find a replacement and slip away from the library. I hope I'm not terribly late!"

"He's still in the basement," the woman said. "I'll show you where the staircase is located. Just give a holler when you're down there. They'll be sure to hear."

"Thank you very much," Miss Mayfield replied. The two women hurried across the lobby floor as a pair of inquisitive eyes watched them disappear around a corner. The lone figure decided to remain at the museum for a while longer to watch what might unfold.

"*Dreadful dictionaries*! What's going on?" Mina Mayfield exclaimed when she saw Mr. and Mrs. Jordan and their son Vergil trapped in the museum lockup. Lucy Easton stood clutching the metal cage, somewhat dizzy and disoriented. Mr. Jordan was attempting to explain to Lucy what had happened and where to find a spare key. Mina took control of the situation at once, and after running back upstairs to get help, the Jordans were quickly released from their temporary prison.

Though insisting she felt fine and wanting to know how she had ended up in the museum, Lucy was finally convinced to see a doctor to get the bump on her head examined. Mr. Jordan asked someone at the museum to drive her there as he had another urgent appointment to keep. Mina would have taken Lucy to the doctor's office herself, but since Mr. and Mrs. Jordan were so evasive about where Artemas and their two other children had gone, she decided to stay and find out.

"I *know* mystery surrounds that man," Mina said. "He was still vague about telling me where he lived when we talked in the park on New Year's Eve. And he can spin giant pieces of candy in midair, for heaven's sake! But he said he hoped our friendship could continue once a certain matter was put to rest." Mina Mayfield gazed at Sam and Sally Jordan with a mix of fear and worry in her eyes. "What *matter* was he talking about? Please let me know. I do value Artemas' friendship, as brief as it has been."

Mr. Jordan glanced at his wife, knowing they didn't have time to stand in the museum lobby and explain the history of the timedoor, Endora *and* Belthasar to Mina. "Our backs are to the wall, so there's only one way to resolve this matter," he said. "You'll have to come with us, Mina, and see for yourself."

Mina smiled gratefully, though unable to imagine what lay in store for her.

Before they left, Mrs. Jordan telephoned a neighbor to look after Magic while they were away, then the four of them departed. Vergil hoped that King Rupert and Queen Eleanor were going to throw another party in their castle.

"Parties in a *castle*? *Kings* and *queens*? Quite an active imagination your son has," Mina commented as they piled into the car.

"That's just the tip of the iceberg. You'll see shortly," Mrs. Jordan replied with a restrained grin.

As they departed, the lone figure in the museum lobby watched them from the main doors and rushed outside, determined to follow.

Mina lightly pinched her arm amid the darkness and the splash of stars, wondering if she would awake from a fantastic dream. She had felt slightly confused earlier when Mr. Jordan parked his car in the empty lot near the restaurant on the side of the road, then shortly after led his wife, young son and herself up the road and through the snow to the area underneath an old bridge stretching across the river. She was *flabbergasted* when he had casually said that they were going to step through a stone wall and take a trip to Artemas' world.

"Finland is *definitely* not in that direction!" Mina had breathlessly replied in the chilly air.

Now Mina Mayfield didn't know *what* to think as she apparently walked through space and time, suddenly noticing a faint light ahead, and shortly after stepping into a stone room with a fireplace and a coat tree, tables laden with parchment scrolls and potions, and everywhere and anywhere bunches and bunches of—*roses*?

"*Where* exactly are we again?" Mina asked Mr. Jordan, holding her chin with one hand and gazing wide-eyed around the castle chamber.

"You are in the kingdom of Endora!" King Rupert proudly said a short time later. They sat around a table in one of his private chambers and enjoyed some spiced apple bread and cinnamon tea that was hastily prepared in the early morning hour. A crackling fire warmed them and freshly cut pine branches tied in small bundles with colorful ribbons hung on the walls, peppering the room with an invigorating scent of the forest.

"Where is this Ulric gentleman *now*?" an astonished Mina asked after everyone took turns explaining about the origin of the timedoor, the geography of Endora and Solárin, and the deviously scheming spirit of Belthasar.

"My chief guard Ulric and two of his men left a short time ago for the Inn of the Twelve Horses. Christopher and Molly have accompanied them," King Rupert said. "They are searching for Artemas as we speak. Or rather for *Belthasar*. Or is it...? Well, they are *searching* at any rate!"

"Then let's follow them!" Mr. Jordan said after the king gave details about Artemas' first mysterious note.

"I know you're anxious to see your children, Sam, but they are quite safe," the king replied as he sliced off another piece of apple bread. "The inn is close to the third outpost. Ulric will send word as soon as he learns something. Trust me!"

"Of course we trust you," Mrs. Jordan said. "It's just that whenever our children gallop off on another adventure somewhere in your kingdom, well, *you* know their track record for landing in a tight spot."

"And for always getting *out* of one," Mr. Jordan reminded her.

"True," she admitted with a slight smile. "I suppose we can wait a while longer for word to arrive back. They shouldn't run into any trouble at an inn, right?"

To her delight, the wait wasn't terribly long. A few hours after sunrise, a carrier pigeon from the first outpost had flown into the castle aviary, relaying a message that originated at the third outpost near the Inn of the Twelve Horses.

"It is from Ardon, one of six soldiers that Ulric secretly sent ahead to the inn as a lookout and backup team," King Rupert explained. He found Mr. and Mrs. Jordan, Vergil and Mina wandering in one of the castle courtyards and hurried with the message to them as soon as it arrived.

"What does it say?" Mina asked.

King Rupert cleared his throat and read the message scrawled on a slip of rolled up parchment.

Ulric and his team traveling along Gray River to Willow Lake, still in pursuit of Artemas. My men and I will follow in secret. Will send further word if possible. Ardon

"Where's Willow Lake?" Vergil asked, imagining a day at the beach. "Can we go?"

"No, honey," his mother said, eyeing King Rupert with a frozen stare. "Now why are they going to a *lake*? And why is *Artemas* going there? And in *this weather*!"

"All very good questions," the king replied, noting the uneasiness in Mrs. Jordan's demeanor. "But Ardon did say he would send further word."

"*If possible*," Mina said, quoting the note.

"True, true," he replied, pacing about the courtyard. "But Ardon is a reliable soldier, so I won't be surprised if we receive another message very soon. *However*," he quickly added, seeing that Mrs. Jordan and Mina were about to interrupt him, "if we don't hear anything by early afternoon, then I shall send out several scouting parties to assess the situation. Agreed?"

Everyone agreed, and then they spent some time wandering about the castle to while away the hours, though Christopher, Molly and Artemas' safety was always on their minds. Around noontime they were invited to lunch with King Rupert, Queen Eleanor and Emma in a small dining area awash in the gray light of day. Mrs. Jordan remarked how they had just celebrated New Year's Eve in their own world and were doing so again now, though with much heavier hearts.

"I look forward more to the arrival of springtime to-morrow than I do to the brand new year itself," Queen Eleanor said. "After a long and dreary winter, there is nothing like the scent of fresh bayla blossoms or the sound of honeybees among the flowers on the edge of a grassy field."

"We're a few months away from that in our world," Mina replied. "This is a lovely respite from the snow back home. I hope Artemas can find the time to show me around your world, providing that we can find *him*. I wish I knew where he was."

Less than an hour later, King Rupert provided them a stunning answer when a member of his guard rushed in with another message from the aviary.

"Sorry to interrupt your lunch, King Rupert, but this was just delivered," he said, handing him the note.

"Thank you," the king said as the man hurried back to his post.

"Good news?" Mr. Jordan inquired as King Rupert scanned the piece of parchment. "Another message from Ardon?"

"No," he replied, sighing. "But it is from one of the other six men." He looked up, his eyes darkened with dismay. "Trouble is brewing, I'm afraid."

"I *knew* it!" Mrs. Jordan whispered, setting down her fork. Her appetite vanished. "Please read us the note, King Rupert."

"Of course," he said, glancing at his wife for encouragement before diving into the dreadful contents.

Belthasar is at Three Frogs with trolls. Other trolls are going to the Alorian River. Will send word to King Jeremiah where to intercept them. The boy Christopher set them up and is safe. He returned to Three Frogs area with Ardon. They will search for Ulric, Garrin, Collus and the girl Molly. The foursome was last seen in a battle with Belthasar's trolls. They may be captives. Will return to the castle at once with a more detailed assessment. Tandrak

"When will I *ever* learn to stop letting Christopher and Molly wander through that timedoor," Mrs. Jordan said, trying to put on a brave face.

Mr. Jordan gently took his wife's hand and smiled. "They've been in worse spots, dear. We'll find them."

"I know," she said.

"And *I* know my next move," King Rupert stated, pounding a fist on the table. "We're going to Three Frogs and confront that blasted Belthasar once and for all! I am *beyond* infuriated with that nuisance. I shall muster the troops at once."

"Just save an extra horse for me," Mr. Jordan said.

"Make that *two*," Mrs. Jordan added.

"You'll ride with me, Sally," her husband replied. "We'll find our children together."

"With me, too?" Vergil asked.

"You will stay here with Queen Eleanor and Emma, young man," his mother said, glancing up at the two women. "Would you *mind*?"

"We'd love to," Emma said.

"But you'll still need that second horse, your highness," Mina informed King Rupert. "I'm going with you."

"Now, Miss Mina, I must strongly advise you against that. For one thing–"

"With all due respect, King Rupert, I was brought up on a farm and can raise, groom and ride a horse in my sleep," Mina bluntly stated. "I can also nail an ace of diamonds dead center with a single rifle shot at two hundred yards without thinking twice about it. I am *quite* prepared for this journey in every way. So now, will you show me to the stables?"

"I guess that settles *that*," Queen Eleanor said with a grin.

King Rupert raised an eyebrow and adjusted the crown on his head of silver hair, glancing at Mr. Jordan. "What *is* it exactly about the women on your side of the timedoor?" he softly inquired.

In less than two hours King Rupert assembled three hundred of his soldiers outside the castle, ready to make the trek to Three Frogs. Though they were only a small portion of his army, the king felt he had more than enough men to counter any trouble Belthasar might send their way. They headed northwest, directly toward Three Frogs, traveling across the deserted plains.

"So this is what the journey must have been like for Christopher and Molly on their first adventure five years ago," Mrs. Jordan said as their horse marched along the uneven terrain. Gray clouds blotted out the mid-afternoon sun as a slight breeze swept through tall grass. "No roads in sight going *this* way!"

"Now you'll have your own fascinating story to tell our grandchildren," her husband said, sitting in front of her and holding onto the reins.

"How long until we reach Three Frogs?" Mina asked King Rupert, riding beside him.

"A few hours," he replied, glancing back at the lines of men and horses. Several green, silver and yellow banners hoisted among the ranks flapped proudly in the wind. "In the meantime, enjoy the grasslands and the approaching mountains as you ride. One can't ask for a lovelier view."

At that same moment, a lone figure curiously watched the passing army through Artemas' telescope high atop his chamber balcony, wondering where to go and what to do next.

Nearly four hours had passed by the time King Rupert's soldiers and supplies had arrived at the edge of the grassy plains. Beyond stretched a vast expanse of bare rock, and sitting in the near distance like a sleeping vulture stood the Three Frogs formation. The king climbed off his horse to meet with his top commanders.

"We will set up camp here and send out teams of scouts along the edge of the plains to encircle the entire area around Three Frogs," he ordered, sweeping a finger across the landscape. "I want Ulric and the others located as soon as possible and Belthasar trapped. He must not escape!"

Mr. and Mrs. Jordan and Mina approached the king shortly after he met with his men. A flurry of activity commenced as soldiers set up tents and built campfires in the remaining daylight.

"I was hoping we could tag along with one of the scouting parties," Mr. Jordan requested. "At least *me* anyway."

"I want to go, too!" his wife insisted.

King Rupert flailed his arms before Mina could add her request to the mix. "I'm sorry, but I have to insist this time that each of you remain here with me. My scouts know how to do their job swiftly and in secrecy. And with all due respect," the king gently said, "they don't need you tagging along and slowing them down."

"But our children are—"

"No, no, no!" King Rupert sputtered. "Not another word on the subject. I am king after all, and I'm putting my foot down this time." Then he sighed, his eyes filled with concern for the plight of his friends. "I know how worried you must be. I truly do. I remember the agony I went through when Rosalind had been kidnapped. But trust me—my men know what they're doing. They will send me reports, and I promise to let you in on even the tiniest detail whenever one reaches my ear." He clapped his hands and tried to smile. "My tent should be up by now, so will you join me for a quick bite to eat? Some food in our stomachs should help us think more rationally."

Then he bounded off to his tent with Mr. and Mrs. Jordan and Mina reluctantly following.

An hour later after full darkness had settled in, Mr. Jordan tossed a piece of wood on a small fire several yards away from their tent. He stood and stared into the flames, his face hardened with concern. His wife and Mina each sat on a folded blanket, warming their hands in front of the snapping blaze. The clouds began to break up and a few stars peeked out as soldiers moved about in the distance attending to their duties.

"Sit down, Sam," his wife said. "You'll think yourself into a trance."

"I don't care. Our children are out there. Waiting by this fire is not going to bring them back."

"Perhaps King Rupert is right," Mina added. "We should wait for the scouts to return."

Mr. Jordan sat next to his wife and looked about. No one else was near at hand. "I'm going after them!" he whispered. "If I just stand around, then I might as well have stayed back at the castle."

"It's too dangerous," Mrs. Jordan said. "Now that it's

dark out, I think the king knew what he was talking about."
Mina nodded in agreement.

"Many of the soldiers are still pitching tents," he said,
keeping his voice low. "I'm sure I can find a spare sword
lying about to borrow."

"*Borrow*?"

"I don't plan to attack the trolls, honey. Just do a little
bit of scouting myself," Mr. Jordan said. "I'd like to get a
closer look at that Three Frogs monument. I should be able
to sneak off easily enough."

"I'll go with you," Mina said. "I'm terribly worried
about Artemas."

"Then count me in too," Mrs. Jordan added, realizing
that her husband's mind was already made up. "We should
circle about the tall grass for a while before heading toward
Three Frogs. In this darkness, who's going to see us?"

"So what are we waiting for?" Mr. Jordan said.
"Let's casually roam about and see if we can find a weapon,
then we'll wander from the campfires and disappear." His
wife and Mina excitedly nodded in agreement. "I have a
good feeling about this plan!"

King Rupert raised his arms in excitement a half hour
later when two soldiers from one of the scouting parties had
returned so soon. They informed the king in his tent that they
had run into Ulric, Christopher, Garrin, Collus and four of
the men he had sent ahead to the inn.

"They were on the edge of the plains, sir, north of
Three Frogs," one of the scouts breathlessly said. He and the
other scout had sprinted back to the encampment.

"Ulric informed us that Ardon was on his way to
meet them and that Artemas and the girl Molly should be
with him," the second scout reported.

"Wonderful news!" King Rupert said, bursting out of
his tent. "Find the Jordans and Miss Mina and send them to
me, then get something to eat. A job well done!"

An instant later the scouts departed.

Twenty minutes after, they returned, shrugging their

shoulders.

"What do you mean you can't *find* them?" King Rupert inquired. "They *have* to be here!"

"We've looked around the encampment several times, sir, but there is no sign of the Jordans or Miss Mayfield," the scout replied. "We even enlisted the assistance of several other soldiers. They're gone!"

"Impossible! Search again! Search again!" King Rupert cried, scratching his head and furrowing his brow as the red-orange light from the blazing campfires cast a devilish glow upon his face. "Just where would they *go*?"

CHAPTER TWENTY

The Climb

Christopher, Molly and Artemas gazed up at Fennic on top of Three Frogs, his eyes tinged with gray as Belthasar's spirit whirled inside him. The sight of Mr. and Mrs. Jordan and Mina standing next to him while surrounded by a clump of brutish trolls proved heartbreaking. Pale dawn crept in from the east, revealing the obvious concern of King Rupert, Ulric and the other soldiers gathered in a semicircle around the eastern side of the rock formation. A handful of troll guards stood at attention near the base of Three Frogs on each side.

"You look surprised!" Fennic said, smirking at his anguished audience perched upon their horses. "So utterly serious. I, on the other hand, find the situation amusing. I have three brand new prisoners to replace the five that escaped yesterday. I'm still getting the short end of the deal, but I can live with it."

"Release them at once!" King Rupert said. "You know there is no escape this time, Belthasar."

"I can't do that, *your highness*," he sarcastically replied. "These three trespassers are spies who infiltrated my kingdom. I have a right to take them prisoner."

"You have no rights here," Ulric said. "These lands

are part of Endora. *You* are the one who is trespassing."

"Let my parents go!" Molly cried.

"We're the ones you want, Belthasar," Christopher said. "Negotiate with *us*!"

A look of mock surprise spread across Fennic's face. "Do I detect a deal in the works? Perhaps an exchange?"

"Don't even *think* about it!" Mr. Jordan said as he glared at Fennic, struggling at the ropes that bound his hands behind his back.

"You're in no position to make demands," Fennic said.

"Maybe not to *you*," Mrs. Jordan jumped in, "but my children still listen to *me*." She looked down upon Christopher and Molly, wishing they were a thousand miles away. "You two stay with King Rupert no matter what happens. Understand?"

Christopher smiled back, hoping to convey a message that everything would turn out all right. "We'll do what needs to be done," he replied. "Trust us, Mom."

"*Christopher...!*"

"Listen to your mother," Mr. Jordan said. "Stay put. No time for heroics today."

Fennic smiled like a snake. "I think the boy has his mind made up no matter *what* you two say." He glanced at Mr. and Mrs. Jordan and shrugged. "So much for all that talk I heard in the museum basement about families sticking together. Where are the smiles *now*? Where is all that sweetness and love?"

"For your information, micro brain, you haven't the foggiest idea how a family works," Molly shouted. "A little tiff now and then is normal. It makes us stronger." Then she laughed. "But look who I'm talking to about *normal*!"

Fennic gritted his teeth. How Molly's laughter grated on his nerves! But he tried not to let on as he stared at his opponents, his eyes filled with loathing for everyone who stood between him and the power he believed he deserved.

"For all the strength you claim to possess, I have you at a slight disadvantage," he replied. Then Fennic glanced at

Artemas, challenging him with a smirk. "You've been awfully quiet, my magician friend. No annoying comments or tedious jokes to offer?"

"You are a friend to no one, Belthasar, except to your twisted ambition and craven deeds," Artemas said. "And that will defeat you in the end." A slight wind carried his sharp voice across a sea of cold rock. "But you do have the upper hand at the moment and I feel partly responsible for that," he added, gazing up at Mina and the Jordans with profound sorrow for drawing them into this situation. "So I shall make you an offer, Belthasar, to atone for some of my mistakes."

"The great Artemas freely admits to a mistake? That by itself is a prize!" Fennic said with glee. "But make your offer and I will consider it."

"I will not bargain with this madman!" King Rupert erupted, glancing wide-eyed at Artemas. "Neither should you!"

"But it must be done," Artemas quietly replied. He breathed deeply and presented a reassuring smile to those gathered around before making his proposal. "I offer myself in place of my three friends whom you have taken prisoner, Belthasar. After all, it is me you really want, is it not?"

"A substantial offer *indeed*," Fennic said, folding his arms and nodding as he considered the magician's words.

"This is lunacy!" King Rupert sputtered, tightly grasping the reins of his horse until his fingers ached.

"This is the only way," Artemas calmly told the king, his ocean-blue eyes dulled by the resignation that this deed must be done.

"Artemas, don't give in to the scoundrel," Mina pleaded. "He's no match for King Rupert's army. Your safety is more important than ours."

Fennic chuckled, glancing at Mina. "Perhaps so, my dear, but the magician's affection for you is foremost on his mind. He can't bear to see you harmed. He'll do anything to save you, including sacrificing himself." Fennic turned and addressed the anxious crowd below. "And as touching and noble a gesture as that is, I'm afraid it's not enough. After all, I have *three* prisoners. Why would I give them up for only *one*?"

Before Artemas and King Rupert could respond, or before Mr. and Mrs. Jordan and Mina even had a chance to react to his words, two voices called out in the gray morning.

"I'll go with Artemas," Christopher said, his voice sure and steady. "That should help even the trade."

"Count me in, too!" Molly added. "Three for three, Belthasar, *if* you have the guts to deal with me again."

"Stop all this nonsense talk!" their mother said, her heart gripped with dread that her children might end up in the same situation which she now found herself entangled. "You will not, I repeat—*will not*—do this!"

Mr. Jordan simply shook his head, gazing at his son and daughter, imploring them with a stern silence that they abandon such a foolish notion.

"But we *have* to do this," Christopher said, realizing the agony and despair that plagued his parents. He tried to smile. "That's what a family is for."

Molly nodded in agreement and offered a wink. Her father looked down in dazed astonishment while Mrs. Jordan tried to hold back her tears.

"You cannot do this!" King Rupert muttered under his breath as Christopher, Molly and Artemas dismounted their horses. "Let my men handle the situation. You must—"

Artemas raised a hand and looked up at his king. "*You* must trust *me*," he softly said, gently laying his hand upon King Rupert's horse to calm its jittery nerves. "This is how it must be done."

Then without another word, he, Christopher and Molly slowly walked to the right side of the Three Frogs formation. The troll guards standing there and gloating quickly separated so the trio could pass. Christopher led the ascent, finding a foothold among the stony crevices and slowly scaling the structure as Molly and Artemas followed.

Fennic signaled to the trolls guarding Mr. and Mrs. Jordan and Mina. "Take them down on the opposite side and release them. Quickly!"

The trolls hustled the three struggling prisoners across to the left side, untied their hands and then ordered them to climb down. The trolls followed the trio to the bottom, leaving Fennic alone on top. The sky lightened in the east while nighttime grudgingly retreated behind the western mountains.

"I hope we know what we're doing," Molly whispered to Artemas and her brother as they climbed up. "We got Mom, Dad and Mina released, but that's as far as our plan goes."

"You're the escape artist, Molly," Christopher joked, hoping to ease the tension. "What should we do next?"

"You tell *me*! Isn't there some scientific formula you can invent in the next five minutes to get us out of this little jam?" she asked, grabbing the cold rock above and placing her boot into a crack to boost herself higher. She briefly recalled climbing down a castle tower on a rope of tattered blanket strips.

"I'm working on it," Christopher muttered. "I'm working on it."

"So am I," Artemas replied, gazing up at the Jordan siblings. He paused for a moment and Christopher and Molly stopped to look down. "There *is* a way to end this."

"*How*?" Molly asked, her face scrunched up with curiosity. "Once we're up there and Belthasar's spirit gets hold of you, well, you know what could happen."

"Artemas, now would be a good time to tell us any ideas you have," Christopher said. He looked up, noting they were halfway to the top. When he glanced down, Christopher saw that his parents and Mina had been released and were reunited with King Rupert. Directly below were several troll guards watching their progress.

Artemas took a deep breath as he wiped his brow. "I'm not the young man I used to be."

"Rest a few moments longer," Christopher said.

"Just a few."

"Tell us your plan," Molly said, noting his reluctance to discuss it.

"Yes, my plan." The magician smiled at his two companions, happy he had visited their world through the timedoor but regretting that his invention had led to so much conflict. "I must put an end to this mess, and I have come to realize that there may be only one way to do it."

"Which is...?" Christopher asked, eyeing Artemas with growing concern. The magician appeared thinner and more careworn than usual, as if the stress of the last few days had taken its toll upon him.

"What's going on?" one of the trolls shouted from below. "Move it!"

"Just a tired magician in need of a brief rest," Artemas calmly said. "We'll be on our way momentarily."

Molly smirked. "Please, allow *me*, Artemas." She scowled at the trolls. "We'll get there when we *get* there! So hold your horses or I'll make you *carry* us up!"

"Much better," Christopher agreed, noting the grin on Artemas' face. "Now tell us quickly, Artemas, before the trolls start following us up. What is your plan? Can you prevent Belthasar's spirit from overtaking you?"

"On the contrary," he replied, indicating for them to climb a few more steps for show. Then he paused again. "The only way I know how to defeat Belthasar is to *let* his spirit invade me. After that, well..."

Molly lowered her eyebrows, gazing suspiciously at their friend. "And *then* what?"

Artemas looked to the top of Three Frogs then glanced at the gathering below. "Quite a dangerous fall if someone accidentally stepped off the edge of this rock."

Christopher's heart grew cold. "*Accidentally?* What are you saying?"

Molly shot a glance at the ground then snapped her head back, looking at the magician in drop-jawed astonishment. "Artemas, you *can't* be serious!"

"*Deadly* serious," he replied. "One small step and all of our troubles are over–if you get my meaning."

"We get it only too well!" Christopher said. "A leap off Three Frogs will clearly put an end to Belthasar, but..."

The magician shrugged. "But I wouldn't fare much better either, is that it?"

"That's a dumb idea, Artemas, in spite of the fact that you're one of the smartest people I know," Molly said.

"Well I'm open to suggestions, Molly, that won't put you or your brother in danger." Artemas indicated that they should again move up. "We're almost out of time."

Molly sighed in exasperation as they started to climb. "Maybe we can make a deal with him? I don't know!"

Christopher flinched. "Make a deal with *Belthasar*?"

"I'm just tossing out ideas!"

"Toss *that* one in the garbage," her brother replied. Christopher turned slightly and looked upon his sister with understanding, knowing how upset she was because of Artemas' idea. "Molly, you have to realize that some people in this world are just rotten to the core, plain and simple. You can never trust them, reason with them or deal with them—*ever*." He shifted his gaze to Artemas. "You can only defeat them."

"My point exactly," Artemas said, closing his eyes for a moment to allow a spasm of pain in his head to subside. Then he glanced at the Jordan siblings and smiled. "Now, Christopher and Molly, let us conclude this journey. Much depends upon it."

"All right, Artemas," Christopher softly said, taking his next step up the rock. "I'm with you all the way, *whatever* happens."

"I'm with you too," Molly said. "But I *don't* like it! I hope there's another way. There *has* to be."

"Well it had better get here soon," Christopher said as he neared the top of Three Frogs. He wondered what fate had in store for them in the next few moments.

CHAPTER TWENTY-ONE

The Last Word

In the lingering gray dawn, Christopher stepped onto the top of Three Frogs, greeted by a cool breeze, a clear sky and the solitary shape of Fennic standing silently in the center of the platform. Christopher ignored him as he offered a helping hand to Molly. Together they assisted Artemas, noting the grim expression upon his face.

The wind off the plains fluttered their garments as they absorbed the breathtaking view. Gently rolling hills in the distant east were tinged along the horizon with a subtle glow from the unrisen sun. Grassy plains stretched north to south, and distant rivers looked like thin strips of gray ribbon meandering through the awakening landscape. To the west, like a legion of sleeping giants, stood the majestic and snow-dusted expanse of the Katánin Mountains. Towering above them all was Mount Maricel, looming directly ahead so proud and quiet, ready to wake from its long winter slumber.

Christopher, Molly and Artemas gazed in wonder upon the stunning sights, for a moment forgetting the chaos that surrounded them. From far below, their family and friends watched helplessly as the trio stood silently in the thinning shadows. Then Fennic stepped into view and the world seemed to stop.

"Have you ever seen a more spectacular view?" he asked, voicing the words of Belthasar. As he approached, Christopher and Molly stepped in front of Artemas to shield him. "Protecting your friend? How very noble. But there's no reason to fear me. My trolls are below and my dagger is sheathed." He looked out across the land again, sweeping his arm through the air. "Soon this will be mine to look at each and every day after my castle is built upon this spot."

"You're delusional," Christopher said.

"A castle will *never* be built here!" King Rupert shouted up to his enemy. "And Belthasaria will never exist. So put an end to this madness before anyone gets hurt."

"This is a parley," Fennic replied, looking down at the king. "We are here merely to talk and sort out our differences. No one is in danger of harm, unless, of course, *you* start something."

The king scowled in reply.

"Don't let his taunting words annoy you," Mrs. Jordan quietly told the king. "That's exactly what he wants."

"What I *want* is for King Rupert's legion of intruders to leave my kingdom," Fennic said, turning to Christopher and Molly. "Is that too much to ask?"

"What you want is *power*," Molly replied, folding her arms in disgust. "For whatever bizarre reason, you need to control people and take what isn't yours. Like Malaban, only he changed in the end. You're *beyond* hope."

Fennic bristled at the mention of the sorcerer's name. "Malaban was a fool! He lost his power, yet I still gave that old man a last chance to be a great ruler. And what did I get for my effort? He betrayed me! Now he's either lost in the wilderness or dead. Well good riddance!"

"Perhaps if you searched hard enough you could join him," Christopher joked.

"Perhaps if *you*–!" Fennic raised a hand then suddenly calmed down. "You see, I try to initiate a civil conversation and all I get are wisecracks."

"You can hardly blame them, Belthasar, for not wanting to speak kindly with you," Artemas said. "You've been a poisonous thorn in their side since the beginning."

"And what would we want to talk to you about anyway?" Molly asked.

"Perhaps I wish to make an offer," Fennic replied.

Christopher smirked. "An offer?"

Fennic nodded. "You fault me for the power and riches I seek, acting as if you're above it all. But would your tune change if you suddenly had the same opportunity?"

Artemas sighed. "What nonsense is this?"

"*Nonsense*? Why, I'm making Christopher and Molly Jordan the offer of a lifetime!" Fennic smiled with an easy manner as if he were speaking with old friends. "You clever children have successfully thwarted me time and time again—which is *not* an easy task. So I have come to the realization that we should join forces. Imagine the treasure we could share and the lands we could conquer!" Fennic pointed across the rock and plains and water as the sky brightened in the east. "All of this could be yours!"

Christopher, Molly and Artemas gazed at Fennic with a mix of puzzlement and disbelief as a cool breeze swept past. The gathering below watched on, equally astounded. The grunting and stomping of the horses punctuated an uneasy silence.

"Quite an offer," Artemas said under his breath, raising an eyebrow.

"Indeed," Fennic replied. "Can't you see yourselves drowning in riches and awash with servants who cater to your every need? Perhaps you might rule your own kingdom someday. Hmmm, let's see… You'll start out as Prince Christopher and Princess Molly, and then who *knows* how far you'll advance in the new order of things. Definitely something to think about!"

Christopher and Molly glanced at each other, their faces void of expression. Christopher took a deep breath as Molly brushed a few strands of hair out of her eyes.

"It *is* something to think about," Christopher said.

"Definitely," Molly replied.

Slowly, and in unison, smiles grew upon their faces,

each knowing the other's thoughts.

"Okay, *thought* about it!" Molly quipped, tapping a finger to her chin as she looked wide-eyed at Fennic. "And on a scale of one to ten, your nutty idea rates, let's say—negative three *million!*"

Christopher shook his head. "Either that's the worst joke I ever heard, Fennic, or you've rocketed light years *beyond* delusional."

"What gives, Belthasar?" Molly asked. "Like we would even consider for a *nanosecond* any kind of pact with you. Are you insane?"

"It is simply a desperate offer from a desperate man," Artemas calmly replied. "Belthasar hasn't been able to physically destroy your family, so he tempts you with outrageous offers, hoping to drive a wedge between you and what you know is right in order to break your family apart." Artemas coolly raised an eye at Belthasar. "But I think deep in his heart he knows he can't do that either. Some bonds are simply too strong."

"What do *you* know, magician!"

"He knows a lot," Christopher said. "And that's why you'll never win, Belthasar, no matter how hard you try. You can hurt us, separate us or even imprison us, but my family's strength goes way beyond that. It carries on through *time.*"

"In other words," Molly added, "we'll simply *outlast* you, Belthasar. Your kind pops up now and then like mold in a dark corner, but eventually we get rid of you. Sometimes it just takes a bit of hard work."

Fennic boiled with rage. "Don't you lecture *me*, little girl!" he shouted, reaching for Artemas like a caged tiger swiping its claw through the bars. Christopher raised his hand and pushed back Fennic's advancing fist as Molly shoved him in the chest. For an instant, Christopher felt an electric chill run through his fingers as the angry spirit of Belthasar swiftly passed in and out of him. Fennic took a step backward, glaring at the trio as he breathed slow and heavy breaths through his clenched teeth.

"Didn't you say a moment ago that this was a parley?" Artemas asked. "Aren't we here merely to *talk*?"

"*I* make the rules," Fennic replied with a snarl, "and I can change them whenever–!" Suddenly his face softened and he stared at the magician with a twisted smile. "Oh, how *interesting*! It seems you have a *plan*, Artemas. So I guess *you* aren't here just to talk either." Christopher and Molly glanced at the magician with a hint of dread in their eyes. "Yes, I now know *everything*," Fennic added, raising an eyebrow as he scowled at Christopher. "I just had another peek at your thoughts."

"What are you talking about, Belthasar?" Artemas anxiously asked as the growing light in the east reflected off his ocean-blue eyes.

"You really *would* give your life to save these people," Fennic said, sauntering toward the edge of Three Frogs and looking down. "My, but that *is* quite a leap. Not a pleasant way to go." Fennic walked back to his prisoners, a smug expression plastered upon his face. "But guess what? It's *not–going*-to *happen*! Your ill-conceived plan to put an end to me will never work, Artemas. I'm too strong to allow you to walk off this rocky tower and destroy my greatness. I *guarantee* it!"

"Brag if you like, Belthasar. And maybe I couldn't destroy you that way," Artemas grudgingly admitted. "But you will never have the one thing *you* want as long as your spirit lives–a new body. And *I* guarantee *that*!"

Christopher and Molly quickly closed ranks in front of Artemas, staring down Fennic with stony defiance.

"And we'll stop you if you try!" Christopher said.

Molly nodded, raising a pair of clenched fists. "That's a promise!"

Fennic chuckled. "So you need children to protect you, Artemas? Not what I expected from a mighty magician. Or are they the best King Rupert's army has to offer?"

Artemas gently laid a hand upon Christopher and Molly's heads, looking at Fennic with a sea of contempt. "These two have shown more courage, bravery and ingenuity in the short time I have known them than you and your legion of trolls could display in a lifetime. I am honored by their unwavering support."

"And you'll have to destroy us first before you get to Artemas," Christopher said, his eyes filled with fiery determination.

"So take your best shot," Molly added, raising her fists even higher.

Fennic grinned like a fox as he advanced a step, his mop of dirty hair blowing in the breeze. "As tempting a prospect as that is, I don't need to *destroy* you to get to Artemas," he said. "I can go *through* you!"

Fennic grabbed Molly's wrist and instantly stumbled backward, holding a hand to his head until the dizziness subsided. Molly felt a tingling chill along the locks of her hair as Belthasar's spirit passed through her and into Artemas. The magician quickly removed his hand from Molly's head as if he had just touched a hot stove, then stepped back and observed his surroundings.

"Ah, this is more like it!" Artemas said, grinning viciously as the spirit of Belthasar took control of his mind and soul. Christopher and Molly spun around and looked at him with heart-pounding fear. "Oh, don't worry, my dear sweet children. Your magician friend is *not* going to walk off this precipice any time soon. I feel the struggle within as he tries to shield his thoughts from me, wishing at the same time he could leap over the edge." Belthasar shrugged, savoring his victory. "Artemas is too overwhelmed and weakened to put up a good fight anymore."

"We'll fight *for* him," Christopher said, standing tall, trying to control his rage.

"Careful so you don't get too riled up," Belthasar replied, pointing over Christopher's shoulder. "I have extra help now."

He and Molly turned around and their hearts sank. Standing before them was Fennic, his dagger raised in the air and the gap in his bottom set of teeth visible through a grim smile. He scratched his whiskered face, the rope burns on his wrist painted dull red in the faint morning light.

"You remember old Blade here, don't you?" he asked Christopher with seething hatred in his voice. The glowing line along the eastern horizon reflected off his sharp knife. "Bet you never expected to see either one of us again, huh?"

Christopher glanced at Molly and smirked. "Just more mold popping up, right?" Molly giggled in reply.

Artemas brushed past them and strode toward the middle of the stone platform. "Guard them closely, Fennic."

"Not a problem!"

Fennic raised his knife, forcing Christopher and Molly to back away to the right side of Three Frogs as their parents watched in horror from below. Artemas, in the meantime, stepped near the edge to address the anxious spectators.

"This is a drastic turn of events," the magician said. "And quite in my favor."

"Get to your point!" King Rupert sputtered, wanting to attack Belthasar at once. Yet he dared not, knowing that Christopher and Molly were in peril. He could easily win the battle but at a tragic cost.

"My point is this–I want you to leave these parts at once. Retreat with your forces to your castle and never return."

"Release my children!" Mr. Jordan shouted. "Or so help me–"

"Or *what*?" Artemas sneered. "You are in even less of a position to bargain than is the king. *I* decide what is to be done around here. So if you hope to see your two precious children ever again, I suggest you convince King Rupert to do as I say. I will not–"

Suddenly Artemas' right arm twitched. He wavered as if losing his balance. The magician gritted his teeth as the real Artemas tried to get through, but Belthasar quickly took control of the situation again, taking a step back in safety.

"I guess you're not deciding *everything* yet, Belthasar. It appears that Artemas still has a little fight left in him," Mrs. Jordan shouted. King Rupert nodded, an ember of hope burning in his heart.

"Your parasite spirit is no match for an actual human being," Christopher said. "As strong as you are, Belthasar, you're still only a flimsy shadow of a real person."

"And that's all you'll *ever* be," Molly said. "Weaker than tissue paper. An invisible nothing!"

"That's what *you* think!" Belthasar cried, flaring his nostrils in rage. He had endured enough torment from the Jordan siblings to last a lifetime. "It's about time you two see who you're *really* dealing with!"

He shook a fist at them before seeking out a small piece of stone on the far side of Three Frogs where the endless wild weather had cracked and weakened the rock. He found a chunk of stone about the size of a brick and pried it loose, then walked back to the spot where he had addressed King Rupert.

"What are you going to do? Throw rocks at us?" Christopher taunted.

"Wait and see," Belthasar hissed, tossing the rock on the ground. "Now prepare to meet your doom!"

Belthasar raised his arms like a vulture spreading its wings and pointed his fingers at the rock. He uttered a series of words and phrases that neither Christopher nor Molly could comprehend, speaking sometimes in soft whispers, other times in harsh commands. His face tightened and his eyes narrowed as the onlookers watched in morbid fascination. At one point, Christopher thought the rock quivered slightly, wondering if he had imagined it. When he looked at Molly and saw her glance back in astonishment, he knew that what was happening was all too real. Belthasar was casting a spell over the rock using Artemas' magic powers, trying to recreate another copy of himself. A moment later Belthasar looked up, his gray eyes as wild as a storm, his face frozen in concentration.

"It is useless to resist any longer, Artemas! You've lost!" Belthasar said to himself, glancing about but looking at no one in particular. "It is time to accept your defeat. Give me the last word of the spell. *Now!*"

"Don't do it, Artemas!" Molly cried.

"Not another word out of you!" Fennic shouted, raising his knife.

"And what are *you* going to do about it?" Christopher said, jumping in front of his sister. "Still haven't learned your lesson?"

Before Fennic could reply, Artemas screamed as if in agony. Everyone turned to look. The magician stood with his fists clenched and his face twisted in rage as the battle between Artemas and Belthasar stormed on. His cloak and tangles of gray hair fluttered in the wind as faint wisps of smoke rose from the piece of rock in the reddening glow of the approaching sunrise.

"Tell me what it is!" Belthasar cried to the skies above, flailing his arms in the air as he battled the magician in his mind. "What is the last word of the spell? Give it to me! Give it to me NOW!"

Then as if hit by an electric shock, Belthasar stood arrow straight. His face softened and his eyes widened as a beaming smile spread across his face. He had finally plowed through all the barriers that Artemas had constructed in his mind. He had overwhelmingly defeated the magician by unearthing the pivotal last word of the spell. Belthasar raised his hands over the piece of rock and shouted.

"*DÉVLIAFATÉLLEGRO!*"

Instantly the rock turned into a gray fluid, looking like a chunk of frozen liquid metal for a split second before collapsing into a small puddle. It reflected the crisp morning sky like a mirror as it slowly spread out a few feet in all directions. Then as if being pulled up by an unseen string, a tiny bead in the center of the puddle began to rise. Suddenly more and more drops of the liquid bubbled up and melted into one another, coalescing into a black solid that grew over a foot high into the familiar yet terrifying shape of a pair of black boots.

And the gray liquid migrated upward, creating a towering being in a pair of brown trousers and a black shirt, topped with a vest of pewter-gray chain mail. A flowing black cape grew downward from the neck like a spreading vine, covered with intricate stitching of silver and gold as it fluttered in the breeze. Lastly, the neck and head developed as the remnants of the puddle disappeared, forming a face both haunting and eerily familiar. A pair of closed eyelids was framed by a shock of iron-gray hair and a pointed jaw on a figure that stood broad shouldered and as tall as a troll. Though slightly different and yet all too familiar to those who looked upon him, there he now stood like a sleeping statue. In the chilly gray dawn, Belthasar had returned to this world like a festering sore, yet at the moment he appeared as lifeless as the rock he was created from.

Molly gulped, feeling the last flicker of hope extinguish in her heart. "What *happened*?" she whispered to her brother, wanting to cry and feeling so cold and alone.

Christopher shook his head, his spirit pummeled to a point miles beyond shock and dismay. "He's really back," he muttered helplessly, staring at the grotesque figure.

Artemas stepped back and looked proudly upon his creation like a sculptor who had just completed a masterpiece. "Now *that's* the power I've always craved!" he said with smug satisfaction. He glanced down at King Rupert and grinned. "Now you'll soon learn what a *real* leader is!"

King Rupert, Mr. and Mrs. Jordan and Mina gazed up in stunned amazement as the frozen figure of Belthasar loomed like an evil giant ready to wake. Ulric saw the fear and confusion in their eyes and shouted out, hoping to break the tension and burst the bubble of Belthasar's mounting pride.

"Looks a little taller than the miserable Belthasar I *used* to know," Ulric said. "Are you tired of having the trolls looking down upon you?"

"Fling your jokes," Belthasar replied with a disgusted sigh. "You won't have many more to make." He looked with satisfaction upon his creation and smiled. "I *tweaked* the spell a little bit. Why should I *not* stand equal with my tallest subjects?"

"A wise decision," Fennic said, viciously grinning as he tried to curry more favor with Belthasar. He felt deliriously happy as if he had finally discovered the path to the wickedly wealthy life he had always desired.

Artemas walked around the frozen shape of Belthasar, scratching his head as he examined it. "Such a handsome figure if I do say so myself," he said. "But something is *missing* which I can't put my finger on. What *could* it be?" His voice dripped with taunting arrogance. He looked down at King Rupert. "Any idea?" The king glared back in reply. Artemas walked confidently toward Christopher and Molly. "How about you two? Any suggestions on improving my wonderful creation?"

"Push it over the edge," Christopher muttered. "That'll make a definite improvement."

"Not fair! You took *my* suggestion," Molly said, grinning at her brother. Then she looked at Belthasar with a mischievous gleam in her eye. "You could stick it in a cornfield. It still looks like an ugly scarecrow, just like the first time I saw you in the great meeting hall in King Jeremiah's castle."

Artemas brushed aside their comments with a flick of his fingers and turned around, his chin in his hand, staring at the motionless shape of his old self. Then his eyes lit up and he spread out his hands, the answer to his question now obvious.

"*I* know! It needs a bit of *me!*" He held up his right hand and extended an index finger. "And all it will take is one small touch." Belthasar smiled, prepared to take on the world once again. "Come, Artemas. Let's finish this task, and then you can crawl away and join Malaban in utter defeat."

He took a few steps toward the frozen figure of Belthasar, now casting a faint shadow in the growing light along the eastern horizon. But as Belthasar extended the magician's arm, Artemas held back, locking the arm in midair.

"You're resisting again," Belthasar said, gritting his teeth. "But it's too late to defeat me, magician. You are under *my* control!"

"Don't let him get near it!" Christopher shouted.

"Fight him, Artemas!" Molly cried, grasping her brother by the arm. "Fight him!"

"Don't think your friend is going to stop him," Fennic said. "The birth of Belthasaria takes place here and now. And you two urchins get to witness it!"

Christopher and Molly saw Artemas putting up a last desperate struggle, but Fennic's sharp dagger prevented them from rushing over to help. Christopher pretended to lunge forward to see if he could catch Fennic off guard, but the man raised both arms, holding his ground.

"You haven't won yet, Fennic!" Christopher shouted.

"Oh, but I think this knife says otherwise," Fennic replied with a smirk.

Molly quickly searched through her pockets. "Oh yeah? Well let's see if that can compete with *this*!" She held out her penlight, causing Fennic to grunt with laughter.

"And what exactly is that strange object, little girl?" he said, tapping the side of the pen with the tip of his dagger. "You're going to fight me with *that*? I don't think so!"

"Take a closer look, brainless, and maybe you won't be so confident!"

Fennic leaned forward, peering closely at the top of the pen. "Looks pretty harmless to–*aaaaahhh*!"

Fennic pulled away the instant Molly clicked on the penlight, sending an icy blue flash directly into his eyes. The glowing beam clouded his vision with an explosion of bright spots as if a flock of wild seagulls had engulfed him. He staggered back for a second, instinctively protecting his eyes with his free hand. Before he had a moment to recover, Christopher seized his other wrist with both hands, twisting in opposite directions. Fennic screamed out in burning pain and dropped the dagger. Molly kicked him hard in the shin at the same time, dropping him to his knees. Christopher shoved Fennic to the ground, grabbed the knife and held him at bay.

"Molly, help Artemas! Hurry!"

"I'm on it!" she yelled, rushing across the rock.

Belthasar saw what had happened out of the corner of his eye, fearing that his mighty plan was in danger from the two children he so vehemently despised. He howled in rage as he tried to walk the final steps toward the towering figure of Belthasar as Artemas resisted, feeling as if his feet and extended arm were made of lead.

"You won't stop me this time, Molly Jordan!" Belthasar cried. "Never again!"

With every ounce of strength left, Belthasar forced Artemas to take one more step, then another, and another, inching his fingertip closer to its goal. It was now a foot away, then only inches. Belthasar pushed his hand through the air as if swimming against a strong current. Molly was nearly upon him as the flash of her blond hair caught his eye. Belthasar knew he had only an instant left to succeed. He suddenly grabbed his own right wrist with his left hand and slammed it hard against the fingers of the sleeping hulk. In the blink of an eye, Belthasar's spirit passed into the motionless figure. Artemas was catapulted backward through the air, flying into Molly so that they both tumbled to the stony surface.

Molly shook her woozy head. "Are you all right, Artemas?" she asked, massaging a bruised arm as she sat up.

"I'll be fine," he muttered, nearly out of breath as he rubbed his burning forehead. "Just give me a moment."

"I don't think we *have* a moment," Christopher replied. "Look!"

Molly and Artemas stood up and saw a commotion brewing among the soldiers and trolls below. Everybody gazed up and pointed at Belthasar, still as motionless as a statue—or so it appeared. Molly and Artemas circled around to the front side to get a better glimpse of his face, gasping at the sight.

"This isn't good," Molly whispered to Artemas, her eyes filled with fear.

Belthasar gazed out over the landscape, though his eyes were still closed. The iron-gray hair and black cloak blew in the breeze, and the pale skin on the face made it seem as if the man had been asleep for ages. But something *was* alive, just barely. Upon closer inspection, Molly noticed a slight movement underneath the eyelids as if Belthasar were in the middle of a deep dream. A faint brush of color slowly returned to his face. The pointed chin and the grim expression grew more hideous by the moment. Belthasar appeared to be nearly his old self again. Then the movement beneath the eyelids suddenly stopped. All stood deathly quiet. And in a flash–it happened!

The eyelids snapped up like wild window shades, revealing Belthasar's dark obsidian-black eyes. They blazed like chunks of burning coal, glowing a garish red and orange fire from deep within. A crazed and vindictive smile crept across his face as he slowly raised one hand, then another, turning each one over to examine as if he had never seen such an amazing sight before. Belthasar wiggled his fingers and grinned, slowly looking up at the clear morning sky and erupting in ghastly laughter. He inhaled the cool fresh air, the first his lungs had tasted in years. Then he raised his arms and cried out in arrogant satisfaction, his voice booming like cannon fire.

"I AM BACK, WORLD!" he shouted, the words echoing sharply off the mountains. Belthasar stared down at King Rupert, then quickly glanced at Christopher, Molly and Artemas, grunting with vicious pride. "So step aside before I plow you down!"

Artemas slumped and bowed his head. "What have I *done?*" he softly said, sighing deeply and despondently.

"You have helped to create one of the world's greatest leaders!" Belthasar replied with robust pride. "I will scale the heights of power and magic beyond Malaban's wildest dreams, and it all starts here and now!" He sliced an arm through the air and aimed a finger at a small boulder lying on the ground about thirty yards behind King Rupert's soldiers. "*FITÉNORES!*" he shouted as loud as he could.

Instantly, the rock exploded like dynamite, bursting into fire, smoke and shards of stone. The horses jumped about, neighing in terror and ready to bolt as their riders tried to calm them. A wave of stunned amazement rippled through the troops. Belthasar immediately voiced another command, exploding a second boulder a short distance away behind the other side of the gathering. The soldiers turned this way and that, wondering what the enemy had in store for them next.

Christopher and Molly watched the scene from above, terrified at how powerful Belthasar had grown, not daring to imagine how much stronger he could get. Trails of gray and black smoke drifted through the air like a brood of poisonous snakes, carried by a fresh breeze and reflecting the golden glow in the east. A chorus of desperate cries tore at their hearts and crushed their souls, sending them into a spiral of hopelessness. And when they saw Artemas standing before them, appearing old and tired and defeated, they realized he had finally lost the battle with Belthasar, at long last succumbing to the enemy's unrelenting cruelty and unquenchable desire for power. Endora was about to fall.

"Molly, take the knife and guard Fennic," Christopher whispered. "I've got to do something *now*!"

"Like *what*?" she asked, noting the determined look in her brother's eyes. It sent a chill up her spine.

"There's no other choice," he said, realizing that Molly had an inkling of his plan. "If I charge at Belthasar while he's distracted, well… This will be our only chance."

Molly looked over her shoulder as Belthasar addressed the crowd below, no doubt setting the stage for a final demonstration of his newfound magical powers. She shook her head, glaring at her brother and wanting to protect him, but knowing he was right.

"You might go over the edge *with* him!" she desperately muttered.

"There *is* no other way, Molly!"

Suddenly Belthasar raised his arms in the air and clenched his fists.

"There *has* to be, Chris!"

Belthasar's voice rang out for all to hear. "Now you shall witness your destiny as a new day, a new season and a new year dawn upon us!"

Christopher handed Molly the dagger and took a deep breath. He planted his feet to the ground, preparing to rush headlong into Belthasar. He nodded at his sister. She flashed a smile back.

"Victory!" Belthasar shouted, pumping his fists into the air as the eastern horizon prepared to erupt with a golden fire. "Victory at last!"

Christopher was a split second from sprinting across the rocky surface to tackle Belthasar, willing to accept any deadly results. His heart pounded and his lungs felt ready to burst. But in the instant before he let loose, Christopher saw Artemas slowly turn his pale and careworn face toward him. The power of his ocean-blue eyes and gentle voice stopped him like a brick wall.

"*Wait,*" he whispered.

Christopher used every ounce of willpower to hold himself back as both he and Molly felt the commanding strength of the magician flow over them—as tender as a warm spring breeze, yet as wild as a raging river. They stood still and silent like everyone gathered below, watching Belthasar triumphantly greet the brand new day as their own dying hearts were wrung dry of the last drops of hope.

"Behold your new destiny!" Belthasar cried, reaching for the sky. "Bow down now to the one and only king of Belthasaria!"

At that moment, the first golden bead of light inched above the horizon as the yellow disc of the sun revealed itself from behind the eastern hills. Steadily it climbed, casting a soft blend of orange, yellow and red upon Belthasar's face and across the cool stone surface of Three Frogs and Mount Maricel. The landscape, still cold beneath the surface from the long dark night, was awash in the delicate pastel light of the first spring day of a brand new year. Yet everyone who watched saw only the hard and bitter edges on Belthasar's face grow clearer and sharper. A swirling rage was evident in the eyes of the tall and sinister figure looming upon the top of Three Frogs like a ravenous vulture preparing to feast. No one at that bleak moment had the strength of mind to imagine what destruction and chaos such an evil being would rain upon them, but all were certain that that would be their fate. It was only a matter of time.

Belthasar lowered his arms and grinned with warped satisfaction. He observed the bewildered faces before him, contemplating his first command as daylight poured into his darkened eyes. He had waited for this moment for so long, for years beyond count. And now, indeed, his time had arrived.

"My first message to all of you is this!" Belthasar announced, feeling the warmth of the rising sun as the golden circle now fully revealed itself from behind the lush green hills like a blazing searchlight blasting away the darkness. "I–"

Then it hit him! A sudden sharp pain surged through his body like an electric jolt. He felt as if he had been punched in the stomach and stabbed in the heart. Belthasar bent over and groaned, tried to stand up straight, but felt dizzy and unsteady as his strength and sharpness of mind poured out of him like a flood of water. His arms trembled and he lifted up a hand, crying out in terror when he saw the rock at his feet right through his own skin and bones. His body faded, turning as transparent and fragile as a bubble of soap. *What is happening to me! This cannot be!*

But his disintegration continued. Belthasar sensed that the magical powers he obtained from Artemas were draining away as his body dissolved. He knew he had to escape now or be destroyed. His spirit had to find a safe haven before it was too late. Belthasar turned his head, but even that small movement proved as difficult as pushing a mountain. He glanced everywhere his eyes could see, looking for someone to take refuge in, but everyone was too far away. Christopher, Molly, Artemas and Fennic stood a few yards to his left, though it might as well have been a mile. Belthasar had neither the strength nor mobility to reach them. He felt as heavy as stone itself. He gazed at the rock beneath his feet as the heat of the sun breathed down upon him like dragon flames, looking for a bug or a fly or a single cricket. But there was no living thing to flee into. *Rock! Stone! Desolation!* Panic flooded through the remnants of his evaporating thoughts. His decaying mind saw everything for the first time with cold clarity. *Why did I come to this wretched place? There is nothing here! Nothing! Nothing!*

Belthasar stood up as straight as he could, unable to scream out in misery or vocalize the injustice being thrust upon him. As he flailed his arms, he saw they were nearly invisible, matching the rest of his dying body. The rays of the sun streamed through him like lasers, burning away the body that housed his spirit. With his last bit of sight, Belthasar gazed down upon King Rupert, trying with all his might to step off the edge of Three Frogs and fall upon him in a last ditch hope to touch something alive and save himself. *I will not be defeated! I cannot be destroyed! I–*

The pale and gauzy body of Belthasar leaned forward and toppled over the edge of Three Frogs, but it was immediately carried off on a current of air like a leaf in the breeze. The rising sun seared away the last traces of his body in a final blast of heat and light. Belthasar's spirit was finally released into the open air in utter and empty silence. It was whisked away on a fresh spring breeze, stretched thin and far and wide, and an instant later, dissolved into nothingness.

Belthasar, at last, was no more.

And as the crisp Endoran morning unfolded, the sun continued its steady ascent across a clear blue sky. Its warm and saving light shined upon those joyfully gathered around Three Frogs, all safe and secure under the protective watch of Mount Maricel now waking from its winter slumber.

CHAPTER TWENTY-TWO

A Magician Reveals His Secrets

Molly glanced at her brother as the morning sunshine danced lightly upon her golden hair. She couldn't speak for several moments, unable to comprehend what she had just witnessed. Christopher, still guarding Fennic with the dagger, stood in a state of wondrous confusion, a crooked grin upon his face. They both gazed at Artemas, their minds whirling with unending questions, though neither knew where to begin.

"Artemas, *what* just happened?" Molly asked, feeling as exhausted as a marathon runner who had crossed the finish line. Yet a strange sense of energy and exhilaration swept over her at the same time.

"That same question was kind of on my mind too," Christopher said with a smirk.

"And a very good question it is," Artemas replied, looking tired and worn out. "But if you would allow me one minute first, there is something I have been waiting to do for about eight days–Endoran time, not yours."

"Sure," Molly replied with a curious shrug.

Artemas placed his hands upon his brow, closed both eyes for a moment and uttered one word that resonated as crisp and clear as a single toll upon a silver bell.

"*Sipárahénic!*"

At once, the ragged lines of care and worry drained out of the magician's face and his eyes brightened to their old cheerful appearance. He stood taller and more assured, looking younger than moments ago. The damage that Belthasar's spirit had inflicted upon him disappeared like morning mist. Their old friend was back.

"That's some trick," Molly said. "What'd you do?"

Artemas inhaled the swirl of invigorating spring air. "Just putting things back in order," he said with a smile.

"You look much better," Christopher remarked.

"I *feel* much better," the magician replied. "Headache gone!"

Molly looked dumbfounded. "*Gone?* If you could have gotten rid of your headache so easily, why didn't you do it before?"

"I had a *very* good reason," Artemas said. "I'll explain in time."

"And is Belthasar really gone?" Molly asked, her eyes filled with hope.

Artemas nodded. "He is gone too–this time for good."

"Which brings me back to Molly's original question," Christopher said. "What happened?"

But before they got another word out of him, a small commotion below suddenly grabbed their attention. The trolls that Belthasar recruited had scattered to the west after realizing their leader had been destroyed. A single horn blared from one of King Rupert's soldiers. Several blasts replied across the plains from the encampment a quarter mile away. Ulric sent out a dozen men on horses to drive the trolls back to the Katánin Mountains, knowing that other men from the encampment were on their way. Those soldiers would ride close to the perimeter on either side of the plains so that no troll could escape to the north or south. Ulric and King Rupert, though, were confident that none of the trolls wanted to engage in battle now. They would take refuge in the mountains for quite a while after this stinging defeat.

At the same time, three more of Ulric's men had scrambled up to the top of Three Frogs to apprehend Fennic. Christopher handed the dagger to one of the soldiers as the other two escorted him down. Fennic muttered to himself, glaring at Christopher as his head disappeared over the side. Molly waved goodbye with a quick wiggle of her fingers.

"I guess King Rupert and King Jeremiah will have to take turns lodging Fennic in their prisons," Christopher joked. "After all, he has a list of offenses as long as his arm in *both* kingdoms."

"I'm confident they'll work it out," Artemas said. Then he raised his hand as Christopher and Molly were about to pepper him with more questions. "But before another word is spoken, I suggest we head down ourselves. Many are waiting to see us."

So after one last look at the vast rolling plains tinted gold in the morning light, and the wall of mountains splashed softly with orange and red, Christopher, Molly and Artemas quietly descended Three Frogs under the gentle hand of a warm spring breeze. Mr. and Mrs. Jordan and Mina rushed over to greet the trio as they stepped onto the ground, smothering them in hugs and tears for several minutes after.

Mina couldn't help but laugh moments later, though still misty eyed because Artemas was safe and sound. "If this is typical of how you greet the New Year, Artemas, then your celebration certainly beats ours!"

"Thankfully it is *not*!" he replied, holding Mina's hand. "When we return to the castle, perhaps we can enjoy a late breakfast and properly celebrate the occasion with a little less commotion."

"*Commotion*? Try mayhem, chaos and pandemonium brought to a boiling point!" Mrs. Jordan said, one arm wrapped around each of her children as though she would never let go.

"That description is an understatement," King Rupert said. "And I hope this kingdom never sees that kind of excitement for a long, long time!"

"I second that!" Mr. Jordan quipped. "It makes it difficult to vacation here."

"Duly noted," the king replied. "So in order to keep the trolls at bay and prevent them from stirring up more trouble, I will consult with King Jeremiah about constructing a string of outposts along the entire mountain range to keep our borders more secure. No longer will Endora sit by and allow those who wish to harm us unfettered access to our lands. If I haven't learned that lesson by now, then I don't deserve to be king."

"I'm sure you'll do the right thing," Ulric said.

Then King Rupert turned to Artemas. "But as king, I *do* deserve some answers from my magician. For instance, what happened to Belthasar? And why did you lead Ulric, Christopher and Molly on a mysterious chase across the countryside?"

Artemas bowed his head, feeling both guilty and embarrassed. "I will be happy to answer your questions, King Rupert, and any others that anybody wishes to ask."

"Stand in line!" Molly joked.

"However, we should commence this conversation on our way back to the castle," Artemas said. "Otherwise we may be here until lunchtime. It *is* quite a long story."

King Rupert directed that everyone return to the encampment while Artemas began his account on the short ride there. All listened in fascination as the steady clip clop of the horses' hooves echoed in the background.

"I suppose everything began when I returned to the Jordans' world for a short vacation—*and* to visit Mina," Artemas said, winking at Mina as the two rode side by side on their horses under a sapphire-blue sky. "When I learned that Belthasar's spirit had taken refuge on the other side of the timedoor, inhabiting the actor Elvin L. Cooper, well, I knew then that my vacation was going to be anything *but* a vacation. I had to stop him. I felt responsible for the entire mess, having created the timedoor in the first place."

"Look on the bright side," Christopher said. "If you had never invented a timedoor, you and King Rupert would have been captured by Malaban five years ago and he would *still* be a powerful sorcerer."

"He would have attacked Endora a second time too," Molly said. "So your invention helped defeat *two* miserable people."

"I never thought of it that way," Artemas mused, stroking his beard. "I suppose I can live with that explanation."

"What happened next?" Mrs. Jordan asked, sitting behind her husband as they trotted along on the same horse. "Don't keep us in suspense, Artemas!"

"I don't intend to, Sally. Thanks to the astuteness of you and Molly at the carnival last summer, Belthasar's whereabouts were discovered when you heard his interview on television. It wasn't until we escorted Emma back to visit Queen Eleanor that I had the first inkling about how to defeat him," Artemas said. "It began after we ran into Ulric's operation to catch that thieving intruder."

"Glad I could assist," Ulric said with a chuckle. "But how did *that* help? My men had only captured a hungry raccoon after all, not a devious troll or goblin."

"True, but after the commotion had settled, you mentioned something that piqued my interest," Artemas reminded him. "You said–*Sometimes to defeat an enemy you must seemingly give it what it wants.* That nugget of wisdom got me to thinking–what did *Belthasar* want? I concluded he desired two things–power, of course, and to be his old self again. I wondered how I could provide them in order to trap and defeat him. As luck would have it, the solution had been given to me by an incident that occurred shortly before we ran into Ulric and the ravenous raccoon, only I didn't know it at the time."

Christopher wrinkled his brow as he gently held the reins of his horse, trying to figure out what *incident* the magician was referring to. He slipped a finger under his ski cap and scratched his head. "Okay, I give up, Artemas. What happened before we met Ulric? All we did was step through the timedoor and hurry out to find King Rupert–except, of course, pausing to watch Molly *obliterate* those dozens and dozens of roses you created in your chamber. That *still* makes me laugh!"

"So glad I can provide you with amusement and entertainment, big brother."

"Appreciate it!"

"Back to normal, I see," Mr. Jordan said with a grin.

"Oh, Christopher is on the right track," Artemas said. "After Molly opened the balcony door and sunlight flooded over the roses I had made with magic, causing them to, well, what *Chris* said... Anyway, that event, coupled with Ulric's advice, got me to thinking—what if I created a new Belthasar and tricked his spirit into inhabiting it? All I'd have to do then is wait for the sun to rise and destroy it, thereby freeing us from all our troubles forever. How's *that* for a plan?"

"Piece of cake!" Mrs. Jordan skeptically replied. "But then again, you actually *did* it, so who am I to talk."

"But *how* did you do it?" Molly asked. "You solved the sunlight problem. Christopher and I saw you create a rose in our backyard and it survived when I carried it into the blazing sunshine in front of the house."

Artemas exhaled a sigh of guilt. "I must confess that everything you saw was *not* what it appeared to be. But I'll explain shortly. It isn't in my power to create life."

"A fascinating story," King Rupert said. "I can't wait to hear more!"

"Me either," Mina said. "But could you clear up one little detail first, Artemas?"

"Certainly."

"Why did you create so many roses in your chamber in the first place?" A puzzled expression clouded Mina's face. "I saw the flowers when I passed through the timedoor, but didn't know what to make of them."

Artemas blushed. "Well, I, um..."

Mr. Jordan jumped in to rescue his friend. "Artemas was simply trying to perfect one of his experiments," he said. Then he whispered across to Mina. "Hoping to impress a lady friend of his next time he saw her!"

Mina understood and smiled, putting the subject to rest. Artemas continued his story.

"So the next step in my plan was threefold–to convince Belthasar that he could have his old body back, make him believe he could be more powerful than ever, and finally, lure him back to Endora." Artemas raised an eyebrow. "Not an easy task. Belthasar was becoming enamored with life in the other world. As a famous actor, he possessed boundless riches and, of course, the phony and fawning adulation of his fans and associates. I feared that Belthasar might not *want* to return home. That's why I had to make him think he could have my magical powers once he recreated himself."

"Those explosions behind us looked pretty real," Mr. Jordan said. "You can't tell us they were make-believe."

"They were quite real, Sam. All part of the illusion to keep Belthasar from discovering what was *really* happening."

"So how'd you do it?" Molly asked with growing impatience.

"Well, after we sent those numerous e-mails to Elvin L. Cooper to draw Belthasar back to us, I needed a plan to deal with him when he arrived," Artemas explained. "I knew sooner or later he would try to attack me, Christopher or Molly, perhaps all three, so I prepared for that possibility. If Belthasar did strike us, he would surely learn of my spell to recreate a living thing and realize he could exist in his old form again–only this time with my magic powers."

Christopher nodded, recalling the terrible time when Belthasar had trapped them in the museum basement. Belthasar had learned about Artemas' spell after inhabiting him and Molly and reading their thoughts about the experiment with the rose. Belthasar fled in the magician's body and returned through the timedoor shortly after, believing he could recreate a more powerful form of his old self.

"Artemas, I still don't understand," Christopher said. "When you demonstrated your spell in our backyard, you created a *real* rose that could survive in sunlight. How come Belthasar was destroyed when the sun rose this morning? It doesn't make sense."

"It will when you understand my elaborate, headache-inducing plan," Artemas replied.

"But you'll have to hold that thought for a moment," King Rupert said as they neared the plains and the encampment. "Ulric and I must consult with our troops on the troll situation, then we'll break camp and head back to the castle. In the meantime, everyone should grab a bite to eat."

Nobody objected, inhaling the fresh scent of grass as their horses waded through the springy green stretch of plains. The world seemed alive again amid a sea of striped round tents, crackling bonfires and the green, silver and yellow banners snapping in the brisk morning breeze. The hungry travelers quickly found soup and bread while King Rupert and Ulric attended to military matters. A few scouts were dispatched to the nearest outpost to send word to Queen Eleanor and King Jeremiah that the situation had been resolved.

Within the hour, tents were swiftly taken down and packed away, campfires were extinguished and King Rupert's three hundred troops made ready to depart. Shortly after, he leisurely led the way southeast across the plains, instructing Artemas to continue his story. As King Rupert, Ulric, Mina and the Jordan family eagerly listened, a lone figure draped in a hooded cloak quietly paid attention as well, riding unassumingly on a horse just behind the others, offering neither comment nor question.

"Now where was I?" Artemas said as he scanned the horizon while riding alongside Mina. "Ah, the details of my plan! I had to work fast, you know, as we only had a short time to linger in Endora after we brought Emma back. While all of you enjoyed a tour of the castle with King Rupert, I was busy in my chamber and the library preparing my battle tactics, so to speak."

"I interrupted you during our tour," Molly said, remembering sticking her head through his chamber door. "You appeared startled, as if you didn't want me to see what you were looking at."

"At that moment I *didn't*," he replied, explaining how he had been studying a map of Endora, specifically an area near the Katánin Mountains. "A short time later I went to the library to continue my work."

Christopher glanced at the magician, feeling just a little bit guilty. "I must confess, Artemas, that Molly and I *accidentally* spied on you in the library. We went to look for you because the timedoor was going to close soon. We heard you talking to someone–only no one was in the library with you."

Artemas grinned. "You must have caught me talking to myself in the mirror. A strange sight, no doubt."

"We didn't want to let on that we saw, so we left and came back shortly after," Molly said, lightly punching her brother in the arm. "You *weren't* supposed to tell, Chris."

"Why would you talk to yourself in a mirror?" Mina asked, perplexed and amused at the same time.

"Forget that we even brought it up," Molly said apologetically, believing that Artemas had followed her suggestion about practicing what he wanted to say to Mina in front of a mirror. Molly hoped that she and her brother hadn't caused him too much embarrassment.

"It's perfectly all right to talk about it now," Artemas said without a hint of care. "I was using the mirror to cast a series of spells upon myself as part of my plan to defeat Belthasar. So *many* spells, in fact, that I ended up with a massive headache!"

"*That's* what you were doing?" Christopher asked.

"Yes. Why *else* would I talk to myself in a mirror?"

"Never mind," Molly said, chuckling to herself.

"What types of spells did you cast?" Mrs. Jordan asked, intrigued by the magician's course of action.

"Where should I begin?" Artemas said. "First, I had to protect my thoughts about my plan to destroy Belthasar *from* Belthasar. If he ever took control of me, he would instantly know my true intentions and the show would have ended before it started. I also cast a spell to give me extra strength to resist Belthasar's influence over my mind and body, though I sometimes pretended that he had the upper hand to make him think he was winning. But it was always a struggle nonetheless."

"What else?" Ulric asked.

"Well, I added a spell to make Belthasar believe that my powers would transfer to him if he recreated another of himself," Artemas continued. "I had to make him really *want* to be himself again. Therefore, I invented a few explosion spells that transferred with him when his spirit inhabited his new body. That perfected the illusion and bought us more time until sunrise." Artemas sighed, recalling the pounding throbs of his former headache. "Plus I had to implant in him the desire to go to Three Frogs and establish his kingdom there. I pinpointed that desolate and lifeless place on my map. It would offer his spirit no escape route as the sun destroyed him."

"Quite clever!" Mr. Jordan said. "You are a crafty magician indeed."

"Clever, yes," Molly said. "But when I found you in the cave, you denied that you deliberately left the clues for us to follow you to Three Frogs. If you made Belthasar *want* to go there, then you must have led us there, too."

"What else *could* I do but deny it? If I admitted that part of the plan to you and then Belthasar found out, well, he would have suspected something was afoot and may have fled."

"So how'd you pull off *that* bit of magic?" Christopher asked.

"Three more *spells*, of course!" Artemas said. "It was *quite* a headache! I had to cast a combination of three temporary sleeping and memory-erasing spells that I could trigger as needed, allowing me to throw Belthasar's spirit into a short sleep without him remembering that he had been affected. That was the most taxing spell. I would never have had the strength to cast it more than three times, and even *that* was a tremendous strain in the end."

"That's how you delivered those notes without arousing Belthasar's suspicion," Ulric said with admiration.

"I activated that spell the first time as soon as Belthasar passed through the timedoor," Artemas said. "I hastily wrote two notes while in my chamber, Ulric, giving the first one to Emmett when I saw him in the corridor, telling him to give it to you. I ended the spell immediately and Belthasar fled the castle, not realizing what had just happened. Next, when near the Inn of the Twelve Horses in the darkness, I triggered the second spell, quickly presenting the other note to Henry Droon after pounding on his door and waking him up. I must apologize to him one of these days for ruining his sleep."

"I think Henry will forgive you," Molly said, hoping to visit the inn one more time before they left Endora. "So I suppose you activated that spell for the last time after you arrived at Willow Lake."

"Precisely. I put Belthasar's spirit to sleep just long enough to build a tiny replica of Three Frogs out of some stones, then I started a small fire and extinguished it, figuring it would smoke awhile afterward to draw your attention at daylight." Artemas smiled. "I believed those three clues were *more* than enough to lead you to Three Frogs where Belthasar awaited."

"It worked like a charm," Christopher said.

"The only other challenge after that was to withhold the final word of the spell from Belthasar until as close to sunrise as possible," Artemas continued, wondering how he had juggled so many spells so successfully. "It was all a matter of timing."

"That's why you were so anxious *not* to leave the cave until morning," Molly said. "You simply had to wait until sunrise before you could proceed."

"And that's why you didn't want the battle to commence until daylight either," Ulric said.

Artemas nodded. "Exactly. If you had launched an attack before I could finish my plan, then Belthasar might have escaped in the darkness and we'd be back to where we started. I doubt such a chance would have ever presented itself again."

"As bad luck would have it, I ended up postponing the attack anyway," King Rupert said. "When I learned that Sam, Sally and Mina had disappeared, I figured something foul had happened and that Belthasar most likely had a hand in it. I couldn't risk putting their lives in danger."

Mr. Jordan couldn't help but laugh at himself . "My *brilliant* plan to rescue Christopher and Molly sort of went awry."

"*Sort of?* After I found out the three of you had left, I was furious," King Rupert said. "Now I'm merely curious." He turned to his chief guard. "Ulric, since I've had time to think about it, you never *did* tell me why you wanted to postpone the attack until morning when you stopped by my tent. I never asked you to explain since I had already changed my mind."

"I had a very good reason," Ulric said. "A visitor in the night told me about Artemas' secret plan."

"What are you talking about?" the magician said, wide-eyed with surprise. The others joined in with exclamations of disbelief. "How did *you* find out about my plan?"

Ulric glanced at Artemas with an awkward grin. "I guess now is as good a time as any to reveal *my* little secret. I was waiting for the right moment during your story."

"Do enlighten us!" Mina said, eager to hear the latest twist in the tale.

"Very well," Ulric replied, glancing back at the cloaked figure riding on the horse behind them. He signaled for the individual to come forward. "Ladies and gentlemen, I'd like you to meet Artemas' secret collaborator over the last several days. Someone working behind the scenes and in the dark."

At that instant the mysterious arrival dropped the hood of his cloak. Everyone gasped in astonishment, though smiles and laughter soon followed.

"*You* again!" King Rupert exclaimed, though more amused than upset. "*Still* spying on us?"

"Not *spying* this time, your highness," Mr. Smithers admitted, blushing slightly. "Merely working behind the scenes. I was following Artemas' instructions after all." The magician was instantly besieged with more questions about how and why Mr. Smithers was recruited in his elaborate scheme.

"As powerful as my magic may be," Artemas said, "I can't do *everything*!" He immediately dived into an explanation. "As soon as we returned from Endora, I knew I would need a reliable ally to help me. So while Sam, Christopher and Molly waited in the restaurant for the car to warm up, I found a perfect time to inform Mr. Smithers about my plan when we went upstairs to get some aspirin for my headache."

"So you were plotting right from the start," Molly said. "*You* should work as a spy for Ulric."

"I had no option. There were a few tasks I couldn't complete myself and Mr. Smithers was a logical choice," Artemas said. "So I quickly explained as much as I could, swearing him to complete secrecy."

"After that moment," Mr. Smithers said, "I couldn't come in contact with any of you for any reason. I had to remain invisible in case Belthasar should notice. If his spirit ever invaded *me*, then the plan would have been discovered and failed. Since Emma was visiting her sister in Endora and the restaurant was closed that week for Christmas, I was the ideal candidate. I had plenty of time to act as a secret agent."

"How did Mr. Smithers help?" Christopher asked, unbuttoning his coat as the warming sun rose higher in the bright blue sky. "And how did you keep in touch?"

"Keeping in touch was easy," the magician admitted. "On the day we sent those e-mails to Elvin L. Cooper, I wrote a long note to Mr. Smithers explaining my plan in detail and what he needed to do for me. I sneaked out of the house later that night and left the letter under a trash receptacle near a mailbox for him to find."

"While in the restaurant, I had instructed Artemas when to place his letter there," Mr. Smithers said. "About a half hour later, I walked by and picked it up."

"The following day we discovered that Belthasar's spirit had followed us to the library," Artemas continued.

"He sure fooled all of us," Molly said. "We were convinced that Belthasar left the woman in the maroon coat and had gone into Mr. Porter when she handed him those bookmarkers. And all the time he was inside Lucy."

Artemas cleared his throat. "I must confess that I had my suspicions that Belthasar did *not* go into Mr. Porter that day. I suspected Lucy right from the start."

"*How*?" Molly asked, taken aback.

"I noticed that Mr. Porter had slipped on a pair of driving gloves while he was checking out his books, just before he was handed the bookmarkers. That lady never touched him on the skin, but Lucy *did* hold her by the hand when she nearly fainted."

"Why didn't you tell us?" Christopher asked.

"I thought it best not to let on so as not to scare Belthasar away," he replied. "Better for us if I could keep an eye on him without *him* knowing it. And since Molly was arranging a tour of the museum for Lucy, I thought Belthasar might find it an ideal place to make a move against your family. That would provide me a perfect opportunity to launch my plan to have Belthasar *discover* that he could recreate another of himself. Luckily, the tour was arranged near the hour when the timedoor reopened, giving Belthasar the added incentive of leaving your world at once."

"I had been following you closely that day," Mr. Smithers said. "I knew the timedoor would reopen then and was assuming Belthasar would make a move. I watched in the museum lobby from behind a newspaper, seeing Artemas, Christopher and Molly rush out of the building. I was about to chase after the three of you when Mina showed up. I eventually followed her and the rest of the Jordans through the timedoor."

"I walked into a complicated mess!" Mina said, patting Artemas on the hand.

The magician smiled and took a deep breath of fresh air, enjoying his time talking with Mina without a headache plaguing his every word. "So to continue, it was on that same night after the fainting incident in the library that I kept watch in your living room. I left the house again in the middle of the night and retrieved some items that Mr. Smithers had placed underneath a park bench for me. He had also left me a note. It was a simple yet effective method of communication."

"A lot of cloak-and-dagger intrigue," Mr. Jordan said. "I like it!"

"Good thing *you* weren't involved, honey," his wife said. "You would have had way too much fun sneaking around in the dark!"

"I'm *still* in the dark," Molly admitted. "What items did Mr. Smithers give you, Artemas? And how do they relate to Belthasar's destruction?"

"Mr. Smithers' role was key to my deception of Belthasar. In order to make him believe that I could recreate another of himself, I first had to make *you* and *Christopher* believe it."

"With the rose demonstration in our backyard?" Christopher asked.

"Exactly! When we gathered in the backyard that sunny wintry morning to begin my experiment, you'll recall that Magic was a bundle of energy," Artemas said. "He would not leave me alone."

"I remember," Molly said with a giggle, hoping that their dog hadn't missed them too much while they were away. "But why is that fact important?"

"It was part of the plan. I concealed a small strip of grilled steak inside my cloak pocket that Magic was trying to get at. It was one of the two items Mr. Smithers had left for me in the park," Artemas said, pleased to explain this bit of cleverness.

"Why would you do *that*?" Mrs. Jordan asked. "Magic gets too many treats as it is."

"Oh, the dog never got the steak, but he *did* keep chasing after me which is what I needed him to do." Artemas observed the puzzled expressions around him. "You see, after I created a rose from the pine needles and held it aloft, Magic was still keyed up, determined to get that piece of steak. After I invited Christopher and Molly to examine the rose, Magic charged at me again and pinned me to the wall, causing me to drop the flower on the other side of the wall. But I dropped it on *purpose* as I had planned."

"There *is* a point to this, isn't there?" Christopher asked.

"If you think like a detective you should have no problem figuring it out," Mr. Jordan told him. He was beginning to see where Artemas' plan was leading.

"I'm not Sherlock Holmes," Christopher said, recalling what Artemas had done next. "So you walked around the wall and retrieved the rose while Molly and I got hold of Magic. He was quite calm when you returned to the yard."

"As calm as a clam!" Artemas said. "Magic no longer pursued me because I had left the piece of steak on the other side of the wall and replaced it with a bar of soap waiting for me there. Magic took one sniff when I passed by him, no longer interested in bothering me."

"As much as I admire detective Holmes, I'm still no match for his intellect," Molly said. "Why was there a bar of soap on the other side of the wall? Who put it there?"

"I did!" Mr. Smithers said. "Ten minutes before you gathered in the backyard, Artemas had me drop off two special items—a bar of soap *and* a red long-stem rose." Christopher and Molly glanced at Artemas, noting the mischievous grin upon his face. "I had parked my car on the street parallel to yours, sneaked through the adjacent yard and left the items behind the wall as instructed."

"So when I dropped the rose over the wall," Artemas explained, "I replaced it with the *real* flower Mr. Smithers had provided. I pretended to be hesitant about taking it into the sunlight to make the demonstration more convincing."

Christopher smirked. "Now I understand why you

came screaming out of the cellar earlier that morning to tell us you had perfected your spell."

"Just more of the act," Artemas confessed. "Another performance to convince you, and ultimately, Belthasar, that he could have his wish. I cannot create a permanent living entity, and that's probably a good thing."

"How ironic," Mina said. "Belthasar inhabits an actor and learns so much of his craft, yet he couldn't see through the very act being staged against him."

"He was blinded by his own arrogance and vanity," Artemas said, "unable to see the world for what it really is."

"That's probably why Belthasar recreated himself taller than he originally was," Mrs. Jordan concluded. "People who crave unlimited power see themselves larger than life, which ultimately leads to their downfall."

"No great loss there," Molly said. "But I have another question, Artemas. After you created a rose, how'd you know it would match the one Mr. Smithers left by the wall?"

"Simple. On that night he left me the piece of grilled steak in the park, he also left a photograph of the rose he planned to leave," Artemas said. "I modified my spell so the two roses would match. I swiftly buried my created rose and the piece of steak under some snow behind the wall, certain that a squirrel or stray cat would devour the meat when it was discovered. And as soon as the sunlight melted the snow in that area, *my* rose would disappear. So I never had any worry about someone finding the evidence."

"Brilliant!" Mr. Jordan said with an enthusiastic pump of his fist. "Now that I know your entire plan, I can say with certainty that Belthasar never had a chance."

"If only *we* had known the details going into the game," Mrs. Jordan replied. "Think of all the gray hairs we could have been spared."

"Oh, that would have been boring," Christopher joked. "Didn't the mystery and intrigue make it more fun?"

"I'm not sure if *fun* is the right word," Molly said. "But I am sure of *one* thing."

"What's that?" King Rupert asked with a contented

smile as the lines of horses marched proudly through the grass.

"I'm sure glad Artemas was on *our* side!"

They traveled for several more hours, urging Artemas to repeat parts of his story which he was more than willing to do. So the morning swiftly passed amid talk and laughter until King Rupert's castle appeared on the horizon against a brilliant blue sky an hour before noontime.

When the front of the line approached the castle drawbridge, standing there to greet everyone were Vergil, Emma and Queen Eleanor. They had heard the good news hours ago and couldn't wait to welcome the returning heroes. Each had a dozen questions to ask and King Rupert knew that that would only be for starters. As Millicent the cat scurried back and forth across the drawbridge soaking in the warm spring sunshine, Artemas laughed to himself, certain he would be retelling his story at least *one* more time before finally getting his proper New Year's day breakfast.

CHAPTER TWENTY-THREE

Goodbye and Hello

During the nearly six days that followed until the timedoor reopened, the Jordan family was blessed with the Endoran vacation they had always dreamed about. At the top of Christopher and Molly's list of things to do was an extended tour of King Rupert's castle. They wandered about the seemingly endless corridors as if they owned the place. King Rupert and Queen Eleanor were delighted to hear the siblings' laughter echo off the stone walls, knowing how deeply they would miss the children in the days to come.

Molly also got her wish for a second visit to the Inn of the Twelve Horses. King Jeremiah and Queen Rosalind joined everyone for a leisurely meal, much to the delight of Henry Droon. The proprietor was honored to have two kings and two queens feast at his tables, and the royal visit was the talk of the inn for weeks to come. Molly later sat down with Queen Rosalind in the common room and chatted about Rosalind's wedding day, at last learning all the specifics about the bouquets, gowns and table settings that Ulric had been unable to provide during their journey to Three Frogs. But Molly thought that the extravagant descriptions were well worth the wait.

At the end of the evening, Christopher and Molly

said goodbye to Rosalind and King Jeremiah, not knowing when they would see the royal couple again. They both hoped to travel to Solárin a few more times to enjoy the peace and beauty of the land that had blossomed after so many years of strife.

The sun shone especially warm the next afternoon, providing ideal weather for lunch in one of the outdoor courtyards. While engrossed in several conversations after their meal, everyone delighted in the honeysweet scent of bayla blossoms wafting through the air as they lingered among ornamental shrubbery and budding flowers along the cobblestone walkways. Mr. Smithers detected a hint of sadness in his wife's eyes as they talked, knowing the reason without having to ask.

"Artemas will do his best to create another timedoor, my dear. Before you know it, you'll be back here visiting your sister as if you'd never left."

Emma smiled. "You're very sweet, Stanley, trying to cheer me up. But I'll be fine once I'm busy in the restaurant. I look forward to opening up our place for another year."

Christopher snapped his fingers. "I have a perfect idea! Queen Eleanor should visit *us* next time. I think it's time she stepped into our world."

Emma burst into a grin. "What a great suggestion! I could show her the sights. Take her to the museum. Even go shopping!"

"Now that our Belthasar problem is solved," Artemas said, "I'll have more time to concentrate on the mechanics of my magical timedoors."

"When will you create another one?" Molly asked.

"Difficult to say, but I'm mulling over a few spells to perfect the process."

"Perfect it as soon as you can!" Mina said. "I want to come back and spend more time with you. Despite the trials of this first visit, I've grown to love Endora very much."

"This kingdom has that effect on people," Mr. Jordan admitted as he proudly eyed Christopher and Molly. "I'm sure you'll be back, Mina. I hope we all will."

"And since *I'll* be living on the other side," Emma added, "Artemas will have a link to Endora to make his job easier."

"That's another problem I hope to solve," Artemas said. "I'll start as soon as the timedoor closes for the final time the day after tomorrow."

"Enough scientific chitchat and making plans about going shopping," King Rupert said as he and his wife pushed their way to the front of the gathering. "Winter is over and a glorious spring day beckons to us. Let's celebrate!"

"Easy for you to say," Vergil remarked. "*We* have a cold winter waiting for us when we get back."

Queen Eleanor smiled as the sunlight gently touched her flowing red hair. "I'll admit my husband is a wonderful king, but he can't solve *every* problem."

"No problem at all," Mrs. Jordan replied. "Now we'll have a *second* spring to look forward to, and my family will all be together when it arrives. I can't ask for *anything* right now more wonderful than that!"

Everyone retired by early evening the next day. The timedoor was to open at the stroke of the fourth hour the following morning when cold and darkness still cloaked the landscape. But few of the travelers got very much sleep that night. Most lay awake at one time or another, contemplating their adventures in Endora and speculating when the timedoor would open next. Some, in the back of their minds, wondered how long such journeys could last.

They awoke when the sky was veiled with a blanket of icy-white stars. They ate breakfast in one of King Rupert's private chambers where a dozen people gathered for their final meal together, hoping to reunite in the near future.

Then King Rupert proposed a toast. "To my family and friends, the people who mean so much to me," he said, his voice slightly cracking as he raised his glass. "May we meet here again soon and often, and may our times together never be forgotten."

In unison, everyone raised their glasses and drank to the king's touching and comforting words. Christopher and Molly glanced at each other, feeling the same mix of emotions. Though it was wonderful to visit this world, their hearts were always torn whenever they had to leave. Today was no exception.

After their meal, Artemas uttered the words that all were expecting but didn't want to hear. "It is near the seventh hour. The timedoor will soon close for the last time," he said, gently resting his hand upon Mina's shoulder as the early morning sunshine spilled into the room. Mina looked up at him with misty eyes. "We must go to my chamber now and get ready."

Minutes later, the five members of the Jordan family, Mr. Smithers, Emma and Mina stood dressed in winter coats, saying their final goodbyes. Artemas and Mina hugged, neither wanting to let go.

"I'll write letters to you and save them," Mina said. "You can read them when you return, Artemas, and see how much I missed you."

The magician smiled through the sadness that filled his eyes. "And I will spare no effort to recreate another timedoor to your world, Mina. So you might not have to use up *that* much writing paper if I have anything to say about it–and I *do*!"

Then after a flurry of handshakes and hugs and teary eyes, the eight travelers stepped through the wavy opening in the stone wall and disappeared through the timedoor. King Rupert and Queen Eleanor watched in melancholy silence as Artemas and Ulric looked on, equally downcast.

"There they go again," King Rupert softly said. "Here–and then gone. It always goes by so fast. *Too* fast."

"They'll be back some day, my dear," his wife said, placing an arm around his shoulder. "In the meantime, let's see what kind of day awaits us." Queen Eleanor opened the balcony doors wide, letting in a flood of warm sunshine. "Apparently a *beautiful* one!"

The four of them stepped outside and gazed across

the northern plains, awed by the beauty and vastness of the greening land and the sun-splashed magnificence of the western mountains. A gentle wind floated in from the south.

"Ulric, I think my wife and I will embark on a short trip to Solárin in a few days to visit Rosalind. It is time that *we* took a vacation," King Rupert said. "I trust that you and your men can handle matters while we're gone."

"Neither troll nor brigand will breach these walls in your absence!"

"Very good."

"And, Artemas, make sure to attend to your timedoor studies," Queen Eleanor said. "I'd like to visit Emma again as soon as possible." She smiled at the magician. "Besides, I think there's someone eager for another visit from *you*."

"I'll be most diligent in my research, your highness," he replied. "All I need is a little time."

"Well, in the *meantime*," King Rupert said, leaning against the stone railing and basking in the warm sunlight, "let's enjoy this fine moment for a little while longer. I'm in no hurry to go to work just yet!"

They walked through a swirl of stars and darkness as if silently passing through a familiar dream, contemplating when–or *if*–they would ever return. Then the eight travelers stepped out of the stone support underneath the river bridge as a blast of frosty January air nipped at their faces. The midnight sky was painted with stars on the brand new Saturday that greeted them.

Mrs. Jordan shivered. "On second thought, maybe a quick spring *wouldn't* be such a bad idea. My, but it *is* cold out here."

"How about some coffee and hot chocolate at the restaurant," Emma suggested. "I'll throw a few sandwiches on the griddle."

"Wonderful idea!" Mr. Smithers said. "Just like on that first morning we went through the timedoor."

"As I recollect, you *sneaked* through!" Molly joked.

"And a good thing," Christopher said, recalling how

Mr. Smithers rescued them from Belthasar's vault.

"I want to see Magic!" Vergil said.

"And I'll call Lucy to tell her I'm okay," Mina added. "How am I *ever* going to explain my absence?"

"You'll find a way," Mr. Jordan said. "You can call her from the restaurant while Vergil and I drive home and get Magic. We'll meet you all back there shortly."

They trudged up the snowy embankment, feeling in better spirits. A few moments after they reached the road, the timedoor closed with a thunderous clap, startling them all.

"Oh my, but is it *always* that noisy?" Mina asked.

Molly nodded. "Artemas needs to work on that. He—"

Then she noticed a dark figure walking down the narrow road that led to their old house. It ran perpendicular to the main road they were standing by. The stranger walked a small dog on a leash and was dressed in a long coat, a fur hat and a thickly knitted scarf. Molly squinted as the pair approached the intersection of the two roads now bathed in the glow of a nearby streetlight. They stared at one another until a flash of recognition illuminated Molly's face.

"Is that *you*, Misty?" she called out.

The dog barked a sharp but familiar greeting, furiously wagging its tail.

"It *is* Misty!" her mother replied, waving at the figure across the road. "Hello, Edna. It's Sally Jordan. What are you doing out so late?"

The woman loosened the scarf around her face as she ambled over to greet her old neighbors. "Misty and I enjoy late night walks. What on earth brings *you* here?"

"We were just, uh, out taking a walk ourselves!" Christopher said. "Nice to see you again, Mrs. Halloway."

Mr. Jordan introduced her to Mr. Smithers, Emma and Mina. "It's been a couple of years since I last ran into you in town," he said. "How are you feeling these days?"

"I'll be seventy next week. Never felt better!" She gazed in amazement at Christopher, Molly and Vergil. "I just can't get over how you three have grown. Especially you, Vergil. You're hardly recognizable!"

"Misty's still as cute as ever," Molly said, bending down to pet the dog.

Mrs. Halloway shook her head. "You must be at least fifteen, Christopher."

"Sixteen," he proudly replied.

"*That old?* It seems like only yesterday that you and Molly were running through the leaves on my property and playing in that old barn on the side of the house." She recalled fond memories viewed through her curtained windows. "I'll bet your imaginations provided for some fine adventures. Make sure you never forget them!"

Christopher and Molly glanced at one another, trying to conceal their grins.

"I *guarantee* that we won't," he promised.

"For once, I agree with my brother!" Molly replied.

"We're heading over to Stanley and Emma's restaurant for a snack," Mrs. Jordan said. "Why don't you join us? It'll give us a chance to catch up."

"Sounds like a wonderful idea!" Mrs. Halloway replied as they walked down the road, chatting up a storm under the sprinkle of winter stars.

Half an hour later, after Mr. Jordan and Vergil returned with Magic, the nine visitors sat around one of the restaurant tables and shared old memories and brand new adventures. Hot drinks and grilled sandwiches were served underneath pine garland and glowing Christmas lights that still adorned the wooden rafters. And amid the celebration, nobody noticed the deep of night fade gently away, replaced by a brilliant sunrise peeking up behind the distant trees in a cold crisp air.

EPILOGUE

A Family Gathering

"Now where did I leave off?" Molly asked herself, sitting down at her desk in the upstairs study. She took a sip of coffee before picking up a pen to write in her journal.

I remember that day vividly. My eleven-year-old brother ran up to me as I worked the soil in my imaginary garden at our old house. The sun was setting on that chilly October evening and Christopher was as excited as a treasure hunter. Everything changed at that moment—for all of us and in so many ways. And now, here we are—

"*Ready?*" a soft voice whispered at the doorway. "I put on my jacket."

Molly set her pen down and glanced at the smiling six-year-old with stringy blond hair. "Come here, silly. We're not leaving *just* yet." Molly removed the girl's purple jacket after she had skipped over to her mother. "You'll be as warm as a toasted muffin by the time we get in the car. Let me write for a few more minutes, Rosalind, and then we'll meet Grandma and Grandpa Jordan for our little get-together."

"Okay. But Daddy told me to check up on you."

"So you're his little spy, is that it?" Molly kissed her daughter on the forehead.

"What are you writing *now*?" Rosalind asked as she tapped a finger on the open journal. "Haven't you finished that story yet, Mom?"

"It's not really a story, Rosalind." Molly lifted her daughter onto her lap. "I'm jotting down interesting things that happen to me as the years go by. I even write things about *you*, sweetheart!"

"*Really*?"

"Sure. You're my best source for material lately."

Rosalind looked wide-eyed at the elegant lines in blue ink. "Can you read some?"

"Maybe when you're a little older and–"

"What's *this*?" Rosalind asked, removing a small folded piece of parchment sticking out of the journal.

"I use that as a bookmarker to keep my place."

"What does it say?" she asked, noticing black ink marks through the paper.

Molly unfolded it, the scent of parchment and ink taking her back to the golden orange glow of a setting sun splashed across the plains. "This is a poem I wrote when I was about twice your age. I planned to work on it some more, but decided I liked it just the way it is. You were only an infant when I last looked at it."

"Read it to me, Mom. We've got time."

Molly smiled and raised an eyebrow. "Only if you promise to go downstairs and keep Daddy company until I finish up here. A deal?"

"Deal!" Rosalind replied with a sharp nod.

Molly glanced at the scribbles of black ink, recalling the day she had written the poem in a horse-drawn carriage on a return trip from Solárin. Some days she wondered if that event had really happened. She looked at her daughter, knowing Rosalind was eagerly awaiting a performance.

"Okay, honey. Here goes. Tell me if you like it. The title is *Family*."

"So *far* I like it, Mom."

"Well thank you. Now here's the rest."

Family is like a gentle breeze
that sweeps across a field of flowers.
Family is like the warming light
that saves you in your darkest hours.

When times are tough and the world is cold
they'll comfort you in your plight.
But when family is away you need only recall
the sweeping breeze and the saving light.

Molly set the poem down and held her daughter close. "So what do you think?"

"It's very nice. Even better than frosted brownies!"

"That's your favorite dessert, so I guess you must *really* like it!" Molly replied, kissing her on the head. "Thank you so much for listening."

"You're welcome." Rosalind climbed off her mother's lap and patted her on the arm. "Now I'll keep Daddy company." She hurried out the door but popped her head in one more time. "Write fast!" Then she disappeared as Molly picked up her pen.

"And now, here we are–" she said, reading the last few words she had written.

–twenty five years later to the very day that King Rupert and Artemas stepped into our lives. Shortly after, we literally walked into their world, and the timedoor would forever become a focal point in our lives. Yet despite the trials of those first few years, we've had many wonderful and joyous visits to Endora and Solárin since.

Still, nearly two years have passed since the timedoor last opened. We are all getting older no matter which side of the magical door we live on. Children grow, parents age and busy lives eat up the hours in each swiftly passing year. So naturally, a walk through the stars cannot occur as often as one would like, even though Artemas has perfected his spells and can now open the timedoor more often and nearly at a time of his choosing.

He was particularly cagey the last time I talked to

him, informing me that he was working on another timedoor spell without revealing the particulars. Artemas promised to share the results whenever we next meet. At that time I didn't know when it would be, so I slipped a note in his cloak pocket as I hugged him and his wife Mina goodbye. I will write more about this later after I learn one way or the other about the success of his secret spell and of my note. In the meantime, I have a party to attend!

The Jordan clan gathered at their parents' house on Maple Street at quarter to five before going to the party. The quiet flicker of candlelight within the glowing jack-o-lanterns on the front porch contrasted with the cheerful bedlam inside.

"Cigam is *not* a horse," Christopher told his five-year-old son Art who wanted to take a ride on the wheaten terrier. He scooped up Art and placed him on his shoulder.

"I told him so," said Samuel Rupert, his older brother by three years. "Art wouldn't listen to me."

"You probably *gave* Art that idea," Samuel's mother said as she walked by to greet Molly and her family as they entered the house.

Vergil and his fiancée sat on the couch, holding hands and giggling. "See what *we* get to look forward to in a few more years?" he whispered into her ear.

"Listen up!" Mr. Jordan said, enjoying his first few months of retirement from the museum. "We can all pile into two cars and head to the restaurant."

"Cigam rides in *your* car, Dad!" Molly shouted.

"Unless the two of them want to walk!" Mrs. Jordan suggested with a laugh.

"Jillian and I will take my car," Vergil said. "Two cars are a bit *too* cramped."

"Can I ride with you, Uncle Vergil?" Rosalind asked.

"No fair! I was going to ask him that," Samuel Rupert shouted.

"Too late, Sam. I was first, slowpoke!"

"But I *thought* of it first–and I'm taller!"

And the bantering continued out the front door into the cool October air. Moments later, three cars pulled out of the driveway and headed to Stanley and Emma Smithers' restaurant in a swirl of leaves and laughter.

Though the restaurant was closed for business that evening, it basked in the glow of warm light when everyone arrived. Mr. and Mrs. Smithers had enlarged their building to accommodate more patrons, the only visible change along the rural road outside the city. The old river bridge lay ahead just beyond the restaurant, its cold metal beams stretching across the water like a sleeping giant.

"Too bad Eleanor and Charles couldn't join us," Mrs. Jordan said as she helped Emma set out appetizers. Her grandchildren's laughter echoed from the adjacent dining section. "How are they doing these days?"

"Busy at school," Emma replied. "Eleanor is a junior at college. She wants to run the restaurant after she gets her degree."

"And I'm ready to let her!" Mr. Smithers replied as he wiped off some drinking glasses behind the bar. "I want to retire soon—at least part of the time."

"You know you love this place," Molly said as she folded a pile of cloth napkins. "You're not fooling anyone."

"You're probably right," he said.

"And how's C. U. doing?" Mr. Jordan asked.

"Charles Ulric is finishing his final year at the military academy," Mr. Smithers proudly said. "Hopes to be a four-star general by the time he's thirty!"

"I wouldn't be the least bit surprised," Emma replied. "After all, your stories about being in King Rupert's army were quite an inspiration to him, Sir Smithers!"

"You must be talking about Endora," Christopher said as he walked by, snitching a piece of cheese from one of the snack platters.

"What else *would* be the topic of conversation today?" Mrs. Jordan said.

"Speaking of which—isn't it about time we headed

over to the bridge?" Mr. Jordan said, glancing at his watch. It was nearly six o'clock.

So after leaving the other adults with the children, Mr. and Mrs. Jordan, Christopher, Molly, Vergil and Stanley and Emma Smithers walked along the side of the road to the bridge. Cigam followed closely behind, his tail wagging contentedly. Christopher and his father turned on flashlights as the group headed down the grassy embankment into the shadows lurking underneath the bridge. The river flowed silently by, speckled with the last light from the setting sun. Though twenty-five years had passed since the timedoor first opened, the area looked nearly unchanged, as if time had forgotten to cast its spell over this quiet section of town.

Mr. Smithers passed out a plastic cup to everyone, then held up a bottle in the glow of the flashlights and popped a cork. "I thought a toast at the stroke of six would be appropriate, the hour when the timedoor first opened to our world." He filled each glass with the bubbling liquid.

"It's only carbonated grape juice," Emma said. "I wasn't sure if the little ones were going to join the celebration."

"It'll be a while yet before Rosalind learns about Endora," Molly said, unable to imagine her daughter walking through the timedoor on her own.

"Same here," Christopher agreed, referring to his two sons. "They're a handful as it is *without* them wanting to run off to another world."

"Now you know how your mother and I felt," Mr. Jordan said. "Welcome to *our* world!"

He raised the flashlight to look upon the grinning faces of his two oldest children. Suddenly his eyes widened as the beam of light hit the outline of an individual standing near the edge of the river, hidden among the thick shadows just beyond the bridge. The tall man walked slowly toward them as everyone turned around in surprise. Cigam barked at once but Vergil calmed him down.

"I heard there was going to be a party tonight," a familiar voice said. "I didn't want to miss it."

"Well if this isn't the icing on the cake!" Mrs. Jordan joyfully replied.

Christopher immediately aimed his flashlight at the bridge support, noticing a hazy distortion amid the solid rock. He smiled. The timedoor was open again.

"Artemas, how'd you get here?"

"The usual way, Christopher. I walked through the timedoor, of course."

"But how did you know *we'd* be here? And at this *moment*?"

Artemas smiled at Molly. "I received some advanced notice."

"It was a wild hope when I slipped you that note," Molly said. "I knew we'd be thinking about you now, but I didn't believe you would actually show up."

"Twenty-five years is a milestone," the magician replied, recalling the first time he had stepped through the magical door into this world. "I worked on my spells with particular diligence over the last few months so I could arrive just at this hour."

"How many years have gone by according to *your* time?" Christopher asked. "Now that forty is creeping up on me, I pay more attention to the passing seasons."

Artemas thought for a moment. "According to the Endoran calendar, I arrived here the first time approximately twenty years, one hundred and sixty-six days and sixteen hours ago." He noted the astonished looks. "Don't be *that* amazed. I performed the calculations before I left in case someone might ask!"

"I would have believed you even if you hadn't admitted that," Mr. Jordan said.

Suddenly Cigam nosed up to Artemas, his tail flapping like a windshield wiper. "And who is *this* excited fellow? Why, he's nearly the spitting image of Magic."

"That's Cigam," Vergil said. "Magic spelled backward."

"After Sam retired, we decided it was time for another dog," Mrs. Jordan said. "We missed Magic, and Cigam was the perfect choice in name *and* breed."

Mr. Jordan walked up to the bridge support, slipping his hand inside the timedoor so that it temporarily disappeared. "You modified your spells to open a timedoor more often and closer to a time of your liking. But this, Artemas, was *perfect* timing."

"I've been *tweaking* the process," he modestly said. "I've made two additional modifications besides."

"Will I be able to make a quick visit to see my sister?" Emma asked.

"Of course. Queen Eleanor is eager to see you. The King and Queen send their regards to one and all," Artemas said. "However, you must go now. The timedoor will remain open for nearly three hours, but it will only open this one time. Or it *should*."

"What about the *three times* rule?" Mr. Smithers asked.

"*That* was one of the two modifications," he replied. "Creating a magical timedoor is no easy feat. By reducing the number of openings from three to one, I saved myself a few headaches. First, I don't have to monitor the subsequent two openings, and second, it's less taxing on my magic. I'm not as young as I used to be," Artemas said with a grin. "In your reckoning, I'm a few years shy of eighty. Nearly as old as King Rupert himself! And since this is my first test of the new spell, Emma, I'd like to have you back here before the timedoor closes to make sure everything works out as I predict."

Molly smirked. "After all these years of research, I doubt you're capable of making any timedoor mistakes." No one else thought so either, but Emma promised nonetheless to be back in under two hours.

"What's the second modification?" Christopher asked.

"*You'll* see," Artemas replied with a playful air of mystery as Mr. Smithers handed him a cup of grape drink.

Then as the setting sun filtered through the distant trees in the cool October air, everyone toasted the timedoor at that special moment. Mr. Smithers escorted his wife back to Endora to visit her sister, then quickly returned to accompany the others to the restaurant for their twenty-five year celebration.

"Artemas, why didn't Mina come with you?" Mrs. Jordan asked as they walked along the road. The tops of the nearby pines and shedding maples stood as silhouettes against a crisp evening sky budding with fire-white stars.

"She's visiting our son Cedric," he replied. "He's working in the village of Osella near the Solárin border. He's just over seventeen years old by your count."

"What's Cedric doing?" Vergil asked.

"Building ships. He's been an apprentice since early spring," the magician said. "With commerce flourishing up and down the Alorian River and across the Baridorn Sea, he couldn't have picked a finer occupation."

"Weren't you training him to be a magician?" Molly asked. "That's what Cedric told me the last time I saw him."

Artemas cleared his throat. "*That* occupation didn't take. Though Cedric still practices magic from time to time as a hobby, he, um…"

"What wrong?" Christopher asked.

"Let's just say that Cedric's magical touch is slightly askew. The last time he cast a freezing spell over a cup of water, I ended up with a charred hole in my working table."

Molly chuckled. "Oops!"

"And as for his one attempt to create a timedoor…" Artemas shrugged his shoulders and sighed. "Well, I suppose the less said about that, the better."

"Don't feel bad, Artemas. Not everyone is suited to be a magician," Mr. Jordan said.

"*Or* a ship builder," his wife added.

"And that's probably the way it should be," Artemas replied as they walked up to the glowing lights of the restaurant and stepped inside.

The partiers indulged in delicious food and drink while discussing old times as so often before. When

Rosalind, Art and Samuel Rupert inquired about the bearded guest, Molly informed them that he was their great Uncle Artemas from Finland who dropped by for a visit. She figured that that explanation should suffice for a few years.

"You must tell us about *your* relatives back home, Artemas," she added with a wink, eager to hear about her friends beyond the timedoor, particularly the royal couple of Solárin.

The magician obliged, filling them in on the latest about Ranen Alexander, Rosalind and Jeremiah's oldest son, and their younger twin daughters, Lily and Molly. He said that Ranen would eventually rule over Endora at Rosalind's request since she would remain beside her husband in Solárin.

"And how is Ulric these days?" Christopher asked.

"He retired as King Rupert's chief guard. Ardon now holds that job," Artemas said. "Ulric, though, remains quite busy. When he's not off exploring the Katánin Mountains, he serves Endora and Solárin as a military advisor. Never a dull moment!"

Christopher fondly recalled his own travels across the sweeping plains and near the mountains. He couldn't wait to arrange another adventure for him and his wife if ever he could find the time.

When two hours had ticked away, Mr. Smithers left the restaurant and returned shortly with Emma, not wanting his wife to walk alone through the timedoor. She was delighted to have spent a warm summer's day with her sister in Endora, asking Artemas to return as soon as possible. He promised to visit again after the tests on his latest timedoor spell were complete. Anyone wishing to go back to Endora then could do so.

"Despite some aches and pains, there are still a few good years left in me!" Artemas said, the youthful gleam in his ocean-blue eyes contradicting the slightly bent frame of his aging body. "I'm sure our worlds will reconnect before all is said and done."

Then after everyone reluctantly said their final goodbyes, Christopher and Molly accompanied Artemas back to the bridge. The night had darkened like coal as they walked down the grassy embankment, guided by a bright white beam from the flashlight. The timedoor silently waited in the stone support underneath, weak and wavy like a veil of fog upon the still surface of a lake. Christopher shook the magician's hand, thanking him for a lifetime of adventure, hoping in his heart that they would meet once again. Molly hugged Artemas as tears welled up in her eyes, wishing the very same thing.

They silently waved goodbye as their friend stepped through the timedoor and disappeared into the dark stone, their hearts heavy and their spirits downcast. Neither was eager to return to the restaurant until the timedoor closed, and so they waited for that moment, saying only a few words or glancing up at the stars. Then Christopher and Molly heard what they thought was a gentle brush of wind through a pile of dried leaves, though the air was still and the ground around them bare. Christopher aimed the light at the stone support and noted that it was completely solid. The timedoor had quietly closed. He glanced at his sister and smiled.

"I guess Artemas tweaked *that* part of the spell, *too*," he said with a laugh.

"Not the usual dramatic closing we were used to, is it," Molly replied.

"No, but that's okay. I like it."

"So do I." Molly gently punched Christopher on the arm. "Well, let's get going, big brother. Tonight's a school night. We both have kids to put to bed."

"No need to tell me twice. They'll probably wake us all up before sunrise!"

Christopher and Molly marched up the grassy embankment and walked along the side of the road to the restaurant, taking their time to get back. They glanced up at the grand display of stars blazing above, wondering if one of them might be the very sun shining down upon Endora at this moment, warming the late summer skies of that faraway land. Both contemplated the many roads they had traveled through that magical place, and through life itself, to arrive at this particular point in time, wondering what drama and adventure the years ahead might bring. Yet deep in their hearts, Christopher and Molly knew that with their families along for the ride, any trip through life would be a joyous and memorable one.

They couldn't wait to continue the journey.

THE END

AUTHOR'S NOTE

When I wrote the winter scenes for **The Saving Light** last year, the grass was green and lush outside my windows as we plunged headlong into summer. Now, as I apply the finishing touches to the final book in the trilogy, an icy wind whips across a trail of shoulder-high snow banks stretching across town, trumpeting the obvious: time marches on no matter what you do. So I hope I have made good use of my time while sitting at my computer desk for the past year or so completing THE ENDORA TRILOGY. To all the readers who have been awaiting its conclusion, thank you very much for your patience and for taking the time to stroll through these pages. It was both a pleasure and a challenge to write them, nurturing the characters and settings that first popped into my head over twenty-two years ago while walking underneath an old bridge one night in my hometown of Little Falls, New York. My sincere thanks are also extended to my sister Theresa Ricci and to Jean, Barry and Quintin Smith and Joyce Leskovar for previewing and proofreading my book. Many thanks also to my sister-in-law Jan Prestopnik for her extensive editing and commentary which helped me get this final volume into shape. Finally, more well-deserved thanks–again!–to my nephew Nathan Prestopnik for all of his time and patience to produce another fantastic cover for the series. And as for my *next* novel? Well, time will tell!

Thomas J. Prestopnik
February 24, 2007

Thomas J. Prestopnik has written four fantasy/adventure novels for children. These include **Gabriel's Journey** and the three volumes in The Endora Trilogy, **The Timedoor**, **The Sword and the Crown** and **The Saving Light**. He lives and writes in Little Falls, New York.

To learn about current and future novels written by Thomas J. Prestopnik, visit his official website at

www.tompresto.com